The music had stopped and Heaven's voice carried across the room. She glanced in Hamid's direction. If his feelings were hurt his eyes, as black as midnight, hid it. She'd not intended that; she was only shouting to be heard over the music.

"Of course, Heaven has failed to mention that I have not asked her for a date and I have no intention of it. My only interest in her is as a teacher. Heaven is not my type." Hamid held Heaven's gaze. "As I am not hers," he continued, putting her in her place.

Indigo Love Spectrum

An imprint of Genesis Press, Inc.
Publishing Company

Genesis Press, Inc.
P.O. Box 101
Columbus, MS 39703

ISBN: 1-58571-210-8
Manufactured in the United States of America

First Edition

Visit us at www.genesis-press.com
or call at 1-888-Indigo-1

DEDICATION

This book is dedicated to the two most important people in my life: my husband, William Davis and our son, William Davis, Jr.
Bill, thank you for making me laugh every single day and for being exactly what the Creator had in mind for my life. You love me, support me and give the best darn massages in the world. You are definitely the yen to my yang. I love you madly.
Billy, for being one person, you've given me the joy of a thousand children. I am so proud of you. Having you in my life has not only made me spiritually richer, it's taught me so many facets about love and the bond between a mother and child. It goes without saying that I love you.

ACKNOWLEDGMENTS

First and foremost all honor and glory go to God.

To my editor, Sidney Rickman, each time we work together I'm more convinced of the psychic connection.

To my family and friends, thank you for your continued love and support

To the readers, may Heaven's and Hamid's love spark renewed love in your life.

To Debbie Williams, the woman in my son's life. You make him happy and that makes me happy.

To Michelle Grajkowski, thanks for being such a wonderful agent.

To Honey, you have enriched my life immeasurably. You are a source of spiritual enrichment and knowledge. You make me dig deeper and accept that which I might otherwise think of as my vivid imagination. You are extremely special to me.

To all the family that he passed away in the past few months. You are not forgotten. My aunts: Lula Lander, Johnnie Mae Pots, my brother-in-law, Terry Davis and my father-in-law, Henry. You all were important in my life and you are missed.

As always, I began my acknowledgements with God, the head of my life and end them with the two people who complete me. This doesn't change because of the dedication. Bill and Billy are the ones who have to deal with papers all over the place and my just starting a conversation that has them thinking I'm talking about someone they know instead of the characters in a book. But, by the time the book is done, they are well acquainted with the characters! So for this and a thousand more reasons, my acknowledgements will always end with the two of you.

CHAPTER ONE

"That's going to kill you."

For the space of a breath, Heaven pretended that the voice was not talking to her.

"Excuse me, miss, perhaps you didn't hear me?"

Oh, she'd heard him alright, and had hoped that perhaps he'd get the message and know she didn't give a darn about his opinion of what she was eating.

"It will kill you," the voice said again.

Heaven rolled her eyes and turned to answer. Her eyes traveled up, and up, and up, and her first thought was, Wow! The man talking to her was magnificent. More than seventy-two inches of long, beautiful male greeted her startled gaze. Masses of curly black hair reached past his shoulders in direct contrast to the neatly trimmed beard that covered his chin. His lips curved in a smile and his dark eyes were enough to fuel her fantasies and make her have wet dreams. She swallowed. "Why do you care what I eat? It's my body, and I'm the one paying for it."

"I care because you're beautiful, and if it will prevent you from doing harm to your body, I will gladly treat you to breakfast."

Heaven glanced behind her at the tray the man had his breakfast on. A box of raisins, a banana, and an apple. Yes, it was healthier than what she had on her tray, but so what? She was in the mood for bacon, eggs, and hash brown potatoes, and even if she wasn't, she wasn't in the mood to hear lectures.

She pushed her tray along the conveyer rail, ignoring the man behind her. Suddenly she felt a tug on her tray and stopped, startled. This was gall. He was trying physically to take her breakfast.

Heaven pulled back. "Stop that! What do you think you're doing?"

"I offered to buy you a healthy breakfast." Hamid looked down at the scowling black woman with the strange hair, wondering why he was getting involved. He'd stood in line behind many Americans in the hospital cafeteria and had always wanted to say something, but this was the first time the words had come out.

Now Hamid found himself doing battle with this diminutive female. He looked her over as she roughly pulled her tray from him. She was no more than five feet tall, if that, with dark chocolate skin, smooth and unblemished. Her hairstyle fascinated him. It must have been a thousand sectioned-off parts. Each section appeared to wrap around itself. From where he stood, she smelled deliciously of lemons. He'd meant it when he'd said she was beautiful. She was ravishing, but the scowl on her face had him wondering why he was taking the time to inventory her.

Hamid tried again. "I wish to buy your breakfast. Take my tray."

"Leave me alone. I didn't ask you to buy my breakfast, and evidently I'm happy with my choices, or I wouldn't have put them on my tray."

One last tug and Heaven had her tray in front of her. She positioned her body so that there was no denying she was serious. If the man touched her tray again, he would get a karate chop, or her heel ground into his foot.

Heaven angrily peeled off bills to pay for her breakfast, and then looked hurriedly around the room for an empty table. Finding one, she picked up her tray and walked in that direction. When she heard footsteps behind her, she stopped abruptly and turned.

She tilted her head skyward. Wanting to make sure the man knew she was not interested, she frowned for all she was worth. Though she felt as though fire were shooting from her eyes, the man merely gave her an amused look and walked ahead of her to the only empty table in the hospital cafeteria, the table she'd been heading for.

For a moment, Heaven stood and watched him as he wiped his apple with a napkin and bit into it. She blinked as apple juice squirted from the fruit and landed, glistening, on his beard. When his hand wiped it away, his eyes locked with hers.

"Are you going to stand there to eat?" he asked before returning his attention to his meal.

A low growl passed through her lips but she sat down at the opposite end of the table and began digging into her food. When she reached for the salt, a brown hand covered hers and she pulled back. "May I have the salt when you're done, please?" She narrowed her eyes, knowing he was not putting salt on fruit.

"Salt is bad for you."

"Who are you?"

"My name is Hamid."

"Okay, Hamid, why are you all up in my business?"

"I don't know really," he smiled. "I just felt compelled to say these things to you."

He stared at her, his head moving a little to the side, making Heaven feel as if she were some type of specimen he was examining.

"Why are you looking at me like that?"

"Your hair."

"What about my hair?"

"What do you call that style?" He started to point, then stopped. "Why do you wear it like that?"

Another growl came from Heaven's throat, this one louder than the first. She deliberately picked up the bacon that had until this moment lain untouched on her plate. She bit into it with gusto before extending it in Hamid's direction. "Excuse me, I forgot my manners. Would you care for some of my breakfast?" She shook the bacon, then brought it to her lips and bit down again. "It's very good."

"No, thank you. I don't eat swine."

"I know."

"How do you know?"

Heaven rolled her eyes. "It's obvious…you're Muslim, right?"

"I am, but how did you know that? Are you making assumptions about me?" He smiled. "What are you basing them on?"

"Apparently you've done the same. You assumed I needed you to tell me what to eat."

"It was apparent to me that you were unaware that your choices in food were bad for your body."

"I've never met anyone like you. Where the heck are you from?"

"Pakistan. I'm Pakistani."

"And Muslim."

"Yes."

"One more question, Hamid. How do you know I'm not Muslim?"

"You're eating swine."

"And it's delicious," Heaven said, taking a bite.

"Yes, and filled with worms."

"So is your apple. Matter of fact, if I were you I would check that hole, it looks like it might contain live worms. At least mine are cooked."

Heaven turned away, wanting to spit the bacon into a napkin, the thought of worms making her nauseous. She wanted to smack Hamid's smug face, but apparently offering him the bacon had made him as ill as he'd made her. At least he'd stopped talking.

When Heaven dumped her breakfast tray, it still contained two uneaten slices of bacon, even though for the first time the hospital had gotten them crispy, just the way she liked.

Hamid sat at the table watching the woman walk away. He'd made her angry; actually, he couldn't much blame her. He had no right to stick his nose in her affairs. If she wanted to kill herself, it was her right. He finished the last bite of the banana and pocketed the raisins for later, smiling to himself, pleased that she'd not been able to finish eating the bacon. At least for today he'd saved her from putting more of the poison into her body. His good deed was done.

Heaven finished her shift and gave her report to the incoming private duty nurse. She liked being a nurse, and liked even better the fact that she worked through a registry, going to different hospitals and the occasional home. It allowed freedom and she earned a lot more money, something that she needed. And she didn't have to put up with the infighting that sometimes went on behind the scenes. She was never at one place long enough to become involved. And after running into that man in the hospital cafeteria, she was definitely glad she was off for the next several days.

She was used to having Muslim men try to tell her what she should eat, especially at Rush Presbyterian St. Luke Hospital. She didn't know why they felt compelled, as though they had a right. Maybe it had something to do with their chauvinistic attitude toward the women in their country. She wanted to shout, 'You're in America now, bub, get used to it. You don't tell women here what to do.' He was lucky that her mind had been preoccupied with other things, or she would have gone off on him.

"Miss, miss!"

Heaven groaned. She didn't believe it. There was Mr. Tall, Dark, and Handsome yelling at her. She kept walking, pretending that she hadn't heard him.

"My car won't start," he offered.

She stopped in her tracks and let out a sigh. *What did she look like, AAA?*

She stomped two rows over to where Hamid was parked. "What's wrong?" she asked, her senses on alert. The hospital staff wasn't off duty, only the private duty help was. "Are you following me?"

"If I am, I'm doing a poor job of it. I didn't know it was you until I saw the little things on your head."

"Twists," Heaven replied angrily, "they're called twists. Now, what do you want me to do?"

"Do you have a cell phone?"

"No."

He frowned. "Thank you for coming over. Maybe I'll just go inside the hospital and ask the security guard for help."

"Does your dome light come on?" Heaven asked, ignoring the way he was looking at her. "Move," she ordered, nudging him aside as she opened his door. "Give me your keys."

She snatched them from his outstretched palm and attempted to start the car.

"Are you a nurse, or a mechanic?"

She didn't answer but found the lever and popped his hood. "Do you have jumper cables? Never mind," she said and walked away.

"Where are you going?"

"To get my truck. Your battery is dead. You didn't expect me to give you a jump with the power of my mind, did you?"

Heaven was being deliberately rude. She would give him a jump but she definitely didn't want him getting the wrong idea. She was not into dating anyone but black men, and since Brandon she wasn't much into them either.

For once luck was on her side. She pulled into the slot directly in front of Hamid's car. Any other position and she would not have been able to help him. For a moment, she wished the space hadn't been open. She popped the hood of her SUV, got out her cables, and went to Hamid's car. She noticed right away the buildup of corrosion around his battery terminals, sighed again, and went for the toolbox she kept in her truck, then set to work.

"What are you doing?"

"Helping."

"I meant specifically."

"Your terminals are dirty. I need to clean them first." She offered the wrench for his inspection. "This is an open-end wrench. I have to loosen the cables."

"Do you know what you're doing?"

"If I didn't, would you be able to tell the difference?"

Heaven watched the expression in his eyes change from curiosity to embarrassment. "I know what I'm doing," she answered.

She cleaned the terminals and the battery posts, then reattached them, she handed the cables to Hamid. "Give me a moment to connect your battery, then you can connect those to my battery." She attached the cables and walked back to Hamid. "Go ahead," she said. He was paused over the post when she slapped his hand away.

"Sorry," she murmured, "You were doing it wrong. You have to put positive to positive and negative to negative or you can blow out the computer on both vehicles." She took the cables from him and connected them herself.

"Go give it a try, turn the key," Heaven ordered. The second she heard the car start, she unhooked the cables, slammed Hamid's hood down, and then her own.

"You should be fine now," she said and got in her truck and waved her hand for him to take off. She drove behind him for a minute or two, just in case. When she was assured that his car was not going to quit, Heaven made a left hand turn at Ashland and drove away before Hamid could follow. She would be more than happy to see this day end. She was going in the wrong direction for home deliberately. *Never can be too cautious*, her *sensei* had always taught them. Sure, the man's car wouldn't start and she knew he had not tampered with it. Still, she wanted that measure of protection. Living in a large city like Chicago had taught Heaven to be cautious.

As she bumped over one pothole after another on Ashland, she cringed at her reasons for being there. A lot of driving, just to throw off someone who wasn't following her. This was ridiculous.

By the time Heaven had done all the backtracking and reached her home, she was royally ticked. For a nanosecond, she thought of skipping her karate class. However, it was the one thing that would allow her to let off some steam in a safe manner.

"Heaven, may I have a word with you?"

Heaven dropped her foot only an inch from her opponent's face, wondering why the *sensei* would stop her in the middle of a fight. She glanced toward the floor before walking into the office. If she had been more aware of her surroundings, she would have known the *sensei* had left the office and was observing her.

"What was all of that?"

She frowned. "I don't know what you're asking me."

"The way you were fighting, you were not in the *dojo*. You looked like a thug, a street fighter. That's not you, Heaven. What's wrong?"

Heaven sawed her teeth back and forth across her top lip. She didn't want to tell the *sensei* what pettiness she was indulging in. Besides, he would think she was saying things she wasn't.

"I'm sorry, I was a little distracted. It was a hard day at the hospital."

"Did one of your patients die?"

"No." Heaven tilted her head and stared at the *sensei*. "But it doesn't look good." She lowered her eyes. Even though her statement was true, it wasn't the reason she was behaving irrationally. It was meeting Hamid.

"For the rest of the evening I want you to practice on your *katas*." The *sensei* smiled. "And if you are frustrated over my words, you may kick the punching bag."

Chastised, Heaven walked back into the *dojo*. She didn't look at any of the other students, even though she knew that they had not heard the conversation. She knew they were thinking it had to be something awful for the *sensei* to call her into the office. Generally he would reprimand a student right then and there, in front of everybody. She shuddered, glad that he hadn't.

Her eyes flicked to the punching bag and she immediately placed Hamid's face there. He was the reason for her bad mood, him and his comments about her being beautiful, then his staring at her as though she were.

She wondered why he'd even bothered to call her beautiful. She wasn't the sort of woman that men preferred. She was short, dark-complexioned with short hair, no breasts to speak of, and very little booty. And, for the past year, she'd worn a perpetual scowl. Since Brandon had dumped her for that white girl, Heaven no longer remembered how to smile.

CHAPTER TWO

As Hamid hung up the phone, the familiar ache of loneliness filled him. He missed his family and Pakistan. His cousin Ahmad's wedding would be in three weeks and he wished he were returning home for that. But his studies would not permit it. He'd come to America to be a doctor, and now was not the time to leave. He had exams in a month. When he earned his license, he would leave and return home with the coveted honor of being a doctor licensed in America, as opposed to one who'd only done his studies there. Then he would allow his family at last to find him a mate.

Hamid smiled. They had begun whispering even in his presence. He was past marrying age and, by now, should have had a baby or two. He had been fighting marriage stubbornly because, somewhere in his gut, he longed for a woman he could fall in love with. Unfortunately it didn't work that way in his culture. There would be no heart-pounding awareness, no sudden burst of lust, no erection that spoke of his desire. It would be a call made, a visit, an exchange of money and jewels, and Hamid would have his bride. They would remain together, maybe for life. Divorce wasn't uncommon, but Hamid had hopes for a marriage that would last forever.

His hand slid beneath the sheets as he tried to imagine the face of his bride, her lovely long black, silky hair, the incense perfuming her body and the ripeness that promised to bear many children.

But as his hand moved up and down, it wasn't the face of a Pakistani woman that he saw, but the dark skin of the angry woman he'd met the day before. He climaxed while trying to wipe her face from his memory. But it was too late, she wouldn't go away.

Hamid wiped his hand on the sheet, disgusted, not by his release but by the fact that a stranger had participated in bringing him satisfaction. His only grace was the woman didn't know. He couldn't help smiling. If she could read minds, he was sure she would send a death ray straight to his heart.

His eyes searched for the clock and he noticed he had very little time. His cousin Sassa was coming over to help him study. At least he would have breakfast at home. He wouldn't have to run the risk of eating in the cafeteria today or next week. He was not working today, and for the next week he would be at John Stroger Hospital. His work as a phlebotomist paid for extras. Money from home took care of most things, but Hamid liked having his own money. It allowed him more freedom in being able to say no. His father had offered to send the money for a plane ticket but Hamid had refused. He didn't tell his father that part of it was due to the way Middle Eastern men and some women were searched in the airports since 9/11.

It was a degrading procedure and Hamid avoided it as much as possible, afraid that one day he would lose his temper and be kicked out of the country. Then he would have failed his family and wasted tens of thousands of dollars, so he held his tongue. And he held it by not putting himself in a position where he might lose it.

Once again, the woman with the funny hair popped into his mind. She had a temper and was not afraid to show it. Hamid rather enjoyed the freedom of that, though he didn't like that her hostility had been directed at him. In his country she would be lucky to have only a switch taken to her for her impudence. He thought of her swatting his hand when she'd assisted with his car.

How dare she hit him! The sting of her hand had stunned Hamid but he'd not reacted, only stared at her as though she were insane. When she'd managed to start his car, he'd remained frozen, his tongue unable to move from the roof of his mouth even to say thank you. He'd felt ignorant and foolish that a woman would know how to make his car run and he didn't.

He made a face, glad that he would never have to see her again, glad that she would never be the kind of woman he would marry. As a matter of fact, he felt sorry for her, and even sorrier for whatever poor man she had in her life. He'd not noticed a ring, but here in America that meant nothing. The women and men indulged easily in sex, and marriage did not seem to be the norm.

Hamid himself had indulged his desires with several women but neither they nor he had ever considered it a relationship. Most times Hamid took care of his own needs. It was easier, no involvement.

He took his shower quickly, even though the sudden urge for a woman that smelled faintly of lemons lingered in his mind, tempting him.

He toweled dry and made his own breakfast, once again thinking of the day he would have a wife to do these things for him. It would make it easier for him to do the things he had to do to follow his path.

When the knock sounded on his door, Hamid was glad for the respite; his mind could now stop wandering roads he could never travel in real life.

"What's up?" His cousin Sassa smiled at him, clapping him on the shoulder. "Are you ready to study?"

"Do you know about cars?" Hamid asked.

"Yes, go to the dealer, see the one you like, buy it, and drive."

Hamid laughed for a moment before turning serious. "I mean, do you know anything about fixing them?"

"Why?"

"My car wouldn't start yesterday when I was ready to leave the hospital."

"Why didn't you just call the tow truck?"

"A truck came and helped me, but I want to know how to do it."

"Why?"

"In case it happens again," Hamid said a bit impatiently.

"You're going to be a doctor, not a mechanic."

"That doesn't mean that I shouldn't know the basics about how to repair my car." Sassa was staring at him as though he'd grown two heads.

"When would you have the time to learn all of this?"

"Sassa, I'm not talking about building a car. I'm merely asking if you know how to start one with a dead battery." He watched while his cousin grinned. When he answered yes, Hamid was suspicious. "Are you sure?"

"How would you know the difference?"

The words packed a punch. That was what the woman had said to him. Hamid wanted to know the difference. "I'm serious," he said, narrowing his eyes and glaring at his cousin. "Do you know how to do it?"

He could tell from the glint in Sassa's eyes that he didn't. "Do you know anyone who can help us?"

"I thought you wanted me to help you study."

"That can wait. This is more important."

"Fixing a car?"

"Yes," Hamid replied. "Come on, Sassa, you know everyone. Don't you know someone who can help?"

"Let me make a call."

Hamid turned away while his cousin made several calls. The fact that Sassa didn't know meant he was not the only male in America who did not know about cars. That made Hamid feel better.

"Hamid, my friend's uncle knows how to fix a dead battery. He said for us to come over before he goes to work."

"What time?"

Sassa looked at his watch. "He leaves at two. That gives us a few hours."

"I want to go and buy the tools." Hamid ignored Sassa's frown. "I know what I need: jumper cables and a wrench." He remembered she called it an open-end wrench.

"He probably has those."

"But I don't. And I need a battery terminal cleaner."

"What? Hamid, what's going on? Why do you need all of this?"

Hamid thought of what to tell his cousin without lying. "The owner of the truck treated me as though I were an imbecile. I didn't like it."

"Did the guy know that in Pakistan you are worth more than the president of this country?"

"What does that have to do with anything? I still required help to fix my car."

"But back home you would have servants to do this for you. Why do you need to learn this? You should have told the ass where to go."

"I didn't say the owner was an ass." Hamid was cringing inwardly. There was no way he was going to admit that the owner of the truck was a woman. Still, he wouldn't allow Sassa to malign her character either.

"Then why would you let a dumb mechanic upset you?" Sassa's nostrils flared with anger at the injustice that had been done to one of his favorite cousins.

"Because this mechanic could fix my car and I couldn't," Hamid replied, "and neither can you, so you need to learn as well."

Sassa scowled, insulted at Hamid's words even though they were true. "I know how to give a jump."

"I thought you didn't."

"I was kidding."

"Do you have cables?"

"No, but that doesn't mean anything."

Hamid knew that it did. The woman had the tools she needed in the back of her truck. Neither he nor Sassa carried anything more than a phone to repair their car, and yesterday even his phone had not worked.

"Let's go to AutoZone." Hamid smiled and headed out of the door.

An hour later, the pair returned to Hamid's apartment and positioned their cars in the parking lot. Sassa opened up the hood of his car and smiled at Hamid. "Now I will show you that I know how to start a car."

"But does it work if the cars are already running?"

"Of course."

Hamid watched while Sassa hooked the cables up to his own car. It looked pretty much like the way the woman had done it, though Hamid wasn't sure.

He lifted the hood of his car and turned just in time to see the cables spark and Sassa drop them on the ground, where they continued sparking. Hamid ran to Sassa's car and yanked the cables from the battery. "What did you do?" he yelled, his heart thundering in his chest.

"Nothing, I didn't do anything wrong."

"You had to. That didn't happen when the...it didn't happen yesterday." Hamid blew out a breath in frustration. He watched his cousin fiddling with the cable, jumping back as they touched and sparked again. He drummed on the fender of the car and looked away from Sassa. Sassa hissed.

"Well, the guy is an expert and I'm not. I don't know what happened. I did it right."

"You couldn't have. Do you know you could have destroyed both of our cars doing that?" Hamid bit his lip, then exhaled his frustration. "And you still think you don't need to learn car repair?"

Three hours later Hamid felt confident that he could now restart any car that only had a dead battery. He smiled to himself, hoping for the chance to run into the woman who had not told him her name as he had offered his.

"Thank you," Hamid said, grinning. "I think we're set."

As an added bonus, the uncle had taught them how to change a flat tire and how to put more air in when it was flat. He'd done it by allowing them to take off the valve cap, place their thumbs directly over the valve stem, and use their fingernail to push the stem to one side, allowing the air to escape. Hamid and Sassa had watched in amazement as the tire went flat and could barely contain themselves as they refilled the tire with the air pump. Hamid knew he would make another trip to the auto parts store. He would buy an air pump.

"You two behave like children. It's hard to imagine you have never done this, or seen it done. Unbelievable," the uncle teased.

This banter Hamid could take. Besides, it didn't matter, for now he knew how to jump start a car, and no one would laugh at him again. An image of the black woman came to him and he imagined her scowl slowly changing into a smile. His heart lurched a bit but he shook himself. Her smile was only in his imagination.

"So have you two learned what you wanted to know?" the uncle asked. "I have to leave for work now."

"Thank you," Sassa laughed.

"Thank you," Hamid mimicked, "you have done more today than you're aware of, and we are in your debt."

Beni looked at him strangely before Sassa spoke. "The tow truck driver, that's why we came." He shrugged, "Hamid wants to prove we're as good as a guy that drives a tow truck."

Hamid only smiled. He wanted to prove he was as good as a woman that drove a dark blue SUV with a sticker he'd noticed that said, 'Nurses do it with precision,' with a picture of a nurse wielding a needle. Hamid would never forget that picture. He'd stared at it the entire time the woman was working on his car, making him feel inept. Now he could only hope that one day fate would allow him to return the favor.

CHAPTER THREE

Heaven took in a whiff of the orange-glazed ribs Peaches was eating. When the tangy barbeque sauce from the pork sandwiches wafted toward her from the sandwiches Latanya and Ongela were eating, Heaven couldn't prevent the longing glances she cast toward her friends' plates. She glanced at her own plate, at her chicken salad, and remembered why she was eating it. Hamid.

Laughter brought her back to the present. She looked at her friends. "What?" she asked, knowing they had been laughing at her.

"If you want some ribs or a pork sandwich, just order it," Ongela said, grinning at her.

"I can't. Ever since talking to that guy in the hospital I haven't been able to eat pork."

"But he wasn't the first guy to try and get you not to eat pork. What was different about him? Was he fine?"

Like I'm really going to answer that, Heaven thought. "I don't know. I only remember him telling me the food was going to kill me and that it had worms."

"Would you please," Latanya snapped, "we're trying to eat."

"See what I mean? When you're eating and someone says something like that, it makes you lose your appetite." Heaven glanced at her friends to make sure they got her point.

"So what are you doing, trying to make us lose ours? Here, girl, you want some ribs, take a taste. You don't have to eat something you don't want, 'cause I'm not giving up the pig." Peaches gave Heaven a meaningful look and bit into the meaty rib she'd been waving.

A round of high fives and hoots followed by laughter filled their area. Heaven ignored the rib her friend held out and instead dug into her salad. She would have to admit the salad was very good with the crunchy pecans, mandarin oranges, and chicken baked with crushed walnuts. It wasn't bad at all. But then everything at Ruby's restaurant was good.

For a few minutes, everyone ate in silence. Then the subject of men was brought up, as it always was. The fact that Heaven was off pork was forgotten.

"So, Heaven, how long has it been since you had a date? I hope you don't give up eating pork as long as you've given up men."

Heaven glared in Peaches's direction. "I haven't given up men, but I'm not in a hurry to rush into a relationship either."

"You should have found a guy the very next day after Brandon dumped you. You should have jumped a white guy."

Heaven frowned. "Why?"

"To get even with Brandon."

"You think me finding a white guy would make Brandon come back to me? And even if it did, why do you think I'd take his sorry ass back?"

"Because we thought he was your soul mate."

Heaven deepened the frown. "You've got to be kidding. If he were my soul mate we'd be together."

"Don't worry about it, the heffa is probably nasty, doing things you wouldn't."

Heaven looked at Ongela but didn't answer immediately. She never got into her sex life. It wasn't her friends' business. If they wanted to tell her all about theirs, that was on them. She shrugged her shoulders. "Who knows?" she said, making her answer as non-committal as possible.

"Look, don't pretend that his going with that stank heffa isn't killing you."

"It bothers me, but it bothers me more that I wasted so much of my time with him on a dream that was going nowhere. But hey, if he's happy, more power to him."

"You know the thing that I can't get is that black men will have a fit if they see us with a man that's not black. They'll almost come to blows. I've been called a bitch more times than I care to remember. Hell, at one time when I was dating Tim, I thought bitch was my name."

They all laughed before Heaven rolled her eyes and asked Peaches, "Is that why you swore never again? You couldn't put up with it?"

"I know it's my business, but I don't like having a brotha look at me like I'm a traitor." Peaches took another bite of her ribs. "Black men have enough problems without us emasculating them."

"That's their problem," Latanya cut in. "We want to protect them from the world and we've made them into cripples that we don't even want. They think nothing of dating or marrying anything with a…excuse me, they don't mind doing whatever they think they're big enough to do. Then they want to write books and brag about being on the down low, as though we're supposed to give them a prize.

"And they think we should admire them for the courage to come out and say it but they don't want to come out and admit to being gay. No, they were just curious, or bi. That's a load of crap."

"Yeah we almost have to go outside of the black man if we want a man." Ongela almost shouted, wanting to be heard after Latanya's tirade.

"But I don't want to," Heaven insisted. "I love black men."

"So do I." Ongela chimed in.

One by one, the women voiced their choices and Heaven reaffirmed for herself that if there was someone else for her it would be a black man, or no man. She would not do what Brandon had done.

"But a sista can look, can't she? I mean sometimes a little looking is good for the soul." Peaches laughed, putting her hand up for high-fives.

"Like cheesecake," Heaven piped in, grinning at Ongela. "It looks good but I don't have any desire to taste it."

"So the dot-head—"

The words grated across her brain and she turned in Peaches's direction. "Don't go there," Heaven stopped her.

"What?"

"Why do we all have to engage in racial slurs?"

"Girl, that ain't no slur. They have a dot on their forehead." Peaches defended her words.

The women laughed, but Heaven turned toward Peaches. "First off, Hamid is from Pakistan, and he's Muslim. I know for a fact that he doesn't have a dot on his forehead. Even if he did it's wrong to say that. How would you like it if they called us colored, or kiffer?" The women stopped and looked at her.

"It doesn't feel so good when it's on the other foot, does it?" Heaven asked. "It's Hindus, who wear the dot in the center of their foreheads. They wear it for religious reasons. It represents divine sight. It's the same as what some people think of as the third eye. They use the dot as a reminder to cultivate the spiritual vision, to see things not just physically but with the mind's eye as well."

"It was only a joke. And we didn't ask for a lesson on religions. Dang, you must have felt something more than nausea when you met this guy. You have been acting crazy ever since it happened."

"It has nothing to do with him. I just don't know why people, and that includes us, have to degrade others with our put-downs."

Heaven took a deep breath and blew it out. "I've done the same thing a million times without thinking. Do you know how long I thought Maxwell Street's real name was Jew Town? I'd heard it said so long and had said it so often that I never thought about it being a slur."

Heaven looked at her friends, knowing they were wishing she would just shut up, not shine a light on their own prejudices. After all, they didn't mean anything by what they said, did they?

"You at least have to admit that we do it all the time and a lot of us don't think about the words. Take, for example, the wife-beater T-shirt. Did you know that term came from Dago tees? Think about it, Dago is a racial slur."

"Dang, Heaven, nobody asked you to police us. You weren't talking like this a month ago."

Heaven glanced at Latanya. "You're right, I wasn't, but I should have been."

"So you want to meet this guy you're defending and go out with him?"

Heaven rolled her eyes. "Look, Latanya, you just heard me say I won't date anyone but a strong black man. Besides, I wasn't defending Hamid. I was voicing my opinion."

"That doesn't answer the question. If you saw this guy again, would you date him if he asked?"

"I don't want to deal with any drama, and to deal with a Muslim man would be too, too much drama, no thank you."

"Heaven, isn't that a contradiction? You're on our case about using slurs and now you're saying you won't give a man a chance if he's not black."

"That has nothing to do with race or ethnicity. I just don't want the drama. A black man comes with more than enough of his own. Another race or ethnicity and a person could get high blood pressure dealing with the problems." Heaven laughed and ran her fingers through her twists, thinking of Hamid asking her what they were called.

"Whatcha doing then, dating Bob?"

"Bob? I don't know any Bob." Heaven frowned.

"You're kidding," Ongela laughed. "I've dated Bob. I think we all have."

"Okay, I know this is a joke. Who is Bob?"

"Battery operated boyfriend," the women shouted in unison and gave each other high fives once again. Heaven groaned inwardly; she should have known. They all laughed again, the mood lightened.

"Yeah, look at you." Peaches hit her playfully. "Not even a date and you're not eating pork. I can't imagine what you would do if you did date him."

Latanya smirked, looking around at the group before adding her comments. "I guess you would start covering up and reading the Koran and stop going to church."

"What's the big deal?" Ongela teased. "It's not like she goes anyway."

"But I believe in God," Heaven cut in.

"Depending on his religion he might also, and you do know different people call God by a different name."

"But I believe in Jesus as my Messiah. As far as I know Muslims believe in him only as a prophet. And I'd give up any man before giving up Jesus. So why even start something that has no possible way of working with someone who doesn't?" Heaven said.

"You've got no choice but to believe. Look at the name your mama gave you."

Heaven ignored the teasing. She'd always taken a razzing about her name and had hated it until her daddy said when she'd been born he looked at her and thought he had everything he had ever wanted, and that at that moment he could have died and gone to Heaven. When he told that to her mother, well, Heaven was the only name that seemed appropriate.

"Peaches, your name is not any better." Heaven looked at her friend. Besides herself, Peaches was the only other one who was teased because of her name.

"But that's a nickname."

"So what?"

For the next two hours the women bantered back and forth, bashing black men in general and the scarcity of good ones, like them or not. Heaven understood them all. She was also wondering when and if she would ever find a good black man. Because, like it or not, a good portion of them were either gay, selling drugs, gang banging, or in prison. And the ones that weren't were trying single-handedly to populate the planet or were dating someone other than black women. It was a wonder that any of them still wanted to keep looking for a black man.

Heaven walked the aisles of the grocery store thinking about the conversation she'd had with her friends the night before. She didn't know why she'd even talked about Hamid, a man she'd met once in her life, a man that she would more than likely not meet again. But she had talked about him.

And the conversation had been the same as it always was with her friends. Date black men only, nurture them. *Baloney.* But she would do it because, one day, she hoped to be the mother of a strong black male.

She picked up a package of ham, determined to put the remark Hamid had made about pork having worms behind her. *This should do it*, she thought. She would buy a bottle of wine and wash the ham down.

She did.

Heaven woke from a dream she'd rather not have had. It was of Brandon and the girl he'd left her for. They were happy. In the dream Brandon told her he'd found his soul mate. Heaven could still feel the sting of tears on her cheeks, the ones she'd shed in her dreams. Hamid had been there in her dreams and had stood a ways off, smiling at her. That in itself was freaky enough. But she'd seen herself walking toward him in a sari. She remembered the knowledge that had been in her heart. She'd forgiven Brandon at last because she had also found her soul mate.

Heaven hopped from the bed and went for water. She knew she could interpret her dream as nothing more than the residue of the night out with her friends, the conversation about Brandon and Hamid, their teasing her about getting off pork. All of that, coupled with the ham sandwich she'd had before bedtime, had likely produced the dream. That and the fact that for the first time in nearly a month she was returning to Rush Presbyterian St. Luke hospital.

She finished her water, returned to bed, punched her pillow, and ordered her mind not to dream. This time it obeyed her.

LET'S GET IT ON

The sound of voices and running feet alerted Heaven. She stopped and looked around the parking garage. She'd been jumpy the entire day. And since the day was over, she could admit it. From the moment she'd set foot inside the hospital, she had been searching for Hamid. Why, she wasn't sure.

As she'd eaten her breakfast and lunch, she'd peeked across the crowded cafeteria, expecting a voice to tell her that her food was going to kill her.

And now in the parking garage she was listening for a helpless male voice. She laughed at her foolishness; the dream had gotten to her.

Hamid whatever-his-last-name-was had gotten to her. She supposed in a way it was a good thing. Alone in the garage she could admit to herself that, for the past year, her animosity toward Brandon had left her feeling angrier than she could ever remember being.

For a year it had all been directed at Brandon, but a few weeks ago it had spilled onto Hamid. She would probably never see the man again, but if she did she might apologize for her abrupt behavior in the garage. She would not apologize for anything else.

Heaven sat in her truck, started it, and drove away, thinking that maybe it was time she put away some of her anger.

CHAPTER FOUR

As Sassa and Hamid walked down Ashland Avenue, Hamid came to a dead stop. He couldn't believe it. He stared at the sticker on the SUV, his heart pounding. He knew there could be another nurse somewhere with the same sticker, but his heart told him this was his nurse.

"Come on, what are you doing?"

Hamid glanced in his cousin's direction. "I know the person who owns this truck."

"Big deal."

"I want to see them."

Sassa came back toward him. "You want to see her."

"I didn't say her."

"I would hope that you're not waiting out here hoping to see a man." Sassa frowned. "Are you?"

"Of course not. I need to find her," Hamid answered, looking up and down the block. "She could be anywhere." He bent down and before he had a chance to stop himself he pulled the valve stem cap off her front tire and was holding his fingernail against the valve stem to allow the air to escape.

"What are you doing?" Sassa hissed angrily, looking up and down the street. "You're going to get us both in trouble."

"What does it look like I'm doing? I told you, I have to see this woman. Fate has put her in my path."

"Fate!" Now Sassa was shouting. "It is not fate when you help yourself."

Hamid grinned before glancing at his handiwork and deciding to let out more air. When the tire was sufficiently flat, he recapped it and stood.

"You think that's fate?" Sassa asked. "That's called vandalism."

"Don't worry, I'm going to fix it for her." Hamid knew the moment his cousin put the pieces together, but he ignored the smug look. "Come on, I have to find her."

After going through most of the stores on the strip and three of the restaurants, Hamid saw her sitting at a table in a *Hala* deli. He rushed inside with Sassa following.

He walked directly to the table and smiled down at her. "Hello."

Heaven glanced at her friends before looking up at Hamid. She needed the time to make sure her face would remain emotionless. She tilted her head to the right as if for a better look. "Do I know you?" she asked at last, knowing that the slight tremble in her voice gave away the fact that she remembered him.

"How's your chicken?" Hamid asked, grinning, knowing she remembered him. "You didn't tell me your name before."

"Heaven," three feminine voices piped in. "Heaven Adams."

Hamid turned in their direction. "Thank you. My name is Hamid Ahmad. I'm sorry to have interrupted your dinner. I just wanted to say hello to Heaven, and to thank her for her previous kindness to me." He slipped his hand into his pocket, withdrew his card case and handed a card to Heaven.

"If you should ever find yourself in need of assistance, please call me. I'd love to return the favor."

"I don't think so." Heaven looked away at the grinning, questioning faces of her friends. She glanced back toward Hamid.

"You never know," he said. "You might find your car disabled one day." He smiled and walked away.

"I think we should stay," Sassa said softly, touching Hamid's arm to stop him in his tracks.

Hamid looked down at his cousin. "Why?"

"For starters, you just told her you disabled her car. Let's eat so she won't suspect us immediately."

Hamid smiled in acquiescence. He definitely wouldn't mind staying in the restaurant and watching Heaven. He almost laughed aloud at her name. Of course, someone with such a sour disposition would be named after the sweetest place man could think of. Regardless of the faith, everyone wanted to go to Heaven. He laughed again, amused that fate had seen fit to send him a woman named Heaven.

Heaven felt her cheeks flaming, and for once in her life was happy that her skin tone was so dark no one would notice. She did her best to pretend that Hamid was not sitting a few tables away staring at her. She knew ignoring her friends wouldn't be quite as easy.

Peaches started the ball rolling. "So that's him."

"Who?" Heaven replied, taking a bite of her food, still pretending.

"Yeah, right, and you tried to pretend that you didn't know what he looked like."

"I didn't notice," Heaven lied.

"How the hell could you not notice? The guy is fine," Ongela almost shouted in a louder than necessary voice. "A blind woman would have noticed it. Look at the way he's staring at you. Come on, Heaven."

"Didn't we have this conversation? I like black men."

"Hamid's close."

"Close, but I'm not ready for more drama in my life."

"Heaven, I didn't hear the guy ask you out. He only said he'd like to help you with your car. Maybe you're all reading too much into it."

Heaven looked at Ongela sharply before turning and catching Hamid smiling at her. That was not the look of a man interested only in starting her battery. Heaven looked again. A*t least not my car battery*, she thought.

She would have to put an end to this before it got started. She would admit that she was glad to see Hamid again and she would make it her business to apologize to him before she left the restaurant. As for any more, well, no thanks.

Hamid picked at his salad, not taking his eyes from Heaven. There was something that intrigued him about her. He thought of what the prophet had said, that if you saved one life, it was like saving a hundred. She was the one he wanted to save. He owed her that much for her help. He would teach her about a better way, but leave the choice to her.

"You should stop staring before the woman thinks you're a stalker."

Hamid turned toward Sassa. He'd almost forgotten that his cousin was there. "I was not staring, merely looking."

"Well, you look any harder and her clothes will melt. Come on, stop it. Besides, I've never seen a black woman with a Pakistani."

Sassa's remarks caused Hamid to frown. "I did not tell you I wanted to bed the woman."

"You didn't have to," Sassa answered. "Your look says it all. You're embarrassing her. Can't you tell?""

"Do you think she would be embarrassed if she wasn't interested?"

"How would I know? I just met her." Sassa smiled. "Is she the tow truck driver?"

※

"I don't believe it," Heaven almost screamed. Her friends had gotten into their vehicles and driven away. How could she have a flat? She stopped and checked the tire. The cap was on; she must have driven over a nail.

Now was not the night to change a tire. Heaven groaned as her eyes fell on the new black pumps she was wearing and the short mini skirt. She was dressed for clubbing, not for this. In fact, she was supposed to be following her friends to the club. Just as she snapped her purse open to retrieve her phone and call for help, she saw Hamid walking out of the door with the man he'd introduced as his cousin.

She glanced at the tire again before glaring at Hamid. This was no accident. The man was a moron, plain and simple. She wondered if he'd been following her, waiting for an opportunity to do this. Was he so macho that he had to prove himself? Would he go to such lengths?

But Hamid appeared to be going in the opposite direction. He wouldn't do that if he had wanted to prove himself. "Hamid," she yelled angrily. She called his name twice more, annoyed when he didn't turn around. Then she remembered. This was a macho game. "Hamid, I need your help," she yelled, barely keeping the anger from her tone.

He immediately turned and smiled, then walked toward her.

"Heaven, what's wrong?"

Innocence, she thought, his voice reeked of it, but his eyes sparkled with mischief.

"Hamid, I do hope you know how to re-inflate my tire. Don't bother denying that you did it, just fix it." She leaned back against the hood of her truck and waited until he walked away. When Hamid returned he was alone, but carrying an air pump. So he'd learned and wanted to show off. Considering the way she'd treated him, she couldn't much blame him. Still, she made him watch while she expertly pumped air into her tire.

"Listen, Hamid," Heaven began as soon as she was done. "I'm sorry that I was so rude to you in the garage. I was having a bad day." She'd wanted to say year but didn't. "Anyway, I took it out on you, so I'm sorry. But you didn't have to flatten my tire."

"I wanted to return the favor."

"But you didn't return the favor," Heaven reprimanded. "You caused a problem. You can only…" She stopped. "Oh, never mind. Listen, Hamid, if you have anything in mind, like hitting on me, forget it. Okay?"

"Why would I hit you?"

His eyes narrowed and he peered at her in such a way that her heart lurched again. Heaven realized he might not know what she meant.

"Hitting on me, I mean trying to date me." Hamid's chin lifted and he held her gaze, his own unwavering. "I only date black men," she explained.

"I didn't ask you for a date, Heaven."

"But…I thought…never mind, I guess I got it wrong. But you were looking for me tonight and you let the air out of my tire. There was a reason for that. What are you looking for?"

Hamid thought over the question. "I'm looking for a friend."

"Why? You seem to have friends."

"That's my cousin. I'm looking to make American friends. I want to learn more about American culture."

If she believed that… "I'll bet," Heaven said softly. "What do you want to know about our culture?"

"Too much for you to answer in one night. I have a proposition for you. I need a tutor and I can pay well. Would you be willing to teach me your culture? Perhaps I could even teach you about mine."

"I didn't ask to learn about yours."

"Do you know about my culture?"

"Why should I?"

Hamid stared at Heaven. "I didn't know Americans chose to be ignorant. I thought it was an accident."

Oh no, he didn't just call me ignorant. "I know we might have a language barrier, Hamid, but you just insulted me. Was that your intent?"

"Is the truth considered an insult in America?"

Not again. Heaven walked away from Hamid and toward the driver's side of her truck. This conversation was over.

"Will you teach me?" Hamid asked, following behind her.

She thought it over for a second. If she didn't, someone was going to kick his ass for the way he went about things.

"How long have you been in this country?" Heaven asked without giving him a direct answer.

"Long enough to know women can repair cars and that you get insulted easily and that you have no knowledge of how what you eat can kill you. Either that or you're deliberately trying to commit suicide."

Heaven climbed in her truck wondering if she should just do Hamid a favor and smack him in the head with the door of her truck, leave him senseless. Perhaps when he woke he would have gained some knowledge.

"Will you help me?" he asked again.

She turned the key in the ignition, snatched the door from his hand and hit the lock. But Heaven couldn't drive away because Hamid stood in the path of her truck. So she stayed as she was, because Hamid stayed as he was. "I'll call you," she said at last. His eyes took on that mischievous look again and he did not move. He didn't believe her and that was a good thing, because she'd been lying.

Heaven tried again. "Okay, seriously, I'll call you."

"Why can't you give me your number and let me call you?"

So Hamid isn't as dumb as I first thought. "I don't have any cards," she answered.

"And you don't know your number?" His lips turned up in a smile. "Where are you going now, Heaven?"

"To a club, my friends are waiting for me."

"Mind if Sassa and I come?"

"This is a dance club."

"I dance."

"This is a blues club."

"I like blues."

"It's a mostly black club."

"Would I not be welcomed there?"

"There's a lot of smoking and drinking that goes on there."

"Would I be required to smoke and drink in order to go inside?" He looked innocently at her. "Do you smoke and drink? A person with the name of Heaven? Surely not."

Heaven rolled her eyes. This was nonsense. It was harder explaining to him than keeping him out. "Just follow me," she said. When she saw he still didn't trust her, she smiled in spite of her annoyance. "I will not leave until you and Sassa get in your car. I give you my word."

And she kept it, but the moment he was in his car Heaven took off as fast as the law allowed, hoping she'd lose him, but not surprised when she didn't.

When they reached the club, Heaven parked and waited for Hamid to pull into the spot beside her. He grinned at her as he walked next to her. Sassa followed behind them, muttering the entire time.

"You attempted to lose me," Hamid said.

"But I didn't."

"I'm a very good driver."

"I see," Heaven answered and pointed to the club across the street. "Ready?"

He took her arm and walked her across the street. She started to tell him she didn't need his assistance to cross the street but didn't. Nor did she speak again until they were inside the club and Hamid was bringing out his wallet.

"I'll pay," she said, taking out her own wallet.

"Why?"

"Because this isn't a date."

"I thought we were going to be friends. Can't I treat a friend?"

Heaven stared at Hamid for a moment and was almost undone by the intensity in his dark eyes. "I'll tell you what," she compromised. "You pay for yourself and Sassa and I'll pay for myself. This way there is no obligation on either of our parts."

"Are you worried that I will expect something for ten dollars?"

"You're a man," Heaven answered and held out her hand to get it stamped. She looked around, spotted her friends and walked toward them without asking Hamid or Sassa to follow, but knowing they would. She ignored the looks cast her way by her friends and pulled two more chairs from the table next to them for Hamid and Sassa, then sat.

Hamid was eyeing her strangely and her conscience pricked her. She'd brought them; it was up to her to make sure they were comfortable, or as comfortable as they could be if they didn't know anything about the blues. Well, Hamid couldn't blame her; he'd said that he did, and apparently, he must have thought Sassa understood the blues. She wouldn't worry about Hamid's cousin. It was Hamid who'd brought him.

"Hamid wanted to come." She pointed toward each of her friends and introduced them. "Hamid wanted to learn some American culture." She looked toward Sassa. "His cousin Sassa, I think, is just along for the ride."

Her friends started laughing. "I'm serious," Heaven said, raising her voice to be heard over the music. "He's going to pay me to tutor him."

"In what exactly?" Ongela made it sound dirty. She looked at Hamid as though he were a tasty treat.

"Like I said, the culture. We haven't worked out the details." Heaven would have blushed if she could. She knew what this sounded like, and if one of them had just announced something so preposterous, she would have laughed.

"Look, we're not dating," she announced harshly. "Hamid understands that I date only black men."

The music had stopped and Heaven's voice carried across the room. She glanced in Hamid's direction. If his feelings were hurt, his eyes, as black as midnight, hid it. She'd not intended that; she was only shouting to be heard over the music.

"Of course, Heaven has failed to mention that I have not asked her for a date and I have no intention of it. My only interest in her is as a teacher. Heaven is not my type." Hamid held Heaven's gaze, "as I am not hers," he continued, putting her in her place.

Neither would drop their gaze. Heaven scowled, trying to look as ferocious as she could. She knew the look on her face. Brandon had told her often enough when she'd done it that she looked evil. Right now, she wanted Hamid to feel the same way, but he wouldn't budge and neither would she.

"Dang, would you two cut it out?" Peaches interrupted. "Hamid, can you dance?" she said, pulling his sleeve to make him move.

Heaven continued glaring at Hamid, noticing that even as he went to the dance floor he positioned himself to return her glare. Only he wasn't glaring. He was looking at her with confusion and amusement. A second or two passed and Latanya had Sassa out on the dance floor.

"Heaven, why are you staring at that man like that?" Ongela whispered in her ear, teasing her. "Have you tired of Bob?" she asked, laughing softly.

"I'm staring at him because he's staring at me."

"Do you think if you stopped staring at him he might stop staring at you?"

Heaven rolled her eyes and finally looked away from Hamid to glare at Ongela. "He's weird and someone needs to put him in his place. He let the air out of my tire so he could put it back in."

Ongela laughed, "Did you let him, or did you do it yourself?"

"What do you think?"

"Are you really planning on hanging out with him to teach him?"

"Of course. I've always wanted to be a teacher, and I can't think of anybody who needs to learn a few things more than Hamid does."

Ongela looked toward the dance floor at Hamid, who was still staring at Heaven. "I get it," she said. "You want to teach him a lesson."

"You got it, a lesson he will never forget. When I'm done with Hamid he'll run screaming back to Pakistan." The women clapped hands and laughed.

Then Ongela said in a more serious tone, "Just be careful that he doesn't teach you a lesson. He's good looking, and he's intelligent and funny."

Ongela glanced again toward the dance floor. "He has moves, I'll give him that. I think you may have met your match. He can take it as well as dish it out. You should have seen your face when he said he didn't want to date you. I wish I'd had a camera."

Heaven spent most of the evening watching her friends flirt with Hamid or dance with him. She wondered what had happened to their pact to nourish and protect the brothers. She glanced quickly toward

Ongela as the high-pitched sound of her laughter carried over the strains of the blues. She'd undoubtedly hit it off with Hamid.

Why not? Heaven thought. He was tall, dark, and handsome to the max, and his silky looking beard gave him a certain something. One more look and Heaven closed her eyes. Damn Brandon anyway. They should have been married by now. If so, she wouldn't have to keep looking away from Hamid every time their eyes met.

With no luck, Hamid kept trying to keep his eyes from drifting in Heaven's direction. *Fate,* he thought again, and smiled at one of Heaven's friends. The women were flirting with him, and while they were attractive, he didn't desire them. He must be a glutton for punishment for preferring the tiny woman whose words were as deadly as snake venom, but he did.

When he'd held her arm to cross the street, he'd felt an electrical surge that had gone from the crown of his head to his groin. This sensation was what Hamid had been searching for his entire adult life. But fate or not, he would not pursue a woman who'd made it plain she considered him incompetent in more ways than just his lack of mechanical knowledge.

Hamid thought of their agreement for her to teach him about American culture. He had a surprise for her. When he was done teaching her, they'd both see just how competent he really was. Even if he didn't pursue her, he wanted her respect.

CHAPTER FIVE

Heaven stared in the mirror, trying hard not to picture Hamid in her mind, the way he'd been in her dreams. Suddenly she had an urge to see his hair loosed from the rubber band. It was jet black and curly. His beard was well groomed and trimmed in the same style that many black men wore.

Try as she might to shake his image from her mind, Hamid's face refused to return to the mist that shrouded her dream. His aura was too potent. Asleep or awake, Hamid's face invaded her thoughts. She knew without a doubt that he would definitely make her friends forget their pact. There was something about him, a gentlemanly quality to go along with his arrogant and somewhat chauvinistic attitude.

His eyes…She hadn't decided if they were a cocoa brown or black; they seemed to shift color. Heaven had no intention to admit it to anyone, but the way his eyes fastened on her as if he could pierce the way to her soul with but a glance had her backing even farther away.

Her friends were right. It had been way too long since she'd had anyone she cared for in her life. She didn't intend to do anything stupid with Hamid simply because he was now in her line of vision. Her pact still stood, whether the others honored it or not. The ringing of her bell startled her out of her reverie. Showtime, she thought and headed for the door.

"Hi," she said to Hamid's grinning face, "what do you want to start on first?"

"I'd like to see your apartment."

"That's not what you're paying me for."

Hamid shrugged his shoulders.

"Why do you need to see my apartment?" Heaven asked suspiciously.

"I don't need to see it, I want to see it."

Heaven hesitated; she still didn't really know anything about this man. She peered up at him, his size not intimidating her. She was a brown belt; she could kick his butt easily. "Come on," she said over her shoulder, determined to not let his charm or sex appeal get to her. *God, but he did look good.*

It was the shortest tour of her apartment in history. Heaven barely paused as she led him through the various rooms and headed back to the living room.

"You've seen my apartment. Now do you want to get started?"

"Do you own this apartment?" Hamid asked.

"You're awfully nosy."

"It was just a question. Are you embarrassed by it?"

"Yes, I own this apartment. Now if you've finished interviewing me, suppose you tell me exactly what you want to learn about American culture." She tilted her head and slanted her eyes. "Or is it African-American culture you're interested in?"

"Are you not American?"

"Yes, of course I am," Heaven stumbled.

"Then why do you qualify yourself as African-American instead of just plain American? In my country we refer to you all as Americans."

Heaven shrugged her shoulder, wondering herself. "Hamid, to be honest with you, I have no idea."

"Do you just do as others do without having a good reason?"

For a moment she wondered if he were being sarcastic, then saw from the curious look on his face that he really didn't understand. *Well, join the club*, she thought, *neither do I.*

"Hamid, you've been in this country long enough to know that everyone is separated into groups: American Indians, Italian Americans, Mexican Americans, Polish Americans, Iranian Americans." She shrugged her shoulders again. "See what I mean?"

"I see, but it is a lot of trouble."

"I know in Pakistan and other parts of the Middle East there are different sects, so why are you judging what we do?"

"Now you speak as though you're a part of all the groups. Did I just offend you or your entire country?"

For a moment, Heaven didn't answer. Then she twisted her mouth to the side and decided to ignore Hamid's question for now. "Hamid, what is it you want to know?"

"I want to know what you call yourself so that I won't make any mistakes with you."

"You mean you want to be politically correct?" She gave him a look, then shook her head and shrugged. "We've been colored, Negro, black, and now African-American. Personally, I prefer black. As for being politically correct, I've had other black people correct me if I didn't say African-American."

"So what do you want me to call you?"

"Call me Heaven, that's my name."

He smiled and Heaven felt pulled by the brilliance of it. She had to get back on an even keel. "Do you want to discuss books, music, food or," she grinned, "how to repair a car?" That lightened the moment. Hamid returned her grin.

"I think I know a bit about car repair," he responded, "and I know something about your taste in music."

Heaven opened her mouth to object but Hamid held her gaze and continued.

"Based on the fact that you attended a blues club, I find it safe to say you like the blues. Is that a fair statement?"

Heaven blinked. She looked at the way his dark lashes fell over his eyes even when they were open. She was held captive by the intensity of his gaze framed by his black curly hair. She wanted to ask…she had to know. "Hamid, are there any African-Americans living in Pakistan?" The words were out before she could think.

"There are Africans living in my country and there are Americans. Whether they are African Americans?" He shrugged his shoulders. "How long have you been a nurse?" he asked, picking up a photograph of her and Brandon from the table.

Heaven leaned over and took the picture from him. "Seven years," she answered.

"Is he a nurse?"

"No."

"A doctor?"

Heaven sighed, "Yes."

"You have feelings for him?"

Again Heaven sighed, but this time she also rolled her eyes. "You could say that." She shot daggers at the picture and only stopped when Hamid laughed.

"I see, you don't like him anymore."

"Hamid, what does my personal life have to do with teaching you?" She watched as he shifted on the couch and shrugged. She shook her head, feeling heat from his nearness. She tossed the picture into the chair on the opposite side of the room.

"Look, Hamid, I'm charging you by the hour so I would suggest you pick a subject." For a long, intense moment, he stared at her before speaking. Heaven watched the way his lips opened slightly. He closed his eyes and was smiling when he reopened them.

"I want to know the difference you find between Middle Eastern men and black men."

"Are you paying for this question?"

Hamid glanced at his watch. "Of course."

"Well, number one, I can't imagine a brother paying anyone to answer that question." She smiled when she caught the slight flaring of Hamid's nose.

"Muslim men believe all men are brothers."

"Are you teaching this class or am I?" Heaven asked.

"I was only making an observation and trying to educate you at the same time."

"I didn't ask to be educated."

"As you wish." He shrugged carelessly.

"For another thing, the brothers eat pork." Heaven smiled at Hamid, but when he didn't return the smile she looked away and, for the life of her, couldn't think of another thing to say.

"Are you saying the only difference in the men of my country and yours is what they eat?"

"Of course not, don't be" Heaven stopped herself. She'd decided if she were going to teach Hamid, she would not be rude.

"What were you going to say?" he asked.

"Nothing."

"Are you certain?"

"Hamid, you're annoying." Heaven turned back to him. "Don't get me wrong. There is something about you that is different and appealing, but the way you turn everything I say into a question really gets on my nerves."

"And you would prefer I didn't do it?"

"See what I mean? That's another question."

"Do you dislike me, Heaven?"

"No."

"Then why do I annoy you? I'm asking only for truthful answers, and I'm paying you for them, so what's the problem?" He cocked his head slightly and waited.

"Do you want to know the difference, Hamid? Right now if you were a *brother*," she said with emphasis, "I would tell you to go to hell and it wouldn't require any explanation. But with you we spend ten minutes debating it, and it's annoying. Don't ask me why, or I might be inclined to answer the way I would answer a brother."

Neither spoke. For a second they stared at each other. Hamid was once again looking at her twists with curiosity. Heaven ignored him. "Why did you try to take my tray from me when we met?"

"I wanted to save you."

"Save me from what?" He smiled and Heaven melted. It was then she knew that tutoring Hamid was a bad idea.

"Why were you so angry that day?"

"Another question?" She watched as he smiled shyly. "I'll tell you what, Hamid, forget about paying me today. Why don't we just get the questions out of the way, get to know each other a little better. What do you say?"

"Thank you."

Laughter followed Hamid's statement. Heaven couldn't help it. She didn't know if it was the way he said things, or that she felt the sincerity behind his words, but he amused her and since she'd found little reason to laugh in the last year she was more than happy to have Hamid around. "What would you like to know about me?"

"I want to know how you got your hair that way."

For three weeks, Heaven had been tutoring Hamid on her off days and his. It was hard coordinating their schedules. When one was off, the other one worked. At times, she almost felt guilty taking the money he paid her. He was making her laugh, and the laughter was healing her soul.

"Heaven, would you rub my back a little before you leave?"

"Of course." Heaven put down her things and walked back over to the bed. Mrs. Reed was one of the nicest patients she'd had at Rush. The woman was in the last stages of cancer, but her concern was for her family and even the staff. She rarely asked for anything.

"Are you in pain?" Heaven asked.

"Just a little."

"You should really think of taking something. There is no need for you to be in pain." Heaven watched while the older woman smiled. Heaven knew the patient would refuse medication, same as always.

"I have no idea how long I have left, Heaven," the woman said quietly. "And all I can do is make memories for my family. I don't want their last memory to be me lying here helpless. I want to talk to them, tell them I love them, how proud I am of them. I want to help them through their grief."

Heaven smiled, a feeling of sadness filling her before she could answer. She poured lotion in her hand and rubbed her palms together to warm the liquid. "They would understand," she said. "They're your family."

"You're young, Heaven," Mrs. Reed whispered and Heaven noticed a tear in the corner of her left eye.

"I want to see my husband's face as long as I can. I've loved him since I was fourteen. He's my soul mate. Haven't you ever been in love, Heaven?"

Of course I have. I once thought Brandon was my soul mate, but look what happened.

"I was in love once, but it didn't work out."

"Then it wasn't love."

"It was." Heaven swallowed, not wanting to argue with the patient. She was sure she'd loved Brandon every bit as much as Mrs. Reed loved her husband. They'd been childhood sweethearts, just as Mrs. Reed and her husband had been.

Heaven rubbed more lotion into the older woman's skin as her mind wandered to her past with Brandon. Soul mates? If there were such a thing, they should have been it.

They'd both known exactly what they wanted, and had spent most of their lives working toward it. Heaven had always wanted to be a nurse and Brandon had wanted to be a doctor. For a short time, Heaven had also thought of going to medical school and becoming a doctor, but decided she liked more hands-on care. Besides, she didn't want to be the one to make the major decisions on a patient's health. The thought of prescribing the wrong treatment terrified her. Her strength lay in her ability to empathize, to nurture, and to give hope. She was born to be a nurse. So she and Brandon had mapped it out. He would be a doctor and she would be his nurse. They would pool their money and open a practice. They would marry and have babies and eventually Heaven would become a nurse practitioner, more than a nurse, but less than a doctor. That suited her.

But a little over a year ago Brandon had changed all of that. They finally had the money saved to buy the practice of an older doctor in Oak Park who was ready to retire. Out of the blue Brandon had come to her and told her that he didn't want her to go into business with him, that he was doing it alone. She could remember the look on his face when he'd dropped the next bombshell: He no longer loved her and he wanted to break up.

Heaven hadn't begged or asked why, but when she'd seen his new office nurse when she'd gone to take him a plant as a show of friendship, she'd known immediately that the woman was the reason he'd left her.

"Heaven, you're rubbing a little too hard."

"I'm sorry," Heaven muttered and stopped. She'd forgotten where she was and what she was doing. For over a year hating Brandon had interfered too often with her life.

Heaven gave the woman a sip of water, checked her IV, and asked if there was anything else she could get for her.

In less than a minute the next private duty nurse was there and Heaven could leave. All this talk of love with Mrs. Reed was getting to her.

"Goodbye, Heaven."

Heaven stopped. The woman had only said goodbye, but there was something in the way she'd said it. For a moment the two women stared at each other. Heaven knew the woman meant the words. "I'll see you tomorrow," Heaven replied softly. This time Mrs. Reed only smiled.

"I'll see you tomorrow." Heaven repeated.

"Heaven, you've been wonderful to me. Thank you. Don't worry, one day you will know the kind of love I mean, and any thoughts of old love will seem like a joke. My husband was not the first man I thought I loved, but he was the one that God made for me. We've fought together for sixty years, and that will be what I know he will miss the most. It's what I would miss."

"Fighting." Heaven paused, her eyes blinking rapidly. "I've never seen you or your husband say a harsh word to each other."

"Honey, I'm dying."

Heaven looked away.

"It's okay. Well, not okay," Mrs. Reed laughed, "but there isn't anything either of us can do about it, now is there? We still fight. I tell him I'm going to die and he stubbornly tells me I'm not. It's always been that way with us. He says black, I say white, I say I love him, he says he loves me more."

Heaven looked at the light shining in the woman's dimming eyes. "How did you ever get past the fighting?"

"As much as we fought, we loved a hundred times stronger. We have never had a dull moment."

Heaven gave the woman's hand a squeeze. She wanted to give her hope, tell her that she would definitely see her the next day. Heaven wanted to make her a promise but it wasn't a promise that she could control. She leaned down, kissed the woman's cheek, and caught the look that passed across the relief nurse's face.

"I'm sure you and your husband will always be together." That was the closest Heaven came to acknowledging that the woman's goodbye might be her last.

Fifteen hours later the registry called and confirmed that Mrs. Reed was gone. Heaven took herself off call. For some reason she needed a couple of days.

"He's dead. Call it."

Hamid looked at the clock. He hated this part of being a doctor. He believed that there was another life after this one, but many didn't, and he'd found that it didn't much make any difference. The family left behind were always sad and it was never easy to tell them the patient had died.

Hamid had no choice. He was an intern. It was his job. He walked slowly to the family waiting room. "Mrs. Stone."

"I know," the woman said and stood.

Hamid blinked and stared, wondering how she knew.

"He's my husband, has been for over thirty years. Do you think I would need you to tell me that his soul had departed his body?" She put her hand over her heart. "I felt it here."

Hamid watched as tears slid down the woman's face.

"Don't worry, Doctor, I'm fine, but a part of me died a few minutes ago."

The woman eyes suddenly rolled to the back of her head. Her body sagged and Hamid caught her in his arms and lowered her to the small couch behind her. He had to be strong, not cry, as he wanted to do. His instructors had once told him he was too soft to be a doctor, that he was better suited to be a nurse.

Hamid called for a nurse to minister to the family. He thought of Heaven, wondering if she was soft. He'd never seen it, perhaps a glimpse when she smiled, but mostly they fought. He was relieved when the nurse touched his arm; he was grateful to have her there. The patient's wife sat up and apologized.

"Don't," Hamid said. "There is no need. Would you like to see your husband?"

"Yes."

"Give the nurses ten minutes to clean him up and you can go in." He glanced at the nurse standing to his side. "Becky will go in with you." He turned toward Becky. "Are you able to remain with them until they can go in?"

"Sure, Doctor." The nurse answered.

Hamid watched as the nurse's arms wrapped around the grieving widow's shoulder. Hamid turned away, licking his lips. "I'm sorry," he said and walked away.

He wanted to talk to Heaven, to fight with her, to have her help him forget the sadness of this moment. But he would not tell her that.

He already appeared weak enough in her eyes; he would not admit to another flaw.

An hour later Hamid was heading home. He pulled his cell out and dialed Heaven, wondering if she would see him.

"I know we don't have an appointment for today, but if you're not busy I would appreciate it if we could talk. Are you free?"

"I am but I was thinking about…"

"What?"

"Well, I was thinking about calling a friend and going to dinner."

"We could go together; we're friends, sort of." Hamid laughed. "If you're ready I'll pick you up. I want you to try *kabouli*. Stop frowning," Hamid teased, knowing that on the other end of the phone Heaven was frowning. This was what he needed. An hour or two of fighting with Heaven and the darkness would go away. He could barely wait to see her.

"Come on, Heaven," Hamid said, reaching for her hand and urging her forward. She was looking with longing at Nancy's Pizza a couple of doors down. "I promise you the meal will be a treat for you."

"I don't like spicy food."

Hamid stopped in the middle of the parking lot and glanced over at Heaven. "I've seen you use hot pepper and Tabasco sauce. You like spicy food."

"I don't like the spices that you use in your food, okay? It doesn't taste like hot sauce."

"What does it taste like?"

"Not good," Heaven answered, and Hamid laughed.

"Maybe it's an acquired taste, Heaven. Some things are." He held her hand and swallowed down his desire. Heaven was off limits; at least this tiny woman with the name of paradise was off limits. It would be much easier to enter the gates of paradise, he was sure, than to enter the private sanctum of this woman.

When they were seated and looking at the menu, Hamid started to order for them but one look at Heaven and he knew she was spoiling for a fight if he did. He wanted to spar with her but not over that.

"Heaven, would you like me to order?" She grinned, and his heart lurched in his chest. He tried to tamp the feelings down. They had a business arrangement that had developed into a suspicious friendship. For them there would be no more. As much as Heaven didn't want the drama involved with dating him, he didn't really want the drama involved with trying to change her.

He would do as he'd said from the beginning and save her, but that would be the extent of it. When he finished his education and got his American license, he would call his family in Pakistan and have them pick the proper bride for him, one who believed in the same things that he did, one who he would not have to convert.

He glanced at Heaven, who was eyeing him with curiosity, and grinned at her. No one in his or her right mind would ever consider converting her. She was much too volatile to make a good Muslim wife.

With Heaven's consent, he ordered for both of them. In a very short time the meal arrived, and Hamid reached for Heaven's plate to fill it. She pushed his hand away, took the serving spoon, and filled her own. When he held his plate up, she looked at him and promptly ignored him.

"Heaven, you're rude."

"Thank you."

"You don't care?"

"Evidently not."

"I was willing to fill your plate."

"I didn't need you to."

"That's not the point," Hamid continued with obvious frustration. "If I could do it for you, why couldn't you do it for me?"

"I didn't want to." Heaven cut into her chicken and took a taste, waiting for the spices to burn her tongue, but all she tasted was juicy chicken. There were some spices but they weren't hot. Heaven helped herself to a second piece of chicken and more rice, ignoring Hamid watching her while he barely ate.

Her skin felt hot and she wanted to scream for him to stop looking at her. She was aware he was trying to hide something from her and had a good idea what it was. At least she thought she did. She wouldn't deny that she felt a charge every time Hamid looked at her or smiled, or ran his tongue lightly across his lips. His nutmeg complexion and curly black hair were more than enough to make any woman's heart flutter and feed her fantasy. She was no different, but she was different about falling for a man simply because he was beyond gorgeous, which Hamid was.

Hamid was watching her eat with his own plate almost empty, Hamid's eyes begged silently for Heaven to put food on it. But she wouldn't. She and Hamid had a business arrangement. She was positive he had more than enough women who would fawn over him and do his bidding. She glanced at him. He would be the type to have a harem. Heaven wanted no part in anything like that.

"Heaven, would you mind giving me a little rice? The spoon is on your side of the dish," Hamid said.

Heaven glanced at the spoon. Not catering to Hamid was one thing, but this, how could she refuse? She put a large amount of rice on the spoon, surprised when her hand shook, more surprised when Hamid placed his hand on hers.

"Thanks," he said softly as she spooned the rice on his plate. For once neither of them could think of a single reason to fight. It felt strange, unfamiliar.

Heaven tore off a piece of pita bread and dipped it in the olive oil. She wanted Hamid to stop looking at her the way he was. Heat shimmered between them and she didn't want it to. It would only lead to hurt and pain and Heaven had no plans to be hurt again.

Hamid wanted to make himself stop looking at Heaven, stop wanting her to be more than a friend, more than his teacher. But she was the missing ingredient in his life, the spark.

He swallowed and looked down at the rice Heaven had heaped on his plate. He wondered who'd hurt her. He'd seen a glimpse of it in her eyes; he'd also seen something other than the fighting woman he was used to. He wondered if it were Brandon, and immediately felt an instant dislike for the man, for any man who'd hurt her.

Stop it, there is no use to go down that road, he chided himself silently. *Pursing a relationship with Heaven would be painful at best*. He dipped his fork into the rice. Look how hard it had been for her even to do that courtesy. He couldn't imagine Heaven living in Pakistan or wearing a sari, and Hamid's plans were to return home. No, Heaven would never make a proper wife. Her instincts were right; they should stay friends only.

His heart seized and heat flamed through his body and touched his soul. Now if he could teach his body and heart to stop wanting her, everything would be as it should be. He blinked. He should stop looking at her; that would be a start. Then she tilted her head, brought her face up and looked him squarely in the eye and thoughts of turning away were forgotten. It had never happened to Hamid before, but he knew it for what it was: he was falling for her big time. He smiled at her and she smiled back, and he knew. Heaven was falling for him despite all of her words to the contrary.

The server brought over their check and broke the spell. He watched Heaven's hand shake as she took a sip of water and reached for her purse.

"Heaven, I invited you, remember?"

"This isn't a date, Hamid. I'll pay my share."

"Not today," Hamid said stubbornly and handed over his charge card to the waitress. "Why are you so stubborn?" He turned to Heaven. "It's only a meal."

He knew why she was behaving as she was. She wanted no strings, and then again, neither did he. "Next time you pay, Heaven. Is that a deal?"

"Sure. Do I get to pick out the restaurant?"

He looked suspiciously at her. "I don't know if I trust you in that."

"I trusted you."

"Just barely. Besides, I brought you to a restaurant that served food that would be good for your body."

"And you don't think I would do the same?"

"Would you?"

"Hamid, I respect your culture even if I could never follow it."

"There is a difference between could and would, Heaven. You could, the question is, would you?"

"I have no plans on changing, Hamid." She looked directly at him. "I will continue to eat ham, bacon, ribs, and whatever else I want. I will wear what I want, drink what I want, and worship in the manner I've always done."

For a moment they were silent as Heaven glared at him. Hamid could have let it stand there, knowing she needed the barrier of their differences to protect her. He needed it also.

"How long has it been since you ate pork?"

A tiny hitch of her lips, followed by a smile, then a full-fledged grin. "I eat it still," she laughed, "but I don't have it as often. How can I? I keep seeing your face."

"Then I've done my job," Hamid joked, the ease of it relaxing the tension between them. "How did you like this food?"

"It was very good."

"Are you ready?" His eyes snagged hers again and when she nodded, he stood. "I'll have to cook for you one day," he said and moved aside for her to pass. He inhaled her fresh lemon scent and wondered if she tasted like lemon. He smiled as he followed behind her. He wasn't doing a very good job of putting his desire for her out of his mind. But she had definitely taken away the pain of losing a patient. "Thanks, Heaven," he said, as they walked out the door.

"Thanks for what?" She turned to him.

"Oh, I needed to forget a few things and you helped me."

"So did I," Heaven admitted, "so I guess I'll thank you also."

Neither said what things they'd needed help forgetting, but when Hamid's hand moved to the side Heaven's hand was there. And when his fingers closed over hers, her thumb brushed his hand. They were both a contradiction.

"I lost a patient today," Hamid said softly. "I needed to unwind."

"I know the feeling," Heaven answered. "The registry called me this morning before I was due to come in to tell me my patient had died. They asked if I wanted to go back on call." She shrugged her shoulder. "I also needed a break."

"Things have changed, haven't they?"

"They have?" Heaven answered.

"You like me."

Heaven grinned, glad Hamid was driving and not likely to dazzle her with his smile. He pretty much kept his eyes on the road when he drove. "Yes, Hamid, I like you."

"But you still wouldn't date me?"

"Too dangerous, Hamid. Beside, are you actually asking me for a date?"

"No, Heaven, I agree it's much too dangerous. You would break my heart," he teased.

"Or you would break mine."

"So it's agreed we will remain friends only?"

"Agreed." Heaven answered even though her stomach felt as though a thousand rocks were pelting it. She swallowed, no longer sure if the mistake was in not dating Hamid, or trying to keep herself from being hurt.

LET'S GET IT ON

Two weeks later Heaven again took Hamid to the blues club, this time issuing the invitation, and this time riding in the same vehicle. She enjoyed his company.

Swinging into the parking lot, Heaven turned toward Hamid. "I invited you tonight, so it's my treat." She waited for him to protest and saw his slight frown before he smiled.

"Agreed," Hamid answered. "Are you picking up the tab for the entire evening?"

"Yes."

"You sure?"

"Yes."

"So whatever I order, you're paying?"

Heaven mentally counted the funds in her wallet before remembering she had her American Express. "Go ahead, Hamid, I'm making extra money now. I guess I can afford to spend a little."

She had the twenty ready to hand over for the admission to the club. She glanced in Hamid's direction to see if he was making a move toward his wallet. He didn't, he merely smiled and waited.

"Your friends are waiting," he whispered in her ear.

Heaven spun around in the direction Hamid was pointing. She'd as much expected their reaction. They were watching them, their eyes widening as they approached.

"Good evening, ladies," Hamid said as he sat next to Latanya. "Tonight is my treat. Whatever you ladies desire, please put it on my tab." He turned and smiled at Heaven.

"That's very generous of you, Hamid, but I'm sure they don't want to take advantage of you." Heaven attempted to give her friends meaningful looks but they were so excited that Hamid was picking up their bar tab that they ignored her.

Heaven watched as the women flirted with Hamid the same as they had the first time they met him, only this time maybe a little more. When Latanya took him onto the dance floor, Heaven turned away to answer the questions her friends were dying to ask.

"Is this a date?"

"Call it a field trip," Heaven replied.

"Yeah, right."

"I'm not kidding. Hamid and I have been all over the city and many of the suburbs. Oh, and before I forget, I'm picking up Hamid's tab tonight so that mess he was talking about, forget it. I'll buy you all one drink and that's it."

"Are you still teaching him a lesson?" Ongela asked.

"Or is he teaching you one?" Peaches chimed in.

"Let's say both, and we called a sort of truce. We haven't fought in a few days."

"What do you call the little stunt he pulled trying to stick you with our tab?"

Heaven smiled. "That's Hamid's idea of being cute, calling my bluff."

"You're falling for the guy," Ongela laughed.

"Maybe a little bit, but not enough to act on it."

"Has he asked you out?"

Heaven glanced toward the dance floor. "We're friends."

"If you don't want to date him do you mind if I ask him out?"

"What about the brothers? We were going to nurture them, remember? We had a pact." Heaven didn't dare look at Ongela. She felt as if her eyes were burning out of their sockets and if she dared to so much as gaze at her friend, Ongela would be burned to a cinder.

"Heaven, I'm tired of dating Bob."

Heaven's mouth flew open. She couldn't believe her friend's implication. She wanted to sleep with Hamid. The idea of it didn't shock Heaven as much as make her angry. *Yes, she minded Ongela dating him.* "No, go ahead and ask," Heaven answered.

The drive home was quiet. Heaven felt Hamid's eyes on her but she refused to say anything unless he did.

"Your friends are nice."

"I know," Heaven answered.

"They have no problems with dating me."

Heaven wasn't going to take the bait. Hamid was an adult, so were her friends. They could all date whomever they wanted.

"Would it bother you if I dated Ongela?"

"Why should it?" The words were said from between clenched teeth.

"Because you have feelings for me and I have feelings for you." Hamid stopped for a moment, blew out a breath, and started again. "But I respect your rules. I don't have any wish to be hurt by you, Heaven. I wasn't joking before. Still, I value your friendship and I don't want anything to get in the way of that. I am truly learning more about American culture from working with you. I think you're learning also."

"I'm not willing to pay you though," Heaven said softly.

"I didn't ask you to."

Heaven rolled her tongue, blew air through it as though it were a pipe, then looked out the window and bit her tongue. She wanted to ask him if he were considering dating Ongela, but his eyes were on her. She didn't have to look at him to know that. She could feel his stare.

"Are you angry that I mentioned dating your friend?"

"Of course not."

"Heaven?"

Chills rushed over her skin, scratching at her like rusty needles, tearing away the scabs, making her bleed afresh. He'd never called her name in that particular way. She wished he would say something, anything that would get them back to fighting.

"Heaven, why are American women such whores?"

Okay, that did it. Heaven gripped the steering wheel, wondering if Hamid too was searching for a way to bring the balance back into their relationship. She turned to glare at him. "Excuse me, but since I know you sometimes mean something different, I'm going to ask you before I overreact. What does the word *whore* mean to you?"

"A woman who easily sleeps with a man she's not married to."

So we both have the same basic understanding of the word. "Tell me something, Hamid, why would a man ask a woman who's not his wife to sleep with him? And the man who did it, wouldn't he be a male whore?"

"It is the worst of insults in Pakistan to call a man a whore."

"It's also an insult in this country to call a woman a whore."

"I'm being truthful in my response. I was only asking you a question," Hamid replied.

"And I'm being truthful in my answer." Heaven turned to look at him, grateful that he'd uttered those words. This was the main reason she would never become involved with Hamid. He was an arrogant…, She saw him smile at her,…very nice guy, she thought but didn't return his smile. Now they could return to what worked for them. They could fight. They could be friends. But they could not, should not, be lovers.

CHAPTER SIX

Hamid placed the tourniquet around the patient's arm, palpated for a vein, found a good one, and uncapped the needle. When the blood filled the vial, he smiled. He liked disproving people's assumptions. Nurses thought they were much better than doctors were when it came to drawing blood or giving injections.

He was good. He knew that, and pretending otherwise would be nothing but a lie.

Hamid removed the filled vial, putting in another and another until he was done. Then he removed the tourniquet, placed a folded sterile cloth over the area, and told the patient to hold it firmly in place.

"I thought you were supposed to bend the arm upwards."

"I find that patients bruise a lot less if they follow the advice I just gave."

"I thought it was the other way around," the patient insisted.

Hamid smiled at the man. "It is your choice, but if you don't want any bruising, just keep your arm outstretched." Hamid took the filled vials, filled out the forms, and put them in the laboratory refrigerator. He removed the gauze from the patient's arm. "There, you don't need a bandage."

"But I want one, and it's your job to give me one. A good nurse would."

"But I'm not a nurse," Hamid answered jokingly.

"That's what I mean."

Hamid looked at the man's hairy arm. "Are you sure?" When the patient didn't answer, Hamid applied the bandage. *Americans*, he thought. They were a bit strange. But he knew a good nurse. At least he wanted to believe Heaven was a good nurse. So far, he didn't have proof of that. She was excellent at fighting with him and repairing a car, but he didn't know for sure if compassion was her strong suit. He would ask her and find out.

Hamid watched the patient leave before he stripped off his gloves, washed his hands, and waited for the next one, allowing his mind time to wander.

For over a month Heaven had never been far from his thoughts. They rarely got to spend time together, because both of their schedules were so erratic. She worked as crazy hours as he did. When he wasn't in class he was working. He barely got to see anyone, but this Sunday he'd offered Heaven triple what he paid her plus her salary from the registry for the day to take the day off and escort him to the museum on the south side of Chicago.

Hamid smiled as the next patient entered the room and sat down. Thinking of Heaven was as always a pleasant diversion. It would be what would get him through the rigorous hours of the next four days.

Heaven yawned and stretched. This case was easy, so easy that Heaven had a hard time staying awake. She hated working the night shift, but with the shift deferential the registry paid, it more than made up for her lack of sleep. She'd been pulling double shifts for the last five days, but she had the next two off and couldn't wait.

Well, she had Saturday to sleep. Sunday she was working in a way. She was taking Hamid to the DuSable Museum. This would be the first time she'd seen him since his date with Ongela. He'd better hope that she was able to keep her away hands from any sharp objects when they were at the museum.

Heaven smiled and tipped out of the room as her relief came on duty. What she wouldn't give to feel as fresh and awake as the nurse standing before her did. She walked away, knowing that sleeping wouldn't make her feel rested. Hamid invaded her dreams as well.

An hour after Heaven was home, her head hit the pillow and, as she'd known, her dreams were of Hamid. Him with his hair down, her with her fingers playing in the curls. That picture faded and Heaven was wearing a sari and waiting on Hamid, hand and foot. She woke in a sweat. "No way," she said, as she punched her pillow. "No damn way."

Seven times Heaven reached for the phone to cancel the meeting with Hamid, and seven times she put it back. Thinking of their outing as a meeting instead of a date was making it easier, but the dream lingered with her still. Hamid was having an effect on her, one she didn't like. She would have to find a way to put him back where he belonged.

When the bell rang, she rushed to answer it, eager to get the day over and done with.

"I'm ready." She rushed down the stairs, bumping Hamid as he attempted to come in.

"What's wrong, Heaven? Why are you behaving as if you don't want me to come into your home?"

"I don't see any reason for us to linger when everything is at the museum."

"I thought maybe we could talk for a few moments. It's been almost three weeks since we've seen each other."

"We can talk in the car."

Heaven continued down the stairs, but stopped when she didn't hear Hamid's footsteps. She turned back. Mistake. She'd not noticed before but his hair, which he usually kept in a band, was down. He was staring at her, and she could see confusion in his eyes, followed by amusement, and by desire.

Heaven blinked. "How did your date with Ongela go?" she asked, wishing she had a twelve-inch blade with which to cut out her tongue.

"It went well. Thanks for asking."

"Are you seeing her again?"

"Perhaps," Hamid answered, smiling slowly, "unless you tell me that you don't want me to see her."

Heaven shrugged her shoulder. "You're an adult, Hamid. You do what you want, and by the way, you're not behaving like a Muslim man. You don't need my permission on whom to date."

"Do you have a lot of experience with Muslim men, Heaven?"

She stared up the stairs at him. His height was made even more impressive. She wanted to scream, she wanted to...Heaven stood three steps below Hamid and moaned inwardly as he quickly swiped his lips with his tongue. She wondered if he was even aware of how sexy he looked when he did that. Probably not.

"Heaven, why aren't you answering the question?"

Her senses were on sensory overload. She took in a deep breath. "You smell good," she said, looking up at him. She shook her head and walked down another step.

"That surprises you, Heaven? What is a Muslim man supposed to smell like? Spices? A disgusting body odor? I bathe, Heaven. I'm fastidious with my body, probably more so than you."

She glanced up the stairs again but continued walking down. Usually she was the one with a chip on her shoulder. "What's your problem, Hamid?"

"I want an answer to my question."

The question? For the life of her, she couldn't remember what the question was. She searched her mind, blinked, and still couldn't remember. All she could think of was her dream, and half of it was real. Only she wasn't in a sari and she wasn't catering to Hamid and didn't intend to.

"Are you a virgin, Heaven?"

If he was trying to stop her in her tracks, he did. "Are you?" Heaven replied.

"I'm a man, I don't have to be."

Heaven couldn't believe her ears. For a moment, she wondered why they were having this particular argument. But it didn't matter; it would have been brought up at some point. The questions would be the same and so would the answer. She glared at him as though he'd lost his mind. "Guess what, Hamid, neither do I. I'm a woman."

Outside Heaven pushed the remote button of her truck and went to the driver's side. She paused when Hamid moved toward his own car parked behind her. "We're taking my truck," she said.

"I want to take my car."

"Then suppose you take your car and I'll take my truck." Heaven got in her truck, slammed the door, and put her key in the ignition. This was stupid. But now she didn't want to sit next to Hamid, either in her truck or his car. Right now, they were a continent apart.

Hamid was livid. He sat in his car, uncertain if he would follow Heaven's truck or not. He didn't know what had made him snap at her the way he had, but suddenly he'd wanted to see some sign from her that she'd missed him. He'd wanted to see a light in her eyes that told him what her words did not.

But it was Heaven, after all. Of course, her eyes would not light up at the sight of him. A small ping went through him. That was a part of his dream, what he was searching for, what he'd heard about from his friends and what he'd witnessed with his own eyes. Hamid wanted it for himself. For a moment when Heaven asked about his date, he'd thought it was because she was jealous. But then she'd backed away from the subject with her inane remark about Muslim men. He'd missed her. He hadn't seen her in weeks. All he'd wanted was a few moments of her time to talk with her, to stare longingly at her and to breathe in her lemony essence. The way Heaven behaved it appeared she'd not missed him at all.

She had not lied to him from the beginning about her feelings for him. She'd said it straight out, that she would never date him because he wasn't black, and she didn't want the drama. And he had admitted to himself that there could never be anything serious between them. He was getting too old for chasing women. He had to think of his future, his family. He had to have his mind set on a proper Muslim woman who would give him sons and raise them in the faith. Heaven would never be able to give him that.

He closed his eyes and prayed. He needed all the help he could get not to become involved with Heaven. She had gotten under his skin; even Sassa had taken note of it. If only it had been possible, he would not have allowed his feelings for Heaven to grow.

He thought of her friend Ongela. Now there was a woman who was willing to adapt. She'd questioned him about his faith, something Heaven had yet to do, and he'd questioned her about Heaven, about the things she had yet to tell. And at the end of the date, they'd laughed. They'd both been on fishing expeditions. She wasn't seriously interested in him. She was aware that his interest was in Heaven.

"You're going to be fighting a hard battle, Hamid. Heaven will not break easily," Ongela had offered.

"Why do you think I want to break her?" he'd asked.

"Because if you're falling in love with her you'll have to break her before she'll admit it. She's been hurt and she's not ready to trust a man right now."

After that Ongela had gone into her home and waved at him.

Hamid didn't like knowing that a man had hurt Heaven. Still, he couldn't understand how having known hurt, she would constantly inflict pain on him.

His last few days of work and classes had been filled with thoughts of her. While he'd rushed to see her, she had rushed away from him as if she not only hadn't missed him, but wanted to get the day done and over with. Sassa had said Heaven was only seeing Hamid because of the money he was paying her, that the color green was all that interested her. He had not wanted to believe it, but it appeared he had no choice.

At last, Hamid pulled out into the traffic, glad that he knew how to get to Fifty-sixth and State. To prove a point, he didn't follow the same direction that Heaven had taken, but instead went a different way.

When he arrived, he parked and went inside, surprised that she was waiting, glad that it was Sunday and admission was free. He didn't want Heaven to pay for him, not even the usual three dollars.

Heaven barely glanced at him. He could tell she was angry. So was he. She walked ahead of him without speaking, her manner in itself commanding him to follow. For a long moment, Hamid stood where he was until Heaven turned back to him.

"Are you coming or not?" Heaven asked, with irritation tinting her voice.

Hamid refused to answer her rude tone, but moved from where he had been standing to come and stand alongside her in the first hall.

"This is the mask room." Heaven spread her arms pointing out one mask after the other. "Masks are many faces of Mother Africa. Masks are used to invoke spirits, exorcise evil, commemorate ancestors, promote healing—"

"I can read, Heaven." He frowned at her, ignoring the same expression on her face. She had no right to frown. "This is the aviation room," she said, going across the hall. Hamid took over the tour and went from exhibit to exhibit and room to room telling Heaven much more about the featured artifacts than was written on the placards. He'd be damned if he allowed her to assume this was another area in which he was incompetent.

He turned toward her once while he was explaining the origin of an exhibit. "What? Did you think that a Muslim man wouldn't know these facts?" She ignored him and, for once, he was glad. It wasn't fun fighting with Heaven today. Today he'd rather be talking with her, finding out if Brandon was the one who'd hurt her and why she was still hurting. He'd like to cook her dinner and rub her feet. He'd like to...

Hamid felt a sudden flush and a thickening in his pants. He was very aware of what he wanted to do with Heaven, and he was aware he wouldn't. She thought getting involved with him was drama. His getting involved with her would also produce drama. Didn't she understand he was willing to risk it?

He saw her staring at the exhibit with the weathered shackles of former slaves, safely hidden behind the glass. She glared at him. He couldn't believe it. She'd glared at him. He tilted his head in question but she walked away. When she stopped at the wall and began reading the notices of slaves being auctioned off, he knew he had not been wrong in thinking she was glaring. When she read the information about the young mulatto woman's body being given away for five nights to any man willing to pay money to enter into the dollar draw Heaven stormed out of the room, leaving Hamid behind.

Hamid caught up with Heaven, pulled her over to a corner, and spoke quietly but with clarity and sternness. "Don't look at me, Heaven, as though I committed those crimes. I did not. And don't assume that slavery was just here in America. Do you know that even today a form of slavery still exists in Pakistan? Bonded labor? What do you think that is? Study your history. Do you know how many nations have practiced this inhumanity? I didn't start it, Heaven, and I've never done it." He stepped away from her. He would not allow her to back away from him because of this. If she didn't want to date him it would be for a much better reason than this.

Hamid walked away and didn't stop until he stood in front of the *Amistad* exhibit. He pulled a pen from his shirt pocket and a scrape of paper and begin writing.

"What are you doing?"

"Writing," he said, not elaborating. Right now he was the one angry with her.

"What do you want to see next, Heaven? The bust of Jean Baptiste Pointe DuSable, born 1745, died 1818, or would you like to see the Harold Washington corner? Chicago's only black mayor or would you—"

"Okay, Hamid, I get it. You've been here before."

"Yes, but I've also studied about cultures other than my own. Can you say the same?" He didn't wait for her answer; he knew what it would be. No, she hadn't studied but he was willing to bet she'd made an assumption about him, his people, and his land.

When they walked out of the door, Hamid reached for his wallet, pulled out several bills, and dropped them in the container for donations.

The seventy-five pound punching bag pulsated and rose in the air several inches as Heaven kicked it repeatedly. She was once again blowing off steam. She glanced over at the *sensei* who was observing her workout. *I'm not hitting students*, she thought. He should be happy.

Heaven finished her workout and was reaching for her bag to put her gloves in and leave, when the *sensei's* hand stopped her.

"It would appear your *chi* is unbalanced."

"I'm not unbalanced."

"Then what is wrong?"

Heaven thought about it for a moment. Maybe she was unbalanced. She'd begun her ridiculous arrangement with Hamid to teach him a lesson; so far, it appeared to be backfiring. Hamid was not only handling everything she had thrown at him but was throwing it back in her face.

A sound escaped her lips as Heaven took in a deep breath, annoyed that Hamid had wormed his way past her defenses. She'd sworn after Brandon that from that point on she would remain in charge of both her emotions and her relationships.

She knew his date with Ongela was part of the problem. She wasn't a fool; she recognized the green-eyed monster in herself. Sure, she'd said she didn't want Hamid, that she wanted only a black man, but Ongela had said the same thing. Hamid had said he had feelings for her, but he was willing to date her friend. She looked longingly at the bag, wanting to give it another punch but held her peace. The *sensei's* eyes followed hers and Heaven held her breath.

"Heaven, you have not behaved so irrationally since, well, it's been almost a year and a half."

The *sensei's* eyebrow quirked upwards and Heaven shook her head viciously. "No, *sensei*, this has nothing to do with Brandon." She clenched her jaw, wishing Brandon had not been one of the *sensei's* best students, that he was not a second-degree black belt and sometimes taught the class. It was hard enough going through their breakup. Heaven had been determined she wouldn't be shoved out of the karate school because of him.

Luckily it hadn't come to that. The *sensei* had of course known of Brandon and Heaven's relationship, everyone had. He'd instead asked Brandon to leave. Still, Heaven knew Brandon was allowed time to practice there when the school was closed. She made sure to go to the *dojo* only when it was open.

The *sensei* had approached her several times and asked if she could work with Brandon again. Every time he asked, Heaven had either kicked or punched the bag with such ferocity and glared so at the instructor that he'd shaken his head in disappointment and left.

Heaven knew he was waiting for the day she would heal enough to share a *dojo* with Brandon. But that would mean eventually they would spar. Heaven didn't trust herself not to pound him silly, or to have him do it to her. But in the mood she was in, Heaven would pit her brown belt against his black belt any day.

But it wasn't because of Brandon that she was now hitting the bag with such force. It was Hamid. She hated that he'd dated Ongela and she wanted to let off some steam before she saw him again. All men should be glad that she used the *dojo* for her release, she thought. It definitely saved them from the things she imagined doing to them.

For two weeks, Hamid had not called for her to show him anything. After their visit to the DuSable Museum, she knew there had really been no need in the first place.

Heaven remembered her words to her friend, that when she finished with him, she was going to have Hamid running back to Pakistan. She thought of Ongela's warning to be careful that Hamid didn't teach her a lesson instead. In many ways he had. She was eating things she'd never thought she'd even taste and not eating things she'd sworn she'd never give up.

Heaven had only an instant to blink before the punching bag struck her and she went flying across the mat.

"Why did you do that?" She hopped up angrily, glaring at the student who'd kicked the bag. Her *sensei* pulled her away.

"I told him to do it. You were not focused on what you were doing, and loss of focus could get you hurt, Heaven. Remember that."

Heaven rubbed her head angrily, feeling a small raised area above her left brow. *Remember it.* She wouldn't have any choice. She snatched her bag from the corner and left the *dojo* without another word.

As they sat miles apart in her small living room, Heaven and Hamid were listening to music, everything from country to hip hop, blues, and jazz. Heaven was surprised that Hamid was familiar with most of it, with the exception of country. He liked "Ease the Fever." *Good choice*, she thought, *me too*.

"What happened to you?" Hamid asked out of the blue.

"What?"

"Your head, you look like someone hit you."

Heaven smiled a little. She'd almost forgotten the fight she'd lost with the punching bag.

"I take karate classes."

"Someone did this to you?"

"Sort of. This happened with a punching bag." Her lids lifted as Hamid moved from his chair and came across the divide toward her. Her breath stilled as his hands gently touched the area. She waited. His hands were soft, and he moved efficiently, asking her questions, making her open her eyes so he could see into them with a penlight. She wanted to laugh, but his concern was genuine.

Still, she wanted him to finish his examination. She was feeling flushed, and the same tingle of electricity that she'd experienced in the restaurant was back. Hot and cold, that described the two of them.

"Are you off tomorrow?"

"Yes," Heaven whispered, finding it hard to talk in a normal voice.

"Good, I think you need to rest and make sure it's nothing. I don't think so," Hamid said looking into her eyes, "but you know the symptoms for a head injury. Watch for them, and call me if you need me."

"I will," Heaven whispered. "Thanks."

All she had to do was reach up, pull him down, and kiss him. And then he would know that his belief that American women were whores was correct. She took a deep breath; *steady,* she urged her body. She sat back; Hamid was the first to pull away.

"Are you a good nurse, Heaven?"

"Yes," Heaven answered without hesitation. "Are you a good doctor?"

"I hope so," Hamid answered.

That surprised her. He was so arrogant she would have thought for sure he would say yes. "Why do you only hope so?"

Hamid looked at her for a moment, and she sensed when he made a decision to share something with her.

"Sometimes I feel too deeply what's happening with my patients. When they die, I take it hard."

She thought of their earlier brief conversation about that. "There's nothing wrong with that. So do I."

His fingers touched the raised area on her head again and he smiled. "We didn't talk specifically about our patients that day, did we?"

"No."

"Was there any particular reason your patient's death was harder?"

"She was a wonderful woman, more concerned about her family than herself. She told me goodbye."

Hamid looked at her. "Your patient knew?"

"Yes."

"Did you acknowledge her dying?"

"I didn't want to, but what could I do? We talked. I wanted to make her a promise that she would be fine."

"I did make a promise." Hamid sighed. "I told both the patient and his family that he had nothing to worry about, but he did."

He looked at Heaven and attempted to smile at her but couldn't pull it off. Feeling the lump in his throat, he looked away from her. "I hate breaking that kind of news to family."

Heaven reached out for his hand and held it. For several minutes, they sat in silence, until Hamid's hand reached out to touch her hair. "So these are called twists, huh?"

He wanted to pull Heaven close, hold her next to his heart. He wanted to ease her fever and erase her pain, just as the song said. Maybe one day he would be able to tell her that.

"A punching bag?" Hamid squinted at Heaven, remembering how she said she'd gotten hurt. "Why were you hit by a bag?"

"I told you; I take karate."

"So there is finally something that you're not good at." He laughed. "Little one, perhaps you need a smaller bag." He raised their combined hands, intending to plant a kiss on the back of Heaven's hand, but she snatched it away and he grinned. He should have known she wouldn't take his words easily.

"Listen, Hamid, for your information I'm very good. I've been studying for three years now, and I have a brown belt."

"Three years? Why not a black belt?"

"Long story. The point is, I can take care of myself." She ignored his pointed glance toward the bump on her head. "That was an accident. I was unfocused...the *sensei*...Never mind, this doesn't mean anything."

"Maybe it means you should stay focused." Hamid laughed before turning serious. "Where do you take classes? I've always wanted to learn."

A sudden and intense change came over Heaven. The playfulness was gone. Instead, she sprang up from her chair as if she were a wind-up toy. "You can't take lessons at my school. Go somewhere else."

For a second Hamid thought Heaven was kidding, that it was just another way for her to blow off steam, a way for her to remove her hand from his. Then he saw she was truly agitated.

"Heaven, what's the big deal? You don't own the school."

"I don't want you there."

"Is the school open to the public?

"Not to you, Hamid. It's not open to you."

Now he was annoyed. Rising, he tilted his head to the side and looked down at her. "What do you mean, it's not open to me? I'm not allowed there?"

"Hamid, this has nothing to do with ethnicity. It's you, I don't want you there, understand? It's my school and I don't want you anywhere near it. Find another place." She walked to her door and flung it open. "Lesson over, leave."

For a second he wanted to grab her, shake some sense into her. What was she talking about? Why didn't she want him to take lessons at her school? He would never understand her. It made no sense.

Hamid walked the few blocks from Heaven's apartment to his. If he lived to be a thousand, he would never understand her. Now he was glad that he'd never told Heaven they lived in the same neighborhood. More than likely, she would have thought of ways to try to have him deported. If she reacted that strongly to the idea of him going to her karate classes, he could just imagine what she'd think if she learned he lived so close.

Then a thought hit him. Maybe the man who'd hurt her was in her class. Perhaps Heaven didn't want him to know of their friendship. That would explain her strange behavior.

Suddenly a possessive urge seized him. He needed to see the man who'd hurt Heaven. The neighborhood wasn't that large, and knowing Heaven she probably took classes close to home. If that were the case, he would check out all of the schools in the area until he found hers and he would attend. His money would guarantee that.

Heaven threw a few punches at the air, bringing discomfort to her head. How dare he? There was no way she wanted Hamid in her class. She'd been through that once already. The school was hers. Brandon had not run her away from it and neither would Hamid. She would not tell him.

Pain came swiftly. As her movements increased, a wave of nausea claimed her, and Heaven sat on the couch remembering Hamid's warning. Her head was much too hard to be hurt by a bump, but she would stop bouncing around.

Thoughts of Hamid in her *dojo* filled her as she closed her eyes and attempted to relax. The *dojo* hadn't been big enough for both her and Brandon, and it definitely wasn't big enough for her and Hamid.

CHAPTER SEVEN

When the phone rang, Heaven glanced at her caller ID. It was Ongela. Heaven had been avoiding her friend's calls since she'd asked to go out with Hamid. Matter of fact, she'd been avoiding going out with all of her friends. She didn't want to get into it with them over Hamid and she wasn't very good at hiding her feelings.

She let the phone ring. After a thousand rings, or so it seemed, Ongela finally gave up. Heaven flicked the television on and began watching a reality show.

Twenty minutes later, her buzzer sounded. She would have ignored that as she had the phone, but the person wouldn't stop. When she finally went to the intercom, it was Ongela. There was no way to pretend now that she wasn't at home. Heaven braced herself and buzzed her friend in, surprised when Peaches and Latanya showed up as well.

"What's up?" Heaven asked, moving away from the door to allow them in.

"You. You're tripping because Ongela went out with Hamid. And you're pretending that you're okay with it. We're not going to allow you to close the door on our friendship; we've been friends way too long for this nonsense."

"Yeah," Latanya chided in, "you should have just told this stank heffa to get her hands off your man."

Heaven laughed and agreed, then caught herself. "Hamid is not my man, and he had a right to go out with anyone he wanted, even a stank heffa," she added, looking at Ongela.

"Do you want to know what we talked about the whole evening?"

"Me, right?" Heaven snickered, "Like I'm going to believe that."

"Believe it or not, we did. He's fallen for you big time."

"Did he say that?" Heaven sat on the arm of the sofa, trying to pretend that she didn't care.

"Of course he didn't. He's as bad as you are. But he kept asking about you. I was so sick of him that I was glad when he took me home."

"Really?"

"Not really, he's fun, but he's too into you and I don't want your dirty seconds."

"I haven't had him," Heaven corrected.

"It's not because you can't. Hamid wants you, and judging from the way you've been avoiding all of us, you want him too. If you had admitted it in the first place, none of this mess would have happened." Peaches splayed her hand on her hips. "Now you two get over it, hug and make up."

Heaven hopped from the arm of the chair, met Ongela halfway, and flung her arms around her friend.

For the next two hours, her friends stayed with her, talking and laughing over ill-fated relationships and men. When they were gone, Heaven felt more relaxed. She hadn't known she'd been stressed, but apparently she had been, because she felt comfortable now that she knew Ongela wasn't interested in Hamid. And more importantly, that Hamid wasn't interested in Ongela.

Hamid had been answering Sassa's questions for over an hour. He'd grown weary of defending his relationship with Heaven. "Enough," he finally admonished.

"That woman has you acting crazy. You don't attend family parties; you spend every free minute of your time with her."

"She's helping me understand American culture."

"Why, Hamid? We get along just fine. I have many American friends but I am content to learn about Americans from the things we do together. I don't require a tutor. You're giving her most of the money you make and you're refusing to take more from your father. Maybe you are crazy. You need money, Hamid, to go out and have a good time, to get a woman." Sassa smiled.

"It takes money to take care of your physical needs. How are you going to do that if you keep giving Heaven all of your cash? Does she know she's leaving you destitute?"

"It isn't her concern. I offered to pay her and she accepted. Besides, we both know I'm far from destitute. It's a business arrangement, Sassa."

"A business arrangement? Lately you can't afford to do anything else since you're refusing to accept even the interest from what's rightfully yours. And I don't see that you're getting anything useful out of your money."

"I'm getting to know American people."

"One person, Hamid, you're getting to know one person and she doesn't appear to be melting in your direction. You forget you were angry when you called. You weren't so happy with her then."

Hamid sighed loudly and groaned. "If I needed a mother, Sassa, I would return home."

"You might mot need me to be a mother, but you do need me to tell you that you had better have your father wire money into your account, or stop blowing all your funds on this woman. Either that, or work more. You're not working as much because you're trying to spend time with her, and every time you do, you have to pay her."

"It's not like that."

"Have you seen her even once when you didn't have to pay her?"

Hamid didn't have to think about it. Yes, he had. They'd had dinner. When he told this to his cousin, Sassa wasn't convinced.

"Who paid for dinner?" Sassa asked.

"I invited her."

"Do you think the two of you are friends, Hamid? Has she ever invited you to her home to cook dinner for you?" Sassa smirked. "Do you think she's invited her girlfriends over?"

"I have never cooked for her either. Thank you. I think I will do that. Besides, I am trying to introduce her to our dishes."

Sassa looked at Hamid and laughed. "How do you plan to buy the food to prepare? You're broke."

"If she comes I will find the money." He put a finger up. "And I will not call home for money." Hamid saw the gleam in Sassa's eyes. "And I will not borrow it from you."

"There will probably be no need, because if she's not getting paid, she's not coming."

Hamid wanted to make a bet with Sassa, to tell him he was wrong. But the truth was he didn't know what Heaven would do. He doubted that even Heaven knew.

Heaven finished her yoga exercise feeling better, more focused. She wasn't working for the next two days because it was time to put her plan into action. She was going to strike out on her own and open up her own health care registry. For the past year, she'd been saving every dime, talking with nurses, X-ray technicians, phlebotomists, and doctors. She now had a contact list and could start putting her plans into motion. She was meeting with a lawyer and accountant in the next few days, and then she would find an office to rent.

Heaven had thought of operating out of her apartment, but knew perception was everything. If clients thought she was a small timer they might not come to her. If they thought she had an exclusive client list, they would beg for the services of her and her staff. She'd worked long and hard for this. Before, the money had been earmarked for Brandon's office; now it was all going to be for her business.

Hamid was about to enter the fourth karate school in the neighborhood when a strange sensation came over him. *This was the one.* This place smelled of musk with a faint lingering aroma of lemons. Stepping inside the door, he felt her energy. He looked around for the instructor and spotted a man in uniform coming toward him.

Hamid stuck his hand out and smiled before beginning the same story he'd given to the last three instructors.

"Hello, I was thinking of starting karate lessons and wanted to ask about your classes and prices."

"Have you ever taken lessons before?" the instructor asked.

"No," Hamid replied and looked innocently around the room before bringing his eyes to rest on the teacher. "I have a friend that takes lessons, Heaven."

He saw a slight flicker in the man's eyes but he did not acknowledge knowing Heaven. He made no comment. Hamid smiled. "I like the energy here. I think I would like to try a few lessons."

In an hour's time, Hamid had paid the fee and ordered a uniform from the instructor. He wanted badly to ask what days Heaven practiced but didn't, his instincts telling him that if he so much as mentioned Heaven's name again the man would kick him out and return his check. There was one more thing Hamid needed to do.

Hamid ran to his class out of breath. In less than a month he would be done. School would be over and he only had to wait a few months until the next scheduled licensing exams to become a doctor and get his license, then he would return home. Having an American license wasn't necessary to practice back home, just as an American education wasn't, but it was highly honored. Most important of all, it was what Hamid's father wanted for him, and the one gift Hamid was able to provide.

The thought of returning home brought mixed emotions. The thought of seeing his homeland and his family and friends filled him with joy, but the thought of never seeing Heaven again filled him with an undeniable pain. Sassa was right; he was falling in love with her.

Forcing himself to focus on the lecture, Hamid pushed thoughts of Heaven away. He needed the information being given. He didn't want there to come a time he needed to know what was being taught and he'd not heard because of his daydreaming. When his class was over, he slipped his cell phone from his pocket and took a deep breath, hoping Sassa was wrong in his assessment of his relationship with Heaven.

"Heaven, where are you?" Hamid asked the moment she answered, not mentioning their last fight. There was no need. They were always fighting. Besides, if he mentioned it he would have to say something about the fact that he had joined her school.

"I'm at Rush. I was just getting ready to go to lunch. Why?"

Hamid smiled to himself. Fate was once again putting things in order.

"I'm only ten minutes from there. If you'll save a place for me at your table, I'll join you." Before she could say no Hamid clicked the phone off and made a mad dash for his car. He made the ten minute drive in seven and was walking toward Heaven within another ten seconds.

"Hi," he said sitting down, ignoring the way she was looking at him. "I want to make dinner for you. Will you come?"

Heaven's lips slid apart and she reached for the fruit on her tray and handed it to him. "Here, I bought this for you."

She'd not answered his question. As Hamid took the fruit, he touched her hand and lingered there for a moment. "Will you come?"

"When?"

"When are you available?" Hamid asked, holding her gaze.

"I don't work tonight and tomorrow I'm off."

"How about tomorrow?" Hamid bit into the apple Heaven had given him in order to hide his nervousness.

She shrugged, "Sure."

"Heaven, you do understand that I'm inviting you as a guest…I'm not paying you?"

Sparks flashed from her eyes. She was insulted. "Don't be angry," he said quickly. "It's just that I wanted to make sure you were aware what I was asking, that's all."

"Hamid, in case you didn't know, I do have an understanding of an invitation and what it means." She shook her head. "You know, I think I might be busy tomorrow night."

"Please, Heaven." He rolled her name on his tongue, loving the way it sounded in his mouth. "I didn't intend to offend you. Please come and I will make you a fantastic meal. We'll have fun, I promise."

She was studying him, making him wonder if she would still rescind her yes.

"Heaven."

She didn't answer, just continued to stare at him. "Heaven," Hamid said softly and reached his hand to touch her. He saw her tremble and pulled back. "I just want to cook you dinner and maybe play some new Marvin Gaye CDs that I bought."

"Marvin Gaye is dead, he's not making music." Heaven shrugged her shoulders. "At least as far as I know he's not making music. So what you bought must be old."

Hamid grinned. She was teasing him. "Next week I have a cousin who's getting married at the mosque in Villa Park. Would you like to go?"

"As your date?"

"Yes."

"Sure, I'll go," Heaven said, then laughed, "but I'll go as your friend."

Hamid would take that. Friend or date, it didn't matter at the moment. She would be there. Three months ago, she would have sworn she'd never go. They were making progress.

He wrote down his address and watched as her eyebrows drew together. But she didn't say a word, leaving Hamid to wonder if her silence was a good thing or a bad thing.

LET'S GET IT ON

Hamid ignored Sassa laughing at him as he stirred the rice and added onions, garlic and peas, then carefully washed the tomatoes for the salad.

"I thought you were tired of cooking for yourself? Now you're cooking for a woman."

"But you're forgetting the woman is Heaven, and that I want to cook for her." Sassa smacked Hamid on the right side of his head. "Sassa, you're the one who said she wouldn't see me if there wasn't money involved."

"Then she must want something else."

"She does, she wants dinner." Hamid opened the oven and basted the chicken with olive oil. He stirred fresh cream and chives into the shrimp he had waiting on the back burner. He wouldn't cook those until Heaven was there.

"You're acting like a school boy."

"I feel like a school boy," Hamid laughed. "Stop trying to spoil it."

"You said you weren't going to pursue her."

"Perhaps I changed my mind."

"Shouldn't you make sure she changed hers? Are you thinking of a future with her? Because I can tell you she isn't thinking of one with you. You heard her, she only dates black guys, and you will need to marry a woman who believes in the same things that you do."

"Sassa, you've dated many American women. What's the big deal?"

"I never fell in love with any of them."

"Were you looking to fall in love?" Hamid noticed that his cousin suddenly looked wistful.

"I guess for a time I was, but it didn't happen. I don't think it will. I called my father and asked him to pick out a bride for me. I'm ready to get married."

"I thought you said you would never allow that to happen, that you would chose your own bride."

"I've changed my mind. I don't think it's such a bad thing to know that the woman I get will be faithful and keep a good home. Besides, I want to be a father."

Hamid gave his cousin a long look before delivering his diagnosis. "Stop going to so many weddings. You're becoming envious, that's all."

"Maybe, but I still plan on going through with it. And I've decided I want to get married in Pakistan. If you don't come I will never speak to you again."

Hamid turned from the stove to face his cousin. "Sassa, if you get married, I will be there. I have not changed my plans to return home."

"With Heaven?"

"Maybe, maybe not."

"It will never work. Take this meal, for instance. You've made it for her taste buds, but will you enjoy it?"

"That's called compromise and being hospitable to my guest. As for the rest of it, sitting across from Heaven, in my home, there will be no way I will not enjoy the meal. Now, why don't you leave?" he said, shoving Sassa toward the door.

"I'm staying to say hello."

"Why?"

"I like Heaven."

Hamid glared at him. "Is that why you're discouraging me?"

"I said *like*, not *love*. I'm not interested in her. Didn't you hear me? I'm going to get married. You're welcome to Heaven."

"Thank you," Hamid said, annoyed at his cousin and not exactly sure why. He didn't want him to want Heaven, but then again he didn't like that he didn't. "Listen, you're leaving five minutes after you speak to her."

Hamid had to have a way to bring control back to his side of the table. Within a short time, the bell was ringing and he was fighting Sassa to get to it. For some strange reason Sassa had appointed himself as a know-it-all. He thought Hamid should make Heaven wait, that he shouldn't appear overeager.

"Heaven." Hamid met her at the door. "Welcome to my home." He opened the door wider and allowed her to enter. "You remember my cousin Sassa," he said by way of acknowledgement.

"Of course."

Heaven smiled at Sassa and a burst of jealousy hit Hamid squarely in the chest. He wanted to snatch Sassa's hand from Heaven but didn't. "Would you like something to drink?" he asked instead.

"Water would be fine," Heaven answered.

Hamid turned toward Sassa. "Would you like something?" He gave a warning glare and Sassa laughed.

"No, thanks," Sassa said after a long pause. "Heaven, it was nice seeing you again, but I'm not staying for dinner."

Heaven moved about nervously after Sassa left. She didn't know why she was feeling so nervous. She'd been alone with Hamid dozens of times, but there was something in his manner, something in the way his cousin had snickered.

She found a chair in his living room and sat down. She took the water from Hamid's hand and took a sip. She needed it. "What did you cook?" she asked, more to make conversation than because she cared. Heaven took in a breath, trying to tell what it was by the aroma. But all she could smell was a delicious blend of garlic and onions.

Hamid turned on the CD player and Marvin Gaye's voice began singing as Hamid brought Heaven a platter of appetizers, bruschetta, cucumber on pita bread, and feta cheese sprinkled over fish. She took one of each, surprised that Hamid could cook. The food was delicious.

"What were you expecting?"

"Just dinner," Heaven replied, "no expectations." Hamid sat opposite her, not eating himself but watching her. "You're making me nervous." Heaven looked into Hamid's eyes as the feeling got stronger.

"I don't understand," Hamid answered. "I'm doing nothing but sitting here."

"It's the way you're looking at me. Stop."

"How am I looking at you?"

"We're friends, Hamid. I want us to remain friends."

"And something about the way I look is making you think we can't be friends?"

"I know that you have certain ideas that I don't like concerning American women."

"You think I'm judging you, Heaven?"

"You've judged every woman in this country. You call us whores." She waited for Hamid to deny it but he didn't. He shrugged his shoulder.

"That was one of the reasons I wanted to learn firsthand about your culture. I have heard stories about American women, but from my time with you I can see that some of the things I was told may not have been true."

He leaned into his chair and gave her a smile. "You do have to admit that the women here in this country do not have the same ideas about sex as the women in Pakistan."

"You don't know that. Probably no one ever asked the women in Pakistan what their ideas are. Maybe you've kept them under your thumb and not allowed them a choice."

Hamid laughed.

"What's so funny?"

"I will admit things in Pakistan and things in your country are different. We are not at the same place, but there was a time that things were done differently in the United States. Women were more under the control of men here than you might know." He laughed again as she looked at him.

"I've studied your history, the dress, for instance, during the Civil War times most especially. I know the type of clothing worn, the traditions, and the customs. Do you, Heaven? Would you wear the clothing the women were made to wear then?"

This time Heaven laughed. "Hamid, I'm sure the books you got this information from didn't have anything in them about black people or their customs and manner of dress. During that time, we wore what we could. As for customs, we had one. Try to stay alive." She took a bite of the pita bread. "Got anything else?"

"What road do you want to travel down?"

"Whichever one you want to travel, I'm game." She pushed her chair back, readying herself.

"Heaven, this is not a battle. I invited you to dinner. I know what you're saying, and I will concede that point. I was only stating that some of the women in this country used to dress a lot more modestly than they do now. And since they couldn't show skin, I'm sure they didn't run and jump into bed with men."

Heaven stared at Hamid. "Isn't that what you're thinking about now, Hamid, going to bed with me, I mean?"

"I'm a man."

"That's your answer for everything, isn't it? That's one of the things that really annoys me about you."

"Would you like me to tell you the things about you that annoy me?" He quirked a brow upward, looking at her in a cockeyed manner.

"Go ahead."

"I'm annoyed that you're letting my appetizers go to waste. Eat up, Heaven, I will not join you in fighting." With that, Hamid got up and went into the kitchen to check on the food, increasing the flame underneath the shrimp dish. Within moments, he was ladling the piping hot food into bowls and serving it to Heaven. He smiled. Every time she tasted something, the look of pleasure in her eyes was worth adjusting the spices to her taste buds.

"Heaven, who hurt you?" He waited. She wasn't going to tell him.

"Brandon."

"Do you still love him?"

"I'm still disappointed in him. We had made plans for years."

"About your future?"

"Yes, but that no longer matters. I now have my own plans."

He wondered what her plans were, but wondering was not getting her to tell him. He needed to know what her future held, because he was sure it would have an impact on his own. "Tell me about your plans, please."

Again, he waited. When she didn't respond, he pulled his chair closer to her and saw her surprise.

"I'm going to open a medical registry for nurses, at least to start, and then I may include others. I'm even hoping to get jobs for doctors." Heaven saw the interest in Hamid's eyes. "It's a dream of mine. Now what's yours?"

"That's an awfully quick explanation for a dream. There has to be more."

"That's enough for now."

"Is that why you need to work so hard? To make money for your dreams?" He looked into her eyes and smiled.

"Hamid, it was your idea to pay me, not mine."

"I wasn't trying to offend you, Heaven. And by the way, you offend easily."

"Maybe I offend easily because something offending is always coming out of your mouth."

"Hmmmm." Hamid smiled at her. "I will have to watch what I say, won't I? Now eat up, Heaven, there is plenty."

"I thought you didn't have enough food for Sassa to stay."

"No one has enough food for Sassa to stay." They laughed, and he smiled again. "I wanted this dinner for the two us. I wanted us to know more about each other. You know, things that are more personal. I wanted you to hear my taste in music. I finally figured out why it's called soul music."

Heaven wanted to hear this explanation.

"You don't believe me," Hamid laughed. "I can tell by the look in your eyes. Okay, here goes. The words in soul music touch your soul; you can feel them down to the marrow of your being."

Okay, Heaven thought, *Hamid may not be a brother, but his game was sure as heck tight.* "Have you found a song that's touched your soul?"

"Yes," Hamid answered softly. "But I don't know if you want to hear it."

"Please go ahead." And she meant it; she wanted to know what words were putting that misty look in his eyes. Damn Marvin Gaye. It wouldn't matter which song he sang; they would all do something to some part of your body.

LET'S GET IT ON

Looking at her, Hamid crooned the words to "'Let's Get It On,'" in his accented voice.

As Heaven listened, she tried to imagine Marvin Gaye singing the words to her. Then she met Hamid's eyes and shivered at what she saw there. Marvin had never looked at her that way; actually, he'd never looked at her at all.

"Heaven, dance with me."

Heaven melted but went into Hamid's arms. His all-consuming maleness made her weak. His arm encircled her and his fingers gently massaged her where they landed on her body. Her head found it's way to his chest.

Hamid sang into her ear, his breath hot on her cheeks, the lyrics and melody burning a home in her soul. Hamid was right; this was soul music at its finest.

She understood only too well what Hamid was trying to say to her. A tremor of desire snaked its way through her body, crawling over her spine and dancing on her nerve endings. Hamid pulled her in tighter and she felt his hardness.

It was the song, she thought, that darn song. She felt her body moving against Hamid's as his hand went below her waist, not quite on her butt but almost. He didn't move for a second. He was asking silently for permission to touch her more intimately. She knew and she wanted it.

There really was nothing wrong with it, Heaven thought, except she still remembered their earlier conversation. He wanted to kiss her and she wanted him to. What would he think of her if she caved? More than likely, he wanted what he couldn't have, and for the moment, she was it.

Heaven danced with Hamid until Marvin Gaye's song "Sexual Healing" came on, and then she marched over and changed the disc. Enough was enough.

"Hamid, you didn't tell me your plans. What are they?" When he smiled, she knew he was aware of her ploy but it didn't matter. She went to the living room and sat in a chair that was only big enough for one. "Tell me your plans."

"I'm going to return home and open up a practice."

"Will that be soon?" Heaven asked, feeling the pain of his leaving sharply. She didn't want to think of Hamid leaving.

"There are too many doctors in this country. My country needs good doctors. Too many Pakistanis come here to go to school to become doctors, receive their license to practice, and make America their home. I will return home and take care of people."

"Aren't there medical schools in Pakistan?"

"Of course there are."

"So why do so many come to America?"

Hamid smiled. "I have met many Americans that have studied abroad."

"I don't doubt it, but that wasn't the question."

"Are you looking for me to say that the medical schools here are superior, Heaven?" He smiled at her before continuing with his answer. "Our schools are very good. So are the schools in England and America. Becoming licensed in America is a coveted prize."

Again, Hamid smiled at Heaven, not adding that it was even more so for the extremely wealthy. They'd never spoken of his worth. Because he drove a modest car most people wrongly assumed that he was a man of modest means. Heaven was good at making assumptions. He had no idea how she would react if she knew he was wealthy.

"How much longer will you remain in this country?"

"I have to stay long enough to pass the licensing exam; that will be less than a year," he answered. "But I can come back for visits."

"Good, I would love to see you come back. I hope we can stay friends. You know, letters, phone calls, that sort of thing."

"Why don't we stop playing games, Heaven? I'm attracted to you."

He could have eased into this slowly, Heaven thought. Now there was no way she could play coy and pretend she didn't know what he meant.

"Heaven, we're not children. I've seen the desire for me in your eyes. Tell me you're not attracted to me."

"Hamid, there are many things I might like the looks of, but things that are bad for me I try my best to avoid."

"And you think I would be bad for you?"

"Yes."

"How about another dance?"

Heaven grinned. "Right. I think I should go now before we get into trouble."

She opened the door to leave but Hamid put his hand over hers to stop her. "I will walk you downstairs," he said.

That she should have expected; he was a gentleman. That was one of the things she liked about him. For once, she would not protest. She would not remind him that she could take care of herself. Heaven was just grateful he'd not asked again to join her karate class. That alone would be reason enough to end their friendship.

At the car, Heaven gave Hamid a hug, leaning into him, feeling dwarfed by his size and hating that he was looking at her as though she were some tiny doll that he wanted to pick up and protect. She should be used to it; men were always treating her like a helpless damsel until she had to show them otherwise. Even Brandon, who'd known her for most of her life, had treated her that way. And when she'd proven she was tough, he'd told her he didn't worry about hurting her because she could handle it. He'd never known about the sea of tears she'd cried.

"Are you still going to the wedding with me?" Hamid asked, bending his head to peer in her window.

"Yes. I never go back on my word." She tilted her head and gave him a meaningful glance. "When I say something, Hamid, I stick by it." She turned her key in the ignition. Now if she could only learn to stop saying things before she thought, maybe there wouldn't be so many decisions she regretted.

In no time at all Heaven made headway with her business. Her accountant convinced her that it would be best to start small in her home and expand after she got off the ground. It was the exact opposite of what Heaven had planned, but in the end she'd seen the wisdom in his words and had yielded.

What she needed was more jobs. She'd lined up several leads simply from having worked for so many different hospitals and private families in the last three years. She used every contact she had. Her lawyer had checked that she did not have a competitor's clause in her contract with the agency. She was simply a private agent, and for whatever reason, no agency thought had been given to nurses striking out on their own.

But she had, and she already had a staff of ten nurses ready, willing, and able to handle the jobs when Heaven got them. Even though she'd not received many positive responses she did have some jobs. But Heaven wouldn't give up. She would wait patiently.

Right now, her agency wasn't receiving enough jobs for her not to work for her competitors. When things were as she wanted them Heaven's primary focus would be to manage her staff from her home office being available to put out brushfires as need. But that time wasn't now. Right now, she was still working as many double shifts as she could through other agencies, socking away the money for her business expenses.

Heaven now felt guilty taking money from Hamid, but they did have their business arrangement and his money was as good as any for building her nest egg.

Heaven was waiting for Hamid to arrive. This would be the first Muslim wedding she'd attended. She hated admitting it but she didn't want to embarrass Hamid by not dressing in a manner that was acceptable by the mosque. She wanted to ask him questions beforehand but refused to. She was determined to dress the same way she always did, and if Hamid didn't like it, tough.

She couldn't help pacing as she waited for her bell to ring. When it did, instead of buzzing Hamid up, she walked down to meet him. She caught a glimpse of him peeping through the mirrored entranceway.

"Heaven, you look beautiful."

"Thanks." Heaven refrained from asking him if what she was wearing was appropriate. She'd vowed to herself she would not change clothes or make any concessions. If she asked about her clothing he'd think she was willing to change if he wanted her to.

When they stood outside, she took several steps back and gave him a good once-over. She couldn't help the smile of approval. He had on a dashiki type dark gray tuxedo, and tonight his curly locks were freed from his usual rubber band. What a disgrace, Heaven thought, to ever bind his hair. He was gorgeous.

"You don't look too shabby," she finally said and he laughed, telling Heaven that he'd undoubtedly seen the look of admiration in her eyes.

Hamid introduced Heaven to every single person in the room, holding her hand as he did so, and Heaven couldn't help noticing that he didn't use the word friend even once. Many of the people seemed to already know her name and didn't seem surprised that she was there.

Heaven and Hamid sat at a table finally, and Heaven looked around at the women. She had to admit she liked the colorful dresses the women wore, and the gold jewelry added a lot.

"What do you think of this?" Hamid whispered in her ear.

She took one more look around. "I love the dresses the women are wearing; they're all so beautiful." She caught his smirk. "What?" she said.

"Of course you would like them. They're very similar to the dress of your people."

"Come again?" Heaven looked at Hamid as if he'd lost his mind.

"I'm talking Africa, Heaven, not America. I knew you would fit in."

The undeniable hum of a microphone brought their attention to the stage, preventing Heaven from answering Hamid. She was surprised that the voice was speaking in English and even more surprised when the man officiating the wedding spoke entirely in English. She looked around the room. There were maybe two or three more Americans there. She wouldn't have thought he would do an entire service in English for so few, but here he was doing it. So she settled in to listen.

Heaven listened to him tell both the husband and wife to respect and love each other. He even admonished them, telling them there would be days of disagreement which they could get through only by showing respect for each other.

Her eyes slid to Hamid and she smiled, wondering if he'd been watching her the entire time. They fought, but she respected him. He was smart, funny, and considerate. Hamid reached out, took her hand, and rubbed his thumb across her hand.

"We're not as different as you might think, Heaven. Someday you will have to let go of your pain and start over again. Brother Marvin knew that. It's okay to love me."

Heaven smiled, almost laughed, and got up. "I'm going to get some food."

"It might be a bit spicy," he said, coming behind her. "I'll tell you what things are less so, but you could just try a taste of everything. It would be the best way."

Hamid shook his head as he followed Heaven. He caught the eye of Sassa, who was grinning at him like a fool. He'd had word from an uncle and would be going to Pakistan in three months to get married to a girl he didn't even know, a first cousin. But Sassa was happy.

Hamid swallowed. He wanted to fulfill his own destiny, to have the love that made him quiver, that gave him wet dreams and had him hard every time he thought of how it could be. He wanted Heaven.

He watched her go through the buffet line, not putting anything on her plate except salad. "Heaven, even if you don't eat, it will save you trouble to just put it on the plate. If you don't, people will continue to try to get you to eat."

Heaven turned back to look at him. "No one can make me do anything I don't want."

Hamid shook his head. No, but they certainly would try. Twenty minutes and ten people later Hamid smiled at Heaven, walked up to the buffet table and returned with a plate with little more than sauce and a couple of tiny slivers of meat.

He was rewarded when Heaven grinned at him. Oh yes, he was falling hard for her, he thought, as he looked at her white teeth, which made her smile even more beautiful. He looked over at the bride and groom, Eunice and Majabeen, and saw the glow on their faces. He wanted that, he wanted Heaven. And whether she would admit it or not, he believed Heaven wanted it too. He would have to find a way to convince her of that.

He watched how easily Heaven blended in with the people in the mosque. She was one of them. He could see her now dressed in traditional garb, but the twists making her stand out. He smiled at Heaven. He'd gotten used to her hair; it was a part of her.

"Why are you staring at me like that, Hamid?"

Heaven touched the napkin to the corner of her mouth. "Do I have something on my face?" He grinned and she grinned back.

"You're so beautiful."

"And that's why you're staring?"

"That, and the vision I just had of you dressed in a sari with your twists," he smiled. "I think you'll like Pakistan, Heaven."

"I have no plans to go to Pakistan."

"Plans change." He kissed her hand before staring into her eyes. "Where a husband reside, Heaven, the wife must reside also."

"Hamid?"

"Don't look so afraid. You must learn to compromise. It will take that to make a marriage work."

"Hamid?"

"Enjoy the wedding, Heaven. I'm speaking of the future, not of today." He gave her a slow smile and then ran his fingers through her hair. "I love your hair," he whispered softly.

Since going to the wedding with Hamid things had changed between them. So much so, that Heaven had asked a man out on a date. Yes, she was falling for Hamid, but after his comment about her living in Pakistan, she knew it was time to put a stop to the fantasy before they both got hurt.

Heaven was anxious she'd ignored Hamid's question several times when he'd asked her what was wrong. They were going way past where they ever intended to go, and she had to do something to get them back on track. When the phone rang, she jumped and saw Hamid looking at her strangely. He knew, she thought.

She went to answer. When she came back, she turned to Hamid. "I have a date, he'll be here in fifteen minutes, sorry, we have to end the session early."

"Didn't you know you had a date when I asked if I could come over?"

"Yes, but I guess I forgot to mention it."

"Forgot? Or are you trying to make me jealous?"

"Not jealous, Hamid."

"Then are you intending to send me a message, hands off? Is your date black, Heaven?"

She ignored that. "Why are you making this more difficult? Why can't you just go?"

"Heaven, you know how I feel about you. I'm in love with you, and I believe you love me."

"We've never spoken about love, Hamid."

"That doesn't make it any less real. We've never spoken about breathing, yet we do."

"There, do you see what I mean? This is what we have between us, Hamid. We fight, and occasionally we have fun, then we fight some more."

"Call your date and tell him not to come."

"I will do no such thing." Heaven glared at Hamid. "You're the most...I don't know what you are, Hamid, but I do know you're getting on my nerves. Stop trying to tell me what to do."

"I love you, Heaven."

This wasn't love. Heaven thought about Brandon; she'd loved him. They'd finished each other's sentences. They had never fought, not even when he'd dumped her. She'd been hurt and angry but they didn't fight.

Yet she fought with Hamid, over everything. She suddenly thought of Mrs. Reed and the words the patient had said to her before she'd died. She said her marriage of sixty years had been successful because she and her husband fought.

Heaven glanced at Hamid; nothing had changed between them except their feelings. Their different backgrounds made for automatic culture clash, and clash they did. But Heaven stood firm by her decision. She had more than enough drama in her life. To think of going to Pakistan with Hamid would only complicate it more.

"Heaven, I will not beg."

"I didn't ask you to."

"I wish to be more than your friend."

"And in a few months you're leaving the States for good. Didn't you tell me those are your plans? Have you changed your mind?"

"No."

"Then you have your answer."

"You could marry me, come to my country with me. You would be welcome."

"Why do you think I would leave my home and go to a place where I don't even speak the language?"

"Stop being ignorant, Heaven. Most of the people in my country speak English. Our schools teach students more than one language. How about you? What other language can you speak?"

"I'm sick of your calling me ignorant. There may be some words in the English language you don't understand, but that isn't one of them. I know you know what you're saying. And for your information, I can talk turkey," Heaven said, between clenched teeth. "Gobble-o tobble-o hobble-e lobble-lobble."

"What's does that nonsense mean?"

"It means go to hell," Heaven said, and started toward the door when the doorbell rang. Hamid caught her arm, stopping her in her tracks.

"If you don't tell me right this second that you love me I'm going to call my father and ask him to contact a matchmaker to find me a bride. When I leave this country, either I leave with you as my wife, or I leave and go home and get married. If that happens, I will not return. Think carefully, Heaven. Don't answer me out of anger."

"I'm not angry, Hamid," Heaven hissed. "Good luck, congratulations, and invite me to the wedding." Heaven snatched her arm away quickly and opened the door for him to leave. "Goodbye, Hamid."

He glared at her but left. She heard him speaking to her date, telling him to have a good time, as if he had that right. Heaven was glad Hamid was gone. She would also be glad when he left for good. That was exactly what she needed, Hamid out of the country. To think he actually thought he could force her to tell him she loved him. That wasn't something that came after hearing a threat. Yes, him leaving would be just what she needed. What she wanted was a different story.

CHAPTER EIGHT

Heaven's mouth dropped opened. She ignored the customary bow before entering the *dojo* and stormed over to where Hamid was sparring. It had been two weeks since he'd stormed out of her house. Not a word from him, not a call, *nada*, and now here he was in her sanctum. She yanked on his arm. "What are you doing here?"

He shrugged his shoulder. "Practicing."

"Don't get cute, you know what I mean. Why are you in my school?"

"It's been my school for over a month. I'm taking lessons."

"I told you I didn't want you here."

Heaven was angry. This was hers. She'd not allowed Brandon to take it from her, and she wouldn't allow Hamid to do it. "Leave," she ordered him. "Now," she said more sharply.

"No," Hamid answered, his eyes narrowing into slits. "Who do you think you are? Why I ever bothered to fall in love with you is a mystery. You're a nasty, sharp-tempered little shrew. Karate is meant to teach discipline. You should know that, Heaven. I do, and I've only been taking it for a month."

Before Hamid could say another word, he felt his arm being yanked forward and Heaven's hip slamming into his right side. The next thing he knew he was landing on the floor with a sharp thud. He stared up from the floor at Heaven in disbelief. He outweighed her by a hundred pounds and he was more than a foot taller, yet she had thrown him as easily as…

Hamid didn't know, he couldn't think. He shook his head a little to clear it but remained on the floor, aware of the commotion of the other students running toward them, offering him a hand up. He was also aware of the scowl on Heaven's face, then of the *sensei* finally coming from the other side of the *dojo*, taking one look and dragging Heaven from the building.

Hamid should have been embarrassed, but that wasn't what he was feeling. He was proud of Heaven. He shouldn't have spoken to her in that manner, not in front of the entire class.

Finally, he accepted a hand up and gave a lopsided grin at the person helping him. "I guess I need a bit more practice," he joked. "I never saw that coming."

Heaven glanced across the room and saw the *sensei* staring at her. His anger was obvious. Before he could come to her, she started to walk toward the office but he stormed outside beckoning her to follow. Her stomach clenched. She wished she'd known he was in the *dojo,* but doubted if it would have made a difference in her action.

"Talk, Heaven, or so help me I'm kicking you out of the school. What has gotten into you? Hamid is a white belt. You could have hurt him. What were you thinking?"

"I wasn't thinking, *sensei*, I'm sorry."

"Sorry is not good enough, Heaven, not in this case. Hamid is right. You're undisciplined, and now you're behaving like a bully. I can't have that in my *dojo*. You're no longer welcome here."

"Please, *sensei*, I'm sorry, don't ban me from the school." Tears formed in Heaven's eyes, but she refused to let them fall. She didn't allow others to witness her crying; that was not a part of her. She watched as the teacher paced back and forth on the sidewalk, his face contorted in thought, looking like a storm cloud.

"You need to apologize to Hamid."

She'd known that was coming, and she groaned low. "I'll do it," she said. "I'll call him."

"No, you will do it in the *dojo*. You humiliated him there and you will make amends there. And you…with your next breath you will tell me what's going on."

"I'm not a bully. Hamid and I are...Well, I guess we're friends, sort of. The night you were trying to teach me a lesson by having the student push the punching bag into me, Hamid came over to my apartment. He's a doctor, so of course he noticed I'd been hurt." Heaven shrugged her shoulder in order to make light of the situation. The look in the instructor's eyes told her to continue. "I told Hamid that I took karate, and he asked me the name of my school. He said he wanted to take lessons. I wouldn't give the name to him, but he found out anyway. He could have gone someplace else; having him here makes me feel as if he's trying to take over my life."

"That's no excuse."

"I don't want him here."

"You do not get to choose the students."

A lone tear slid down Heaven's cheek. "This is a sanctuary for me. For Hamid, it's only something he can take away from me."

"He's not trying to take the school, Heaven. He's been coming for over a month. He's a good student and a fast learner. He has never come when you're here. This is a different night for you or he wouldn't have been here."

"How do you know that he's trying to avoid me here?"

"Because the day he joined he mentioned your name."

Heaven felt betrayed. She swallowed the sudden lump and closed her eyes for a moment; she didn't want to look at the teacher. When she opened them, she looked instead at the traffic light a half block away, at the trees swaying gently with the evening breeze. She couldn't let go of the feeling of betrayal.

At last Heaven turned back to face the *sensei*. "Why did you allow him to join?"

"Because he wants to learn. As for his being in your school, you need to let go of the pain, Heaven. You've kept it bottled up for so long that now it's coming out when it shouldn't. You can't beat up on Hamid for the hurt Brandon caused you. If you're angry with Brandon you should confront him."

The *sensei* folded his hands. "But I don't suggest you try that little maneuver on Brandon. He's your equal." He stared intently at her for a second. "Actually, Heaven, he's much better. Brandon always remains focused. He doesn't allow his anger to control him. Look at you. You should have earned your black belt a year ago. You don't have it because you refuse to test for it. But you still have the skills, and you will not use those skills to intimidate my students."

Heaven ground the palms of her hands against her eyes. "Hamid asked me to marry him."

"And for that you attack him?"

Heaven smiled slowly. "It seemed a good enough reason at the time."

"Are you in love with Hamid?"

"He says he's in love with me."

"That wasn't my question. I asked if you love Hamid."

"I think I might, but I'm not sure I want to. We do nothing but fight, *sensei*. From the day I met him we have fought. Can you imagine us together? Brandon and I loved each other for years. We never fought, and look what happened. A relationship between Hamid and me doesn't stand a chance of surviving."

"You can't be sure, but it might be fun finding out."

"Can I remain at the school if I apologize to Hamid?"

The teacher looked her over as he rubbed his chin with a closed fist. "If you do that and if you talk to Brandon. He's the source of your pain. You need to address it, for if this happens again, I will not be moved by your pleas or your tears."

"I didn't cry." Heaven looked at him in amazement. Surely one tear didn't constitute crying.

"You were crying in your heart," the teacher said and walked away. Heaven walked in the opposite direction. She would apologize to Hamid just as she'd promised, but there was still too much hostility in her to do it now.

Just the thought of confronting Brandon gave her a chill. She didn't want to. She'd seen him several times with the white girl he'd left her for. She had to admit those times had filled her with rage.

She'd seen them fighting a couple of times and wondered why he'd left her for someone with whom he now seemed to have such a volatile life. No, they'd never fought, but at the moment she couldn't get over wanting to best him in a ring. True, his skills were better and he was more disciplined, but it didn't keep her from wanting to fight him.

It took two weeks for Heaven to venture back to the *dojo*. She didn't know if Hamid would be there, given his schedule, but it was Wednesday night, the same night he'd been there before, so she decided to take her chances.

Heaven allowed a sigh to escape when she entered the *dojo*. She did the customary bow of respect to the *dojo* and spotted Hamid sparring with another student. She watched him for a moment before making her way to the office. He was getting good. She stood for a moment while the *sensei* finished the papers he was working on.

"It took you two weeks in order to come back?" he asked.

Heaven shrugged her shoulder. "I'm here now."

"What about Brandon? He's the reason you took your hostilities out on Hamid. Are you going to talk to him?"

"Yes, that was our agreement."

"When?"

"I don't know, but I give you my word. I will talk to him."

"Have you apologized to Hamid?"

"Not yet."

The *sensei* rose from his chair. "Then I think it's time," he said.

"You're going to make a big production out of this, aren't you? You could wait until class is over."

She saw the man smiling at her. "I could, but I won't. What fun would that be? Besides, you could use a dose of humility. Hamid has been taking quite a ribbing about your kicking his butt. Now I think it's you who should eat a little of that crow. Come on, Heaven," the teacher said and went out to the *dojo*.

"Attention please," he said, immediately gathering the attention of the instructors and students. "Heaven is here to rejoin us, but before she does, she has something to say. Heaven," he said, moving away and giving the floor to her.

Heaven could feel her face burning with shame. She didn't want to do this, but she had no choice if she wanted to remain in the school that had kept her sane in the past year.

She cleared her throat. "I regret my slight transgression of two weeks ago." Her head snapped up and she saw Hamid watching her intently.

"Hamid, I apologize for using superior power in order to bring you to the mat. It won't happen again." Heaven looked toward the *sensei*.

"You may rejoin the class," he said.

"Was that supposed to be an apology?" Hamid asked in a loud voice, bringing the attention of all in the room to rest on him.

"For Heaven it is, and we will all accept it." The sensei spoke with authority. "Heaven, lead the class," he ordered and returned to the office.

Great, Heaven thought. She knew he was doing this just to teach her a lesson. No one in the class wanted her to be in charge, not tonight anyway, but they were bound by the *sensei*'s rules, same as she was. She saw a hint of malice in several of the instructors' eyes, and that made her want to laugh. They didn't think she was up to the challenge. She'd show them.

When the class was over, everyone was soaking wet with sweat and too tired to do more than look at Heaven. She smiled and went to the punching bag and hit it several times, then kicked high in the air. She was showing off, and she knew it, but she was also sending a message. She might be little but she was not one to be messed with. Heaven stuffed her gear into her bag and walked out. Walking home always calmed her down.

High on the adrenaline rush, all Heaven could think of was the exhausted state she'd left Hamid in. She doubted if he'd ever want to take a class from her again. The image of his body sweating and going through the torture of intense exercise quickened her step. Lost in her thoughts, she didn't notice that the shadow on the brick building was actually a man. When she did, it was too late. He was in front of her and pulling on her gym bag.

Thoughts whirled in her mind. She could let the bag go; it had nothing of real value in it. And even if it had, her life was more important. She knew this but rational thought did not translate into action.

"You little bitch, let it go."

Heaven's eyes flickered, then rested on the man's face. She froze. She tried to make her body move, drop the bag, kick him, punch him, anything, but she couldn't move.

A meaty fist slammed into her eye, sending blinding hot pain from the socket throughout her skull. She stumbled backwards, still clutching the bag.

"Bitch," the man yelled angrily. Blinking her rapidly swelling eye, Heaven saw a man's fist smash into her assailant's face, then a couple more punches followed by a full round house kick. When she got a good look at the man, it was Hamid.

"Hamid," she said softly, not thinking. Hamid turned toward her, taking his attention off the assailant. In that second the man ran off. Heaven could see Hamid's indecision about giving chase or remaining with her. He shrugged and came to her side. Heaven turned her back to him. The pain in her eye was blinding, and she didn't want him to know.

Hamid was breathing hard, thankful that he'd been walking the same route as Heaven. Once again, fate had put them on the same path. When he'd first glimpsed the man, he'd thought it was someone Heaven knew. When he realized what was happening, for a second he'd paused, waiting for Heaven to flatten the guy. When she appeared immobile, it had momentarily rooted him to the spot. Then the certain knowledge of what was going to happen to Heaven broke the spell. Hamid ran faster than he ever had in his life, the oxygen pumping to his lungs. He felt a burning in his calves that traveled upwards to his thighs and ran even faster. He had to save Heaven.

He'd tried to get there before anything happened, but hadn't. That he regretted. Still, he didn't understand why Heaven hadn't defended herself.

He touched his hand to her shoulder to turn her to face him. "Heaven, are you okay?" He felt the tremble in her body and worried. "Heaven," he called to her again softly, "answer me please, you're scaring me."

She held her hands out; they were shaking. "Look at me," she said through clenched teeth. "This shouldn't have happened. I can take care of myself. I shouldn't need rescuing. I shouldn't need a hero. I shouldn't need you rushing in to save the day."

Hamid tilted her face up for a better look and saw the flesh on the left side of her face raised, her eye already swelling. "You're wrong, little one, you did need a hero. Tonight you needed me. Come on," he said, reaching for her hand, holding on to her as he'd wanted to do a thousand times in the past two weeks since he'd seen her.

He met with some resistance. That much, he'd expected. If he said black, she said white. If he saw rain, she saw sunshine.

But tonight he didn't want to fight with her. No, tonight he wanted…

Despite his stance over the past month, despite his having called his father to find him a bride, Hamid still wanted Heaven. He gripped her hand more firmly in his own and felt the warmth.

It seemed the short distance to her apartment passed in but a single step. So far, Heaven had not removed her hand. He climbed the stairs still holding on to her. When they were inside, he went to her bathroom and found a towel to fill with ice. When he returned, she was watching him from her one good eye, suspicion on her face. He knew she doubted his motives.

"Why are you being nice to me?" Heaven finally asked.

"What would you have me do? Should I have seen a man hitting you and done nothing? Should I leave your eye to swell even more? It's ice, Heaven, nothing more."

He pressed the cold compress gently against her swollen flesh. His fingers lingered on her brown skin and he felt a surge of desire so strong that he was forced into silence.

"You do know that nothing has changed, don't you?" Heaven asked.

Hamid groaned inwardly, wishing that Heaven's tongue for one night could also have remained as frozen as she had been when attacked. He smiled.

"Why are you smiling?"

"I just thought of something funny," Hamid replied, his smile now turning to a full-fledged grin.

"What?" Heaven asked.

"The way to make you stop fighting." With that, he leaned down and brushed her lips with his. He felt her freeze but she did not order him away so he continued kissing her lips softly, not asking or pressing for the intimacy of his tongue inside her mouth. Now it was he who was trembling.

When he didn't think he could continue kissing her without deepening the kiss, he pulled away. He heard Heaven take in a breath and could almost see her thoughts.

"Hamid, I'm not changing my mind."

"I didn't ask you to. It was merely a kiss. By the way, you taste like mangoes."

"And I suppose you hate mangoes, but no matter—"

"Goodnight, Heaven," Hamid said, interrupting what would more than likely turn into a tirade. "I see you're not any the worse for wear."

He left, pulling his phone from his pocket as he went down the stairs. "Father," he said as soon as the phone was answered, "I'm sorry to have put you through so much trouble but I'm calling about the matchmaker. Would you please tell her that her services are no longer required? Fate has provided me with a bride, a most unwilling one," he laughed.

"The woman that Sassa told us about?" his father asked.

"Yes," Hamid replied, a bit surprised that Sassa had mentioned Heaven to his family.

"Does this woman love you enough to convert?"

"I have no idea," Hamid answered, "But I know she's the one. Fate has dumped her in my lap and besides loving her, I think she needs saving. I want to save her."

His father laughed. "Of course you do. Satisfy this itch, then return home. And, Hamid, I did not make the call for a bride for you. Your cousin forewarned me. It would have proved quite embarrassing to have two members of the family break a marriage agreement."

"What?" Hamid asked.

"It seems fate has also found your cousin."

That was news to Hamid. He and Sassa had always told each other everything. But he asked no questions. The roaming charges were already going to kill him. Instead, he would go home and find the best way to break through Heaven's defenses. He would marry her and begin his family and, as he'd told his father, he would manage to save her from herself. He would be her hero, whether she thought she needed one or not.

Heaven woke with a splitting headache and pain shooting through her left eye. She was angry with herself and her reaction last night, or rather her lack of reaction. She'd trained for years and should have been prepared for an attack. She would have been, except she'd been unable to stop thinking of Hamid, of his body sweating as she'd put him through his paces. To put it bluntly, she'd been unfocused and she'd gotten her butt kicked.

Daring to peep into the mirror, Heaven frowned at the swelling, glad that Hamid had been around. She was thankful that the man who'd done this to her was probably looking and feeling worse than she was this morning.

Heaven touched her fingers to the tender flesh. "Ouch," she moaned. Maybe this was a warning. She knew very well what the problem was. She hadn't seen or really talked to Hamid in a month. In that time she'd at least admitted to herself that she cared for him, and she missed his not being around.

Their last fight was always at the back of her mind. Hamid had threatened to return to Pakistan to find a bride. If he did, it would be too late for her. She would never see him again. She didn't want that.

Heaven blamed herself for her disorientation and hated that she'd behaved worse than someone who'd never set foot inside a *dojo*. Her *sensei* would be disappointed in her if she told him, which she had no plans to do.

Heaven touched her fingers to her lips. Hamid had told her she tasted of mangoes. She laughed to herself. It was her lipstick. She wondered if she'd ever tell him. He must think she was a fruit farmer. He'd commented so many times how much he liked her lemony scent that she hadn't dared to change her perfume.

What happened last night wasn't as much a surprise as it should have been. Him swooping down like her dark knight...That was Hamid, chauvinistic and yet the defender of women. She knew he would never allow her to live it down.

What she was thinking of now was the kiss. She could feel his breath warm and sweet fanning her face, his lips soft and lush, just the right feel to them. She had felt his straining not to push and she had appreciated that. Still, she'd wanted to yank him down and kiss him so hard that she'd forget her own pain and his, kiss him so hard that the thought of finding a bride in Pakistan would be the last thing on his mind.

But she hadn't done it, because when Hamid kissed her she'd thought of Brandon, and realized the *sensei* was right. She would have to take care of her feelings for Brandon before she did anything about Hamid. Heaven shook her head; she didn't want to be in love with Hamid because she was lonely.

Heaven looked at the wet spot on her blouse from the soggy towel and wished that she had more ice. She could also do with a strong cup of coffee.

A knock sounded on her door and Heaven moaned. Who would be so insensitive as to come to her home so early in the morning? Then she smiled in spite of herself, thinking she knew who the early morning caller was.

She yanked the door open without asking who was there. "What are you doing here? And how did you get in?"

"I came to bring you coffee." Hamid held a tray from McDonald's with coffee and cinnamon rolls. "Your neighbor was coming out and let me in."

"Are you here to be my nursemaid?" Heaven asked, trying to keep the smile from her face.

"No, but there is a saying that if you save a man's life that life belongs to you."

Heaven laughed; she couldn't help it. "Number one, I'm not a man. Number two, you didn't save my life."

"May I come in?"

She moved aside and held the door open. "Sure, come on in." She snatched the pastry from the cardboard box and took a bite. "Hamid, I have a strange question to ask you. Have you ever thought you heard my voice in your head?" His eyes narrowed and she thought he was going to call her crazy but he didn't.

"All the time, Heaven. Since the moment I first met you in the hospital, I have heard your voice in my head." He sat at the table, removed the lid from the coffee, and slanted his eyes toward her. "And since then, I've been trying to get rid of the sound."

Heaven blinked. "Why?"

"Do you like my voice in your head?"

"I never said I heard yours."

"You didn't have to. Now, are you going to answer the question?" Hamid took a sip of coffee and waited.

"I've wondered what it meant. You've annoyed me, amused me, and…"

"And stirred your passion, but because of some silly rule you made for yourself to only date black men, you think you have to save face with your girlfriends and ignore what your heart is telling you."

He moved his hand toward her arm. "We're both black, Heaven."

"But there is only one of us who's allowed to have a harem. I won't be a part of that."

"Heaven, you say the silliest things. You know nothing about me really, about my culture, yet you constantly spout off all of these facts as though you've lived the life." He peered intently at her. "You haven't, have you, Heaven?"

Heaven pulled her hand away. "You do the same, Hamid. You asked me if all American women were whores. You had judged us in your mind before you even came to this country. You were also guilty of being ignorant and biased."

"Guilty as charged," Hamid smiled. "We've been acquainted for many months. Now, don't you think it's time the two of us stop playing these silly games and really get to know each other?"

"Maybe after you answer one question for me. Are you allowed to have harems?"

"Me personally or Muslim men in general?"

"Both."

"I'm allowed because I can afford it. But what man would want more than one wife, unless there were good reasons for it? Look at us. We fight constantly. Do you think I would want to do that with more than one wife?"

"I don't think Muslim men marry women for their conversation."

Hamid took a slow sip of the coffee. "You're wrong, Heaven, it's not about the sex. The prophet Mohammed instituted what you in this country call polygamy in order to protect the women who were without men to protect them. If a man cannot provide for more than one wife, then he shouldn't have more than one."

"Why did the prophet think women needed to be protected? Perhaps if rights had been given they wouldn't have needed it."

"All women need protecting, Heaven, even in this century. Whether you like it or not, the fact is that women on the whole are not physically as strong as men. Take last night, for instance—"

"I wondered how long it would take for you to bring that up."

"As I was saying, you can handle yourself when you're in a ring and can see your opponent. You could have easily kicked that guy's butt, but you froze. You needed a man with brute strength last night, not skills, or years of practice, but strength."

"And you wonder why I won't agree to date you." Heaven laughed and looked at him in wonder. "You're so full of yourself. You're an arrogant—"

His lips were on hers before she could say another word. He was down on his knees, his arms around her. He was not going to hold back on the kiss, and for God's sake, she hadn't brushed. And she didn't have on lipstick, and she wouldn't taste like mangoes.

"Hamid, stop, not now."

"Hush, Heaven, for once in your life just shut up."

And for once in her life, she did. She shivered as his tongue parted her lips she tasted the coffee and sweetness from the apple Danish and hoped he also tasted the sweetness from what she'd eaten. Heaven gave herself over to the kiss. Her head was spinning. She felt weightless, as though her entire body had melted into a puddle.

She should be doing something other than kissing Hamid as though her next breath came from him. She shouldn't be sucking on his tongue as if it contained oxygen. He'd just uttered the most ridiculous nonsense she'd ever heard. She didn't need a man. Heaven moaned. But if he stopped kissing her, she would die.

When the kiss ended, Hamid remained on his knees in front of her. "Let's get to know each other, Heaven."

What a silly man. Did he think after kissing her like that she could talk? Heaven nodded her head, it was the best she could do. Then Hamid smiled and she melted again. She wanted him to kiss her again. She swallowed, her eyes fastened on his lips. She sighed, and a low moan escaped her, making her feel embarrassed.

"Ask for what you want." Hamid whispered softly.

Did she dare? "Kiss me, Hamid." *She dared.*

CHAPTER NINE

It amazed Heaven how quickly her life had changed. She would admit that she was happier now than she'd been in a year and a half. She and Hamid had been redefining their relationship for the past month, trying to see if they could make it work.

Heaven had done as she'd said she would. She was giving Hamid a chance. She'd already been to a mosque with him for the wedding, and now she wanted him to go to a Baptist church with her.

Neither of them said much on the ride to the church or after they'd been seated. Heaven opened her Bible and followed along. She sang hymns, glancing sideways from time to time to see how uncomfortable Hamid was. He didn't appear to have a problem, but she didn't ask until they were in her truck and heading to her apartment.

"What did you think?" Heaven asked.

"About the service?" Hamid gave a quick laugh. "Heaven, this is not the first time I've been in a Christian church."

"You didn't say that you had been."

"You didn't ask."

"You could have said."

"Why? You have all of these assumptions about me that I allow."

"Allow? You don't allow me to do anything."

"Heaven, please watch the road before you run into something."

Heaven hit the steering wheel and glanced at Hamid. "This is never going to work."

"I think it's working just fine." He pushed the button to her CD. Heaven's eyes followed his fingers. Number three, of course.

"Hamid, you always try to use that song to shut me up." Heaven looked down. "Marvin Gaye doesn't control me."

"But he controls your sensual nature and makes you more prone to listen to me."

Heaven couldn't help laughing. He was right. She wanted to close her eyes as the music washed over her.

"Better pay attention, Heaven."

"Then I would suggest you turn off Marvin," she answered, knowing he wouldn't, knowing that the moment it was safe to do so, she would lean toward him for a quick kiss. *What the heck?* Heaven leaned over and smiled as Hamid kissed her.

This was every bit as hard as she'd thought it would be but she was committed to at least giving them a chance. She smiled, wondering how Hamid would react when he found out he'd made some mighty big assumptions of his own. She wouldn't tell him, not until the time was right.

"Hamid, can you come for dinner tonight? Ongela and Latanya are coming."

Minute after minute passed without Hamid answering her. She knew he was wondering what she would cook. She could have ended his doubt by telling him she was having catfish, home fries and salad, maybe spaghetti, but she didn't.

She started talking to herself. "Ham hocks, greens, baked ham, macaroni and cheese. I wonder what I've forgotten?" Heaven didn't smile, nor did she look in Hamid's direction. Let him wonder, she thought.

"Of course, I can come. How's it going with your business?" he asked, switching the subject.

This one Heaven would give him because she was extremely excited to tell Hamid that she had three new clients. Still not enough for her to be able to stop working herself, but she was getting there. Thank God, she had three of the best nurses in the city on the cases. If they did a good job, and they would, Heaven would soon be given more work than her staff could handle.

When they were done talking about her, Heaven remembered that Hamid was still waiting to see if he received his medical license.

"Have you heard anything?"

"I think I'll tell you when we get upstairs," Hamid said sadly.

Not another word was spoken until they were in Hamid's apartment.

"Okay, tell me." Heaven rubbed his arms. "I'm sorry, you can try again in a few months."

She was lifted from her feet. "I'm a doctor, Heaven. I did it. I passed. I can return home and work." He spun her around and around. "My dreams have come true."

And Heaven's nightmare had begun.

It was time to get her life in order. Heaven didn't know what was going to happen with Hamid but it had little bearing on her decision to put things to rest with Brandon. If she didn't, she wouldn't trust her decisions.

Heaven sat in the waiting room of Brandon's office, ignoring the perky woman who'd taken her place in Brandon's life. The woman was not to blame anyway. It was Brandon with whom she'd had a commitment, and Brandon who'd broken her trust.

When the nurse called her in, Heaven stuck her arm out woodenly and allowed her to check her blood pressure. She'd given a bogus tale and could barely wait until the nurse left the room.

She heard Brandon's voice outside the door, harsh, cold, not easy-going and warm, the way he'd always been. She heard him turn the knob and swallowed. Suddenly the urge to cry filled her throat. It was going on two years. She had not allowed Brandon to see her cry then and she wasn't about to do so now.

"Hello, Miss Smith."

Heaven turned from the wall to stare at him. She gave a smile as his mouth opened wide.

"Heaven?" Brandon looked down at the chart in his hand. "But I thought...there must be some mistake." His eyes widened in understanding. "Did you give a false name?"

"I wanted to talk to you."

"You could have called, Heaven. You didn't have to go through this. I'm busy, I have patients."

Good, Heaven thought. His brusque treatment of her was what she needed. She hadn't known how she was going to handle this, but now she did.

"Brandon, I think I'm worth ten minutes of your time. I think the years we spent together entitle me to that."

"Heaven, we were over two years ago."

"It doesn't matter. I never told you what I'm going to tell you now. I think it's time you heard."

First Brandon glared at her, then frowned. "Then let's do this in my office after I'm done with my patients."

Heaven almost laughed. "Do you seriously think I'm going to wait an hour or two in your office before you come to see me? You think I'm going to give up, or come to my senses and leave, but I'm not. You either go to your office right now with me or we do this here in this room."

"Have you gone crazy?" He walked over to her and attempted to take her arm. "You know how thin these exam room walls are. What are you looking for, an audience?"

"I'm looking for an answer, Brandon."

"Why?"

"I never asked and you never told me."

"And you want to know now? I don't get it. I have someone else. I don't want you back, Heaven. It's over, it's been over."

This time Heaven did laugh. "Don't flatter yourself. I didn't come here for you. I came for me. It's taken me this long to realize that we never had the perfect relationship that I thought we had. I haven't been able to so much as share the *dojo* with you because of everything I've kept inside. You hurt me, Brandon, and you pissed me off. I never told you that. I just accepted your decision and faded quietly into the scenery the way that you wanted. I never got a chance to have my say."

"Okay, fine, Heaven, I pissed you off. You've told me. Now that you've gotten that off your chest, will you leave?"

Heaven hopped down from the table. Before she knew what she was doing, she had shoved Brandon into the wall and was jabbing her finger into his chest. "No, I'm not leaving. Why did you do it the way that you did? Why didn't you tell me you no longer loved me? Why did I have to find out you had someone when I came to visit your office?"

"Heaven, get your finger out of my chest."

"No." Heaven gritted her teeth. "You owe me an explanation."

"You're only pissed, Heaven, because she's white. If she were black, you wouldn't be here right now pulling this crap. Cut the drama. Since when did you start acting like your crazy ass girlfriends? This isn't you. Someone put you up to this. Who? Latanya, Peaches, or Ongela?"

"No one, Brandon. Don't you understand? I need to know this for myself." She shook her head, disappointed in him, disappointed in herself for spending so many years of her life loving him, and another two years hurting.

"Do you really want to know, Heaven?"

"I wouldn't be here if I didn't."

"How long did you think I was going to go without sex? I could almost understand when we were in high school that you didn't want to do it, but after that…My God, Heaven, what were you saving it for? Are you still a virgin?"

Heaven moved away. "Brandon, are you telling me you left me because of sex?"

"That was a big part of it. I grew tired of living like a monk, and I also grew tired of our predictable life, your scheduling everything to death, not spending a dime because we had to save it for our business, not having fun because we had to stay on track. I left you because you were no damn fun. Look at you. It's taken you two years to get angry over my leaving. What did you do, wake up and have a sudden revelation?"

Heaven blinked. Unlike her, Brandon's anger was showing in his face. With his high yellow complexion, his face was now blotched and red, his eyes bulging out.

"It didn't take me two years to get angry, Brandon. I was angry the moment you said it."

"Then why didn't you say so then? Why didn't you tell me how you felt? Why didn't you ask me to stay? You say you loved me, but Heaven, you loved your plan, our working together. I was only a cog in your plans, the sperm donor for those babies you wanted to have."

"It wasn't just me. If you had wanted things to be different, why didn't you ever say anything? We never once fought over our plans. How was I to know you didn't want it? How was I to know how you felt? If you were looking around because I wouldn't sleep with you, you should have just told me that." Heaven backed away from Brandon. She didn't like the way her voice was trembling or the sick feeling in her gut. She'd never known he thought she was no fun, that he was only going along with her plans. *Oh, God,* she thought, feeling sicker. She'd been wrong about their love. "Why didn't you ever tell me how unhappy you were?" Heaven asked.

"What good would it have done? Would you have said yes and then made me feel guilty about it for the rest of my life?"

"It seems like you have unresolved issues with me also, Brandon. You said I should have said something. It sounds like you were angry as well as unhappy. You never let me know it."

"Like you said, Heaven, we didn't fight. It wasn't our thing. We were in love, remember? Our love had to be perfect. Fighting would spoil it. Making love would have spoiled your perfect vision of being a virginal bride."

His bitter look felt like a slap to Heaven. She sucked in air as though she were drowning. She blinked to stop the tears. Could she have been so wrong about the two of them for so long?

"I never knew you had a problem with my remaining a virgin until we married. I always thought we were in agreement on that. I never went looking for anyone else," she said. "I was happy."

"I wasn't. And you want to know what else? I fight with Jeannie all the time, ten times a day, and it doesn't matter. At least I know she's alive."

Heaven held her head up high. "You two getting married?"

"Eventually. I love her. She's my soul mate, Heaven."

She moved toward the door. "The *sensei* said I needed to make peace with you, fight with you, whatever. I've done that now."

He was eyeing her strangely. "Does this little visit mean I can come back to the school and not have to act like a thief, sneaking in through the back door when you're not there?"

Heaven laughed, "You've gotten very good at showing your anger, haven't you?"

"You should try it, Heaven. Believe me, it feels good, and the make-up sex is wonderful." He gave her a tiny smile. "But I'm sure you still don't know about that, do you?"

"You're wrong, Brandon. I do. And that's another thing. I'm truly glad you and I never made love, considering all that's happened. I was able to give myself to Hamid knowing he was the first, that I'd not been soiled by you." She lied, not wanting to hear any more insults about her still being a virgin.

"Hamid? Is he a brother?"

Heaven walked toward the door, then turned around. "What difference does it make?"

"I know Miss-Black-Soul-Sister wouldn't date anyone other than a black man, not you who dogged my having a white girlfriend."

"I never said anything to you about her."

"You didn't have to say it to me. I've seen it in your eyes every time you've seen us together, and I know your friends. I know you dogged her and me. Now you're with a...what is he, Arab?"

Heaven shrugged her shoulder before answering. "He's a man, Brandon. Take care," she said, and closed the door.

Heaven marched out of the building. *Didn't that just take the cake?* she thought. Hamid thought American women were whores, and Brandon thought she was frigid. She was neither. She wanted to have sex so badly that her womb ached. But look what had happened. Brandon had left her for Jeannie, and Hamid was leaving her for his country. She'd made the right choice to keep her drawers on.

Since he'd gotten his license, something had been wrong with Heaven. She was subdued. It was if someone had closed the drapes on her. She still spent time with him listening to music, eating, going to different churches. You name it, they did it. And they continued to fight. That was the only time Heaven seemed to behave normally.

It was when he'd take her in his arms that he noticed a change. She was pulling away from him; emotionally he could feel it. She was not there, and it made him wonder if she had discovered she didn't love him.

She told him it was due to her business taking off, but he didn't believe it. He'd even taken a couple of jobs for her, just to let her know that he supported her business.

Things should have been going well for them, but they weren't. They were dating, but in dating, they had lost something. He almost wished they had not made it official. The kisses they'd shared only weeks ago were what kept him going. He wanted to find that woman again.

Hamid let out a breath. He didn't know how Heaven would take it when he told her that he was going to Pakistan. He hoped she would be here when he returned, but he had to go, he had received the coveted prize. Now he had to go home and share that moment with his family. Besides that, another favorite cousin was getting married. Both he and Sassa were expected to attend.

"Heaven, I need to tell you something."

"I already know."

"How could you know?" Hamid moved to kiss her but she turned away.

"You're going to Pakistan. I know."

It hit Hamid like a titanic gust of wind, nearly knocking him over. He'd told Heaven that when he received his license he'd return to Pakistan. Heaven must think he was leaving her. He had to clear that up.

"Heaven, Sassa and I are returning home for a wedding of a cousin. We'll return in a couple of months."

"Whatever."

"Not whatever. I'm coming back. Do you think I could leave you and have you believe I could live without you? I love you. I want to make you my wife."

"And live where? You told me your dream was to return home with an American license. Has your dream changed?"

"Not my dream, but my life. You're a part of my life, Heaven, a very important part."

"Then don't go. Don't leave me, Hamid."

"Don't you trust my word to you?"

"No."

"I'm not Brandon, Heaven. I'm not going to hurt you. I will be back, one month, perhaps, but no more than two."

"Whatever, Hamid."

This time he took her into his arms and kissed her hard, trying with his lips and his tongue to show her she owned his heart. *Silly woman*, there was no way he could leave her forever. He had no idea how he would convince his family that he needed to return to American for an extended period. Nor did he know how he would get out of his commitment to his family to return home, especially since he didn't want to get out of it, even if he could. It was a matter of honor. Heaven was a matter of his heart. Hamid would have to find a way to have them both. As soon as he could after the wedding, he would return to Heaven and remain, until he could convince her to marry him and move to Pakistan.

Hamid glanced at Heaven as airport security detained him. He'd wanted to make a grand gesture, show Heaven how much he wanted a future with her. So he'd suggested they fly to San Francisco to visit her father.

Now he stood there being humiliated as first one airport official, then another, checked him over. Their hands brushed his genitals. Hamid pulled back, anger flaring rapidly. *Pigs,* he thought. This only gave them license for their sickness.

He glanced toward Heaven. She was pleading with her eyes. When her mouth opened, he wanted to warn her but didn't have a chance.

"Hamid," she said softly, looking at him. "It will be over in a moment." He shook his head at the flicker of recognition that crossed the security guards' faces. They seemed to swivel around in slow motion. Hamid knew what was coming next.

He saw surprise widen Heaven's eyes as she was led away. He saw her gaze land on him as she tried to smile. Hamid watched helplessly, as a wand was passed through Heaven's legs repeatedly. The woman examining her appeared to take perverse pleasure in touching Heaven's breasts, going so slowly that when his eyes connected with Heaven's at last, he saw the tears that glimmered like diamonds in their depth. A part of Hamid died then. It was one thing to have to endure this himself, quite another to have to witness Heaven going thorough it.

As the woman readied her hands for another pass at Heaven's breasts, Hamid jerked away, went, and stood in front of Heaven. "That's enough," he said defiantly.

"Hamid, don't," Heaven pleaded. Her hand was reaching out to touch him when a male officer pushed her back. Red hot rage filled Hamid as he swiveled to confront the man.

"Hamid, don't please. It's okay."

It wasn't okay. It would never be okay. He was a man and she was his woman. She was not to be treated like a chattel. Hamid hated it. He hated the terrorist acts that had been perpetrated across the entire world, not just in America. If he had a way to stop it, he would. It was not just Americans who had died in terrorist attacks, and it was not just Middle Easterners who had committed those acts.

"Take your hands off her," Hamid said, all the anger in him fueling his words. He said it with deadly calm, no longer giving a damn if they tossed him out of the country forever. He would not stand by and allow this indignity to take place, not to Heaven.

The guards were looking at him. He could see the fear in their eyes. That was good, they should fear him. But it was Heaven who broke his heart.

"Hamid, it's okay. They have to make sure the plane is safe. It's all because of Homeland Security, Hamid. It's just because of 9/11. It's not personal."

Hamid couldn't believe what he was hearing. He swung his gaze to Heaven in disbelief. "Do you think that only Arab citizens have blood on their hands? Heaven, look at you. Did your ancestors come to America on cruise ships? Were they invited? Were they allowed to leave when they wanted to go? Don't you think America has bloody hands for that? And what about the so-called savages that lived here before this land became America? They were called heathens and devils. Why, Heaven? Because they wanted to protect what was theirs, their land, their women, their children, their way of life. You don't think there is blood there?"

"Hamid, let's talk about this later," Heaven pleaded. Her eyes closed and she nodded toward the guards. Hamid's gaze followed her. Did she think he gave a damn that the guards heard what he was saying?

Hamid glared at Heaven and the guards. "Everyone in America is angry and suspicious of anyone from an Arab nation, whether that person abhors the acts or not. I don't agree with the acts of violence, Heaven, but I can understand some of the thinking behind it.

"Hamid, please," Heaven warned again, and again Hamid ignored her warning, now angry with her also.

"Don't you think I know that was part of the reason you didn't want to date me? Do you think I believed that nonsense that you date only black men? Of course there are differences, but you assumed many things about me."

Heaven was released. "And you assume many things about me." She glanced at the guard and walked toward Hamid. They walked a few steps away and then she turned to him.

"I didn't base my not wanting to date you on a war, on the blood of either of our countries. I may have assumed things, but that doesn't mean that was the reason for my refusal to date you. Initially I worried about a culture clash, a personal matter, not a global one."

"If that were true, Heaven, why did you so easily accept the guard's treatment? You're American; you think your country has clean hands."

"I'll be the first person to tell you America has blood on her hands, but so does your country. What are you going to do, blame me for the way we were treated here today? And don't forget, Hamid, I was treated badly as well. Do you think I liked it any better not being able to help you? I may be a woman, but I want to protect you as much as you want to protect me."

"You will not emasculate me, Heaven. It is not your job to protect me; it is my job to protect you." Hamid started walking. He was too angry to continue talking to her as they walked to the gate, too angry when they loaded the plane, and even more furious when the plane landed in San Francisco.

What could he offer Heaven in this country, and what, he wondered, could he offer her in his own? Would she be any safer there than he was here?

They waited in silence for Heaven's luggage. Hamid had only an overnight bag.

"Hamid, you couldn't do anything."

"And you think that makes me feel better about it? You don't understand, Heaven, how belittling it is to a man not to be able to protect the woman he loves." He grabbed her hand and pulled her to him. "Why would you respect me when I can't do that? Why would you love a man you don't respect? Is that the reason you've never told me that you love me?"

He put a finger to her lips to still her words. "Don't tell me now, Heaven. I won't believe you. I've never asked for your pity, only your love, and right now there is so much pity in your eyes that I'm drowning in it."

He picked up her bag from the carousel and marched out the door.

Heaven watched Hamid as he walked away from her. The incident at the airport had angered her also, but she wasn't angry enough to jeopardize Hamid's freedom. Yes, they'd overdone it. Yes, they had no right to touch either of them in the manner they had. With the new heightened state of security, their rights were being stripped away daily.

Heaven did not intend to let the matter drop. As soon as they returned home she would file a complaint. Hamid was behaving as though he was the only one embarrassed.

When he kept his silent treatment up in the taxi to the Jack Tar Hotel, Heaven kept hers up as well. If he wasn't talking to her, then she wouldn't talk to him.

In the elevator Heaven could finally take it no longer. "Why are you treating me like the enemy? I didn't do a thing besides try to save you from being tossed in jail. Don't you understand that people have been detained at the airports for much less than shouting and demanding that they stop their search?"

"I didn't want you saving me. I would have gladly gone to jail for you, if it had come down to it. Don't you understand that?"

"I understand it, but there was no need for you to do that, Hamid, I didn't need you to prove anything to me by getting in trouble."

"That is not your call, Heaven," he said between clenched teeth.

"You are the most stubborn, arrogant man I have ever met in my entire life. You act as though you are the first person it's happened to," she yelled. "It happens, Hamid, and it happens to a lot of people, not just to Muslim men."

He glared at her, held her gaze, then swallowed his words before walking out of the elevator. He proceeded down the hall carrying both of their bags, unlocked the door to her room, went in, put her luggage on the bed and turned to face her.

"I will not argue with you about this, Heaven. I am not attempting to tell you that an insult to a Muslim man is more than an insult to a black woman. I am telling you that for a Muslim man to have to watch others trail their hands over his woman's body, the insult is unforgivable. In this case, I will accept your calling me arrogant and a male chauvinist. I am a man. You are not."

With that, he walked out of her room, down the hall and into his own room.

Heaven stood, fuming for a moment. If only, she thought…but if only what? If only men from the Middle East had not bombed the World Trade Center? If only American forces had not marched full force into a Muslim country and blown their world to bits? If only she had not met Hamid? If only she had not fallen in love with him, and if only he weren't leaving her? This trip was meant to cement their relationship, not tear them farther apart. This argument was different from any they'd ever had. It involved Hamid's manhood, his idea of who he was.

Heaven dialed the phone to alert her father that she was in San Francisco. "Remember I told you Hamid is from Pakistan. Please don't say or do anything to offend him," she warned, wishing that for once her opinionated father would be able to keep his opinions to himself.

❧

"John and Ernestine Ross, meet Hamid Ahmad. Hamid, my father and stepmother." Hamid's hand was already out to shake her father's hand. Heaven saw the question in his eyes and smiled. "It's a long story. I'll explain later."

When they returned to the hotel later that evening, they stood in the hall outside of Heaven's door. She didn't ask Hamid to come in and he didn't ask if he could.

"Are you going to tell me now?"

"My father never married my mother. I use my mother's maiden name."

"Does it still hurt?" Hamid asked.

"My mother's death?" Heaven asked, looking at him in surprise. "Of course it still hurts. She gave me life, and I loved her with all my heart. I wish she were alive to see my business, to cheer me on. She would have been happy for me."

"Would she have approved of me?"

Heaven studied Hamid for a moment. "She would have approved."

"Your mother, what was her name?"

"Katherine," Heaven answered. "Frances Katherine Terrell."

"But you once told me the story of your birth, and you said when you were born your father said he had everything he wanted."

"He did," Heaven answered, "and maybe something he didn't want. He had a wife." She looked at Hamid. "Good night, Hamid," she said, and went into her room.

Heaven took in a deep breath. She'd never told that truth to anyone. Not even Brandon was aware of the circumstances that surrounded her birth, and they had known each other practically all their lives, at least since they were six. That was a long time not to share such an intimate detail.

For a long time Heaven had always felt shame for the circumstances attached to her birth. She'd finally let go of it. She didn't know when it had happened, but it must have been the same time as when she'd decided to let go of her anger over Brandon leaving her.

Fifteen minutes later a knock sounded on the door and startled her.

"Who is it," she asked, her voice sticking in her throat.

"It's Hamid."

Heaven opened the door, wondering if he were going to ask if he could come in, if he could sleep with her. If he hadn't understood the meaning behind her story, then she had no other way to tell him. Crap happened when you weren't looking. She would not take the chance of having a child out of wedlock. The stigma might have lessened, but she still didn't want to pass it to a child.

Hamid was holding his hand open. In it was a basket from the hotel restaurant. Two perfectly ripened mangos lay side by side; a knife and napkin lay next to them.

"This is for you. I told you I like the taste of mangoes." He kissed her lightly on her lips, shoved the basket in her hand. "Heaven, do you know the story of the great flood and God's promise to Abraham? He sealed that pledge with a rainbow in the sky. I will seal my pledge to you with mangoes."

"What pledge?"

"My pledge, my sacred pledge. To be used only when I have been really ignorant. This will be the bond between us. When I give you mangoes you will know that I am sorry for whatever offense I have done. You will know this is my way of renewing my commitment to you. It will be my declaration of love and devotion."

"Mangoes, Hamid?"

"Mangoes, Heaven. Think about it. No one will know how impor-tant this symbol is to us. It will be our private declaration of love." He held her gaze. "Do you understand how important this is, Heaven?"

"I understand that instead of saying the words that you should, you're trying to make amends with fruit."

"Not just any fruit, Heaven, mangoes. Giving you mangoes will tell you what's in my heart. They will remind you and me of the first time I kissed you and tasted mangoes." Heaven smiled. "Now do you understand?"

Heaven moved into the room. "Do you want to come in?"

"No, I don't think it's proper for us to be in your bedroom alone."

"Hamid, you've been in my home many times and we were alone."

"But never in your bedroom." He kissed her, then turned and walked back to his room.

"Heaven, you know I'm leaving in three days. Is there anything you would like for me to bring you back?"

She wanted to tell him she only wanted him to return. She licked her lips, pulling her top lip into her mouth, chewing nervously on it. "Are you truly coming back in a month?"

"Yes, I'll be gone no longer than two months, no matter what. Now tell me what gift you would like me to bring you when I return?"

"Bring me a sari."

"It's improper for men to buy clothes for women. What else would you like?"

"If you didn't want to bring me what I wanted, you shouldn't have asked."

"Heaven, what's wrong? Why are we fighting? My plane could go down and you want harsh words between us?" He smiled at her, but she was frowning, not taking his words as a joke.

"Heaven, I'm coming back."

"But you *are* going back for good at some point. You told me that was your plan, that you want to open a clinic there."

"Yes, I do."

"So your coming back is only temporary. You're going to be back for a few months, and then you're going to be out of my life."

"Heaven, I will be back."

She refused to look at him. "Sure, you will," she said, in a voice devoid of emotion.

"Trust me, Heaven."

This time she looked at him for a long while before speaking. She wished she had stuck to her plan. Hamid was breaking her heart without meaning to, but that didn't lessen the pain. "I want you to know before you leave that I went to see Brandon," she muttered, waiting for his response."

"Why?"

"When I attacked you, *sensei* said I had to make things right with Brandon, so I did."

"Did you settle things?"

"I tried."

"Is he the reason you didn't want me there?"

"Partially," Heaven said, looking directly in his eyes. "But not because of the reason you think. I didn't want to be around Brandon after he'd hurt me. I couldn't be at the *dojo* when he was there, so the *sensei* let me stay and made him leave. When you wanted to join, it brought up too many bad memories. I didn't want something to happen with us," She laughed. "Come on, Hamid, the way we're always fighting, how long would it take before it spilled over into the *dojo*?"

"It took you less than two minutes to throw me to the ground when you saw me there, so I'm guessing you'd thought of this."

"Not exactly, she laughed. "But I didn't want our private fights to spoil my ability to relax at the *dojo*."

"Are you over Brandon?"

"I already was."

"Will he be rejoining classes at the *dojo*?"

She lifted her shoulder and shook her head slightly. "I don't care if he does, if that's what you're asking me."

"Will you still attend?"

"Most likely."

"There is just one more thing. I don't understand what you're saying to me, make things right. Would that mean there is a chance for you to have Brandon, the man who hurt you, back in your life?"

Heaven saw the quick spark of jealousy that laced Hamid's brown eyes. She reached her hand up to touch his dark curls. "I didn't go to see Brandon because you're leaving."

"No?"

"No. I wanted to make sure I'm with you for the right reasons."

"And?"

"And I am."

"Will you be here when I return?"

"Of course, where do you think I'm going?"

"I mean, will you be here waiting for me, Heaven?"

Heaven swallowed. "We'll talk when you return, Hamid." She walked to her desk and pulled out folders and began making calls to the nurses she had scheduled to work. She saw Hamid watching her and ignored him. She had to get used to not having him around.

"You're making assumptions again, aren't you, Heaven?"

"No assumptions. I'm replaying every conversation we've ever had in my head."

"You can't be replaying them all, because if you are, you must have surely missed the one where I told you I loved you."

Heaven pushed her tongue around in her mouth. She wasn't going to debate love with Hamid. She dialed another client. She had her dream and Hamid had his.

Hamid sat next to Sassa on the plane. They both had almost been ordered to return home. That, he had not told Heaven. Things did work a bit differently in their country, and respect for family was still something that he valued. The family wanted to have them home to get a feel for exactly what was going on. True, there was a wedding, and true, he was going home in order for his family to share in the joy of his being a doctor licensed in America. But the larger truth was that if neither of those two things had occurred, he and Sassa would still be sitting on the plane bound for Pakistan.

"Hamid, you know we're in for it, don't you? First me, then you."

"I know. Why didn't you warn me that you had called off the matchmaker?"

"You didn't care what I was doing. Your only concern was Heaven."

Hamid growled low, not wishing to fight with Sassa on the small plane. "I didn't go looking for her, everything just happened. Even my father believes in fate."

"Right."

"It was." Hamid insisted. "Why do you think we met if it wasn't meant to be?"

"You've met many women. Have you fallen for them like a complete fool? Don't answer. The answer is no. You've kept your head.

LET'S GET IT ON

You've slept with women in this country, and none have been able to turn your head. And this woman, she's beautiful, granted, but she's so tiny. You're a big man." Sassa looked slyly at Hamid. "I'm sure you're much too big for her."

"Sassa, if that's your way of asking about my relationship with Heaven, I'm going to tell you the same thing I've told you the last million times that you've asked: What I do with Heaven is none of your business, and don't ask me again."

"She's what? Is she even five feet, Hamid?"

"Not quite, she's more like four-eleven."

"And you're six-three and a half?" The two of you look funny together. Have you ever gotten a good look at the two of you in a mirror? She's like this little doll. You would smother her in a short time if you married her."

Hamid laughed. This was Sassa's way of trying once again to ask him if he were sleeping with Heaven. He wasn't, but it wasn't Sassa's business. He hadn't asked Heaven and she hadn't volunteered. He was doing penance for having said American women shouldn't have sex with men they were not married to.

Sometimes Hamid hated that he spoke before thinking. He didn't know that Heaven would have allowed him to make love to her if he hadn't said those words, but he did think they would have been closer.

"Sassa, have you ever gone into a women's dress store?" He laughed at the look on his cousin's face. "Heaven wants me to bring her a sari."

"Have one of the cousins buy it for you."

"I don't know how, but she would know if I didn't pick it out myself. I will do this."

"See what I mean? If she asks you to put those little things in your hair, will you do that as well?"

"They're called twists, Sassa. And if she asked me to do it, yes, I believe I would."

His cousin slapped playfully at him and he slapped back.

He had not even arrived on the soil of his homeland and already he was wanting to be back in the States.

From the instant the plane touched down, a difference came over Hamid. He was home, and he felt it in his spirit. This would be perfect if he were not so far from Heaven.

Hamid sat waiting for the plane to empty. He hated being bumped and shoved. Sassa gave him an annoyed look, but waited also. What was five more minutes?

The last of the stragglers were gone when Hamid and Sassa stood and stretched, their bodies tired from the long flight. Hamid looked out the window of the plane and smiled before turning toward his cousin.

"You'd better wipe that look off your face before the family sees us."

"What look?" Hamid asked in surprise. He didn't believe he wore any special look.

"That dopey, homesick look."

"Sassa, I was homesick. I'm home."

"That's not the look on your face. You're wanting to be back in Chicago. You are already missing Heaven, and if the family sees just how much, they are going to work on you big time to keep you here."

"I'm leaving in a month, no more than two months, Sassa, no matter what. I promised Heaven."

"Like I said, then you'd better stop looking like you want to be somewhere else."

They walked off the plane still bickering. Hamid didn't believe he had a goofy look on his face. He was glad to be home.

"This must really be serious." Sassa punched Hamid in the ribs. "There's your father waiting for us. They didn't send a servant."

"It could be my father missed me."

"Right."

Hamid turned to frown at Sassa before turning back to look at his father. Sassa was right. There was trouble brewing on the horizon.

As soon as they were done with customs, which was nothing more than a glance, he and Sassa were free to leave. Each carried only a small bag.

"Where are your things?" his father asked both of them.

"We're going back in a month, so we left most of them."

"Hamid, you have what you went for. You should have brought all of your belongings. Your mother is not expecting this to be a short visit. You promised you were coming home. The two of you were summoned home because it seems you've forgotten our customs. Both of you, calling your fathers to find brides. Both of you, calling your fathers to cancel the contracts. It is not right. You need to be here in Pakistan. As for you, Hamid, we have even found a clinic for you to run."

This had been the agreement, the plan. Suddenly the sound of Marvin Gaye filled Hamid's head. He'd used one of his songs to tell Heaven he loved her, to ask her to open up to him. She didn't believe he was returning. She thought he would hurt her as Brandon had.

"Hamid, I'm talking to you. Where is your mind?" His father squinted, grabbed his head between his hands and kissed him on each cheek. "Give it time and you will forget her. You're home now."

"I don't think..." He saw Sassa shaking his head gently. "I won't forget her, Abba. I love her and I'm going to marry her." He saw his father's shoulders lift but he didn't answer.

"You couldn't keep your mouth shut for five minutes," Sassa whispered viciously. "Now I'm going to get dragged into this. Thanks."

Hamid's father turned to Sassa and frowned at his nephew. "Sassa, your father is angry that you called off the plans with the matchmaker. You will go to the girl's home while you're here to make amends, and you will tell them the reason."

"But that whole thing is over. It's been months. Why do I need to go there?"

"Because this is the way it's done. Now do you two see why it was urgent for you to return home? You remember nothing."

"I don't have to go," Sassa answered his uncle.

"No, but if you have respect for your family you will do it. Then we can set about finding wives for both of you. You can return to the States for visits, but you will return with wives to help keep you out of trouble."

Sassa grabbed Hamid's arm and pulled him. "Hamid, if you say anything they will have us married off within the week. Keep your mouth closed."

"I have no intention of my family finding me a bride. I've found my own. I'm not going to marry anyone else."

"But you did give your word to return home. Let it go for now."

Hamid looked around him at the soil, at the building, and then his eyes came to rest on the new Mercedes his father was driving. A lump formed in his throat. No, it had not been a financial burden for his family to send him to receive a western education, but he had promised to return, and his father knew he would keep his word.

For now, it was best to do as his cousin had suggested, push his thoughts of Heaven to the back of his mind. He took a deep breath of the air and could swear he smelled the gunpowder from hundreds of miles away.

Things had changed here in his country, but it was still home. The ache eased as they rode through the streets. Sounds of Arabic hung on the winds. Mostly his friends and he spoke English now. They'd quickly learned that people were offended when a language was spoken they didn't understand. There were many hospitals where the doctors and other health care workers were forbidden to speak in another language unless it was on their break.

The rule had annoyed Hamid at first, until he saw that many different ethnic groups were relegated to the same rules. He'd noticed small groups of Africans and Filipinos talking in their native tongues, huddled in small groups during lunch. Hamid had also seen the look of disdain from Americans. He had not come to America to make waves. And besides, with the new terrorist threats, Hamid's nationality was always at question. It was a wise choice to speak English.

As he thought of these things, anger filled him and a real homecoming took place within his soul. For the first time since he'd stepped off the plane, Hamid was glad to be home.

The smells from his mother's kitchen, the aroma of curry, filled him with longing and made it complete. He would bet that his mother had instructed the servants to make all of his favorite dishes. There might be a chance that his mother had cooked for him herself.

"This is home," Sassa said, and ran from the car kissing relatives along the way. "I bet you miss this, don't you, Hamid?"

Hamid didn't fail to notice his father glance over his shoulder toward him. "Yes, Sassa, I've missed my mother's cooking." That was enough for now. They would not get into a long debate over what Hamid was or wasn't eating. He'd only moderated the foods to make them more palatable for Heaven. He had not done anything wrong.

Hamid caught his mother up in a big bear hug, enduring her numerous slaps on his face and body for being away so long. He was laughing, and then suddenly tears were running down his cheeks. Everyone was crying at once, rejoicing over his becoming a doctor.

This was what Hamid wanted from Heaven. He wanted to believe she was happy that he'd gotten his license, but that was not the look in her eyes. She'd hugged him when he'd lifted her high in the air, but there was fear in Heaven.

Hamid's heart seized, and he knew that even then she had been afraid that he was leaving her.

"Hamid, what's wrong?" his mother crooned.

"Nothing, I'm just glad to be home." He kissed her forehead. After stuffing himself with so much food, followed by many sweets, Hamid was finally pushing the offered dishes away. He grinned at Sassa. He loved his mother's cooking, he would admit that, and yes, he could do with a bit more curry in the dishes he was making for Heaven. A couple of times he'd sprinkled it in his own dish, but later when he'd kissed Heaven she'd pulled away. Since then he'd done without.

"You can't stop thinking of Heaven, can you?" Sassa asked.

Hamid grinned. "I tried." He cocked his head to the side at the sound of a familiar voice and blinked. He saw Heaven in his mother's kitchen wearing a sari, a thousand twists in her hair, and laughing with the female cousins and the servants as she stirred a pot. "Heaven," he said softly before blinking again. The image disappeared. But he'd seen her in a golden sari that accented her dark beauty.

"Hamid, what's wrong?"

Hamid glanced at Sassa. "She's coming here, Sassa. She's going to come to Pakistan. I just had a vision."

"You're crazy."

"I don't think so."

"Okay, what was she doing in this vision of yours, yelling and screaming at you for kidnapping her? Kicking your behind? What?"

"I saw her laughing and happy and a part of this culture. It's going to happen."

A few weeks later, after the wedding, after the parties, after visiting all the relatives, Hamid looked at the place his father had picked out for the clinic. It was only a few miles from his family's home. He saw the need in the community, and knew the work would be most satisfying. He knew most of the people wouldn't have money to pay him, but that had not been his primary interest. His family had money, lots of money. So that was not his focus.

"Hamid, you're licensed so we can start hiring nurses and get you started, have the clinic open in a week or two."

"Father, I have business to attend to in the States. I can't open it right now."

His father narrowed his eyes and squinted at him in disappointment. "Does your word mean nothing, Hamid? Is that why we sent you away to receive the best education, for you to turn your back on your people and on your word?"

"I'm not doing either. I fully intend to honor my commitments."

"Then there is no reason why you can't open the clinic. I didn't say you couldn't return to the States for a visit every now and then, but if you're serious, if you really intend to honor your obligations, you will get this clinic open and start to work here."

Hamid stood facing his father. "I've already been here longer than I planned to stay. I told her I would return in a month."

"This woman you've known less than a year, is she more important than your family, than your word?"

Hamid didn't answer. A lump formed in his throat, his chest felt tight and his stomach filled with knots. Hamid recognized it as stress, something he'd never experienced before. He thought of Heaven. He wasn't able to talk to her as often as he wanted, but he could tell from the tone of her voice that she was thinking he was not coming home and was mentally distancing herself from him. He didn't want that. How was he going to call her and tell her he had to stay a little longer?

"How long do you think I need to stay before I can leave again?"

"It will take at least six months to get the clinic running, Hamid. You're a doctor. You know that it will be your business to manage. You will be the one the people will come looking for."

Hamid licked his lips and turned away from his father.

"It's better this way, Hamid, trust me." His father patted his shoulder and walked out of the building, leaving Hamid alone, truly alone. His honor or his heart? Which was more important? Surely if fate had really had a hand in his falling in love with Heaven, fate would find him a way out of this mess.

CHAPTER TEN

Hamid stared at the retreating back of his father, knowing his father had left him to deal with his decision in privacy. At the sound of footsteps, Hamid turned. From the look on Sassa's face, Hamid knew his cousin had been somewhere in the clinic listening. He stood and waited for his cousin's remark.

"I didn't sabotage you, Hamid."

"I know that."

"I just wanted to be sure you knew. I spoke up for you and Heaven. I tried to get Uncle to allow you to return and gather your things. He told me clearly to keep them for you or to get rid of them. He wants me to get the key to your apartment so I can clean it out."

Hamid reached his hand into his pocket, pulled out the keys, and handed them over to Sassa. They stared at each other for a few moments before Hamid walked away.

At the sound of Heaven's voice Hamid regretted that he'd made a vow to his family. He missed her and wanted her with him. "Heaven, you've been avoiding my calls."

"No," she answered. "I've been busy. My registry is really taking off."

"You've been too busy to talk to me?"

"You should have been back more than a week ago."

"Are you punishing me?"

"When are you returning?"

"Heaven." Hamid closed his eyes. He heard the panic in Heaven's voice. How could he tell her?

"You're not coming back, are you?"

"Heaven, my father found a clinic for me to run. I have to get it started. It has to be running smoothly...before...before I can come back to America." He took a deep breath. There was no easy way to say it. "Heaven, it will be at least another six months before I can return to you."

"Do us both a favor and lose my phone number, Hamid. I'm not waiting for you."

Before the phone was slammed down and disconnected him from her, Hamid had heard the catch in Heaven's voice. He'd never known her to cry, but this time she sounded on the verge of it. He called her repeatedly, even trying her cell. It was apparent she'd cut off all communication with him. He'd just have to wait until she was willing to listen.

Hamid pulled a deep breath into his lungs. Didn't Heaven know that he missed her? Didn't she know that he was unsure if he possessed the will to keep his vow to his father, to remain in Pakistan for six more months without her? He loved her. Heaven was the first thought in his mind when he woke up and the last thought before he drifted off to sleep each night. He had to find a way to make her understand her place in his life, to know that he'd not really gone back on his promise to her, that it had only been delayed for a little while. He would return for Heaven, that much he did know.

A few days later Hamid went to his uncle's house to look for Sassa. He'd been trying for days to get Heaven to talk to him and she wouldn't. He needed a friend who understood.

"You don't have to stay here, Hamid. You can just go back," Sassa said after Hamid told him he was staying.

"I know that."

"Then why are you staying?"

"Are you telling me if your father ordered you to stay you would return, regardless of his wishes?"

"I didn't make a promise to give anyone my life. You did that, but it's not fair for Uncle to hold you to that promise."

"If I don't honor my vow my father will bear my shame, not I. We know the ribbing he's always gotten about the special treatment he gives his youngest and favored son."

"Your birth order is not your fault. Nor is it your fault that your father favors you."

"It may not be my fault, but try telling that to my brothers."

"Your brothers love you and your sisters worship you. They are thrilled that you're remaining here."

"Of course my sisters want me here. They have no concept of time. They still think they will be able to dress me." Hamid laughed. "And my brothers love me, you're right, but I can see in their eyes that they're all waiting for me to fail. They're waiting for me to go back on my word, to break my promise. I want their respect, Sassa. I owe it to my father to prove to the entire family that his trust in me is not ill placed. I can't let him down."

"Looks like being the favored son comes with a heavy price."

"I've enjoyed all of the privileges. Now it's time to take my place. I should have done it years ago."

"What about Heaven?"

Hamid's eyes closed and he sucked in his pain. "My staying does not mean I love her any less, or that I'm choosing my honor over her."

"But if you stay, you are."

"I'm going back for her."

"When?"

"Someday."

"And you think she will be there waiting for you?"

An idea came to Hamid, a way to give him a shot at having Heaven wait for him. "I'm going to send her a present, Sassa, the sari I bought for her and a few other things. Will you take it to her when you return?"

"Just mail it."

"Sassa, please, this is too important to trust to the mail. Will you take it to her?"

"Yes."

"Do you promise?"

"I said that I would, but I don't see how a gift will do anything."

"The gift that I'm going to send her will. She'll understand."

"But will she wait?"

"The gift is only to soften her up so she will listen to me. She's been hanging up. When I called to tell her I had to stay here for at least six months, she told me to lose her number. I do not intend to do that, but I need her to understand."

"Get your gift, Hamid. I'll deliver it."

Heaven eyed the punching bag. She imagined a coconut, then a melon, then Hamid's head and then…her gaze settled on Brandon. He was back in the class. The *sensei* shot her a warning look, but she didn't need it. She was over Brandon, she no longer had the desire to beat him senseless, or at least she had enough sense to know that wouldn't happen with Brandon.

She remained focused, remembering what had happened the last time she'd forgotten that basic rule. Maybe, just maybe, that was what she needed, for someone to hit her and knock some sense into her.

"Heaven, why are you standing there? Does this look like a ballet to you?"

"I was waiting for instructions."

Brandon glared. "I thought you said you were over me."

Heaven laughed, "Brandon, you are so full of yourself. Get over it. You have no impact on my life, none. Do you understand? *Nada*, not a bit, get it?"

She turned on her heel to walk away, went a few paces, gave a loud yell, and ran back toward Brandon. She kicked out, catching him off guard. She pulled the kick back mere inches from his face.

"Now do you get it, Brandon? I can control myself. You have nothing to do with my life." Heaven fell in line and did the *katas* with the lower belts. She needed the intensity to bring back her focus. For the first time in two years, she felt nothing for Brandon. He was merely a memory. Gone was the ache she'd carried for all that time. She felt nothing. She wasn't in love with him and she no longer cared that he'd left her. Good for him, she thought. She hoped he was happy.

One stance after another and Brandon was pushed even farther away. Heaven was thinking of Hamid. What a fool she'd been.

Month after month passed and Heaven missed Hamid more with each passing day. The ache for him had not lessened. She still loved him, but she wasn't going to hold her breath waiting for him to return for her. Instead, she was spending time with her friends. She'd even had a date or two. Now she was faking a laugh as her friends joked about her lack of a love life.

"Dang, Heaven, your batting record with men is zero. You were right not to fall for Hamid," Peaches almost shouted. "He's been gone for what, five months now?"

"She did fall for him. Don't you remember how crazy she got when Ongela went out with him?"

Heaven looked at Peaches and Latanya. "Hamid had no choice but to stay in Pakistan. He gave his word."

"But he gave his word to you that he'd come back. You should be glad he's gone."

"Why should I be glad he's gone?"

"Because now you can go back to doing what you want. You don't have to be bothered with him looking over your shoulder or trying to please him."

Heaven gave a snort of derision. "Do you think I was doing the things that I was to please Hamid? Get real. I began feeling better when I started eating better. As for being glad he's gone, I'm not going to lie. I miss him like crazy."

"Then why did you get your number changed to avoid his calls?"

"Because I was crazy."

"Heaven, if he really loved you he would have come back regardless of what his family said. Who the heck wants a little baby that can't make up his own damn mind?" Peaches asked.

Just like that, a ping went off in Heaven's brain. "You're right. Who wants a little boy, one who would ignore his word because he fell in love? I wouldn't."

"Are you saying that you're okay with Hamid's leaving you?"

"I'm saying I respect Hamid's honoring his commitment. I don't think he should have come back if it meant going back on his word to his father."

"So, you're over him?"

"I'm not over him, but I'm over wanting to hurt him."

"Are you going to contact his cousin and try to get in touch with him?"

Heaven looked toward Ongela, wondering if she'd read her mind. "I thought about it, but nope, I'm going to leave well enough alone. Hamid still has a couple of months to remain in Pakistan. And who knows, something can happen and I'll get my hopes up and he'll have to stay longer. No, I'm going to enjoy having met him and having loved him. Being with Hamid helped me to finally get over Brandon, and it helped me to put that nonsense we've been spouting about black men back in the closet where it belongs."

"So, are you now swearing off the brothers?"

Heaven laughed. "Every one of you has dated outside, so don't give me that. I'm just saying that I'm open. If the guy touches something in me, I'm going to give him a chance. Right now, my business is growing so fast that I don't have time to think of dating anyone, not even Hamid."

But Heaven would finally open the gift that Sassa had brought to her. In the long run, it wouldn't make any difference. She was not putting her life on hold for Hamid, and she would not waste any energy wishing for things that wouldn't be. She had her dream. Her business was a huge success; there were four or five medical personnel filling out applications every day, and the jobs were pouring in. Her accountant had been right. In the end, operating out of her apartment had not made a difference in her ability to secure jobs, but it had made her bank account fatter.

When the last person was gone from her home-slash-office, Heaven went to her closet and pulled out the box she'd stuck in there several months before.

She pulled the sari from the box and smiled. She loved it. Studded with rhinestones, the brownish-colored silk was beautiful. It was very intricately designed, with tiny birds and flowers woven into the material. There was also a matching scarf.

Heaven held the sari to her cheek, trying to imagine Hamid in a clothing store picking out women's clothing. She was positive he'd picked it out because there was a mango tree sewn into the fabric.

Gold glittered in the box and she pulled out a dozen gold bracelets, earrings, and more scarves. Then she spotted a small package wrapped in tissue paper lying there amidst the jewelry. She sucked in a breath. It wasn't mangoes, or the rotted fruit would be creating a horrible stench. She opened the tissue and then she let her breath out. Dried mangoes. She should have known Hamid would find a way. She spotted a card with his tiny scrawl.

"Heaven, I will return. Don't give up on me—don't give up on us. Put the mangoes on your desk so you will see them every day and know our bond remains intact. You know how to reach me if you need me. I can only assume that you're too angry to talk to me since you've disconnected your phone and won't answer my letters. Even so, I remain firm in my commitment. I love you and I will return for you. Hamid."

Heaven's hands trembled as she held the dried mangoes to her heart. She would put them on her desk as a reminder that she shouldn't have gotten involved with Hamid. But also, she would be grateful to him for reminding her that there was more to life than hating.

Heaven received letters from Hamid almost on a daily basis. She didn't open them, but something prevented her from throwing them away, maybe the sight of the mangoes.

LET'S GET IT ON

As the weeks passed, she told herself it didn't matter. Her life was full. She was working and going out with her friends, even dating on occasion. And at the *dojo,* things were much better than she would have ever thought. It didn't even bother her when Brandon's obviously pregnant girlfriend came in to watch the matches.

To Heaven's credit, she didn't attempt to kick Brandon any harder than she would have anyone else she was sparring with, but she couldn't deny the momentary pleasure she felt when she fell on the mat and Brandon attempted to stomp her. Her leg shot up automatically and she landed a solid groin kick.

When Brandon dropped to his knees and glared at her, she meant it when she told him she was sorry. She blinked. "Brandon, why didn't you have your cup on?"

"Because I didn't expect to get kicked by you," he said between clenched teeth.

Heaven held out her hand and then she smiled. "Come on, Brandon, I didn't do it deliberately. You should have had a cup on. Besides, you were trying to stomp me."

"But I wasn't really going to do it."

"Right," Heaven answered, then broke into a full grin. "Maybe we both wanted to get in one last shot. Come on, let me help you up." She grinned even wider when Brandon finally smiled at her and took her hand.

"I guess you deserved to land that kick." He stood bent over with his hands on both knees and looked across the room. "It's a good thing I've already reproduced or I think I wouldn't be able to. Good block."

Brandon stuck his hand out and grinned at Heaven. She shook it, looked over his shoulder, and spotted the *sensei* watching them and beckoning her to come into his office.

Heaven's heart sank to her stomach. She'd been warned about being overly aggressive. Now she was going to be kicked out for something she hadn't done deliberately. Her mind was whirling as she walked toward the office, wondering if Brandon would vouch for her.

"Close the door, Heaven."

She let out all of the air in her lungs, took a deep breath, closed the door and turned back to face the teacher. "*Sensei*, that was a legal block, I didn't know Brandon wasn't wearing a cup."

"What?"

Heaven stopped her explanation when she realized the teacher had not even seen her and Brandon sparring. She followed his eyes as he looked toward the phone. "Talk to Hamid," he said.

Heaven glanced toward the door, then at the instructor who took the hint and left the room, closing the door behind him.

"Hi," Heaven said as she waited for Hamid's voice.

"It isn't fair of you to initiate a fight and not give me a chance to fight back," Hamid said softly.

For the first time in months, Heaven felt reconnected to the universe. "That wasn't what I was doing," she said after a long pause.

"Of course it was. You like being in control. You're there, and I'm here. So you assumed you'd win this by changing your number, not answering my letters, running away from me." He paused and said softly, "How childish, Heaven."

"You tracked me down to tell me I'm acting childish?"

"Well, aren't you?"

"You arrogant—"

"I love you, Heaven."

"I love you too."

"Do we have a bad connection?"

"I don't think so."

"What did you just say?"

"You heard me," Heaven laughed.

"Repeat it."

"You should have been listening."

Hamid was laughing. "I've missed you."

"I've missed you also," Heaven replied, without a second of hesitation.

"Then why didn't you get in touch with me? Why did you make it so hard?"

"I don't know, Hamid. I thought it was for the best. What good would it do either of us to let this go any farther? You're there and I'm here, and I do understand why you stayed."

"Doing this is not more important to me than you are, Heaven."

For a moment she didn't answer, but she understood what Hamid meant. "You had to live up to your word, your commitment."

"I made a commitment to you also, and I will find a way to live up to that as well."

"You're not married yet?"

Hamid laughed and the sound washed over her. She really had missed him.

"How could I be? You're there and I'm here."

"Easily." Heaven held the phone to her heart and gave thanks. She swallowed the tears, wishing Hamid were standing in front of her, wishing she could kiss him, wishing she'd not waited so long to tell him that she loved him.

"Heaven, are we going to fight about that as well?"

"Why not? We fight about everything else," she said softly.

"Are you going to give me your new number or will I have to find other means of talking to you? I have a carrier pigeon, but I'm not sure if it can travel that far."

"You won't need a pigeon, Hamid."

"How are things between you and Brandon?"

"No war," Heaven laughed.

"No love?" Hamid asked.

Heaven thought for a moment, wanting to be certain.

"Heaven," Hamid said, "don't tease me."

"No love," she answered at last.

"Any regrets?"

"Some," she answered truthfully.

"Any regrets about us?"

"Some." Heaven smiled, knowing that on the other line Hamid would know it. "I regret not telling you sooner that I loved you."

"Can we get through this?"

"I'm willing to try," Heaven said. She heard the click of the door behind her and finally gave Hamid her new number. "I love you, and avoiding you hasn't changed that. Listen, the *sensei* wants his office back. I'll talk to you later."

"I thought you weren't going to wait for Hamid to return to this country," Peaches said as she picked up the dried mangoes from Heaven's desk. Heaven took them from her.

"I'm not just sitting at home." Heaven held the dried fruit in her hand for a moment before continuing. "But I'm not slamming the door on him either. He loves me." Heaven took another look at the dried mangoes. "And I love him. He went to a lot of trouble to reach me. I don't have my hopes up, but we'll see what happens."

For the next couple of months, Heaven continued to date occasionally when she could find the time from her business. She was forever being paged in the middle of the night. It was time she hired someone to help put out the brush fires. Fulfilling dreams could be a lot of work.

Hamid looked around the clinic. It was running smoothly. He was working sixteen-hour days to get it that way. The place was spotless, and he had the best help he could find. He could see the pride his father showed, the initial disbelief from his brothers, and then the pride from them also.

His mother and sisters continued their clucking over him, saying that he was working too hard and needed a woman to take care of him. Hamid agreed, but not a woman of their choosing. He had his own woman in mind, and it was time he returned to claim her. At least things had gotten easier since she'd relented and begun talking to him.

Now that Sassa was getting married to the woman he'd found in America, Hamid was expected to return for the wedding.

He had made arrangements for two doctors he trusted to take over the running of the clinic until he returned. His father was in charge of the clinic finances, not much of a duty since they were operating at a loss. Still, the main thing had been to get the clinic up and running and to give care to people who couldn't afford much more than a chicken for payment. His father believed in the adage, 'To whom much is given, much is required.' Hamid supposed he believed that as well, only he was beginning to think that too much had been required of him and of Heaven.

Hamid looked around, wondering how he could ask Heaven to return with him to a business that made no money. He knew her business was booming. It would be unfair of him to ask her to give that up. Still, he wanted her with him. And it wasn't as though he were penniless; no, he was far from that. But he didn't want money to be the deciding factor.

A week later, he was ringing Heaven's bell unannounced. She buzzed him in and surprised him by running down the stairs. He looked up as she came down and for the first time in his life, he had what he'd been waiting for. Heaven's eyes were glittery with tears, tears of joy and love. The look she was giving him as she ran toward him was worth dying for. This was the look he'd thought she'd never give him. It was true; absence did make the heart grow fonder.

Hamid caught Heaven, lifting her off the steps, wrapping her securely in his arms and kissing her for long minutes. They stood on the stairs unable to talk, able only to kiss and cry tears of joy.

"Hamid, why didn't you tell me you were coming?" Heaven said when she was finally able to form words.

"I started to, but now I'm glad I didn't. I don't think I would have received this reception."

"You would have received it. You came back as you promised."

Hamid licked his lips, his eyes fastened on Heaven's face. He would not lie to her about the timing of his visit.

She read the truth in his face. "You didn't come back for me, did you?"

This time instead of the light of love that had been in her eyes only moments ago, there was fire. Hamid prayed for understanding before answering her.

"Not entirely. Sassa is getting married." Heaven was pulling away from him. He could see the freeze come over her as though she'd willed the love she had for him to turn to ice. "I was coming back for you, Heaven."

"When?"

"I don't know," Hamid answered honestly. "This just made it easier. I didn't have to explain."

"Loving me requires an explanation?" Heaven tilted her head to look up at him. *What nerve.* "Get out."

"You don't mean that."

"Hamid, if you don't get out of my face this moment you will regret it for the rest of your life."

Heaven moved away from him and stood with her legs apart. "Get out or so help me I'll…"

Hamid's hand caught her closed fist and he narrowed his eyes. "Stop it, Heaven, don't be a fool. Do you really think I only came back to attend a wedding? Look at me," he ordered. "You are the reason I returned. Are you not listening to me? I said Sassa's wedding made it easier. I didn't have to feel as though I'd gone back on my commitment. As for explaining about you, do you think there's one person in my entire family that doesn't know about you? Do you think anyone could force me to marry a woman I don't want? I love you and by God, you're going to accept that."

Heaven struggled to get away. "This is deja vu, Hamid. Didn't you learn that you can't order me to love you?"

He pulled and brought her within inches of his chest. "So you'll tell me freely. Do you still love me?"

"You're holding my arms and you consider that freely?"

"Heaven, stop being so damn stubborn. Do you love me?"

"I love you." Heaven stared into his brown eyes and shook her head. "I love you, Hamid."

"Good."

"But I still want you to get out." Heaven brought her foot down and missed his toe by a centimeter.

He dropped a kiss on her forehead. "I'll see you later."

The ringing phone was a blessing to Heaven. For twenty minutes she'd stood where she was after Hamid left, wanting to continue being angry with him, knowing that he'd not come back for her, but for a wedding. Then suddenly it dawned on her that she didn't much care why he'd come back. He was here, and for now that was what mattered. The possibility of having a long distance relationship where she would see Hamid once or twice a year occurred to her.

Heaven thought of Mrs. Reed and the advice she'd given her. She thought of Brandon, who had complained and said he wished they had fought. And she thought of herself and Hamid. Together they were the proverbial oil and water. Cliché or not, that's exactly what they were. But she could not imagine them ever having a dull moment. She wondered, though, if the fighting would ever come to be all they had. That wouldn't be enough to sustain them through the hard times if it were.

Two hours later Hamid was back at her door. This time she didn't race down the stairs, but buzzed him in, opened the door and sat down to wait for him.

"I see you're not as happy to see me as you were earlier."

"I think I may have overreacted and it went to your head."

"I like seeing your eyes light up when you see me enter the room."

"Then I would suggest you don't tell me that you came to see me because of your cousin."

Heaven stood watching him, noticing his hand was behind his back. "What do you have?" she asked.

"Something for you but I'm wondering if I should give it to you now. You should treat me nicer than you do."

"I treat you the way you deserve to be treated." Heaven tilted her head and grinned at Hamid. She waited for the next words from Hamid. She was trying so hard to shield her heart from him, but there was only so much she could do. She breathed in and knew what Hamid held behind his back.

Hamid smiled and pulled a basket from behind his back. It was filled with fresh mangoes. Heaven stared at the ripened fruit. They were perfect. She could smell the sweetness. She remembered Hamid's vow. "What are those for?" she asked.

"I told you I would always give you mangoes by way of apology. I've messed up with you again, but the obvious solution has been staring me in the face for months."

Heaven's breath hitched in her throat. "What do you mean?"

"Remember that song you played for me when you first started tutoring me?"

"Which one? We played a lot of music."

"The country song."

"We played a lot of those also." Heaven watched as Hamid slipped a slim CD case from the basket and marched over to the stereo. He popped it in. "Do you remember now," he asked, as the music filled the air.

"I remember," Heaven said softly.

"Well, I have a surprise."

Heaven laughed as Hamid began singing. After she got over the accented country twang, she realized he didn't sound half-bad. In fact, he sounded pretty good, not R. Kelly good, but Hamid good.

He sang several love songs before sitting next to her. "All those things I want."

Hamid spoke so softly and earnestly that Heaven held her breath. "What do you want?" Heaven asked, as Hamid gazed intently into her eyes.

"Let me ease your fear," he answered.

"What?"

"Heaven, I want to erase your pain."

"I don't have any pain."

"Yes, you do. And I want to take it away. I want you to love me, Heaven, and I want you to let me love you. I want us. All of this, our madness, all of it."

Heaven could feel the beginning of tears. The madness Hamid spoke of, this wasn't what she'd had with Brandon. It was never what she'd ever thought love was like. But she knew this was love. His hand caressed her cheek.

"Heaven, let me make you believe in love again. Allow me to give you so much love that your tears will disappear forever." He bent and kissed her softly on the lips. "Let me love you, Heaven."

"Are you talking making love to me or loving me?"

"Both."

"Why would you ask a woman that's not your wife to sleep with you?"

"I wouldn't, not you." He licked his top lip, his eyes never leaving her face. "Marry me, Heaven, and ease my pain. Make my dream come true," he whispered softly and then knelt on the floor on his knees. "We were meant to be together, you know that. Ignore whatever reason brought me back to this country and listen to your heart. I love you. Marry me, and I'll prove it to you."

Tears were now streaming fully down her cheeks. "We would kill each other, and you know it."

"Yes, I know it, but we would save the world from having to be saddled with either of us. Let me indulge my taste for mangoes. Will you marry me, Heaven?"

"Yes," she answered, feeling the tears, hot and salty, rush in a flood from her eyes, skip over her nose and land on her lips. Hamid begin kissing them. "I promised I would kiss your tears away," he said. "When do you want to get married?" He leaned on his knees, holding her.

"Hamid, this is serious. I'm not converting."

"I didn't ask you to."

"Do you realize what that means?"

"It means my dreams will become realities."

Heaven shook her head before smiling. "We're going to have a ton of problems, probably more fighting than you ever imagined. I'm not moving to Pakistan and you can't move back here. How are we going to handle it?"

"We'll find a way."

"Hamid, what if we don't?"

"Are you trying to go back on your word, Heaven?"

"No," she answered, "I just want you to know I haven't changed."

"But you're wrong," Hamid said softly, looking into her eyes, outlining her lip with the pad of his thumb. "You have changed. A year and a half ago you hated me. Now you love me."

CHAPTER ELEVEN

Heaven stood next to Hamid after witnessing Sassa and Isha take their vows. This wedding wasn't all in English, but Heaven found it didn't matter. She was happy for Sassa that he'd found his soul mate, almost as happy as she was that she'd found hers.

Two weeks after Sassa's wedding Hamid stood with Heaven in a park and they took wedding vows from a non-denominational minister, with Ongela, Peaches and Latanya as her bridesmaids. Sassa and cousins of theirs she'd yet to meet were there for Hamid. He and Heaven had both compromised; The ceremony was not Christian, not Muslim.

Hamid gazed at Heaven before looking at the friends and family from both sides gathered there. He was hurting his parents by not having a traditional ceremony and by not returning to Pakistan to marry, but this was the best he could do. Their reception foods were also unorthodox: catfish and hala meats, steaks, chicken, salad, and rice.

"You're my wife," Hamid said to Heaven as they danced together, the breeze blowing over them.

"And you're my husband," she answered.

Hamid grinned down at her. "My words were not meant to be the start of a fight," he said.

"Nor were mine," Heaven answered.

Hamid laughed, kissed her forehead, and continued dancing.

Hamid sat on the bed in his pajamas waiting for Heaven to come from the bathroom. She was taking three times as long with her shower as he'd taken.

He went to open the bathroom door and found it locked. He knocked. "Heaven, are you coming out?"

He couldn't understand the sudden shyness. "Heaven?"

The door opened and the sight of her took his breath away. She was beautiful. He stood for a moment, just looking at her in the silky mango-colored gown. His eyes trailed over her body, noting how the fabric clung to her. He bent suddenly, lifted her up and took her to the bed.

"You're trembling, Heaven. Are you cold?" he asked.

"No."

"Then why are you trembling?"

"No reason."

Hamid kissed her. She was not as combative as usual. *Good,* he thought. He'd imagined they would fight before, during, and after they made love.

Keeping one arm around Heaven, he managed to flip the lamp switch off. His hands searched tentatively under the silk gown Heaven wore. He felt her pulling away.

"Heaven, is something wrong?"

"No, you tickled me, that's all," she answered. But Hamid heard the nervousness in her voice. *Surely... Of course she has,* he answered his own thought. She was American; this would not be her first time.

His hand slipped between her thighs and again he felt her pulling away. "Heaven, I love you," he whispered. "I will not hurt you. Whatever you've heard about Arab men, I'm not a monster. Don't assume I am, not on our wedding night."

His lips found hers and he kissed her until she was breathless, until she pulled him close and he felt her loosen her legs. This time when he eased his hand between her thighs and found her nether lips, he dipped a finger in and found her moist.

Touching her made him hard. He remembered the first time he'd met her and had dreamt of her touching him, caressing his hardness. Now he had to guide her hand. He heard the sound she was making in her throat. She was touching him so gently that the thought again crossed his mind. *It's the first time she's touched a man.* Surely that wasn't the case. He kissed her ears and felt her shiver. This was better, he thought. They had to get to know each other in this fashion to find the proper rhythm. Still, he wondered what was going on in his wife's head. He knew Heaven well, was aware of her penchant for making assumptions without checking into the facts.

He peered at her. "Do you not want to make love with me, Heaven?" he asked quietly.

She nodded her head in the affirmative.

"You're usually so chatty, why not now?"

"I want to make love with you, Hamid."

"Then why are you moving away from me? We need to be close in order to make love, closer than we've ever been before. I will not hold anything back from you. I want to touch you all over. I want to taste every inch of you, and," he looked at her, "I want you to want to taste every inch of me, but that is strictly up to you."

Hamid watched as Heaven closed her eyes again. If he didn't know better he would swear that she really was a virgin. She was behaving like one. But he'd asked her straight out. *Wedding night jitters, most likely*, he decided.

He finally pulled her gown over her head and removed his own clothing. Just having her touch him through the slit in the pajamas hadn't been enough.

Hamid felt Heaven's heart beating beneath his palm. He smelled her sweetness and moaned, then studied her for a long moment, wanting to read her, to see desire for him in her brown eyes.

There it was, what he was looking for. When she grinned and her eyes flamed with heat, he sank down into her lush softness, suckling one breast after the other, tasting her skin, lapping away hungrily. He moved downward, kissing her belly, her thighs and feeling the hot moistness that flowed like lava from her.

He moved to taste her nectar and she closed her legs. "Not yet, Hamid. I want to feel you inside me first," she whispered in a voice made husky by desire. Hamid smiled. He wouldn't argue with that request; he wanted that also.

"I want to please you, Heaven."

"You will, don't worry," she said.

He eased away and positioned himself to enter her. Going in he was stopped by a look on Heaven's face. For the third time the thought entered his mind and this time he knew it was true. "Heaven?"

"Don't stop, Hamid," she whispered in the semi-darkness.

He pushed gently against her opening, felt the resistance, felt her tense. Her nails dug into his back as she moaned and ordered him to continue.

"You're a virgin."

"Yes."

"But I asked."

"You assumed, Hamid. I didn't tell you I wasn't."

"Why?"

"Can't this fight wait, Hamid?"

Heaven's hips lifted and she pushed herself forward, forcing Hamid to drive forward also. He felt the thin membrane rip, felt Heaven's nails dig deeper into his flesh and heard her intake of breath as she took in the pain.

"Hamid, I love you," she said, and he slid all the way in.

"I love you too," he said. She was smiling with her eyes closed tightly. He knew the instant the initial pain subsided. He felt her limbs loosen and heard the moaning deep in her throat. He laughed before finding her lips and kissing her.

He wanted to make sure she enjoyed this. He timed his strokes to her breaths. When she breathed in, he went deeper, stroking her, feeling her heat, and when she exhaled, he pulled out.

Hamid watched Heaven's face. Her eyes opened and ecstasy filled him at the look in her eyes. He saw the desire blazing hotter and hotter, heard her moans of delight increase, felt her body tense, but this time the tensing was expected. She was fast approaching her climax.

Heaven writhed beneath her husband. For only a half second did she think of Brandon. She'd never felt for Brandon what she felt for Hamid. She was overjoyed that she'd waited, overjoyed that she was making love to her husband. He filled her and she moaned, wanting to take him deeper into her body, enjoying the thrusts, the rhythmical rotations of his hips. She loved the way he was touching her, his finger trying to touch parts of her that were already filled.

A fire different than what she had experienced covered her entire body from head to toe and she felt as if she were falling headlong into a pool. *What a glorious ride.*

She held on to Hamid, her eyes on him. He must have known what was happening, for he lifted her hips and Heaven was now sitting on his lap. He was so deeply embedded in her body that she could barely breathe. Hot needles exploded in her toes and quickly traveled upward, exploding in the place where they were joined.

Heaven screamed out in ecstasy, her body tightening, her muscle clenching around her husband. "Hamid," she moaned. Then she couldn't speak. She was thrust into a world of wonder. Pleasure seared every cell of her body, and her very breathing caused a new wave of bliss.

Hamid rocked against her gently, sending aftershocks of delight rippling through her. She saw the look on his face and held on. It seemed he came forever as spasm after spasm gripped his muscular body and passed from him into her, causing a deep contentment.

Heaven had been told she wouldn't enjoy her first time. That wasn't true; she'd not only enjoyed it, she wanted to do it again, and again, and again.

Heaven couldn't help laughing in delight at the grunting sounds Hamid was making as he came. He fell forward, surprising her how swiftly he moved to his back and brought her body to rest on his chest.

For a long moment, she lay on his chest, trying to remember how to breathe while his hands played in her hair.

"You lied to me," he finally said.

Heaven didn't pretend, not now. She finally wanted to do something with Hamid other than fight. And as soon as she could breathe again, she would ask him to repeat the things he'd done that made her entire body quiver.

"I didn't lie," Heaven said, rubbing her hand on the inside of his thigh. "You assumed, Hamid, and I let you."

"I asked if you were a virgin. You allowed me to believe you weren't. Why?"

"Because it wasn't any of your business, because you were being such a…such a…man and I didn't like it."

"Then why didn't you ever tell me?"

"It was never any of your business."

"Not even when you agreed to marry me?"

"I figured you'd find out soon enough, and I didn't want you thinking of my virginity as a prize."

"Heaven, you're too much." Hamid ran his hand down her hips and paused. "How was it?"

She laughed. "What if I told you it was horrible?"

"I would try and do better next time."

"And if I told you it was the most wonderful experience I've ever had in my entire life, and that I'm glad that I had it with you, what would you do?"

"I would make sure it was even better next time."

Heaven looked up into her husband's eyes and laughed. "In that case, it was wonderful."

"And?"

"And I'm glad I had it with you."

"You sure you're ready to go again?"

"I can handle it if you can." Heaven looked at him and grinned. Her words made Hamid laugh. Like Heaven, he'd done his own assuming. He'd assumed wrongly that as a virgin she would not enjoy it. He certainly didn't anticipate her ravenous appetite. But he thanked the fates for it.

During that two weeks as man and wife, both Heaven and Hamid avoided the one thing they should be talking about, Hamid leaving. They both knew it was coming.

"Do you have a valid passport?" Hamid asked Heaven as they lay in bed.

"Yes," she answered, knowing what was coming. She couldn't leave her business, not now. There was too much to do. Besides, her business was her dream. She couldn't just give it up.

"I bought you a ticket." Hamid looked at her intently.

"I can't go."

"You can go. You always have a choice."

"So did you, Hamid."

"I'm your husband. You're supposed to follow me wherever I go."

"Stop talking crazy. You knew that wasn't going to happen. And as if you didn't know what my answer was going to be before you spouted off that nonsense, here's a surprise for you. I'm your wife; your place is here with me."

Hamid rolled over and looked down at Heaven. "Why do you have to turn everything into a fight? I have to return home, and I want you to go with me."

"Just like that? You want me to pack my things and go. What do you think will happen to my business? I worked like crazy to make it happen, and now that it's off the ground I can't just walk away."

"Does your business mean more to you than I do?"

"Does your clinic mean more to you than I do?" Heaven stared up into her husband's eyes, then closed her own. She'd known from the beginning that getting involved with Hamid would mean far more drama than she was willing to put up with.

"Heaven, this has to be the shortest honeymoon period in history. I didn't think that even the two of us would find a reason to fight so soon."

"I'm not trying to start a fight with you, Hamid, but you sprung this on me. Maybe, just maybe, you should have thought of asking me."

"If I had asked you, Heaven, would you have said yes?"

Heaven opened her eyes again and stared into the intense brown eyes of her two-week husband. "I wouldn't have gone, but we wouldn't have had a fight."

"Heaven, we have to learn to compromise. We both promised that we would. We're married now, we have to try."

"I'm willing to compromise, I am, but you can't expect me to change. I warned you. You can't expect me to just up and move to a foreign country where I don't know anyone."

"You know me."

"What am I supposed to do when you're not there, Hamid? And what's going to happen to my business?"

Heaven moved away from him. "I think maybe we should have put a little more thought into it before we got married. I think maybe the romance of the moment got in the way of the reality. We could end it, Hamid, if that's what you want. We could end it with no hard feelings. We could both return to our lives the way they were before we ever met."

He reached for her and she moved away. "Not now, okay? Not this moment. You'll hold me and I'll think about how much I love you and forget the problems. And when we're done, the problem will still be there. We have to find a way to take care of the problems."

Heaven got up from the bed. "I have some work to do," she said, over her shoulder. "Please, Hamid, don't come after me." When he didn't she was a little disappointed, but turned on her computer and did the work that had piled up in the last five days. She tried to think of ways she could run her business from out of the country, but didn't think it would work. Her business was a hands-on affair. Cases changed hourly and she had to be there to oversee it all. Sickness and death couldn't be planned, and neither could the nursing availability. There was no way she could leave the country with Hamid.

LET'S GET IT ON

She loved him. She would not lie about that, but the real possibility was that perhaps they shouldn't have gotten married. They had both been wearing masks, pretending, compromising so much they they'd ignored what was important to them. They had even managed to forget who they were. One of them had to make them remember.

"Where were you?" Hamid asked, meeting Heaven at the door. He looked at the bag in her hand and took it from her.

"I went to the store. Take your shower and I'll start breakfast." Heaven gave Hamid a mild peck on the lips and started the coffee. She knew he was wondering what she was doing. He'd know when he came from the shower.

Heaven sucked in a breath, pulled out pots and pans and began. She didn't know what would happen when Hamid came into the kitchen, but it was time they both put their cards on the table.

It didn't take long. Within fifteen minutes, Heaven heard Hamid coming toward the kitchen. She braced herself.

"What's that smell?" he called out to her.

It was now or never. "It's breakfast," Heaven yelled back.

"What is it?" Hamid said, coming to stand beside her. He started to put his arm around her, wanting to make up for their fight, wanting them to not fight any more. When he saw what was in the pans, he stopped and pulled away.

"What is this, Heaven?"

"Breakfast." Heaven turned from the stove to face him. "Bacon, ham, sausage, grits, eggs, pancakes and fresh fruit."

"You know I don't eat pork."

"But I do, Hamid. You can choose the foods you want to eat." She looked at the table filled with food. "This is my compromise."

"I don't think that this is meant to be a compromise, Heaven. I think this is more your declaration of war."

"It's who I am."

Hamid looked at the table. "I think I need to leave for a while to clear my head. I have things to think about."

"There is food there that you can eat, Hamid. A compromise requires two people. I'm not going to be the only one giving up something in this relationship."

"Relationship? This is more than a relationship. This is a marriage. And I believe it's not wrong of me to expect that my wife not put food on the table that is offensive to me."

"And I—"

"Save it, Heaven, I know your answer. I'll be back later. We'll talk then."

She licked her lips and pressed her tears back. She had offered a compromise, not war. She wanted her marriage to work, but she didn't want to lose her own identity.

Heaven removed the last of the bacon from the pan, turned off the stove and sat down to her solitary meal. She heaped her plate, ignoring the tears that coursed down her face. She wasn't even hungry, but she forced herself to eat. Otherwise it would have been a meaningless gesture.

Hamid paced back and forth through Sassa's apartment. He glanced up from time to time, opened his mouth to speak, but couldn't bring himself to do it.

"What did she do that was so horrible, Hamid?" Sassa asked at last, as though bored with his pacing.

"She made breakfast for me. Bacon, sausage, and ham. She had tons of the stuff."

"Did you eat it?"

"No."

"Why did she make it?"

"To prove a point."

"What was her point?"

"That she is not going to change for me."

Sassa laughed. "You knew that from the moment you declared that fate had sent her to you. You knew it."

"That was then. This is now," Hamid said angrily. "I'm her husband."

"She knows that, Hamid. Be honest, this is not about your wanting to control Heaven. This is about your having to leave her, and that's more than likely the reason she made the breakfast for you that she did."

Hamid sighed and shook his head. "You know me so well, Sassa. I don't want to leave her. How can I leave her?" He sighed again. "I bought her a ticket to go with me, but she refused." He stretched his long legs out in front of him. "What am I going to do?"

"Only you can answer that. Which do you want more, Heaven or to remain faithful to a vow?" Sassa shrugged his shoulders. "It's a hard choice, I know, but it is just that, a choice."

"You think I have a choice in this?" Hamid shook his head and looked sadly at his cousin. "I have no choice. If I did, I know what I would do. I would remain here with my wife."

"Then maybe you should be telling her that and not me."

"That still doesn't solve the problem."

"It doesn't solve the problem, but it might buy you a little time to figure out something."

"I have to leave in two weeks. Nothing is going to be figured out in that time."

"No, but you would still have a wife." Sassa peered at him. "You still want to be married to Heaven, don't you? You're not thinking about divorcing her, are you?"

"Divorcing Heaven?" Hamid glared at Sassa. "Heaven gave that to me as an option." He shook his head. "It's not an option. I love her. I will always love her. I want our marriage to work. I just don't see how it's going to happen with us in two different countries. I can't be that far away. I'm afraid she might try to find a reason she doesn't want to remain married."

Sassa asked the obvious. "Did you speak to your father?"

"I did, and he said the marriage still didn't release me from my obligations. In fact, they're all extremely angry that I would get married without them. They want Heaven to come there and repeat the vows, or they will not accept that we're married."

Sassa laughed. "So that's why you bought the ticket. You were trying to trick her into another wedding."

"No," Hamid answered, "I was trying to keep my wife by my side. How would you like it if Isha decided to go and live somewhere else?"

"I would follow her," Sassa answered quickly.

"You have no vow."

"And you shouldn't have one. No one in this day and age would put himself into deliberate servitude. Well, not the very wealthy anyway. And Uncle shouldn't ask so much of you."

"My family has given me a lot, and you know my father's adage. 'To whom much is given, much is required.'"

"Then if you feel the price to pay is your happiness, then pay it. But, Hamid, it is still a choice."

Hamid wondered as he put his key in the lock what kind of mood he would find Heaven in. He opened the door and found her staring at the computer monitor. He went to her and stood looking down at her for a moment.

"Tell me not to leave, Heaven, and I will not go."

He watched as her eyes found his. He saw the tears glistening and shook his head. His finger moved to wipe the first tear that came. "You do not have to cry," he said, bending before her. His arms went around her and he held her. "I told you I would love your tears away. I never said I would make you cry. Tell me not to go and I will stay here with you."

"I don't want you to go," Heaven said, and burst into sobs. She held him so tightly that he felt her entire body tremble with her sadness.

"Are you telling me to remain here?" More sobs followed. And he caressed her back. How could he leave her?

"I can't ask you to break your vow, Hamid, but no, I don't want you to go."

"I can't do both, Heaven. Either I go or I remain here with you."

"How long will you have to remain there? When would you return?"

"I suppose I could stay three months at a time and return here for a month."

"Would it be like before? You told me you were coming home in a month, no more than two. You were gone eight months."

"If I go, I give you my word I will return in three months."

"Is that a promise, Hamid?"

"It is a promise I will not break, Heaven. Are you thinking about allowing me to leave? Are you saying you will be here waiting for me each time I return?"

"I'm thinking about compromising. I want our marriage to work and it won't if I ask you to stay here with me. You won't be happy with that choice."

"I won't be happy if I leave you. I don't want to leave you, Heaven. I'm weak; all it would take to make me stay is for you to tell me to do so."

He held her face in his hand. "Nothing is as important to me as you are, my beautiful little wife, not my vow, nothing."

Heaven smiled. "If that were true we would not be having this conversation."

"About that compromise you offered. I'll take it. No more fighting," Hamid said. "We have two weeks left. I want to put at least three months of loving into that time so my thoughts will keep me warm on the coldest of nights."

For the next two weeks, Heaven and Hamid made love as if each time would be their last. Then the time arrived when it actually was their last. They lay in bed entwined in each other's arms.

"We're going to need to go to the airport soon," Heaven said softly, playing with the thick, black hair on Hamid's chest.

"I don't know if I can tear myself away from you." Hamid held her tighter, caught up in his own feelings, not wanting to leave yet knowing he couldn't stay, not the way he'd left things in Pakistan with his family. He'd done enough already by deliberately marrying Heaven regardless of their wishes. That was the one thing he was not sorry for. No one could have made him take a bride that wasn't Heaven. He'd not given a vow about that.

He smiled at Heaven. "You never did tell me how you manage to smell like lemons, yet taste like mangoes."

Heaven laughed. "That's my secret."

For a split second, they were both silent, both lost in their thoughts. "It's not too late, Heaven," Hamid said at last, "either to come with me or to demand I stay."

"Demand?" She laughed. "You're saying I can demand and you will do it? I don't think so, Hamid. Don't worry. We're going to be okay. I'll be here waiting for you."

"I changed your ticket, it's open-ended. You can come whenever you want and I'll be there, waiting for you the moment the plane lands."

"And I will be here waiting for you."

"I'll call you every night."

"Those calls are going to kill us."

"Don't worry," Hamid assured her. "I've opened a checking account for you. Use it to take care of bills, and your personal needs. If you need more, just tell me when I call and I will wire more into the account immediately. I left the checkbook on the nightstand for you with a note."

"Hamid, I didn't need you to open a checking account for me. I have my own. And I don't need you to send me money, I make enough." Heaven saw the look that came into her husband's eyes and decided to tease him. "I can send you money."

He kissed her to shut her up. She was aware of it and it didn't matter. His hands traveled the length of her body, roaming so slowly over her that shivers of anticipation claimed her. How would she ever get by without having Hamid make love to her? Three months was a long time.

She touched him, felt his wetness, but took it as slowly as he was doing. They had to make the moment last. This would be the last time they would touch each other for three months.

"Hamid, will you sleep with anyone else?"

He nuzzled her neck for an answer.

"You said you could have more wives. Will you take another while I'm here at home? There would be no way for me to find out."

"I won't dignify that question, Heaven. You have no need to feel I will betray our marriage bed. My vow to you is sacred."

"Are you going to ask the same of me?" Heaven whispered softly into the lightened room.

"There is no need," Hamid replied, "because, unlike you, I trust you and I know that you will not betray our marriage."

"How do you know that?" Heaven teased, wanting to see the jealous light go off in his dazzling gaze. He didn't take the bait. Instead his hands moved over her body, between her thighs and came to rest in her wetness.

"When I touched you again, I would know."

He pressed a finger, two, and then three into her, cutting off her words. Heaven moaned and a tremor trailed over her back. She gripped his hardness in the palms of her hands, rubbing up and down the length of him. She smiled as he trembled at her touch.

"Not yet, wife," Hamid ground out, his voice rough, filled with need, with wanting. "I haven't kissed you all over yet. I have to have the taste of you to make this horror bearable."

He pulled out one finger at a time, scraping each against Heaven's cervix before removing it. She was having a mini orgasm with his touch, but she would have the big one when they were done.

When he removed the last finger, he heard Heaven's soft, "Hamid, no," and laughed as he reinserted the finger deep inside her. He felt her muscles loosen slightly before clamping around his finger and pulling him in even deeper, so he reinserted a second and then again the third. When she arched upward, he pulled out a little and waited.

"Not yet, Heaven, there's so much more." He kissed her ear, then suckled the lobe, pulling it into his mouth, allowing his hunger for her to be satisfied for the moment with devouring her ear.

He twirled his tongue into the shell shaped organ, blew his warm breath gently inside, and at the same time pressed his fingers deeper into her body. He felt the hot liquids cascading over his fingers and grunted. Neither of them was capable of having a conversation.

Hamid then lavished the same attention on Heaven's other ear. He moved to her face, kissing her nose, her eyes, her cheeks and finally her lips.

The nectar of the gods was on her lips and in her mouth. Her tongue drew him in deeply. Their tongues battled for dominance but when he pressed his fingers against the soft fleshy hidden delights, Heaven gave in and allowed him to take control. She moaned, her eyes glazed with desire. "Hamid, I love you," she said.

Allah, *how am I going to leave her?* he thought and closed his eyes to the sudden pain he saw in hers. He wondered if she'd perhaps spotted his pain.

He dipped his head and lapped away at the hollow of her throat, pulling her soft skin between his lips, placing little kisses all over her. He nibbled his way to the opposite side. He would make sure Heaven was well loved. He would make sure she waited for him and him alone.

At last, he slid down her body. He circled one nipple with his free hand while his tongue circled the other. He pulled a taunt nipple into his mouth and bit down until she squealed. Then he released her and repeated the act, each time making sure his fingers fed her fires from below.

The way her body was arching into him, he knew he couldn't keep the big orgasm away for long. And he didn't know if he wanted to. She was touching him, fondling him, kissing and licking him as he was doing to her and the heat between them sizzled. His own fluids were running from his body, covering his hairy thighs and her hand. But he wasn't done. He'd promised and this would be the last time for three long months. He pulled his fingers from inside her body and tweaked her gently. He wanted her to hold on just a little longer.

"Hamid," Heaven pleaded.

"Just a little longer, my love."

He kissed her abdomen, allowing his tongue to swirl circles across her flesh. He dipped his tongue into her navel, felt a spasm rip through her and stopped. When it subsided, he returned to pleasuring her. He kissed his way down one leg and then went for the other.

He made sure every inch of her body was lavished with attention from his tongue, his fingers, and his teeth and then he moved lower and tasted the juices that he'd made her spill.

He pulled away quickly and worked his way farther down her legs, nibbling the calves, kissing her toes, kissing his way back up. Then he stopped once again at the entrance to all of her secrets and he again tasted her sweetness. He held her tightly, not letting her go as her nails dug into him and she attempted to push him away. This would be the first time he'd brought her to orgasm in this manner.

"Hamid, I can't hold back," Heaven moaned.

If he had been able to talk, he would have told her that was the plan. He felt every muscle in her body tense, felt her hips undulate as she ground herself into him while at the same time tried to pull away. Still he held her to himself. His tongue raced farther than he'd thought possible, and he felt the moment when there was no turning back. Hamid heard the sound deep in her throat, felt it on his lips, felt it in her womb. Then he tasted her relief and as he did tears of joy poured from his eyes and mixed with her juices. This was the big one for his new bride. He remained where he was, tenderly kissing her, his tongue caressing her, taking every drop she had to give. When her legs went limp, he continued still, until he heard her sigh of satisfaction.

"Hamid," she called softly. Then he went into her arms and entered her, gently at first. Then his thrusts became harder and harder and faster. He pumped for all he was worth, for the three months he would be away from her.

And again, the thought, "Allah, how am I going to do it?" floated through his mind. Heaven's legs wrapped around his back and drove him home. Hamid screamed out. The sound to his ears was like that of a madman. His release tore through him and filled the space that would separate them. They would be a continent apart but this would bind them for that time and forever.

He kept pumping even after he was spent and satisfied, and then he saw the tears in Heaven's eyes and they cried together. Fate had brought them together and fate would find a way for them to stay together.

He had time for only a quick shower but there was something he needed to do first. He ushered Heaven into the shower, gave her the lemon-scented bath gel and kissed the tip of her nose. "Give me a second," he said, and moved away then turned to watch the water cascading over her. He sucked in his desire and ignored his burgeoning arousal. He'd been in that state since he'd returned to Heaven. Since it looked as if neither fate nor Allah was going to intervene, Hamid had no choice but to make his leaving easier for both of them.

He held the phone to his chest. *It was done*, he thought as he entered the bathroom and stepped into the shower with Heaven. He lathered her and accepted the same from her, not acting on his desire or hers.

Finally, when they could draw it out no longer, he climbed from the shower, wrapped a towel around his wife, and marched from the bathroom. "We have to get dressed," he called to her and hurried away.

In less than twenty minutes Heaven and Hamid were dressed. When the bell rang, Hamid buzzed the caller in without asking who it was. A chill claimed Heaven's soul. Something was very wrong.

"Who's at the door, Hamid?"

"Sassa."

"Is he going with us?" Heaven watched her husband's face as it fell. She saw determination in his eyes when he finally looked at her.

"Sassa is taking me to the airport."

"You mean he's going with us?"

"I don't want you to go. It will be much easier if you stay here."

"Are you crazy? Of course I'm going with you."

"No, Heaven, you're not." Hamid turned from her and opened the door to Sassa. He gave him his bag. "I'll be down in a second," he said.

"We're coming down now," Heaven said, glaring at Sassa and Hamid. "The two of you cooked up this little plan, but it's not going to work." She rushed forward, shoving Hamid, who wouldn't budge. She shoved harder, intending to bring her husband down if she had to. She was not staying home.

"Go, Sassa, I'm coming," Hamid said quietly.

"I'm going, Hamid." Heaven made for the door and struggled against Hamid's strong arms. She elbowed him, her arm landing on his chest, but he had her in a bear hug.

"Don't fight me on this. I need you to stay home, pretend that I'm just going with Sassa for a drive and I'll be back soon." He struggled with her for a minute, trying to push away the sound of the pain in her sobs.

"Heaven, you must stop it," he said. "We agreed."

"We didn't agree to this," came her tearful reply. "How could you just decide to shut me out like this? You can't make my decisions for me, Hamid. I know you're trying to make your leaving easier for me, but you have no right to do it."

Hamid tilted his wife's head and looked into her eyes. "I didn't do this for you. I did it to make it easier for me. This is very hard for me, Heaven. I don't want to leave you, and if you're there at the airport, I will not be able to get on the plane. So please, as a favor to me, please this one time do as I ask, remain home."

Heaven closed her eyes and sank against her husband. Fighting pain, her heart breaking, she whispered, "So this is love." She opened her eyes and stared at Hamid through the tears. Compromise or sacrifice, this too was a part of love. "Can I at least come downstairs?"

"I would prefer it if you didn't. But I won't try to stop you if you give me your word that you will say goodbye on the porch." To his surprise, Heaven smiled.

"You're just going to have to trust me," Heaven said, and went down the stairs.

Hamid took a quick look around the apartment that he'd come to think of as home. Few of his personal belongings were there, but the one thing that was the closet to his heart was. And it was killing them both for him to leave. One last look and he followed his wife.

Sassa was standing outside the car waiting, staring up at them. For a long moment, no one spoke, as if by agreement. Then they all began to play their parts. Sassa got into the car and Hamid took Heaven into his arms.

He held her close to his body, kissed her lightly on the lips. He felt her body start to tremble. It was now or never. "I'll talk to you soon," he said. Heaven nodded her head, her eyes brimming with tears. He understood her inability to speak. He pulled away from her and tried to ignore the fact that her body was shaking as if she'd suddenly developed some dreaded disease. He licked his lips in order to speak. "Are you going to be okay?" This time she didn't nod her head, just stared at him with the tears streaming down her face.

He should have asked her not to cry, he thought, and blinked before turning and bolting down the stairs without reaching to comfort his wife or tell her that he loved her. She knew that already, and she knew if he touched her again, he would not have the strength to do what had to be done. "Drive," he ordered Sassa the moment he was in the car. He didn't look back but closed his eyes.

"Is she going to be okay?"

"You're worrying about the wrong one, Sassa."

CHAPTER TWELVE

If someone had told her that, in the space of six weeks, she would become little more than a zombie, Heaven would not have believed them. But that was exactly what had happened. Hamid had been gone for six weeks. And all she seemed able to do was call him, wait for his next call, read his letters, or write him her own letters. Her every thought was of her husband. They were at the halfway mark, six weeks left to go. Heaven wondered how on earth they would continue this way for a lifetime.

A pile of mail lay in front of Heaven, half checks, half bills. The accountant had called to tell her that she needed to get the checks to him so he could meet payroll. Twice she'd started and twice she'd not been able to finish. Since Hamid had returned to Pakistan, Heaven had been unable to concentrate. His promise to call her was not a promise easily kept. She didn't blame him, but it was hard just the same. The times they talked were almost as painful as their parting had been.

A pink envelope caught her eye and she picked it up. There were foreign stamps on it and a name that she didn't know, but it was from Pakistan.

Heaven opened the envelope, curious to know who was writing her.

> *Dear Sister,*
>
> *Welcome to the family. I am Fatima. Surely my brother has spoken of me. My brother has told us much about you. We would like to plan a party for the two of you. Please tell us when you will come here to your new home. Everyone is waiting to give you a proper welcome. Abba is upset with Hamid that he did not bring you. So I have decided that maybe what you need is an invita-*

*tion from your new sister, to let you know how much you are
welcomed. You are loved by us because you are loved by my
brother. I hope to meet you soon.*

Much Love
Fatima

Heaven smiled. The first smile she'd had since Hamid had left.
Pulling out pen and paper she immediately wrote a letter to her new
sister, liking the idea of having one. After all the things Hamid had
told her about Fatima, Heaven was anxious to meet her. She issued an
invitation to the entire family to come to America.

The letter from Fatima was the catalyst that got Heaven moving
again. She was aware she couldn't sit in a chair and just wait for Hamid
to return; even he'd known that. He'd told her to go out with her
friends. She'd tried, but listening to the blues with Ongela and Peaches
had reduced her to a blubbering mess. She hadn't wanted to do it
again. It seemed everything she did made her think of Hamid, as if her
life had only started the day she met him. Latanya had tried to get her
out of her stupor by advising her that her dream, her business, was
going to go down the toilet if she didn't refocus her energies.

That was what Heaven was trying to do now, refocus. At the *dojo*
the *sensei* had taken her aside to tell her to cut it out. No preamble,
just cut it out. It had been the kick in the butt she'd needed. Heaven
went through the bills finally and organized them, and then she signed
the checks and put them into a manila envelope for the accountant.

She checked the clock, deciding to ignore that it was three A.M. in
Pakistan. She called Hamid's cell.

"Hello my beautiful wife. I was just dreaming of you," he
answered the phone. And just like that, her day was made brighter.
She talked to Hamid until the ache in her heart receded. He loved her
and was miserable. That knowledge made her smile; she selfishly
wanted her husband to be miserable without her. Several minutes later
she told him that she loved him and that he could go back to sleep.

She smiled, knowing he would wait until the early morning hour to call her back. It would be payback, but a very sweet payback.

Each time Hamid returned to America was like the first time he'd returned right before they got married. Three months in Pakistan, one in America, and then it would start all over again.

The third time Hamid left the leaving wasn't as hard, and that had Heaven worried. She didn't want them to become used to being separated.

She was wondering if Hamid was as lonely as he'd been in the beginning. She knew she was. But she was trying to survive, not have him worrying about her the entire time he was away from her.

Her business was good. But it was not her business she wanted in bed at night. Still, Heaven had the routine down to a science. It had been almost a year. Three times Hamid had returned to Pakistan, and three times he'd returned to her. But this time there was something different in his leaving, a kind of resolve, and she thought it was easier for him to leave than before. Their anniversary would fall two days after his flight back to Pakistan. It annoyed Heaven that her husband had not done better planning.

"I am going with Sassa for a few hours to talk with the uncles. I'll be back shortly." Hamid was standing near her desk and not looking directly at her.

Heaven looked at Hamid but didn't answer. He had every right to see his family and friends when he returned to America. She had no right to try and stop him, and she wouldn't; only she didn't want him to want to leave her.

For the longest time they stared at each other until Hamid blew out a breath, looking defeated. He shook his head slightly and bit down on his bottom lip as if he wanted to say something. But he didn't, just turned and left the apartment.

Instant clarity hit Heaven. She would not allow this to go on. This was not the marriage she wanted, seeing her husband for a month at a time.

Fear skittered down her spine, but she refused to allow it to take hold. Before she could change her mind, Heaven was on the phone calling a friend, then calling her clients, her accountant, and her employees. Next, she called the health department about the Hepatitis A and the Typhoid shots and the malaria pills she knew she would have to take.

Then she called the airlines. It was time to redeem that ticket. She was going to Pakistan with Hamid. She muttered a prayer that she was making the right choice. She was planning to be there for three months. She would remain there with Hamid until he returned. At least then, they would have four months together as man and wife. She would get to spend her first anniversary in her husband's arms.

Hamid paced back and forth, feeling as though he'd aged ten years in the twenty-one days he'd been in America. "This is getting to be way too hard." Hamid looked at Sassa. "Maybe Heaven was right. Maybe we should have given this more thought."

"Are you no longer in love with her?" Sassa asked.

"I think she may no longer be in love with me. Why does she continue to allow me to leave her here? Why hasn't she once mentioned that she would like to see Pakistan with me, Sassa? We promised to compromise, but it is I who appears to be doing all of the compromising. I sit there alone waiting for her letters, which have become fewer and fewer, I might add. In the beginning, she would call me in the middle of the night and she would awake when I called her, eager to hear my voice. It seems I spend a lot of my time waiting for calls that never come. I think if I never called Heaven, she wouldn't notice. And when we're together, it is no longer as it was."

"Are the two of you fighting more than usual?" Sassa asked.

"No, we don't fight at all. We talk to each other like polite strangers. She no longer cries when I leave her to return. She doesn't even bother to come to the porch. Do you remember the first time? I felt her pain until the moment I landed and even after. Now there is nothing but dead silence between us."

"What are you going to do?"

"I have no idea. Reason tells me to release her, to allow her to seek her happiness with another man. My heart says I would rather die first."

"Hamid, it would seem you are still faced with the same choice. And as I told you earlier, it is up to you. I will pray that you will make the right decision."

"I already have." Hamid closed his eyes for a second, prayed, and then opened them. "When I return to America, it will be to remain. I will not leave my wife again."

"And your vow?"

"What of it?" Hamid sighed. "I will dishonor my father by breaking it, but I will break it."

"Have you told this to Heaven?"

"No."

"What if she doesn't want you to break your vow?"

"Like you said, Sassa, the choice is mine to make, not Heaven's."

"Then at least talk to her. Tell her that you plan to be a fulltime husband. That will take a bit of adjusting."

"Are you saying that she likes having me gone?" Hamid's nostrils flared.

"You're the one that's questioning her feelings for you. I'm just voicing what you think." Sassa shrugged. "I didn't tell you, Isha is going to have a baby." Sassa's face beamed. "I'm going to be a father."

Hamid pounded his cousin on the back, hugging and kissing him, envious that he was not with his wife long enough to make a baby, wishing he had the same kind of news, wondering why he didn't. He'd never spoken to Heaven about not using birth control. He was against it and didn't want to get into a fight with her over it, knowing that with her feminist views she would spout off things about it being her body. So he'd avoided the conversation. And he had no babies planted in Heaven's womb to show for it.

Hamid wished that he'd not gone to Sassa. His cousin never failed to be honest with him, a trait he admired and yet hated at the same time. He went into the apartment for the first time since their marriage feeling like a stranger. Everything in the apartment belonged to Heaven. They had bought no furniture together, no dishes, not even food. When he came home, the cupboards were well stocked, and while he slept she refilled them.

This place was only a place he came to visit once every three months to hold his wife in his arms, to make love to her and to return to his homeland.

A sadness came over Hamid as he thought how the apartment he shared with his wife was little better than a hotel lately. Nothing other than Heaven's presence in it spoke of home to him. He'd asked her once why she didn't wake him to go with her to the market and she'd smiled and said she liked doing it alone.

Hamid didn't know if Heaven needed the time to be away from him, so he hadn't pushed it. A lump formed in his throat. This life was not working, and the fate he'd praised was being unnecessarily cruel.

Heaven packed her bags in record time and put them away until the time was right. She had no idea of the type of clothing she would need in Pakistan, but she was going. It was done. She watched Hamid as he came in and she winced at the tiredness around his eyes. He looked at her, barely smiling, and sat across from her.

"What would you like to do before I leave? I should have thought of the date of our anniversary and planned more carefully. I'm sorry, but the price of the ticket..." Hamid stopped, embarrassed. Money had not been the reason, and he was aware that she knew that. He'd just forgotten. This traveling back and forth, always bartering with another doctor to cover the clinic, was having a tremendous effect on him. Hamid felt as if he'd been reduced to begging.

"I'd like to go and listen to some blues if you feel up to it. As for our anniversary, don't worry about it," Heaven said.

He stared at her. Surely this, more than anything else, told him her feelings for him had changed. *Don't worry about our anniversary.* Hamid swallowed and closed his eyes. The habit of not saying the important things was getting to be too much for him.

They went to the club and spent the next week together in spurts. Heaven was so busy working that Hamid wondered why he'd bothered coming to visit. When the day finally arrived and it was time to leave, Hamid looked at Heaven and wondered if she would cry this time.

"I called a limo. Sassa has to work. Do you need anything before I go? Money or anything?"

Heaven was smiling. Allah, *no*, he thought. She was happy that he was leaving. He went to the room to get his luggage and stopped at the sight of two more bags on the bed. Where was Heaven going, he wondered.

"Hamid, don't forget my bags," Heaven said, coming up behind him.

"Where are you going?" He turned to her, not hoping, just waiting.

"Where do you think, silly? I'm going with you."

Before she could finish the statement, he had her in his arms twirling her around in disbelief. "You're coming to Pakistan?"

"Yes."

"When, why?"

"Because I can't stand this. It's killing me to stay away from you. This isn't working, Hamid, not like this, and besides, it doesn't feel much like a compromise."

"Did you talk to Sassa?"

"Sassa? What are you talking about?" Heaven tilted her head.

"Never mind. You're really going? How long?"

"Three months. I'm staying until you're ready to return."

"Three months? What will happen with your business?"

Heaven took in a breath and looked at her husband. "What will happen to us if I don't?"

"You've felt it?"

"Yes."

"Do you still love me, Heaven?" Hamid held her eyes for a second. "It hasn't felt like it for some time. You stopped crying when I left." He smiled. "Not that I wanted to have your tears be the last thing I remembered, but…"

"I know. You just wanted to know I cared. I was beginning to wonder too, Hamid. You don't hold me as tightly. You don't look as if you heart is breaking to leave me."

"But it was."

She shrugged. "Either way, I thought it best for us, for our marriage, for me to go to Pakistan. You're important to me, Hamid, too important for me not to try. You're my husband. I intend to keep it that way." She paused before picking up her luggage from the bed. "Have you kept your vow, Hamid?"

For a moment he didn't understand. Then it hit him. "Heaven, if you're coming with me because you don't trust me…"

"No."

"I haven't dishonored you. You do not have to come with me to ensure that." A sudden burning filled his chest. As much as he wanted his wife to accompany him, he did not want her thinking he'd defiled their marriage bed.

"I'm tired of not being with you." Heaven shrugged her shoulders and smiled at him. "I want to be with you."

"You're giving up an awful lot to come with me."

"I gave up more having you leave me. I love you, Hamid."

Hamid brought Heaven's hands to his lips and kissed them. His heart was too full for words. Then he remembered. "Heaven, you need shots. As much as I want you to come with me, I want you protected. You'll have to take a later flight." *Damn fate*, he thought.

"You've forgotten I'm a nurse, Hamid. I went to the health department a week ago for the shots, and I've been taking the malaria pills since then."

"Is that why you were complaining of an upset stomach a couple of nights ago?"

"It could have been that, or the side effects from the typhoid shot." She smiled at him. "But it's getting better."

"Do you have enough pills to take the entire time we will be gone, and for a month after we return?"

"Yes, Hamid."

"I just want to be sure. I don't want to risk your health."

"Neither do I."

"I can't believe you planned all of this."

"The moment I knew we needed this, yes, I planned it."

Hamid kissed her forehead. "I love you, Heaven, thank you."

"You don't have to thank me. I'm coming because I can't stand it anymore. Being away from you for so long is killing me and you, and it's tearing our marriage apart."

Hamid grabbed the bags from her and carried them down the stairs. When the last bag was in the limo, he placed a call to Sassa.

"My wife is coming to Pakistan with me."

"I know," Sassa answered.

"When did she tell you?"

"A few days ago. She called, said you were in the shower and told me she was going with you, that it was a surprise. I guess you have your answer, Hamid. She does love you and wants your marriage to succeed."

"Praise Allah," Hamid said softly before closing the cover on his phone.

He grinned at Heaven. She would take the country by storm. With her strange hair and penchant for fighting, he wondered how their stay in Pakistan would be received, and if before the three months were over they'd all wish she had remained here at home in America. And America was now home to him. Regardless of feeling like a stranger in the apartment, America was where his heart was. It was where Heaven was.

After twenty-three hours of riding on the plane, and a seven-hour layover in England, Heaven felt stiff. She also realized how much of a sacrifice Hamid had made in order to be with her. The plane wasn't in the least comfortable for her, and she couldn't imagine how uncomfortable a tall man like Hamid must be. She leaned forward trying to stretch, but wasn't able to. Then she felt strong fingers kneading her tired muscles and she closed her eyes. "Umm," she moaned softly, "thank you." She heard her husband chuckle beside her.

After a few minutes, she sat back and asked him to turn from her so she could massage his neck. Just touching him relieved some of her strain. Heaven knew part of the tenseness was because she was about to meet the family she'd married into. She couldn't help wondering what would happen when she landed on foreign soil. Would she be accepted? Would they see her as an infidel? Would she still be married to Hamid after she left Pakistan? She closed her eyes and sat back, holding on tightly to Hamid's hand. She felt him squeeze her fingers in reassurance.

"There's only an hour left," Hamid whispered into her ear. "It won't be long."

"I think I want to use the bathroom before we land," Heaven whispered back. "Would you hand me my bag from the overhead bin. I want to brush my teeth," she said in answer to the questioning look on his face.

Without a lot of trouble, Heaven managed to do what she wanted in the small space. She glanced at her reflection in the mirror and bit her lips. Then she opened the door and stepped outside.

Hamid glanced up, saw a woman walking toward him and almost looked away. But there was something about the woman that begged a second look, something familiar. He looked at the clothes she had on. They were also familiar. He'd bought the same outfit for Heaven over a year ago.

Suddenly the woman was only a couple of seats from him and he was looking into her face with his mouth open. It couldn't be. But it was. Heaven was wearing the gift he'd bought for her.

"Heaven." He smiled, saw that she was looking nervous, and stood to allow her to pass. When she sat he couldn't take his eyes from her. "You're beautiful, so beautiful. Why did you change?"

"I thought it would be nice, and I love the sari."

He squeezed her hand, wishing they were in America where he would have kissed her with all he passion that was in him. Now it would have to wait until they were alone.

"Hamid, what if they don't like me?"

"They will love you," he answered.

"What if they don't?"

"Heaven, I don't understand what you're asking."

She wouldn't meet his gaze. "Us, Hamid. I'm asking what will happen to us if your family disapproves."

"You're my wife," he said, looking at her, wondering where this was coming from. "If they love you, you will be my wife. If they don't, you will still be my wife."

He caught the look in her brown eyes and understood at last. "No one will make me stop loving you, Heaven, not my family, and not a vow. I give you my solemn promise."

Hamid watched as the tiny quiver claimed the corner of her lips but didn't quite make it to her eyes. "Heaven, I will love you forever, trust me."

There was lingering doubt in her eyes, doubt that he wanted to erase. He ignored the plane filled with Muslims, leaned over, and kissed his wife. She smiled then, and he kissed her lips softly for a few more seconds. "You are the pathway to my soul. I will love you forever."

He heard her relived sigh as she finally leaned into the small cushion of the airplane seat. He wondered if her fears had kept her from returning with him before. No matter, she was here beside him now, and he'd meant his words to her. He didn't care how his family felt about Heaven, he would love her forever. But for assurance, he whispered a little prayer. *"Please, Allah, let them love her."*

As they filed off the plane, Heaven could swear she could hear Hamid's heartbeat. Then again it might have been her own. Everything about the airport in Pakistan was different, the smells, the sounds, the sights. *"Okay, Dorothy, 'we're not in Kansas anymore,'"* she said under her breath.

"What did you say?" Hamid asked, stopping to look at her.

"Nothing, just something silly."

Still Hamid stared at his wife, his eyes narrowing. "You're afraid." He tilted his head slightly. He was confused and a little hurt that Heaven would be afraid. "Don't you trust me to protect you?" he asked.

His look was scorching her. As she stared into his gaze, the fear began to drain away. She would wait and see, not base her opinion of the country on things she'd heard. Besides, she was with her husband. He would not let anything happen to her.

"I trust you to protect me, Hamid," Heaven said softly, smiling at him. When he returned the smile she knew they would be fine.

They made their way through the crowded lines and when they stepped out into the bright sun, Heaven took a deep breath. The air smelled clean. And then she took in a mouthful of heat and coughed. The heat was dry, and her eyes teared for a moment, adjusting to the difference, and then she blinked and blinked again.

A group of at least thirty people was swarming toward them. It was obvious who they were. She'd thought they'd have a few minutes before meeting Hamid's family. There was no doubt they were his family. They were running toward them, some crying, some laughing. To her surprise, Hamid's hand found hers and gave her fingers a squeeze, and he smiled down at her. Sassa had warned her that in Pakistan public displays of affection between a man and woman, even husband and wife, were avoided.

"My family, your new family." Hamid smiled at her and slid his arms around her waist, guiding her toward the group. Again, he was doing what she'd not been expecting, touching her. It wasn't that Heaven had plans on making out in public, but at the moment Hamid's touch gave her confidence she had done the right thing in coming. "I should have warned you to never trust Sassa with a secret," Hamid whispered.

"Sister, I'm Fatima," the woman hugged Heaven tightly. This was her new sister-in-law she'd been writing letters to. As soon as Fatima let go of her, one woman after another, came up to Heaven, calling her Sister, kissing her on the cheeks, hugging her so tightly that she could barely breathe the dry, almost dusty air.

Then an older woman who was a bit plump came to the front of the line, and the women stepped to either side, as though parting a veil, and allowed her to come forward. For a long moment, she stared at Hamid, then turned her attention to Heaven.

"Ammi," Hamid said, "this is your new daughter. This is my wife. This is Heaven."

Heaven trembled slightly, moving her body toward Hamid, until she saw that the woman had come to a decision. She nodded her head and her lips turned up in a smile. Heaven waited. The woman nodded her head some more and Heaven grinned and bowed her head slightly, not knowing why she'd done it. When she looked back up, the older woman was smiling broadly. Then she reached for Heaven and hugged her, then hugged Hamid. She spoke in Urdu, and her words were spoken so fast that Heaven knew without understanding the language that Hamid had been reprimanded for Heaven's not having visited before.

Then, apparently, the scope of the conversation changed. The group of women huddled nearby beamed and laughed as they looked toward her. Hamid was shaking his head and saying something to them that appeared to be argumentative as he looked at Heaven helplessly.

Heaven watched as her new mother-in-law hit Hamid several times on the shoulder. Then she put her arm around Heaven and led her away. She glanced back at Hamid and, to her surprise, his mother hit her several times, the way she'd done Hamid, and pointed toward the front.

Heaven got the picture. The older woman didn't want her looking at Hamid. Okay, Heaven thought, what's going on? What happened to all the protecting her husband was going to do? She smiled. She didn't really need protecting, and she knew that.

"Sister, you're getting married," one of the women finally said in English and Heaven's mouth flew open.

"We're already married."

"Not to Ammi you're not. She's arranged everything. You will be married in two days."

"Wait a second. How could she arrange everything? My coming was a surprise. Even Hamid didn't know."

"Sassa called," the woman explained. Heaven had not retained the names. "I'm sorry," she said, "tell me your name again."

"Aisiha."

"Aisiha, Fatima," Heaven said turning to include the woman she had at least a writing relationship with. "Hamid and I have been married for a year. Our anniversary is two days from now."

"That's perfect. You will become man and wife here with a traditional, well, not quite traditional, wedding. But you will marry, and we'll have a feast, and you'll receive a lot of gifts."

Fatima jingled her bracelets in Heaven's face. "Hamid is the favorite son, and everyone will come to the wedding, you'll see.

"What about Hamid? Where is he going?"

"He'll come to the house, but tonight and tomorrow you will not sleep with him, not until after the wedding."

This was not the deal. Heaven had not followed her husband halfway around the world to be told she could not be with him. That was defeating her reasons for being there.

"I have to talk to Hamid about all of this first to see if he approves." She was given a little push into a van and the rest of the women filed into the other waiting vehicles. She managed to catch a peep of Hamid before he climbed in a van. The butterflies were back in her stomach.

"I'm not Muslim." Heaven looked at Fatima. "Didn't Hamid tell you that? I'm Christian."

Fatima looked embarrassed. "He told us."

"So why has your mother arranged a wedding? I'm not changing my religion."

"Allah will take care of that. We were not there to see Hamid get married, Sister. Would you deny us that?"

"Fatima, let me repeat, we're already married." Fatima smiled and spoke to the rest of the women. They nodded a few times, laughed, and talked among themselves. It was then Heaven knew she was going to have a wedding.

"I know it's against your religion for a Muslim to marry a Christian," Heaven offered.

"Didn't Hamid tell you? Islam says that Muslim men can marry women of the book."

"Pardon, what book?"

"Your book. Your Bible. It was okay for Hamid to marry you, a non-Muslim woman, a Christian, a woman of the book." Fatima smiled.

"Then why was your family so upset that he had?"

"We wanted to celebrate with him; he has the position in our family as favored son. That's an important role, and then he would not bring his bride to meet his new family."

Ahh, Heaven thought, so Hamid had been more than likely taking flak about her unwillingness to come to Pakistan.

"Hamid wanted me to come." She waited to make sure Fatima knew what she was saying. Fatima looked at her for a moment, said a few words to her mother, and then looked inquiringly at Heaven.

"You did not wish to come?"

A knot formed in Heaven's belly. "It wasn't that I didn't want to come. I had just started a new business, and I needed to be there to make sure everything was okay. It takes a lot of time. It was important to me. I used all of my money for the business."

"Wasn't it important to be with your husband?"

"That's why I'm here now." Heaven took a deep breath. "I love Hamid. We tried to have a marriage from two countries, but it wasn't working. I miss him too much." Heaven saw the old woman smile and she looked at Fatima.

"Oh, we all speak English," Fatima explained and shrugged her shoulders.

Heaven laughed. Her new mother-in-law had been testing her. When the woman turned from the front seat to pat her cheeks Heaven knew she'd passed. She didn't blame Hamid's mother for questioning her love for her son.

"So now, Heaven, do you agree? Are we having a wedding?"

Heaven looked at each woman in turn, wondering if they were still testing her. "I have to ask my husband," she said. The women smiled and she knew her answer had been the correct one.

Nah, Hamid will agree.

Damn Sassa and his big mouth. Hamid had promised Heaven that his family would love her. That part was covered because they did. He was grateful to Sassa for having them welcome Heaven at the airport. But he wondered how his wife would feel having the women attack her, telling her they weren't married, that she couldn't sleep with him tonight.

Hamid groaned. He'd dreamt so long of bringing his wife to Pakistan and making love to her under the stars.

"Hamid, you're so quiet."

Hamid looked at his father, who'd waited in the van, not getting out to meet Heaven. He'd wanted to wait until they were home and had chosen instead to observe Heaven's interaction with the women.

"I didn't expect all of this," Hamid said.

His father laughed, and said, "Then you shouldn't have told Sassa."

"I didn't, Heaven did. Truthfully, I guess we both did, but Heaven told him days before she told me. She told him she wanted to surprise me." Hamid smiled. "She did. She didn't tell me until it was time for me to leave for the airport."

"It's a good thing Heaven told Sassa. Don't worry, the women will take care of Heaven, and surely one night of not sleeping with your wife will not kill you."

"No, but Heaven just might." Hamid smiled. "This is all nice, but if Heaven doesn't want it we're not going to do it. Besides, it's not customary for a married couple to sleep apart. We've been married for a year now. No one would force a couple to do this."

"No one is forcing you, Hamid. But I think since you did not have the decency to bring your bride here to meet us or to ask our permission in the first place, you deserve to sleep alone for a night."

"So this is penance."

"More like a joke that your ammi wants to play on you. Now are you getting married here?"

"If Heaven agrees."

"Are you saying that she is the one who controls your home?"

"Abba, for the last year I haven't been able to establish exactly where home is. But I leave my heart with Heaven every time that I come here. So I would have to say where Heaven is is home and..." he shrugged. "Make of it what you will, but she controls my heart." Hamid waited. "Abba, Heaven is here in Pakistan for a visit, for three months. After that she will return to America. Abba, my heart and my home is with Heaven."

Hamid held his father's gaze, not saying more. He'd planted the seed, and he and his father both knew it. Hamid was going to dishonor his father and break his vow.

"She means that much to you?"

"More. I didn't choose her, Abba, fate did. I had no choice in the matter, but I do love her."

His father laughed. "Hamid, don't lie to me. Your cousin has told us all about your meeting Heaven in the hospital. Maybe that was fate," he grinned, "but you gave fate a great shove, letting the air out of her tire." He laughed. "And pretending you needed her to learn American culture."

"I learned a lot from my wife," Hamid insisted.

"I'm sure you did."

"I'm serious."

"So am I," his father laughed. "Hamid, don't tell me that there was something about America that you didn't already know. You probably know more about America than the ones that live there." He grinned. "Did she think you were really that ignorant?"

Hamid smiled a little, remembering his first encounters with Heaven. "In the beginning, but I gave her reason to believe that. My car stalled, I needed assistance, and she helped. She started my car."

"And your heart too."

"Yes," Hamid agreed. "She did. But I thought I would never see her again. I dreamt of her, could think of nothing but her and when I saw her truck, I truly believed fate had intervened, that it was the will of Allah."

"And Allah told you to flatten her tire?" his father asked for the second time.

"Maybe not exactly, but just the fact that I knew how to do it, that I could assist her in fixing it, seemed to be Allah's will."

"Did Allah tell you to play the imbecile for this woman, pretend that you have not studied America since you were a boy?"

"Abba, that was genuine."

"Ha."

"It was."

This time the others in the van joined in laughing, even Hamid laughed.

"What can I say?" Hamid argued. "My heart was struck by an arrow and I fell in love with her. When I saw her again I wasn't going to let her get away. I couldn't."

"Are you happy, Hamid?"

"No, Abba," Hamid sighed. They all knew what his father was asking. "I hate leaving my wife in America. It breaks her heart, and it breaks mine."

CHAPTER THIRTEEN

After the laughter died down in the van Hamid stared at his father, holding his gaze, grateful to be so loved, to be the favorite son. He swallowed around the sudden lump. Hamid did not want to hurt his father. But in order not to do it he would have to continue hurting his wife. The price he'd agreed to pay had become much too high. Sassa was right, it was Hamid's choice, a choice where no one would be truly happy, but one that must be made just the same.

Hamid would once again disappoint his father and bring about the sneer of his older brothers. He thought all of this as the caravan holding his family pulled up to his parents' home. He stood for a moment watching the women unload, waiting to see Heaven. When she got out, she was laughing, looking at Fatima. Hamid let go of the breath he hadn't been aware he'd held.

He watched her smiling, and then he saw her head turn slowly in his direction. She grinned widely and stood there for a second before his mother whacked her about the shoulders again and pulled her away. Still, he heard Heaven laughing at it all.

"You can stop worrying, Hamid. I don't think fate would have chosen a wife for you that your family could not love."

Startled, Hamid turned. He opened his mouth to speak but no words came. For a moment, heaviness filled his chest, but it was instantly replaced with the feeling that he was floating on air. "Abba."

"Come on." His father swung his meaty arm around his shoulder. "Come and introduce me to my new daughter."

"Praise Allah, thanks be to him," Hamid prayed silently as he followed his father into the house.

Hamid walked with his father up to Heaven. "Abba, I would like to present your new daughter. This is Heaven. Heaven, my father, now yours."

Heaven was holding her breath. Hamid could see it. He laughed as Heaven craned her neck to look at his father. And to think she'd thought he was tall at six-three and a half. His father was six nine, an impressive figure. Seconds ticked away and Heaven still did not speak, just continued looking at his father.

He moved closer to her and touched her gently. Her eyes swung to meet his and it seemed to loosen her tongue. She blinked and spoke.

"Hello sir, it's nice to meet you," Heaven said. But Hamid saw something else in the depth of her eyes and wondered what it was.

"Heaven, what do you think of Pakistan?"

"Truthfully, I haven't had much of a chance to see anything." Heaven replied. "From the airport we talked," her eyes swung to Hamid, "about the wedding."

"Are you pleased with the wedding arrangements?"

Again, Heaven looked toward Hamid. "I think it's very nice for you all to go to so much trouble for us," Heaven kept staring upward, "considering we're already married."

His father shook his head. "So that's the reason you're staring at me. You're afraid I'm going to object to the first wedding." He rubbed his hand across his beard. "It is true we did have a problem with that."

"That's not why I'm staring, and I'm sorry that I was. But no, that's not the reason."

"*Nah?*"

"*Nah,*" Heaven repeated obviously knowing it meant no.

"Then why are you staring?"

"You look exactly like my uncle."

For a moment, the room went quiet. Then he laughed. "Who knows, Heaven, maybe I am. Come sit with me," he ordered mildly, "tell me about yourself. You're Christian, *nah?*"

"Yes," Heaven answered.

"And you plan to remain so."

"Yes."

He nodded his head. "And the children, what will they be taught?"

"We haven't really talked about it."

"You should. It's important, don't you agree?"

"Hamid and I are learning to compromise. We will on that also."

"You can't compromise on God."

"But you're not speaking of God. You're speaking of religions, beliefs, and customs. On those things Hamid and I can compromise."

"What do you believe about God, Heaven? Do you believe in an eternal resting place? Do you believe in soul sleep or judgment day, or purgatory, or in attaining heaven, the dwelling place?" He frowned at having to make a difference between her name and the place of men's dreams. "Do you believe in hell?" he asked, getting up.

"Some days I do, some days I don't. I was taught they both exist. I don't always agree with that, but I do believe God created the universes and I do believe in Jesus."

"We also believe in Jesus' existence."

"I believe In Jesus as my savior."

"And we believe Mohammad is ours."

Heaven smiled. "There is no compromising on this point. I also believe in Mohammad's existence, but he is not my savior."

"You're in a strange land and you are disagreeing with me. Are you doing this out of disrespect?"

"*Nah.*"

Abba narrowed his eyes and glanced at Heaven from his lofty position. "*Nah*, then what are you doing?"

"Answering your question. You asked my beliefs, and I attempted to tell you. I also attempted to tell you the points on which a man and wife, Hamid and I, can compromise and the ones where we can't."

"What if we disagree?"

"Begging your pardon," Heaven smiled, "but I'm not married to you. I'm married to your son."

Hamid watched as Heaven smiled at his father. She smiled the same smile that never failed to melt Hamid's heart. Now she turned it toward his father.

"I am honored to be accepted into your family," Heaven said softly. Then she bowed her head slightly and waited, leaving Hamid flabbergasted.

Where had Heaven learned this? She had only planned a little over a week to return with him, as far as he knew. Still, she was being as respectful as Heaven could be, almost as agreeable as any Pakistani woman would be.

She was holding her own. Hamid looked at his father, then went to stand beside Heaven. He smiled at her. "We could raise all the boys as Muslims and all the girls as Christians. That's a compromise," Hamid offered. He heard his sisters laughing in the background. Heaven smiled but didn't speak.

"Are you willing to go through the traditional ceremony that you and my son robbed us of?"

Hamid wondered why his father was addressing all of his questions to Heaven, why he was engaging her in verbal war. And he wondered how long Heaven would play his game.

"While everything you want to do for us is incredible, I can't answer that question until I have some time alone to talk with my husband." This time Heaven spoke firmly, with a no- nonsense attitude.

"But here when a man and woman are getting married the parents take care of the details. It is left up to them."

"But you forget Hamid and I are already married."

"Was this a Christian ceremony?"

"No. Will the wedding ceremony you're planning be Islamic?"

Heaven watched while Hamid's father's cheeks filled with air. Then he smiled.

"My brother is a *Kazi*. He will perform the ceremony. He will not ask you to renounce your faith. He will ask you to say vows to each other, and he will ask Allah to bless your marriage."

"Nothing else?"

"Nothing else. I too can compromise, Heaven. Now ask your husband before I forget that enough of the traditions have been broken already."

Heaven smiled at Hamid. "Can we go for a walk?"

Hamid was bursting with pride. Heaven handled herself beautifully. "Yes, we can go for a walk," he said, ignoring his mother telling them they had to eat. "Ammi, we'll eat when we return."

He took Heaven's hand and walked with her out the door, wishing he could hear the conversation his parents, sisters, and cousins were having behind their back. He was thankful his brothers were not there yet. There was something he wanted to show his wife. Hamid wanted Heaven to see the clinic. It was a long walk, but that was what he wanted her to see.

"Are you tired?" he thought to ask.

"Yes," Heaven answered, not bothering to pretend.

"Think you have the energy to walk to the clinic?"

"Can't we drive there?"

"I thought you wanted to walk."

"I have the feeling the clinic is farther than I want to walk. Is it?" She glanced up at him.

"More than likely," he said, and took her hand, pulling her after him. "If you get tired, I'll carry you in my arms." She laughed and his arm slid around her shoulders as easily as it did in America. He wondered if his family was watching them, and if they were stunned by his affection toward his wife. If this shocked them, they'd better not spend too much time with them.

"Hamid, how far is the clinic?"

"About five miles," he laughed. "It will go quickly." He wasn't surprised when Heaven stopped walking.

"I can't walk five miles, Hamid."

"Of course you can."

"Okay, put it this way. I'm not going to walk five miles there and five miles back."

"How far will you walk?"

"I don't know. It could be a block or it could be two steps. When I get tired, I'll stop walking."

Hamid turned and called out and in seconds, a servant was beside them waiting for Hamid's instructions.

"Now you don't have to worry. Jhonni will drive the car ahead of us."

As they walked, for the first time Hamid saw Heaven's reaction to Pakistan. She looked around the area.

"What is this community called?" Heaven asked.

"Area of Defense."

"Defense?"

Hamid saw the startled look in her eyes and smiled. "It's just a name, Heaven, it doesn't mean anything."

"Everyone that lives here is rich, I take it?"

"Yes."

"And everyone has what?" she tilted her head and looked at him. "Help, servants?"

"Ahh, I see where you're going, Heaven. Everyone in Pakistan has servants."

"Does Jhonni have servants?"

Hamid laughed and squeezed Heaven's shoulders. He saw several of the neighbors look toward them and knew they would be gossiping. But his family was much too powerful for anyone to do anything more than gossip. Still Hamid decided to remove his hand from around Heaven's shoulder and be satisfied holding her hand. She laughed.

"So we're going to go three months without touching, huh?"

"I don't think we can do that," Hamid answered honestly, "but I suppose we should try." He gave her fingers another squeeze, bumped his hip into her, and laughed. "Don't worry, Heaven, we will have the nights to make up for the days."

"Dr. Hamid, you're back."

Heaven looked down at the little boy with the coal black eyes and skin the same color brown as a leather wallet she owned. The wallet was sort of cinnamon, but Heaven had never found the right color description. She smiled at the child as Hamid's hand tousled the boy's hair.

"Armand, what are you doing here?"

"I had a cut." He held his hand up for Hamid to examine. "Dr. Youseff stitched it for me."

"Then you'd better be careful." Hamid looked over the boy's head to Dr. Youseff. He smiled. "Thank you for taking care of everything."

"Who's the lady?" Armand asked.

"She's my wife."

Heaven and Hamid waited while the child examined Heaven with his eyes.

"Is she an African princess?" he asked when he'd completed his visual inspection.

"Yes," Hamid laughed, "she's also an American princess."

"She's very beautiful."

"Thank you, Armand, I think so."

"I heard that you're getting married. Are you getting a second wife?"

Heaven laughed and tilted her head at Hamid.

"No second wife," Hamid answered. "I love this one too much to think of having another one. Besides, this wife would not like it very much if I did that. She would stop loving me. I would die if she did that."

Armand laughed. "What's your wife's name, Dr. Hamid?"

"Her name's Heaven." He looked at Heaven. "You may speak directly to her, Armand."

The boy smiled and turned to Heaven, showing a mouth filled with the straightest, whitest teeth she'd ever seen. He would have been the perfect child for any mouth care ad.

"Hello," Armand spoke softly.

"Hello," Heaven answered, "it's very nice to meet you. I'm glad that I came to the clinic." She reached out to shake his tiny hand. Armand looked at her hand a second, then turned and ran out the door. Both Heaven and Hamid laughed.

"One more thing and then we may leave. I want to show you my office," Hamid said.

Heaven followed behind Hamid, the strain of the flight beginning to tell on her. She thought she'd be able to sleep standing up if Hamid would stop making her walk. She watched as Hamid's hand went into his pocket and brought out a set of keys. It was the only room in the building that he'd used a key to enter. Heaven wondered about that.

When they stepped inside, Heaven smiled. The room was painted in the same colors as their bedroom in Chicago. She looked at the pale peach color, surprised. Hamid had told her the bedroom in Chicago was a girl's room.

Her mouth opened when she saw their wedding picture framed and on the wall. She walked around picking up small objects that had come up missing in the past year. Things she'd thought misplaced were in Hamid's office. She continued surveying the room, walking slowly, looking at the items. She picked up framed movie theater stubs and looked at the date. It was the first movie she'd seen with Hamid.

"You kept these?" she turned to Hamid and asked.

"Of course," he answered.

"Why? We weren't even dating at the time."

"That didn't make any difference to me," Hamid said, coming to stand beside her as she continued looking at his mementos.

Heaven frowned as she lifted the framed menu. She'd not known Hamid had taken one. "Why this? I wouldn't even serve you rice."

"But you did in the end," Hamid said. "I knew even then that you loved me, that we would be together."

"You were that sure?"

"Yes, weren't you?"

Heaven moved toward a brochure from DuSable Museum. "No, Hamid, I wasn't sure at all."

"Then it's a good thing I was sure enough for both of us." Hamid pulled her to him and kissed her.

"What's that?" Heaven moved away, despite Hamid's trying to keep her in his arms. She saw for the first time that he was embarrassed by his collection. This was one thing he obviously had not meant for her to see.

"I want to see it," she said as she moved to stand in front of a shadow box. She stared for a long moment at what appeared to be a Pakistani doll. She wasn't sure, there was something a little odd about the doll. She frowned at Hamid and picked the doll up. The cover fell from her head and Heaven saw the doll's hair was in twists, and a tiny diamond sparkled from a thin gold chain on the doll's neck. As she picked up the scarf to replace it, she saw her name, Heaven, stitched into it.

"Hamid." She walked toward her husband, who was leaning against the desk watching her. She saw another picture of her on his desk and finally realized the purpose of it all. This entire office was a testament to them, to their love. "Hamid." she smiled, unable to say more.

"A touch of home," Hamid answered. "I couldn't have remained here so long if I hadn't had this room to come into. This is the place from which I call you. It's here I feel close to you."

Heaven smiled, went and stood between his legs, and threw her arms around him. "You should have told me."

"What good would it have done?" He kissed her. "Telling you wouldn't make me miss you less."

"Now I'm here. Just think, Hamid, for the first time in our marriage we will be together for four months."

"You want to know what I've thought about when I've dreamed of you here in Pakistan?"

"What?"

"Making love to you under the stars." He grinned. "Now I won't even be allowed to sleep with you for the next two days." He kissed her nose. "How do you feel about my family's plans?"

"What do you think?" Heaven countered.

"I told my father it's your decision."

"And I told your mother it's yours."

They both laughed. Heaven drew in more of the hot, dry Pakistani air. "How can they rent a hall that quickly?"

"I'm sure they won't. There's a new law forbidding serving food for weddings in public places. Don't ask," he said in answer to Heaven's questioning look. "The government is trying to discourage lavish parties because even the very poor are expected to participate in the three-day custom and a good part of Pakistan can't afford it."

"Where are they planning to do it?"

"More than likely on our land. We own a lot of land, so it will be easy to put up tents and have the caterers bring food and food and more food." Hamid laughed. "It would be fun."

"You want to do it, don't you?"

"I don't want you to feel forced into anything. There are no customs, no religions, nothing I will ever attempt to force on you."

"But still?"

Hamid laughed. "Okay. Still, I would love to marry you again and I would love to introduce you to the entire community as my wife." He felt longing fill him. Yes, he did want to marry Heaven again.

"Hamid, do you not feel married to me now?"

He blinked, looked at Heaven and decided to tell her the truth. "Because of our arrangement, sometimes it's hard to feel that way."

"Would you feel more that way if we have this ceremony?"

"Would it influence your decision?"

"Yes. Would you use this ceremony to add to your room of memories?"

Hamid didn't tell Heaven that he would no longer need the room, that he did not intend to leave her again. He didn't want her three months with his family to be used to make Heaven feel guilty. His family was good at that.

He would not tell Heaven until much later, though he knew his father was aware it was on his mind. Hamid smiled at her. It wasn't an easy decision to make. But he'd tried for a year to live up to his vow. But he'd also taken a vow to Heaven to be her husband, and he couldn't be her husband one month out of four.

"Heaven, you will not be able to turn this into a fight, no matter how much you try." He held her tightly in his arms.

"I want to do it," she announced, "if you don't think it's silly."

"I don't think it's silly."

"Okay, now that we have that all settled, tell me about the doll. I didn't know you played with dolls." She pulled back to look into her husband's eyes, to show him she was teasing.

"This was to be a present for you. I took it to a beautician in Chicago and had her put the twists in. I had the outfit made here in Pakistan. I was going to give it to you, but kept it hidden in my luggage to keep you from finding it before I was ready to give it to you. Then I forgot it and brought it back. And then I realized I needed it much more than you did."

"Hamid," Heaven breathed slowly in and out. "I'm so glad I came. I've missed you so much."

For an answer, he crushed her to him. After a few more minutes, he heard the patients outside the door and drew back. "I think we should leave now."

"Tell me again. Why do we have to sleep alone tonight?"

Hamid laughed. "We don't, there is no custom that dictates that. Any married couple would be given a room together. This is their way of getting even with us for having married in the first place without their blessing on our union." He shrugged and smiled at her. "If you don't want to follow through on that one, we won't."

"I don't want to follow through on it." Heaven grinned. "But I will. Just know that I'll be thinking about you every minute that I'm asleep."

"Are we having a wedding?" Fatima asked the moment they walked back into the door.

Heaven and Hamid looked at the preparations that were undoubtedly for a wedding and laughed together. "Yes, we're having a wedding," Heaven said.

"And tonight?" Fatima asked.

Hamid looked at his sister. "Tonight will be our official engagement." He laughed. "Both Heaven and I are tired. I want to show her where to rest."

Before he could do that, his mother came, grabbed Heaven's hand, and pulled her to the kitchen where they uncovered a pot. Heaven stirred and tasted at his mother's insistence.

Heaven's face lifted and her gaze met his. For a moment, Hamid's breathing stopped. This was the vision he'd had, Heaven in a sari in the kitchen, with his mother, sisters, cousins, and aunts, while the servants moved about. His chest felt tight, as though it would burst from the love he was feeling.

"Hamid, what's wrong? You look as though you've seen a ghost."

"Nah, Abba, I had a vision and it's come true."

His father frowned. "What vision?"

"This." He inclined his head toward the kitchen, "This, my wife dressed as she is now, here in Pakistan cooking with the women in the family. This was my vision before we ever married."

His father looked at him. "Maybe fate did play a hand in your finding her."

Hamid smiled and went back to watching Heaven until the tiredness in his body told him of the weariness she must be feeling. He walked toward her. "Heaven's tired, Ammi. I'm going to show her to her room. She is sleeping in my room, isn't she?"

"You didn't eat. You have to eat. Look at all this food."

"There will be even more food when we wake. Thank you, Ammi, for understanding."

Hamid didn't wait for an answer. He held out his hand to Heaven and she took it. First, he showed her the rest of the mansion, laughing when she was so tired that all she said was, 'nice house.' Nice house indeed.

His bedroom he saved for last. Hamid smiled, a bit embarrassed when she grinned at the pictures of them that covered the dresser. He shrugged. "You'll sleep here tonight, alone," he whispered in her ear. "At least part of my dreams will come true." He showed her the bathroom. "I'll have someone bring in your bags," he said, hearing his father's voice outside the door.

He kissed her quickly. "Sleep, and I'll see you soon."

"Will you be here, or will you have to go somewhere else to sleep?"

"Do you want me to remain in the house?"

"Yes," Heaven said immediately. "Will it be okay? I mean the customs…"

"This is one custom we will ignore. You want me in the house, I'll be here. Now, sleep." He kissed her once more and walked out the room, looking back at her, wanting more than anything to crawl into the bed with her. But he would wait and play out this game to please his family. And maybe in the end it would ease the pain of what he would do, of making his father regret him being the favorite son.

"Hamid, it's time for you to go and stay at your brother's home," his father called out to him. "You will not see Heaven until the *Mehndi*."

"Sorry, Heaven," Hamid said, "I have to leave you now." He saw the look on her face. "*Nah*, I will not leave the house, only this room."

"Hamid, you agreed to this wedding; it is custom." His father said the moment he closed the door. "Heaven's parents are not here so we will stand in their stead. It would not look right for you to be in the home with her before you marry her."

"Abba, I married her already. This ceremony is for you and Ammi, not for Heaven or me. We don't need it."

"Hamid?"

"*Nay*, Abba, I promised my wife that I would be here should she need me. And I will not go back on that promise."

His father looked at him. "You are very good at keeping your word. I might say even when you don't want to. That's an admirable trait."

Hamid stared at his father, trying to decipher the meaning of his words.

"Sometimes, though, Hamid, we find ourselves breaking our vows, our promises."

Now Hamid knew what his father meant. He understood what Hamid meant to do. "I'm not breaking this promise to my wife," Hamid said, and made his way to the living room. "I will not go in to her, unless she calls me," Hamid added, and laughed.

CHAPTER FOURTEEN

Heaven woke feeling almost as tired as when she lay down. She rolled over and landed on the pillow she knew her husband must have slept on. It was on the left side of the bed, the side Hamid liked. She knew his scent wouldn't be in the freshly laundered sheets, but still she searched for it.

The smell of strong coffee was drifting toward her. She wondered if Hamid had been allowed to stay the night. It didn't matter, she knew he would. She didn't know why it was so important to her that he remain, just that it was.

She wondered what the morning protocol was, and wished she'd asked Hamid. She needed a cup of coffee to get her going. Could she throw on a robe and go into the kitchen? A knock sounded on the door, and she pulled the covers to her chin.

"Sister?" It was Fatima's voice. "Are you awake, sister?"

"Yes," Heaven answered.

"May I come in?"

"Yes," Heaven answered.

Fatima came in with a tray. Smells of food pulled at Heaven and made her remember that it had been many hours since she'd had anything to eat.

"Fatima, thank you, but I was thinking about taking a quick shower and brushing my teeth." She tried to peek out the open door. "Where is Hamid?"

"He's outside. He refused to leave last night, but tonight he must. You will have to tell him."

"Is it okay if I take a shower?" Heaven didn't want to offend, and wondered if it would if she got out of bed to get her robe.

Fatima was smiling. "You're still in the bed. What's wrong?"

Heaven looked at her for a moment. "I don't want to offend anyone. Is it proper for me to…I have on a gown. Is it okay?"

"There are no men in the house, only women. You may shower and I will wait here for you and have tea with you."

Heaven had her answer. "Thanks, Fatima." Heaven pushed away the urge to ask if they used bottled water to make the coffee and tea. She thought of her malaria pills, and decided when she came from her shower she would take a chance.

"Anything else I can get for you?" Fatima asked. She smiled. "Hamid wants to know if you need anything. My father wants him to go, and he won't leave until he checks on you."

Heaven smiled. There were a lot of things she needed, and wanted but she couldn't tell this to her new sister-in-law.

"Don't worry, Heaven, we will take care of you. You're family now. What do you want me to tell Hamid?"

"Tell him good morning, and tell him I saw the stars." Heaven pointed to the ceiling and waited a second for Fatima to leave. When she saw she wasn't, Heaven got out of bed and reached for her robe. She hadn't known Fatima meant her words literally, that she would wait right there for Heaven to finish her shower.

"You can have breakfast when you're done. We have a lot to do today," Fatima said. "Today is your *mehndi*."

This was the second time Heaven had heard the word. She started to ask what it meant, but didn't. Instead, she hurried into the shower and finished as quickly as she could. When she was done, she felt a thousand times better. Her mouth now felt fresh, not full of cotton. For a moment, she worried whether the water had been safe for brushing her teeth. But it was too late; the deed was done.

Hamid was nowhere in sight when Heaven came out, but the bedroom was filled with women, some in jeans, some in saris. They laughed, pulling her into the main room of the house. Heaven was glad she'd taken her jeans and shirt into the bathroom with her. She wanted to ask for the coffee Fatima had brought in earlier and the food. The tray was now empty. Heaven grinned. Some of the women must have gotten hungry. She didn't have time to ponder that as the women surrounded her and started taking measurements.

"Quickly, quickly." Hamid's mother was waving her hands at the woman taking Heaven's measurements, apparently the dressmaker. Before Heaven could protest, the women had her arms spread wide and the dressmaker had the measuring tape wrapped around her waist. They showed Heaven bolt after bolt of material to pick from. Yellow, they told her, had to be the color of the dress she wore tonight.

Tomorrow for the actual wedding, she could wear red, white, or gold. The gold material was a champagne color, more what Heaven wanted, and she chose that. "There're going to have two dresses ready by tonight?" she asked in astonishment.

"There are two dressmakers." Fatima extended her hand. "Don't worry, it will be ready. Now, would you like breakfast?"

"Can I have something hot to drink?" Heaven asked.

Before the words were out a cup was placed in front of her and she was instructed to sit and drink. Finding it was tea, Heaven was a little disappointed since she remembered smelling the coffee earlier.

"Is there any coffee left?" she asked.

"Yes, but tea is better for you," Hamid's mother said and placed dates, toast, and butter and jelly in front of Heaven.

"Here," Fatima said, handing Heaven a note. "Hamid wanted me to give this to you."

"The water is safe. Hamid." Heaven smiled at her husband's consideration.

She'd barely finished eating when the women begin fussing over her, shaping her nails and wanting to redo her twists. Heaven looked at all of their shiny long braids or jet-black curls and knew they wouldn't know how to do her hair. Even Heaven didn't know. She only knew that she sat in a chair for ten hours at a time and plopped down two hundred bucks. The style would last a good month before she had to plop down another fifty to have the twists taken out. Since she was far away from her beautician, Heaven knew she had to learn, or her hair would be a mess by the time she returned home.

"*Nah*," Heaven said getting the hang of it. She wondered when she returned home if she would ever use the word *no* again. *Nah* seemed so much more, she laughed into her cup, more sophisticated.

"What's funny?" one of the women asked.

"Nothing," Heaven replied. "I was just thinking of something."

"You don't have much time for thinking. We have to get you ready."

The door opened again and a group of women rushed in. Three more sisters, Isha, Hannah, and Irim. And five cousins. Heaven couldn't even attempt to remember their names without coffee.

It turned out the women had been right. She hadn't had much time. When it was evening, Heaven found her hair entwined with decorations and gold bracelets shoved on her arms.

"Whose are these?" she asked.

"They're yours," Fatima answered. "Now come on, hurry." Just then the dressmaker came in and the same group of women began fussing over Heaven again, painting her body with red dye.

"Hold it, stop it! What are you doing?" Heaven pulled her hand back.

"This is *Mehndi*."

"Will this stuff come off?" Heaven asked.

"In about a week. Now come on. Hamid's coming, and we have to have the rest of your body painted."

"Hamid can come tonight?"

"Yes. Usually he wouldn't be allowed to attend, but since we're the family for you both it will be done together."

"Hamid's having his body painted?"

"Yes."

Within an hour, Heaven had been shoved into a beautiful yellow gown. Despite the red dye, she felt like the princess Hamid had told Armand that she was. Then Hamid was there, along with the brothers she hadn't met: Imran, Irfan, and Ali. Heaven laughed softly as she looked at them. And here she'd always thought her husband tall; he was the runt of the litter, it appeared. They were seated side by side and the women began painting their palms.

"What's the meaning of the paint? What are we going to do?" No one answered Heaven. The women giggled, but wouldn't answer. Hamid sat quietly, barely looking at Heaven. That should have been her first clue that something was coming she might not like.

Then the men and women separated and the women begin throwing food at Heaven, pelting her with cake, sweets, and even pieces of fruit. She blinked and noticed that the men were doing the same to Hamid. She wondered why she needed to have a special dress made for this, and wondered also about the meaning.

As soon as they were cleaned and the partying commenced, she no longer needed an explanation. It was just an excuse for a party. Besides, she'd asked Fatima what the dye meant and could tell Fatima didn't know. She'd said, simply, "Custom." Heaven wanted to know what was behind the custom. When it was obvious that the women Fatima asked also didn't know and began making up explanations, Heaven laughed and told them to forget it. It was just one of those things that had been done so long that no one questioned the why, except Heaven.

The next day Heaven was awake before any member of the household. She wanted to take a long shower, intending to get off the henna the women had painted her body with, but found she couldn't wash it away. Lucky for her, with her dark skin, the dye wasn't an eyesore. Then she remembered. This was her wedding day, and the butterflies began. Heaven was more nervous than she had been the day she married Hamid a year before. Then she remembered that this was their anniversary. How perfect.

Before long, the planning culminated in the main event. Between the women speaking Urdu and the ones speaking English, Heaven figured things out. Her stomach was rumbling, especially watching the other women eat, but she was permitted only strong tea and bread and little else. They thought she would be too nervous to eat. She was nervous, but she was also hungry.

"Heaven, the *Nikal* is here. You can't come out now." Fatima's face was flushed.

"The *Nikal*," Heaven repeated.

"Yes. Hamid is coming with our uncle to sign the marriage papers. Our father will stand in for you also. Then you can come out. After that you will go to the wedding feast. Now we need to get you dressed."

If Heaven had thought the yellow dress was beautiful, she had no idea what to think of the champagne dress. It was the most stunning dress she'd ever seen, and the women had been able to make it into the full Cinderella look that she wanted. It was not traditional but hey, she was the bride. From the ohhs and ahhs from the women, it was apparent they were happy with Heaven's choice. The last thing was to have Fatima and two of the cousins place the hair adornments throughout her hair. They were in the same pale gold color.

Hamid's mother came in and brought her several bags. "Heaven," she looked at her sternly for a second, "you're my daughter now. You will call me *Ammi*, like Hamid, and his father is your *Abba*. Okay?"

"Okay," Heaven agreed. She wouldn't have felt comfortable calling them Mom and Dad but *Ammi* and *Abba* she could handle.

"Here, this is for you." Hamid's mother shoved the bags at Heaven. "These are from your new family, and this is from your husband."

Heaven's desire was to open the gift from Hamid, but she was polite and first opened the ones from his parents. The beautiful necklace encrusted with jewels and matching earrings, several heavy gold bracelets, and a sapphire set left Heaven speechless.

"Thank you, Ammi," Heaven said taking the jewelry from the wrappings. "They're beautiful." She hugged her new second mother tightly. Then she opened the box from Hamid. A ring with a diamond so large that at first she thought it was a cubic zirconium winked at her. She blinked. "Did Hamid pick this out himself?"

"Of course. He wouldn't let anyone help, and everyone offered to. Put it on," Fatima said.

Heaven closed the lid. "*Nah*, I want Hamid to do it."

"That's not the custom."

"But we're compromising, remember? It's our custom in America. It means more to the bride when the groom places the ring on her finger." She looked at the ring she'd been wearing for a year. She didn't want to replace it, but then again, she did want Hamid to slip the new one on her finger. She moved her old ring to her right hand.

In thirty minutes a bell sounded and the women began pushing Heaven out the door of Hamid's bedroom. "It's time for the marriage ceremony to begin," they said. "What are you going to say?"

Heaven had no idea what she would say.

They stood in a circle and, for the first time that day, Heaven gave a thought to what this was about, what it meant to Hamid and her new family.

"Hamid, your pledge," the Kazi said.

"With my heart and soul I pledge my devotion and undying love. I will care for you and the children you will bear me with infinite love and gentleness. I will provide for their care and their education, and when we leave this world, I will thank Allah for gracing me with your love and your smile."

"Now, Heaven," the Kazi said, "you may speak."

For a moment Heaven was silent, then she licked her lips. "With my heart and soul I will return your devotion and undying love," she began. She gazed up at Hamid, the words she wanted to say finally coming to her lips. "'Whither thou goest, I will go, and where thou lodgest, I will lodge; thy people will be my people and thy lands my lands. And naught but death part thee and me.' I pledge to be the wife that you will be proud of."

For a long moment, Heaven stared at Hamid and he stared back. The Kazi blessed their union and the babies they would have. Then Heaven slipped the ring from her hand to Hamid. He smiled and placed it on her finger, and they were pronounced husband and wife.

When Hamid kissed her hands, Heaven tried to stop the tremor that was slowly washing over her. But the liquid fire poured through her veins and she sucked in her breath.

"I love you," Hamid said softly.

"I love you too," she whispered and was wondering what would happen next when Hamid wrapped her in his arms and kissed her. It wasn't the kind of kiss he usually gave her, but it was one that promised her more to come. Heaven thought of the stars in the ceiling of Hamid's bedroom and smiled at him.

"What are you thinking about?" he whispered.

"The stars," she answered.

And just like that, they were pulled apart to receive the good wishes, kisses, and gifts from family and friends. There must have been hundreds of people who filed in and handed Heaven fistfuls of cash, envelopes with more cash, jewelry, and all kinds of things.

When that was done, they drove to a field where tents stretched across the land for miles. The smell of cooked meat permeated the air and music sounded off in the distance.

Heaven smiled at Hamid. At least they were now permitted to ride in the same car. "What are they cooking?" she asked, ignoring the look of amusement on Hamid's face. "Come on, I need to know, or you need to stay close and tell me what I'm eating."

"You could always as the bride plead a nervous stomach."

"Forget that. I'm hungry. I'll try almost anything that's not too spicy."

Hamid laughed. "Don't worry, I'll tell you what things you might want to eat."

Some things Heaven didn't have to ask about. She recognized the kabobs, lamb, chicken, and beef. She didn't try the lamb, but the other meats were succulent and the rice was good. She tried what Hamid told her was samosas and chicken tikka and chicken korma. Then for desert she had ras gullah. It looked like the doughnut holes she got from Dunkin' Donuts, but was soaked in a dark brown, warm syrup. She was finally overstuffed. They danced and Hamid sang to her, words that she didn't understand. But she did understand the look in his eyes and the love in his smile.

When it was dark, they were finally able to leave the party in full swing and go away for their official honeymoon.

"Now do you feel married to me, Hamid?"

"Now I feel married to you," he laughed. "And I've thought that maybe I would just hide your passport and keep you here. How was the wedding for you?"

"I loved it. I'm glad we did it," Heaven admitted.

The luxury of the presidential suite of the Avari Towers Hotel in Karachi had taken Heaven by surprise. "Hamid, how in the world did you get all of this accomplished? You had no idea we were getting married again, did you?"

"No, but once I knew we were going to get married, I wanted to make this right for you. Has it been right?"

"Being with you is right."

"I'm glad you came." Hamid rolled over on his back, bringing Heaven to rest on top of him. "I've wanted this for a long time."

He was serious. Heaven could see it in his eyes and wondered why he'd never asked, maybe the same reason she'd never asked him not to return to Pakistan. "What do you do when I'm not here?"

"Think of you," Hamid answered, and watched as his wife smiled.

"I'm serious." Hamid pinched her lightly. "All I do is think of you. Now, tell me what do you do at home when I'm not there?"

"Well, I work hard, I go to the blues club with my friends, I go out to eat, I shop, ouch…" Heaven laughed as Hamid bit her ear. "I miss you and I can hardly wait for the time to pass for you to return."

"We're going to have to change our arrangement. This long-distance marriage in which I see you one out of every four months isn't working."

"I know, Hamid, I agree. It isn't working."

"The words you said to the *Kazi*, why did you say that?"

Heaven had been wondering during the three days they'd been on their honeymoon when he would ask her that question. She was looking down at him as she toyed with the hair on his chest. "First, I didn't say the words to the *Kazi*, I said them to you."

"So we're going to fight over my choice of words?"

"*Nah*, to tell you the truth, Hamid, I don't know what made me say it. It's a passage from the Bible. It's from the book of Ruth. It's a story about love. It just popped in my head when I looked at you.

"I like it," he stared into her eyes. "Did you mean it?"

"I guess I did."

"So, my people are your people?"

"Yes."

"And my land, your land?"

"Yes."

"And whither I goest, you will go?" He felt Heaven's limbs tremble. "Is that part true also, Heaven? Will you go wherever I go?"

Heaven closed her eyes and thought about it, what saying the word 'yes' to her husband would mean, and what saying the word 'no' would mean. She felt a shiver that played down her spine. "Yes, Hamid, I will go wherever you go. At least for a season," she added and smiled.

"That wasn't in your vow, the season part."

"I know, but it's kind of what I'm doing now. I'm here for a season." She waited for him to ask her to stay for more than a season. She'd just given him her word.

Hamid kissed Heaven's eyes closed before bringing her head to rest on his chest. He didn't know what her answer would be if he asked her at this moment to stay. But he knew one thing-it wouldn't be fair.

"I love you," he said instead, and made love to her. More than a continent separated them, and they were both trying as hard as they knew how to make it work. Vows between them, vows they'd made to themselves and promises given to others, made them both a part of who they were. And it was what was keeping them apart.

Hamid knew how badly Heaven wanted her business, how she'd worked for it. He also knew it somehow involved her failed relationship with Brandon. She'd told him they were going to work together. Hamid knew that that hadn't happened. He'd never asked her what happened, but from the moment he'd met Heaven, she'd been obsessed with the idea of opening her registry. He couldn't ask her to give up her dream now that she held it in her hands.

As he plunged deeper and deeper into her body, the more certain he felt that she was his soul and he could not survive without her. He would not lie and say his vow to his father meant nothing. It would break his father's heart, and he didn't want to do it. But he was now Heaven's husband, though for the past year he'd not been acting like it. She was not some paramour that he visited for a month here and there. She was his wife. And his place was beside her.

"Whether thou goest, dear wife, I will go," he whispered softly. Then he pulled her closer as his orgasm overpowered him. Hamid meant his words to Heaven, the same as she'd meant hers to him.

CHAPTER FIFTEEN

"Heaven, I hate leaving you here all alone. I could really use your help down at the clinic."

"Did you want me to come here to work?" Heaven teased. She knew Hamid was a little disappointed that she didn't want to work alongside him. When he'd first mentioned it, images of what she'd planned for years came rushing back. She and Brandon, working side by side. That had been their dream, or at least hers. When he'd dumped her, Heaven's dream had changed. Her business was quite different and working in a clinic with Hamid would seem like retreating, going backwards. She didn't want to do that.

"I can't stay focused knowing that you're a short walk away." He shrugged and grinned. "I'm beginning to believe that maybe you didn't miss me as much as I missed you."

"That's not true. I missed you terribly." Just as Heaven started to defend her action, she realized her husband was teasing her.

"You're spending more time with my family than with me."

Now he had a certain tone in his voice that warned her he wasn't altogether teasing. "Isn't that what you wanted, for me to become part of your family?"

Hamid took a moment to answer. "It isn't quite what I had in mind. I would much prefer if we had our own home, but then I suppose for a few months it doesn't make much sense."

He heard a knock on the door, then his mother calling their names, warning him it was time for him to leave the house for work, telling Heaven it was time for the day's work to begin.

"*Nah*, Heaven, this is not what I had in mind."

Though Hamid was grateful to his family for giving them the guest quarters, which consisted of a bedroom, sitting room and private bath, the operative word was privacy. And they had very little of that.

Besides, this wasn't his Heaven, this quiet imitation. They hadn't fought in three weeks. There had really been no need to fight, but still if they were in America, they would have had a dozen fights by now. And they would have been followed by the most thrilling lovemaking, with Heaven screaming out his name over and over. Though they made love here, it wasn't with the wild abandon they were used to. They made love in whispers as though they didn't have the right. Pakistan was changing Heaven, and he had to get her back to America so she could change back. He turned to stare at her.

"You really like it here, don't you?"

"I like being with you."

"But you're not with me if you sit here in this house and I only get to see you for a few hours a day."

"Hamid, why don't you tell me what you want?"

Her voice was raised and Hamid smiled. "That's what I want. The fiery little spitfire that I met at Rush Presbyterian, the same woman I fell in love with. Since you've been in Pakistan…you're…you're too nice."

"Too nice? Are you crazy?"

To that Hamid could only laugh. Perhaps he was crazy. Why would any sane man complain that his wife was being nice, that she was getting along with his family? But when he thought again of their making up, he knew for sure he wasn't crazy. He pulled Heaven to him. "I guess I'm a little jealous that you seem content to spend so much time away from me."

"What if I bring you lunch and stay a couple of hours with you at the clinic?"

"Will you make the lunch yourself?"

"I'll try, if your mother will allow me."

"I only want it if it's prepared by your hands. You tell that to my mother." He kissed her then with all the passion that was in him.

"We're going to have to have another honeymoon. I need to hear you scream out my name." With the next bang on the door, he turned toward Heaven. "How would you feel if I found a house for us to rent for the remainder of your stay here?"

"Hamid, even I know they would be insulted."

"That wasn't my question. I asked how you would like it."

Heaven grinned. "I would love it."

"Hamid, Heaven," Ammi called.

"Consider it done." Hamid pulled Heaven out with him and they sat down for breakfast.

Heaven sat in Hamid's office dishing out the food for him. She saw him glancing at her and knew what he was thinking. She remembered when they were eating at the Indian restaurant in Woodridge and she refused to pick up the spoon to give him food. She'd come a long way.

"This smells good," Hamid commented.

"Believe me, I had to fight with your mother. First, she insisted that it was the servant's job to cook, and then she wanted to add curry and I wouldn't allow her. When I added the vegetables, she said I was ruining good meat."

"You and Ammi got into a fight?" Hamid paused from taking a bite.

"And Fatima, and Jana, and every other woman that was there. When they continued, I had your father take me to the market, and I bought food with my own money and made your lunch."

"I don't believe you did that."

"You said you wanted me to make it myself."

"*Nah*, I meant I don't believe you took on all the female members of my family in one battle." He bit into the beef and chicken stir-fry. *Welcome back*, he thought, and continued to shove food into his mouth.

Hamid was laughing at his father's retelling of the fight that had ensued at the house.

"You should have seen her, Hamid. All this time she's been as quiet as a little mouse. Then it happened. She told your mother and sisters that she wanted to make your lunch. At first, they were pleasant about it, telling Heaven that it wasn't necessary, that it was not her job to do the cooking, that the servants did that work. Your wife politely told them it wasn't the servants' job to cook for you, that it was hers."

"What happened after that?"

"They smiled at her and Ammi gave her permission to make your lunch. But that was when the real trouble started. All the women started trying to tell her what to make you and how to do it. There was yelling and screaming and your wife was like a little tornado. She told them, 'Fine, if you want to make that, you eat it. I'll cook my husband's lunch myself.' Then she asked me if I would drive her to the market."

Hamid was laughing. "I'll bet Ammi had something to say about that, Abba."

"I saw the way Ammi was looking at me, but I did not want to offend your new wife. I wanted to tell her that maybe it would be better to let your mother cook your food. But when I opened my mouth, her eyes shot liquid fire out at me. She said, 'If you don't want to drive me, then loan me your car.'"

"Abba."

"Of course not. I said, 'Heaven, you don't know the way.' And she said, 'That's what you think. Let me drive.' So I did, and she drove us to the market. I couldn't believe it. She's really something. She has fire."

"Is Ammi upset?"

"Oh yes, all the women are, but Heaven didn't seem to care. She was singing and laughing as if they didn't exist. And after she placed your lunch in a container to bring it to you, she gave them this smile that was like...I can't explain, except to say it was a victory smile. Before she left, she turned back and said, 'I made enough food for everyone.' With that, she went outside and asked Jhonni to drive her to your office. All the women stared after her when she was gone, and

Ammi hit me a couple of times for taking her to the market. At first, no one was willing to try the food Heaven made, but I took a plate and sampled it. It was very good."

"Did anyone else try it, Abba?"

"They all did. First, of course, Fatima. I think because she really likes Heaven. The last was Ammi, of course. She had to admit the food was very good."

"What did Ammi say?"

"She said, 'Not enough spice,' but I saw her go back in the pot for seconds. There was none left for Heaven when she returned."

"What did Heaven do?"

"She took food from the pot your mother made and ate it. Then she said, 'Too much curry,' and then she went and got a second helping." His father laughed. "Hamid, you married well. Not only do you have a woman who loves you and can cook well, but today she truly earned your mother's respect."

"Is Ammi still mad at Heaven?"

"Maybe just a little, but she likes Heaven, she'll get over it. Now I can see what you found so fascinating about your wife. She would keep a man on his toes. I'm surprised she fought with the women, she has been so...so..."

"So, not Heaven," Hamid laughed. "I asked her today where the real Heaven had been hiding. I told her that I missed her. I know she's been trying to make a good impression on all of you, but even when we're alone she seemed unsure, not herself."

"The fight was your fault then?"

"I only asked her to make me lunch. Actually, she offered. I didn't tell her to take on the entire family." Hamid laughed. "But I do love the fire in her eyes."

"You're very much in love with her, aren't you?"

For a second Hamid was stunned. He'd thought his father understood that. It was then he realized that for the past year his father had only had Hamid's word to go on. It was wrong that they had never met their new daughter until recently.

Hamid smiled at his father. "Yes, Abba, I love her very much." He held his father's gaze. "I can't continue the way we've been living—her in America, me here. I'm her husband. I made a vow to be that to her. I made the vow twice." His father and he held glances for a long moment.

"I'll see you later, Hamid. I think I should go back to the house in case the women need to be refereed."

Hamid watched his father leave, knowing that neither of them wanted to have the necessary talk, and knowing he would put it off as long as possible. Heaven would be leaving Pakistan in another two months, and Hamid planned to leave with her. He would have to tell his father before they left for America that he was not coming back, at least not to work in the clinic.

"Dr. Hamid, we need you," Dr. Youseff called. Hamid groaned. Right now he didn't have the luxury of worrying. He had patients to take care of. Patients with no money needed him.

The heaviness in his heart grew as he dialed the phone. There was at least one thing he could give Heaven here in his homeland. He would return their passion and bring it back to their bed where it belonged. His goal accomplished, he walked into the exam room and apologized to Dr. Youseff.

Hours later Hamid sat in the sitting room of his family home with his arm around Heaven. He'd seen his mother look disapprovingly at him a couple of times but he didn't remove his arm. Heaven was his wife.

"I have a surprise for you," he whispered. "I rented us a house."

"A house? Why?" she asked.

This wasn't what he'd expected. He'd thought he would see a smile spread across her face.

"Why now, Hamid?" Heaven repeated. "Does your family want us to leave?"

"*Nah*, it's not that. I thought you'd like some privacy. We talked about it this morning. Aren't you tired of the knock on the door each morning?"

"I find it amusing."

He whispered in her ear, "What about us?" She blinked. "I want to make love to you without either of us worrying about the noise." She laughed. "I thought you promised that where I go you would go also." Heaven sobered. Hamid smiled.

"They're going to think it's because of what happened this morning."

"Are you going back on your marriage vows so quickly?" Hamid laughed. "Don't worry, Heaven, I will take the heat for this one."

Before Heaven could persuade him to wait, Hamid called out to his parents. "Abba, Ammi, I have an announcement. Heaven and I will be moving into a rental home. We need our privacy." He saw his mother's eyes, and then he glanced at his father and knew he understood.

"If it's okay I would like to come in the mornings and visit."

"I'm sorry, Heaven," Hamid interrupted. "I want you to come to the clinic with me."

"Hamid, I'm not going to stay with you all day while you work."

"Then you can help me. You're a nurse, there's enough work for both of us."

"I haven't worked as a nurse in over a year."

"But you're still a nurse. You haven't forgotten your training."

"I didn't come here to work in your clinic."

"*Nah*, you came to be with me, not to spend all of your hours with my mother in the kitchen." He was pushing her with his words, he saw her eyes dart to his mother and Heaven blinked. A sparkle appeared in her eyes.

"You're my husband, Hamid, not my father. You don't give me orders."

"*Nah*, I'm making you remember. Where I go, you will go, and I'm going tonight. A husband takes his wife to his home, not the home of his parents. Tonight we go to our home. Now pack some things, just a few, and tomorrow we will have Jhonni bring the rest." He gave Heaven a stern look. "Now."

Heaven turned to look at the family, then back to Hamid and again to the family. "I'm sorry, but we have to leave tonight. Please forgive us. I want to thank you for welcoming me into the family. I've enjoyed being with you. Don't worry, we will have you over and we will come to visit."

"Heaven," Hamid said, "we need to leave."

Heaven exhaled before turning to Hamid. "Yes, my lord." Then she went and packed, trying to hold back the giggle that threaten to erupt. She tamped it down as she kissed the family and even after she got into the car. She didn't let loose until they had been in the car for five minutes. Then and only then did Heaven start laughing.

"Hamid, what got into you, what made you do this?"

"You did. Today I saw a glimpse of my true wife, and I wasn't going to lose her to a kitchen or shopping. I'm being selfish, I know, but I've missed you far too much to only see you a few hours a day. I was serious about you coming to the clinic with me. You don't have to work if you don't want to, but I would love it if you were just…just there, so that when I have a difficult patient I can come into the office and kiss you after, or just kiss you anyway. What do you think?"

"Every day?"

Hamid looked sideways at Heaven. "What, do you have a better offer?"

She grinned. "No better offer, but what if I want to sleep late? You're getting up before dawn to work."

"Aren't you going to make my breakfast each morning?"

"I wasn't planning on it."

"Hmm, maybe I moved too quickly. Perhaps we should have stayed in my parents' home." He laughed and reached his hand over to Heaven.

When they arrived at the house, something popped in Hamid's chest. This was a new beginning for them. This was the first home he'd provided. In America, they lived in Heaven's apartment. The three weeks she'd been in Pakistan, they'd lived with his parents. Now he was the provider. And he felt a surge of pride, then a hope, that his wife would like it.

He opened the car door and swept Heaven up into his arms. "Welcome to our new home, Mrs. Ahmad."

Heaven smiled, comfortable in her husband's arms. She'd not known they needed this, or that she'd ever wanted to be the kind of woman that expected to be carried over a threshold, but she found she was. She didn't know if Hamid understood the custom, but decided it didn't matter. He was doing it. She'd heard the slight hesitation in his voice and for the first time in their year of marriage, she thought about the fact that their apartment was really hers. Very little there belonged to Hamid, with the exception of his clothes.

Waiting for Hamid to put her down seemed an act of futility. He seemed perfectly content to keep her in his arms as he carried her from room to room. She heard his breath deepening as he headed for the bedroom. Then and only then did he put her down.

"Tonight we get to live my dream."

Heaven eyed the bed. "And exactly what dream is that?" She couldn't help laughing when he grinned, showing off his perfect white teeth. Her heart swelled with love for him. "Hamid, can we afford this?"

"My family is quite wealthy. Haven't you noticed?"

"I've noticed, but that has nothing to do with us. We're adults. We take care of our bills, not your family. This place is like a palace, so you'll have to forgive me for wondering if we can afford this."

"Trust me, Heaven."

She watched as he went into the closet and brought out something rolled. She looked again. A mattress, she realized in surprise. Then she watched as he pulled back the heavy drapes with the ripcord and carried the mattress out onto the enclosed alcove.

"This is beautiful," Heaven said, admiring what was the American equivalent of a patio.

"Come on," Hamid urged, his voice husky.

Shivers traveled up and down Heaven's spine at the thought of what Hamid meant to do. Of course, she should have known he wanted to make love under the stars, literally. She'd thought he'd meant the stars that could be seen through the glass set into the ceiling of his bedroom. But no, not Hamid, she should have known.

"We can't do this, someone will see us."

"I think we can do this," Hamid answered from the doorway. He spread the mattress and returned and scooped Heaven into his arms. "I have everything ready."

"You're crazy."

"I don't deny that."

"What if someone sees us?"

"Then I say we'd better be good at what we do."

"Hamid." Heaven smiled, for some reason feeling embarrassed, yet at the same time as giddy as a new bride on her wedding night. She'd made the right decision to follow her husband. Somehow, this felt like the first night of their married life together. Heat rushed through her body, flushing her skin. "This is nice," she whispered.

His eyes bore into hers. And then his lips found hers and kissed her until she was breathless with desire. "Do you feel it, Heaven?" he asked.

"I feel it," she answered, knowing exactly what he meant. This night was somehow the beginning of their marriage, or maybe just a turning point. She didn't know how but she did feel it.

"Look up, Heaven."

She did, amazed at the brightness of the night, of the millions of stars twinkling overhead. She suddenly was overcome by the fragrance of flowers. She took in a breath filled with the perfumed air. It was only then she noticed that the entire alcove was covered in flowers, beautiful and fragrant flowers. She spotted a small table and a champagne bucket and smiled.

"How did you know I would go along with this?"

"Because of your vow, Heaven. I knew you meant the words when you said them. Besides, if you had not come along willingly, I would have thrown you over my shoulder and brought you here by force." He smiled. "Want some champagne?"

Heaven smiled back as Hamid lifted the bottle of non-alcoholic champagne and filled their glasses.

A bright light woke Heaven from her dream of her dark-skinned prince, with lashes so long they touched his cheek, and hair so black someone should invent a new word for the color.

She moaned, wanting to return to the dream of the prince making love to her, slowly, tenderly and lovingly. He kissed every inch of her body, dipped her toe in his champagne glass, and then slid her toe into his mouth. She'd squealed at that and had felt deliciously wicked, refusing to kiss him until he sipped from her glass, telling him he needed to sterilize his mouth. He'd looked at her and said, 'There, is that better?' They'd made love for hours, laughing and talking and making love some more. And she'd fallen asleep in his arms. Now this light was shining on her, annoying her and bringing her back to reality.

Then she felt his body, naked and warm against her. She felt his flesh, hard and firm, pressed against her rear. It hadn't been a dream. She peeked out of one eye. She should have known the sun was up and shining brightly down on them. She attempted to move and Hamid pulled her even closer than she'd been.

"I thought you were asleep," she whispered.

"I was. I was dreaming of making love to this beautiful American princess with the wild hair. And I was dreaming she was kissing me all over, and that she took me in her mouth. I left my body for a moment and joined the stars that shine over Pakistan. And I thought, surely that must be a dream because in a year of marriage my American princess has never before done that. Then I drifted back off to sleep and I thought I could feel her pressed against my erection. I could smell her, the lemony mango scent. And I could smell the scent of love. Then you moved and I knew it was not a dream. Was it?"

"It was not a dream." Heaven's head settled on his chest.

"Did you dream?" he asked.

"Almost the same dream, only in mine, there was a prince."

"Tell me what he did."

"Well, his fingers were hot and all over my body."

"Like this?" Hamid asked, touching her. Feeling her jump slightly he chuckled deep in his throat.

"Yes, just like that."

"Then what?"

"He turned me over on my back."

"Like this?" Hamid asked, moving away from her body and shifting her just the tiniest bit.

"Yes, like that."

"Then what?"

"He suckled my breasts."

"Oh, let's see." Hamid's head bent over Heaven and his tongue found her nipples hard.

"In your dream were your nipples hard?"

"I don't remember. Are they now?"

"Yes." He suckled both breasts repeatedly until he thought he felt a shudder in his wife's body.

"What did your prince do next?" He looked down at Heaven's glazed eyes. "Tell me, wife, what did your prince do next?"

"He kissed me."

"Where?"

"I'm not telling," Heaven laughed.

"I can't have a man in your dreams doing things that I want to do." Then he began his descent, kissing her wildly.

"Anything else?"

"His hands traveled my body as he kissed me."

Hamid laughed. "Forgive me, my princess if I didn't do all that the man of your dream did. I'll remedy that immediately." He caressed her, feeling her brown skin heat with his ministrations. He kissed his way down to her belly, blew a breath of air into her navel, and stopped abruptly.

"Was there anything else he did, Heaven?" He waited a nanosecond, then an eternity, wondering if she would tell him what she wanted, what he knew she needed. "What did he do next, Heaven?"

"He tasted me."

"Tasted you where?"

"A little lower than you are."

He stayed just above where he knew she wanted him to be. "Is this where he kissed you, Heaven?"

She moaned and he smiled. "You need to tell me what he did."

"He kissed me between my legs."

"Ah, let me see if I can reenact it." Hamid placed a tiny kiss on her entrance.

"Like that?" he asked.

"Not quite."

"Then tell me, what did he do?"

"Hamid."

"Heaven, I don't know unless you tell me."

"He didn't do it nearly as quickly as you just did. He lingered, as though he enjoyed what he was doing. What can I say? Later when he kissed me, he tasted like...me."

"Ahh, so he didn't just kiss you?"

"In a way, but it was more of a French kiss."

"And exactly what is a French kiss?"

"He used his tongue." Heaven could barely get the words out.

"I see," Hamid answered, running his fingers over her body. "Would you like for me to do that also, dear wife?"

"Hamid," Heaven groaned.

"I didn't understand your response. You must tell me what you want."

"I want it." Heaven groaned again, more urgently.

"You want what? Tell me exactly what you want."

"I want you to French kiss me there."

He did and Heaven felt desire shoot through her and opened her eyes to the bright sun. This was her prince, her husband. How could she ever go back to living months at a time without him? How could she give up her home, America, and everything that meant? She thought of her business. She'd worked so hard to have it. She needed to have something of her own. Once more unwanted thoughts of Brandon popped into her head. She couldn't allow Hamid's dream to become her own.

A moan escaped her lips. But she also couldn't continue living apart from her husband. They would have to find a better compromise. Then she quit thinking altogether and gave herself over completely to the orgasm that was claming her, knowing that in a few minutes she would become Hamid's dream princess. And she would make sure he enjoyed it as much as she was enjoying having her dream come a reality.

CHAPTER SIXTEEN

When breakfast was placed on the table, Hamid looked up and saw Heaven entering the room. "It looks like you waited until I was done to come out. That was awfully convenient." He was grinning as he took in her jeans and top. "Are you going somewhere? I thought you wanted to lie in bed all day?"

"I have other plans."

"Such as?" he asked, hope surging in his chest. "Are you planning to visit my mother?"

"*Nah.*"

"Going shopping?"

"*Nah.*"

"Are you going to hire help to do the cooking and cleaning?"

"I don't think we need any help, especially if you plan on continuing the practice of making love under the stars." She grinned. "Do you?"

"I do."

"In that case we definitely can't have anyone else here with us."

"I agree. Now tell me where you are going."

"I'm going to the clinic with you."

Hamid tried to stop the grin but he couldn't. It spread over his face and seemed to envelope his entire body. He could swear his skin was bursting apart at the seams, grinning.

"You're looking very cocky, as if you knew this would happen."

"With you, Heaven, one never knows. I'm just happy that you're coming with me."

"Is this also one of your dreams?"

He grinned and kissed her. "One of my minor dreams maybe, but the other dreams, they've been fulfilled."

"So you don't want to repeat them?"

Hamid swatted her lightly on the behind. "What do you think? Now eat up. If we're going to the clinic we have to be there to open in an hour. When we're done I'll take you to the market to stock up on food."

Heaven dumped the bag of books on the desk in Hamid's office, glad she'd brought all of them with her. If she stayed in his office and read, she would not be what she'd planned to be with Brandon. She would be merely Hamid's wife waiting for him, reading. She wouldn't be trading in her dream for his.

She looked at the title of the books she'd brought with her, *Kite Runner* by Khaled Hosseini, *In My Heart* by Melody Thomas and *In My Bedroom* by Donna Hill. She was familiar with Donna Hill and Melody Thomas's work and loved both of their voices. Khaled she didn't know, but the book had been highly recommended, so she picked that one up, deciding to read it first. By the second page, she was totally hooked.

Two hours later Hamid poked his head in the door and Heaven barely looked up.

"How soon they forget." Hamid looked down at Heaven cuddled in the huge chair in his office and smiled.

"What?"

His laughter broke her concentration and she blinked rapidly. "I'm sorry, what did you say?" Heaven laid the book spine open across her chest.

"I said, how soon they forget."

She frowned.

"I fulfilled the things your dream prince did, and now you don't even remember. I'm wounded, Heaven. Surely the things I did, the things I made you feel should linger in your mind for a few hours." He grinned and took the book from her chest. "It must be very good," he said.

"It is. I think it's going to turn out to be the best book I've read in a long, long time."

"You're not getting bored in here?"

"Meaning, do I want to come out and help?"

"I've never seen you be a nurse, I mean at your job. Maybe you're not any good."

"Maybe you're not a good doctor."

"There's only one way to find out. Of course if you don't think you can handle it…" He laid her book back in the position he'd found it and walked out the door, grinning.

Heaven shook her head and smiled, noting the page number. As good as the book was, Hamid had issued her a challenge, one that he'd undoubtedly known she would not pass up. What would it hurt, she thought, if she just observed him for a little while? She could watch him and think of him fulfilling her fantasies.

Heaven opened the door and laughed when she spotted Hamid standing there like a sentinel waiting for her. "You think you know me, don't you?"

"Not well enough," he said, taking her hand and pulling her toward an examination room. He introduced her to the patient. "This is my wife. She's a nurse."

From patient to patient, Heaven followed Hamid, feeling pride in the way he talked with the patients. Even though he spoke in Urdu instead of English, she could tell he was gentle. For a moment she missed working, but pushed the feeling away.

"Dr. Ahmad, could you try to take a patient's blood for me?"

Heaven's eyes swung to the nurse who'd entered the room, then back to Hamid.

"Can't this wait?" Hamid asked, without taking his attention from the patient.

"It's Mrs. Chaudhry. We've tried to get her in here for two months. She hates needles. I've stuck her four times, and she's angry."

Heaven studied the nurse's face. When their gazes connected, the nurse looked away and her head dropped in embarrassment.

"I can't leave now. Tell her to wait until I'm done."

"She's getting ready to leave, I can't keep her here," the nurse answered softly, and Heaven knew the woman hated admitting she couldn't draw the blood.

"Then she will have to leave." Hamid finally turned from the patient. "I'm busy, as you can see."

"I'll do it." The words popped from Heaven's mouth before she could bring them back.

"What?"

"Hamid, if you'd like me to try, I will."

His eyes lit up and the look of gratitude was worth more than…she didn't know, but it was definitely the look of a man ready to fulfill another fantasy.

The nurse exchanged looks with Hamid before looking at Heaven. "What's wrong?" Heaven asked.

"The patient doesn't speak English," the nurse answered.

"That doesn't matter." Heaven smiled. "I've taken care of many patients that didn't speak English. We got along just fine. Don't worry, you'll see. By the way, I haven't met you before. My name is Heaven, what's yours?"

"I'm Saddia."

"It's nice to meet you." Then Heaven followed Saddia out the door.

"Don't be upset if she doesn't allow you to touch her."

Heaven smiled at Saddia. That was Heaven's least worry; she had a way with patients. "Hello, Mrs. Chaudhry," she said, pasting on her biggest smile as she followed Saddia into the room where the elderly woman was struggling against her daughter's efforts to keep her in the room. Heaven grinned even wider as the woman said something and eyed her suspiciously.

"*Nah, nah,*" Heaven answered, not knowing what the woman had said, but knowing she needed to say no.

Heaven sat on the stool and waved her hand toward the woman offering her the chair. The woman pointed to her hair and Heaven laughed and touched her twists. The woman frowned and Heaven scrunched her own face up. "Ouch," she said, and pinched her skin. "Ouch." She pinched her skin again, then laughed. Mrs. Chaudhry laughed too.

"It hurt?"

"Yes," Heaven replied, opening her arms wide to show just how much. Then she tilted her head to the side. "It hurt?" She pointed at the patient's arms and saw fear begin to creep back into the patient's eyes, replacing the earlier laughter.

"*Nah, nah,*" Heaven said. She put her arm across her chest and shook her head. "I won't hurt you," she said, and shook her head again. "I won't hurt you." She patted the woman's shoulder. "Ouch," Heaven said softly. "*Nah, nah.*" She laughed at the way she was butchering the language, but she could see a glimmer of trust in the patient's eyes.

"Please?" Heaven asked for permission and held up one finger, allowing her facial expression and gestures to convey her words. "One time." She shook her head again. "One time." She knew Mrs. Chaudhry understood her. Then Heaven opened an alcohol swab and gently rubbed the patient's skin and began palpating for a vein. When she found one, she smiled. She put on her gloves, rubbed the skin once more with the alcohol swab, and put the needle into the vacotainer. Again, she palpated, then eased the needle gently down.

Before she inserted it, Heaven smiled. She knew the problem. The patient had rolling veins. Heaven shook her head up and down and smiled again at the woman. "One time," she said again. This time when she palpated she kept a finger over the vein and inserted the needle. She pushed the tube inside the vacutainer and watched the dark red blood fill the tube.

She looked at Saddia. "How much do you need?" The nurse hesitated and said, "Three more."

"Give me the tubes," Heaven said softly as she filled one after the other and handed them over to Saddia. She eased the needle from the vein, applied a cotton ball, and kept Mrs. Chaudhry's arm outstretched while she applied gentle pressure.

"Your vein," Heaven said, "it ran." She worked her fingers in a running motion and laughed. She watched as Mrs. Chaudhry's daughter explained what happened and saw understanding in the patient's smile.

Heaven pointed to the woman and touched her hair. She waved her hands between the two. "Would you like?" Heaven asked.

"*Nah, nah,*" was the quick reply. Heaven laughed, patted Mrs. Chaudhry on the shoulder again, and said goodbye. Her gaze connected with Hamid. She hadn't known he'd come into the room. Her concentration had been on the patient. She tilted her head slightly and looked at him for several seconds before walking toward him.

"You were wonderful," Hamid said softly, in amazement.

"In exactly what way?"

"With Mrs. Chaudhry. You had her trusting you, eating out of the palm of your hand and," he looked at Heaven in amazement, "you did it without even speaking the language."

Heaven put her hands on her hips and looked her husband in the eye. "Honey, there is one universal language that I speak and it's called compassion, love, understanding. Take your pick. We all speak it." She sashayed away, went back into Hamid's office, picked up *The Kite Runner*, and began reading. Within seconds, the nurse had returned.

"Thank you, Mrs. Ahmad, you were wonderful. Do you think you could help out some more? We're really swamped and could use the extra hands. Two of the staff didn't come in today."

Yes was on the tip of her tongue but she'd told her husband no. How could she possibly say yes to someone else? Heaven licked her lips and sucked in her desire to help. "I don't think so," she answered instead.

Hamid stood just outside the door to his office waiting as Saddia came out alone. He was disappointed.

"What did she say?" he asked.

Saddia shrugged her shoulders. "She said no."

Hamid tried to tell himself that it was okay. Heaven had not come to the clinic to work, but to be with him. She'd already helped, and now she was reading her book. He should be grateful that she'd drawn Mrs. Chaudhry's blood. Now he had a new dream, one he'd not known he'd wanted, not until this moment. But it was a real dream that was taking root. He wanted to work with his wife as a team.

"She did look as if she wanted to say yes, for just a moment anyway," Saddia said as she hurried away. Then Hamid walked into the office. He circled Heaven with his arms. "You smell good," he whispered softly.

"And you smell sweaty." She pulled back and looked into his eyes. "You're tired."

"Yes, it's so busy here today. Too many patients not enough..." He stopped. He was using blackmail, and they both knew it.

"Not enough help," Heaven finished for him. He rewarded her with a smile.

"No, not enough help," Hamid answered truthfully.

"Would you like me to help, just for today, Hamid? Today only?" He kissed her, and kissed her again and Heaven grinned. "I don't have a uniform."

"You don't need one. We just need your skills." He looked in his closet, came back with a lab coat of his, and put it on her, laughing as it almost brushed the floor. "That'll do nicely, my princess," he said, "let's go to work."

Hour after hour Hamid and Heaven worked, stopping once for a thirty-minute lunch and once for a ten-minute break. By the time they were done and on their way home, Heaven was too tired to think of making love or anything else. "Aren't there any fast food places?" she asked.

"Pizza Hut and Kentucky Fried Chicken."

"Good, we can get both. I'm too tired to go to the market, and too tired to cook." She lay against the cushions of the car. "Do you work like this every day?" she asked.

"Every day, and if we were open longer, we'd still be working."

"How can you do it?"

"It needs doing."

"How did you have energy to…spend time with me?"

"If you're asking how I find the energy to make love to you, then that's easy. I will always have the energy to love you. How about you?"

"I'm much too tired."

"Even if I bathe you?"

"I don't care what you do tonight, Hamid. I'm too tired."

"Are you saying the honeymoon is over, that you're refusing me for the first time?"

"Put it like this. You can do what you want. I won't be participating. I'm tired."

He surprised her when he laughed. "Doing it without you isn't any fun." He pulled into the parking lot for the pizza. "I'll guess we'll wait," he grinned.

"It seems you gave up a little too quickly."

"You said you were tired."

"And you said you were going to bathe me. I'll make you a deal. Feed me first, and then bathe me, and maybe that will revive me."

Hamid kissed Heaven under the stars after having made love to her. "I think we may have found our own custom, your working by my side, my feeding and bathing you and then our making love under the stars. What do you think of doing this every night?"

"Hamid, I don't think I will ever be too tired to enjoy our own special custom," Heaven said, and readied herself once again to receive him.

The weeks were passing quickly since Heaven had begun helping Hamid at the clinic. In three weeks, she would be returning home to America. And part of her was glad. She couldn't say she wasn't enjoying the work, but somewhere in the back of her mind, the worry hung about her like a mist. She was once again living on the fringes of the dreams of a man she loved. She'd thought more than once of remaining in Pakistan with Hamid for more than the agreed on three months. She'd found herself wanting to help Hamid fulfill his vow to his family and that, more than anything, worried Heaven the most. She needed to return home to her own business before she lost herself completely in Hamid's vow.

Heaven waited at the front of the clinic while Hamid did a last check. Tonight she really was tired. She didn't know if even Hamid's bathing her would revive her.

"You're looking worn out," Hamid said joining her.

"I am."

"Too tired for our custom?"

"I don't want to be, Hamid, but I am pretty tired."

Hamid couldn't believe it an hour later when he scooped Heaven from the tub and into his arms. She really was tired. She'd fallen asleep in the tub while he bathed her. He couldn't believe it. For the first time since they'd moved into the rented house, Hamid placed Heaven in the bed. And for the first time they would not sleep outside under the stars, they would not make love. He curled his body around hers, feeling tired himself.

If Heaven thought the past weeks had been hectic, she didn't have the words to describe what that day had brought. Hamid was impatient; something she rarely saw in him. She tried to put it down to the fact that for the past two nights, they'd not made love and he was a bit grumpy. She intended to take care of that when they returned home-if they returned home.

If she didn't know better she would think Hamid was hiring someone to bring the patients in. They never stopped coming. The entire staff was overworked. Heaven had just taken a couple of minutes to get off her feet when Saddia had come looking for her to do an EKG. Sighing and putting her shoes back on, Heaven went to take care of the patient.

"Heaven," Hamid shouted.

Heaven looked toward the door. If her husband didn't stop shouting at her like that, she wasn't so sure she'd be in the mood to make him feel better. She smiled down at the patient.

The leads were firmly in place when Heaven turned the EKG machine on. She was in the process of attempting to explain the procedure again and to tell the patient to remain still, when she heard Hamid's raised voice again and wondered what was wrong.

"Heaven, I need you out here, stat."

"I'm in the middle of an EKG," she yelled back, deciding to ignore the annoyance in his voice.

"I said stat. Do you understand what that means?"

Heaven looked down at the patient. "I understand that I'm busy," she shouted back.

"I said stat!"

Heaven glanced toward the now open door and glared at Hamid. "I understand that you'd better not talk to me in that tone of voice." She smiled at the patient, hoping he'd not noticed the tension, glad that he spoke little English.

Hamid stared back at her. She watched while he rubbed his hand across his face and shook his head as though he were coming out of a fog. "I'm sorry," he said. "As soon as you're done, will you come and help Saddia? She has about fifty kids out here that need injections."

Before Heaven could even tell him yes, he was gone. Her feelings were a bit hurt, but she understood. He was tired. They were all tired. They'd worked ten fifteen-hour days in a row. And that was the reason Heaven would be glad when she hopped aboard a jet and returned home.

When the last shot had been given, Hamid gave her a look that might have been another apology or might have meant he was just plain tired.

"Hamid, why are we working like this?"

"I don't have a choice. We're leaving in less than three weeks. I have to make sure I take care of as many things as I can."

"But you're behaving as if you're never coming back." She glanced at him. "Hamid, do you hate returning to the States with me?"

"Of course not."

"Then I don't understand why you're working like this. It's as though you're attempting to put in enough work to make up for the month you'll be gone. You can't do that or you'll get sick. We all will. It's probably why your staff calls in so often or just fails to show. You're working everyone too hard."

He looked at her. He'd not told her yet that he wasn't returning to Pakistan. He guessed maybe she was right. Maybe he was trying to work off his guilt for not returning. "Let's go home," he said quietly and began turning off the lights.

When they were home, they showered together. Neither wanted to eat, but in bed they turned toward each other and made love, each desperate to wipe out the harshness that had come between them. This would all be over soon, Hamid thought, but in a few hours, it was worse.

The morning started out with a thousand things going wrong. Everyone was giving a hundred and fifty percent, but it wasn't nearly enough. No matter how he looked at it, there were too many patients for them to handle. While he was grateful for Heaven's help, it still was only a drop in the bucket. He was trying to remember his gratitude when he called Heaven for the tenth time. She was spending way too much time with a group of children, talking with them, playing with them, when he needed her to move.

"Heaven, let those kids go, and get over here," he yelled. "I need you to draw blood on Mr. Singh, and then do an EKG on Mr. Meah. I need a urinalysis on room two and a throat culture on room five."

When she just stared at him, Hamid saw the warning sign for a blowup. But he didn't heed it. He needed the work done. "Heaven, now," he screamed even louder. "We don't have all day."

"You might not, Hamid, but I do. I'm not your employee, I'm your wife." She threw the lab coat at him and walked out the door, ignoring the nurse begging her not to leave. Heaven knew her leaving would make it harder on everyone else, but she wasn't going to ignore Hamid's foul mood. She'd never seen such a display of temper from him in all the time they'd been married.

Suddenly a wave of homesickness washed over her. She wanted to go home now, not in three weeks. She missed Chicago, she missed her friends, and she missed leisure time. She began walking down the same road they drove, wondering if she would remember every turn and find the right house. Tears began seeping beneath her lashes.

"Heaven."

She heard Hamid calling her, heard his footsteps running over the gravel but she didn't stop, nor did she turn around. Within moments, he'd caught up with her.

"Heaven, forgive me please."

"No," she said. "You asked for my help, Hamid, but I don't like being talked to like that. You've never talked to me like that. I'm leaving."

"You don't even know how to get back. You might get lost. Where are you going?"

"I'm going home, Hamid."

"You don't know the way."

"Home, Hamid, back to America, back to Chicago. I've had enough." She burst into tears and began sobbing.

For one brief panic-stricken moment, Hamid stared helplessly at his wife as she stood in the middle of the road and cried. Then he caught her up in his arms. Damn what anyone thought. "Heaven, don't cry," he soothed. "We're leaving in three weeks."

"I'm leaving tonight."

"Please, Heaven, don't leave without me, please. I'm sorry. I'm so sorry. You don't have to work anymore, you don't have to come to the clinic again."

He was holding her, her sobs breaking his heart. This wasn't how Heaven handled things, not with tears. She fought back. She only cried when she was hurting, when she was missing him, he thought. Damn.

"I thought you were so busy. Why are you out here with me? Why aren't you in the clinic?" Heaven attempted to push away. "You never touch me in public, why now?"

"I'm out here with you because nothing is as important to me as you are, nothing. And I had no right to talk to you in that manner. I promise I will never do it again."

"You promised that yesterday, and today you were even worse." Heaven glared at him. "Your promises are worthless, Hamid."

He stared at her. She didn't know how right she was. His promises *were* worthless. He swallowed. No matter what his reasons for being driven, he truly regretted taking it out on Heaven. "This promise I will keep. I will not yell at you again."

"I know you're not, because I'm going home," Heaven stubbornly insisted. "You stay here, Hamid. This is your dream, not mine." She turned and pointed toward the clinic.

"You're my dream, Heaven, that's my vow. I asked you over a year ago to tell me to give it up. And you didn't. That's why I keep returning."

"Then maybe you should think about just staying here." Heaven pulled away from him and began walking again, not surprised when a few seconds later the car pulled alongside her and he was asking her to get in.

"Please, Heaven. If you allow me to take you home I can return and help at the clinic."

She glared at him but got in. It was bad enough that she'd left the others with all the work. Hamid shouldn't leave as well, not because of her.

All the way home, Heaven refused to speak to Hamid. The moment she was in the door, she pulled her stored luggage from the closet and began throwing her clothes in it.

"Heaven, don't. Just give me until tonight, just until tonight."

She started sobbing again. This time Heaven began to worry about herself. She didn't cry like this when she was angry. She should be telling Hamid where to go, not bawling like a baby.

"Heaven, don't you think you're being a little overly emotional?" Her reaction was worrying him. There was something out of sync. This was not Heaven. And then it hit him.

"Heaven, I'm not trying to fight with you, but I want to say something. Just think about it, okay? You don't usually cry, Heaven, not when we fight."

For a nanosecond, neither of them breathed. Then Heaven brought her head up. The tears were still streaming down her cheeks, but she had ceased sobbing.

"I'm just tired."

"No, Heaven, that's not it. Think about it."

"How can you tell me what's wrong? It's my body."

"Remember a few nights ago your breasts were tender?"

"So?"

"Heaven."

She looked at him, understanding dawning when he smiled, but she didn't smile back.

Hamid mentally calculated. "Heaven, you've been in Pakistan for two and a half months, but you've had only one cycle. I think you're…"

"*Nah*," Heaven whispered, reverting back to using Urdu.

"Yes."

"*Nah*," Heaven repeated. "I'm not." But she stopped crying and ran for her calendar. Hamid was right; it had been almost seven weeks. She was way overdue. He didn't give her a chance to say it. He grabbed the calendar from her hand and began flipping the pages, counting the weeks.

"You're pregnant," he whispered softly.

Heaven stared back at him in disbelief. His eyes had such a look of wonder that she didn't know how to tell him that if she were, she didn't know if she shared in his excitement. She didn't want to raise a baby with Hamid leaving her for three months at a time.

"Heaven, you're not happy about this. Why?"

"I want to go home, Hamid. I can't do this. I can't live like this, me in one place and you in another. I don't want to work in the clinic with you being the doctor and me being your nurse. I had that dream once. I don't have it anymore."

Words that had nothing to do with the baby were tumbling out of her mouth. She wanted to make herself stop talking. She could see Hamid's happiness was draining away.

"I don't understand. What dream? You told me your dream was to have your own business." He stopped again. He knew the answer to his question.

"Your dream was to work with Brandon?" He frowned, careful to keep his voice calm regardless of how this was killing him. "And you can't...you don't want to work with me because of him? You're my wife and you can't work with me? Is that why you're not excited that we're having a baby? Did you also dream of having babies with Brandon?"

Hamid had to calm himself. He'd made a promise to Heaven that he wouldn't break. He licked his lips and took in a deep breath, trying hard not to allow his pain to show. He was concerned now with Heaven.

"Let me say this and you can correct me if I'm wrong. You wanted a baby with Brandon, and now you're stuck with having mine. Is that what's bothering you?"

Heaven's hand shot out to slap her husband, but he caught her hand in his and kissed it.

"No hitting, Heaven."

"You're wrong," she said.

"I'm not wrong that you don't want this baby."

"We don't even know for sure that I'm pregnant."

"I'm a doctor, you're a nurse. You're seven weeks late. It's easy to do the math. We know, Heaven."

"Not for sure," Heaven repeated.

"Still, that doesn't answer my question. Why are you not happy?"

"Because, Hamid, you're coming back to Chicago for only a month. I don't want to raise a baby by myself." She ran into the bedroom and locked the door. "Give me time to think, Hamid. I'm tired, let me rest." She could almost feel his body pressing against the door. She knew her husband and knew the idea of leaving her alone in the bedroom wasn't going over too well. Hamid was a fixer. He wanted to fix the problem.

"Heaven, let me in."

"Go back to the clinic. They need you there."

When he didn't answer, Heaven knew Hamid was thinking she would take off. "I'll be here when you get home, Hamid."

"Do you promise?"

"*Nah*, I don't promise." Then Heaven lay on the bed, closed her eyes, and went to sleep.

CHAPTER SEVENTEEN

Hamid stared at the closed door, wanting to comfort his wife, who wouldn't need comforting if he had not yelled at her. This was enough. What good would it do to work away his guilt at leaving the clinic to be with his wife if he were going to kill his wife's love in the process? Not one bit. It was time he told his wife the truth, the reason for his sudden craziness. And he would. Soon.

Heaven was right. He needed to return to the clinic, but first he had another stop to make. He had to say what needed saying. They were having a baby. He smiled at the thought. Heaven would come around once he revealed to her that he would never leave her again. Then she would be as happy as he was.

For now, Hamid would put aside his hurt feelings. She loved him, not Brandon. He'd never had any doubts about that. And he would not allow doubt to creep in now. As for everything else, he put it down to her just being tired.

In fifteen minutes, Hamid was walking in the door of his parents' home and calling to his father. He kissed his mother and his sister Fatima, hugged them briefly, and continued out to the back gardens. He kissed his father's cheeks, embracing him as he did so.

"There is a very strong possibility that Heaven might be pregnant." Hamid watched as his father's eyes sparkled with joy.

"Are you happy?" his father asked.

"You can't imagine how happy I am, Abba."

"And Heaven. Is she happy?"

"Heaven's tired. We've been working very hard at the clinic."

"She's not happy?"

Hamid shrugged. "She will be. Right now, she's angry with me. I've been trying to get as much done as I could before it's time to leave. I've been yelling at everyone. I yelled at Heaven and she walked out of the clinic." He shrugged his shoulder. "My wife fights when she's angry, Abba. Once she gets over being angry she will be happy."

"Are you sure?"

"I'm sure."

"Won't Heaven be angry when you return here to work?"

Hamid looked his father directly in the eye. "I am not going to allow Heaven to go through her pregnancy alone."

"What are you saying? Are you breaking your vow?"

"Abba, you forget. I made a vow also to my wife."

"Does she know you're breaking your vow?"

"*Nah.*"

"Does she want you to do this?"

Hamid closed his eyes. "Yes, but she will not say the words. She knows how important the clinic is, how important you are to me, and how important keeping my word to you is. But, Abba, she's my wife. We're going to have a baby."

"Your mother's heart will be broken that your first child will not be born here, and so will your father's."

After moments of silence, Hamid looked hard at his father, then looked away. "My wife's heart will be broken if I leave her. I will not break her heart, not again. You can come to America, Abba."

His father nodded, but didn't answer the invitation.

"I have to go now. There's a lot of work to do at the clinic."

"Hamid, you've been working too hard, too many hours. Your wife needs you as much in Pakistan as she does in America. Close up like a normal person. The poor and the sick will be with us always. Those you don't care for one day will return the next. You must not forget that. I never asked you to kill yourself, Hamid. I only asked you to give back some for the blessings Allah has given you. Let Heaven shop, allow her to visit with the women. You mustn't forget that your wife is an American woman."

"She's a very strong American woman, Abba."

"But you've been forcing her to work as hard as you've been doing, and she doesn't even know the reason why. It was not Heaven who made the vow, nor is it Heaven who is breaking it. You have made your guilt hers. We accepted her as our daughter. You will not abuse her, Hamid. I'm not surprised that she's not happy about the baby. Right now she's probably not happy with you as a husband."

A stab of pain went through him at his father's words. "I don't blame Heaven for this, Abba. I don't want you or Ammi to blame her, either. The fault is mine."

"I know that. I have accepted many things that are not custom because of my love for you. I accepted your marriage to Heaven because I saw how much you loved her and how much she loves you. Too many angry words can stop her from loving you, Hamid. Be careful."

"Don't worry, I will not allow our love to erode."

"Where is Heaven now?"

"She's home resting."

"Do you think she'll be up to coming for dinner tomorrow night?" He looked sternly at Hamid. "At a decent hour, Hamid. Today go work for a couple more hours and let the others go home to their family, and you go home to your wife. Do you understand?"

"Yes, Abba."

"Good, now tell Fatima to go to your home and stay with Heaven."

Hamid smiled and embraced his father, again kissing him on each cheek. Then he sought out Fatima, kissed her and thanked her for going to be with Heaven. "Just let her rest for a couple of hours before you go," he instructed, "I think she needs it."

"You should not have worked her so hard," Fatima admonished.

"Don't worry, it won't happen again." In spite of the mess he'd made of things, Hamid was now happy. He'd at last told his father his decision. He was sure Heaven would be forgiving when he returned home.

"Sister, open the door." Fatima banged louder. "Sister."

Heaven thought for a moment of not answering, but she knew Fatima was not going away. She wondered if Hamid had sent her to sit guard duty.

"Heaven, please open the door."

Heaven walked slowly to the door, admonishing herself for her behavior. There was no need to be rude to Fatima. She was not involved with her and Hamid's fight.

"I'm sorry, Fatima," Heaven said as she opened the door. "I was sleeping and didn't hear you."

"You were angry at Hamid and didn't want to be bothered."

Heaven couldn't help laughing at her sister-in-law's matter-of-fact explanation. "You're right, I was, and still am, upset with Hamid. Did he tell you to come to make sure I didn't get on a plane?"

"No, he didn't say what was wrong or what he'd done. But he was talking with Abba, so I knew it was something serious. I don't think Ammi or Abba know that you're planning on leaving. You can't leave; we have not had enough time with you. Especially since you moved here with Hamid, we haven't seen you. We want to take you shopping. I want you to go to Dow Hospital and meet my friend Anjum."

"Fatima, don't worry. I'm not getting on a plane tonight." Heaven moved into the sitting room. "I'm sorry we don't have a lot to offer, but we do have some sweets and bottled water and juice, or I could make you tea."

"You'll make me nothing. I came to care for you, not for you to care for me. Now, let's talk like sisters. What did the favorite son do?"

Again Heaven laughed. "He's working so hard at the clinic. I don't think he wants to leave, and I think he's angry with me that he has to. He yelled at me in front of everyone. He's never done that before."

"What do you mean, he doesn't want to leave? When you weren't here he walked around with this sour face from missing you."

Heaven shook her head. "It just doesn't seem that we're hitting the right note." She saw Fatima had no idea what she meant. "When you're married it takes time to become one." Heaven stopped when Fatima started laughing.

"What's so funny?"

Fatima covered her mouth and laughed harder.

Heaven frowned, then started taking the twists apart. The same thing she'd been doing when Fatima had knocked.

"What are you doing?"

"I'm redoing my hair."

"Why don't you wear your hair long?"

"I don't have long hair."

"Why?"

"Not everyone has long hair."

"Here in Pakistan they do."

"In America they don't."

Heaven had more than half of the twists out when she noticed Fatima staring at her in an odd manner. "What's wrong?" she asked.

"Your hair." Fatima smiled. "It looks beautiful, wild, and sexy."

"Sexy?" Heaven's hands left her head and she sat stunned, staring at Fatima.

"What, you think I don't know about sexy? I've been married."

"Married!" Now Fatima definitely had Heaven's attention. "I didn't know that."

"Of course you didn't. I'm the family shame. Hamid would not have told you."

"But why?" Heaven asked. "Divorce is permitted in your religion."

"Yes, of course, but I was married twice. I have no children from either marriage, so I'm now thought of as damaged goods. Only I know it isn't true."

Heaven couldn't believe what Fatima was saying. "Did you take birth control pills?" she asked in a whisper.

Fatima just looked at her for a moment and Heaven thought she'd crossed the line, that maybe Fatima wouldn't answer. But then a change came over Fatima's face and Heaven sat ready to listen.

"Neither of my marriages was for love, not like you and Hamid. I was the dutiful daughter. I agreed to an arranged marriage with my first cousin. I have a friend that is a doctor. She said if I didn't produce sons or daughters, after some time passed, my husband would divorce me. So she helped me. When Abba arranged a second marriage, with another cousin, Anjun helped me again. After this divorce, no one wanted to marry me. Because I have no prospects and I'm now in my forties, I am free to do what I want. I can go on holiday with my friend and neither of us has to worry."

"Is your friend divorced as well?" Heaven asked, curious.

"No, she refused to marry. She said a man is a hypocrite, that he wants us to cover ourselves in the daytime and be wicked in bed." Fatima laughed. "All men are like that, I think." She looked slyly at Heaven. "How about Hamid? Is he like that?"

Heaven laughed. This conversation was the last thing she'd expected. She remembered a conversation she'd had with Hamid about Pakistani women and sex, and she laughed harder.

"Why are you laughing, Sister? Is Hamid bad?"

"I'm not answering your questions."

"Why not? Both of my husbands were bad. Neither cared if what they did pleased me. They climbed on top and did their business."

Questions roared through Heaven's mind, things she wanted to ask but didn't dare; she was bowing out of this conversation. "Fatima, I haven't seen much of your sisters or your brothers."

"They're coming again, don't worry. They live far away. Now tell me, is my brother like all men?"

"I'm not telling you that."

"Oh Sister, I'm so sorry that Hamid doesn't please you."

Heaven laughed. So, Fatima thought she could use psychology and make her talk. "Hamid makes me very happy." The words popped out and Heaven smiled. Apparently Fatima's psychology had worked.

"I knew he made you happy. I see how you always look at him, how you touch him in secret when you think no one is watching. And I see Hamid, how he watches you when you cross the room, when you drink tea. In everything you do my brother's eyes are always on you. I can see in his eyes how much he loves you. We all know the excuses he makes to touch you when he pretends to help you. He will do anything to touch you and when he does, the two of you look at each other the way couples do in the movies. You make me believe in love. I think I would do anything to feel that way."

For the space of a breath, neither Heaven nor Fatima spoke. Then Heaven noticed a serious look cross Fatima's features. "Can I tell you a secret?" Fatima asked.

Heaven was positive Fatima was going to confess to being lesbian. "Sure, go ahead," she said, "I won't tell."

"Not even Hamid?"

"*Nah,* not even Hamid."

"I've eaten pork."

Heaven blinked. Her new sister was full of surprises. For a second Heaven didn't know whether Fatima wanted something from her, or just to say the words aloud. Who better to say them to than to a pork eater? Heaven shook her head and smiled. "Did you like it?"

"Very much."

"Fatima, when did you do this? When you went on holiday with your friend?" Heaven asked, guessing at the answer. *Now Heaven had to meet Fatima's friend.*

"Yes, we were in London. I ordered every pork product on the menu, we both did, and we both liked it."

"Are you still eating pork?"

"Nah, I said too many prayers afterward; it's not worth the worry. Do you want to know what else we do?"

Heaven gave the question serious consideration. "I'm not sure I do."

"Why?"

"Because there is only so much I want to keep from Hamid. And I don't want to betray your secrets, so maybe that's enough for now."

"My friend and I have dated non-Muslim men and we—"

"Enough." Heaven cut her off, knowing where this conversation was heading.

"Why are you so embarrassed?" Fatima laughed. "You should understand."

"You thought I would understand because I'm married to Hamid?"

"Yes. It's different being with someone who's not like you; it's exciting."

"I guess that's where we differ. I wasn't looking for excitement when I met Hamid. I didn't want anyone different."

"But you married Hamid twice."

"I fell in love with Hamid and I respect him. That is why I would be uncomfortable keeping secrets from him. So from here on out, nothing that you say is going to be a secret."

"Are you going to tell Hamid?"

"Not the things I've given my word not to mention, but I'm not giving you a promise on keeping more secrets, Fatima. Hamid and I have enough problems already."

"If you're angry with him, why are you worried about keeping secrets from him? You behave more like a Muslim than I do. You're obedient to your husband."

Now it was Heaven's turn to laugh. "Fatima, Hamid and I had a fight, but it doesn't mean that I've stopped loving him or that anything's changed with us. You should try sharing some of these secrets with Hamid, and then the three of us would know." Heaven smiled. "Just don't tell him anything about your love life. I don't think he would be able to handle that."

"How do you and Hamid get around your faith?"

"We don't get around it. We respect each other and our faith is a part of us, so we respect that." Heaven rubbed her chin and stared at Fatima. She was the one Heaven would miss the most when she left Pakistan.

She licked her lips, wanting her words to come out right, not wanting to offend or preach but wanting to answer Fatima's question. "I've always tried to respect other faiths and their manner of worship. I've always thought we were all heading for the same destination, just taking different paths to get there."

"Do you adhere to everything your faith tells you?"

"*Nah*," Heaven admitted honestly. "I'm not wired that way. I can't blindly accept things that I question. And I question many things about my faith. So I believe more in having a personal relationship with God, asking and listening for the answers."

"So if you question your faith, maybe you can become Muslim. Hamid would love that."

"He probably would," Heaven laughed again, "but like I said, I can't do things blindly just because everyone else is doing it. It has to make logical sense for me. I suppose that's why I respect the faith of others. If I question my own faith, how can I judge anyone else's? I think people have a right to worship God in the manner they chose, or not worship. It's their choice."

"So why not Islam for you?"

"Because I believe in Jesus."

"Oh, that's a little thing; maybe we can work it in."

"That's a big thing," Heaven laughed. "A really big thing, no changing, no compromising."

"Anything else?" Fatima asked.

"Probably, but when people start talking about the differences in their beliefs it gets wacky."

"That happens with everything, even about putting curry into food." Fatima gave Heaven a look and they both started to laugh, remembering the fight.

"See what I mean? We were all ready to kill each other over curry powder," Heaven said.

"Not kill, I don't like war," Fatima corrected.

"Neither do I," Heaven answered, "too many innocent people dying without even knowing why."

"In Jihad it's different; people know why they're fighting."

"I don't believe in holy wars, and I don't believe in Christians or Muslims killing and claiming the victory for God. To me if God welcomed those victories it would make him evil, and I could not worship an evil God."

"Heaven, you're strange. Don't you worry about your soul when you say such things?"

"Apparently not, and Fatima, that is our little secret." Heaven put her finger to her lips. "Don't even tell what I just said to God." Fatima looked serious until she realized Heaven was joking.

"Do you and Hamid talk about faith a lot?" Fatima asked.

"*Nah.*"

"You and Hamid don't care about fighting, do you?"

"We love to fight."

"But not today."

"*Nah*, not today. We didn't fight by the rules."

"You have rules for fighting?"

"Yeah, I'm supposed to be the last man standing." Heaven laughed. "Usually we don't have hurt feelings when we fight. Today we did."

"I'm going to miss you when you leave, Heaven. I like talking to you."

"I like talking to you too, Fatima, but it's not like we won't see each other again. You and your friend Anjun can come and visit us in Chicago, and we'll come again to Pakistan."

For another two hours, Heaven and Fatima sat and talked and, once again, Heaven's beliefs were proven correct. People were basically the same, wanting the same things, mainly love and a certain amount of freedom to express their wants and needs. Now more than ever Heaven was glad she'd come to Pakistan. She'd always thought she was open, but since meeting Hamid she'd become aware that she had been guilty of a lot of assumptions. No one should assume, Heaven thought.

And when Hamid walked in as Fatima was preparing to leave, carrying a basket of mangoes, she had the same thought. Even Hamid should not assume that his pledge to her would get him out of trouble so easily. After all, it was only fruit. He was going to have to tell her what was going on.

CHAPTER EIGHTEEN

Hand in hand, Heaven and Hamid walked to the car. The tension between them had eased in the past couple of days, and they were once again comfortable in their silence.

Hamid slid his arm around her waist. "Fatima told me you thought I was angry with you because we're leaving soon. That's not true."

"Then tell me what's wrong. There's been something going on with you for weeks, and if it's not me you're angry with, then your getting so angry with me at the clinic doesn't make any sense."

"I'm so sorry about all of that. I should have explained everything to you, but I was waiting until things were final. It's time you know the truth." Hamid stopped walking and held Heaven's gaze. "I was never angry with you. I'm not coming back to Pakistan. I'm not going to remain at the clinic."

"You're breaking your vow?"

"I have no choice."

"The baby," Heaven whispered. She'd almost forgotten, and had not taken a test out of spite. She would have to do that, they needed to know.

"Hamid, I…" she wanted badly to tell him that she didn't want this for him, that she didn't want him to be with her. But she didn't know how to tell that lie. It was way too big. "Hamid, I don't want you hating me for this decision. How can you be happy about a baby that forced you to break your vow?"

"This has nothing to do with the baby. I decided more than three months ago, before you surprised me and accompanied me. I knew that I could not take this any longer. Seeing you for a month here and there, it wasn't working. I love you. My vow now is to you."

"What about Abba and Ammi and your family?"

"That's the good thing about families. In time they forgive, and they forget your transgressions. They will be hurt, but they will not stop loving me, I'm sure of that."

"Is that why Abba was looking sort of sad tonight?"

"I'm not sure. I think maybe he wants his grandson born here."

"You told them," Heaven gasped. "Hamid, what if I'm not?"

"But you will be one day, and I want to be involved in every moment of your pregnancy. I will not be in another country while you have our baby alone."

"Hamid, are you certain? If not, I promise we can work something out. I can come here and stay for a few months just like I did now. Maybe we can spend six months here and six months there."

"Heaven, nah." He shook his head. "This is not up for negotiation. No compromise. I want to spend all my nights and days near you, in our bed. I made this decision, Heaven, not you. I didn't make it because of you, but because of me. I will not ever lay blame for this decision on your doorstep. You don't have to worry about that."

She stared at him. "I'm sorry for what I said about the clinic and my not wanting to work with you."

"Did you mean it?"

"I had been working toward having a partnership with Brandon. That was my dream for years. It was what we," she smiled, "it was what *I* planned for. I saved every dime for it, and would have been still saving if he hadn't decided that he no longer wanted me or my plans, that he wasn't in love with me." She shrugged her shoulders. "I didn't dump him, Hamid, he dumped me."

"And you were sad that he dumped you?"

"I was, then I got angry. It's not a good feeling being dumped."

He held her hands in his. "Do you love him still, Heaven?"

"Of course not. It's been a long time since I loved him."

"You told me that things were settled between you months ago, that you no longer hated him. Do you still hate him?"

"No, I'm not angry with him any longer. I was honest with you about that. I let that go and realized that if things hadn't happened as they had I would not have been available for my true prince." She stood on tiptoe and kissed him. "And you are my true prince. Why did you think I wanted Brandon's baby?"

"I guess I was hurt that you weren't happy." He grinned. "We're going to have a beautiful little baby with twists." He touched Heaven's hair.

"After hours in a salon," Heaven laughed. "Come on, Hamid, let's go home."

The ride home was filled with promises, and when they arrived home, Hamid turned the covers on the bed, glanced at Heaven and smiled as she shook her head no. "I want to sleep under the stars," she said. "Until we leave I want to make love with the open sky above and wake to the sun shining on our faces."

She waited until he went into the shower and then she followed him. This was the way for them to put their argument behind them for good. They'd let their angry words go down the drain with the dirty water. Heaven climbed in, content to be with her husband. And later, after they made love under the stars, she lay back while her husband rested his head on her belly, cooing to someone who might or might not be. Her hand was tangled in his hair and a smile was on her lips.

"I have the name for our first two babies."

"First two?" Heaven asked. "How many are we having?"

"I'm not sure."

"What are the names?"

"Fabanna and Tsukama."

"Suppose you tell me where you came up with those names and what they mean."

"Don't you remember?" Hamid asked. "When we went to the DuSable Museum, they were listed as the names of two of the slaves on the *Amistad* ship."

"How did you remember that?"

"I wrote it down. I knew we would need the names one day."

Heaven laughed. "I still don't know what they mean."

"Fabanna means remember, and Tsukama means learner."

"Are they names for males or females?"

"It won't matter. Do you agree to the names?" Hamid nibbled her stomach and she laughed.

"Yes, husband, I agree."

The sun definitely shone brighter in Pakistan, or maybe it was that Heaven had never slept outdoors in Chicago. Either way, it was definitely a different way to wake each morning. This morning Heaven didn't feel her husband's body pressed against her. She rolled over and still didn't feel him. Her eyes flew open. "Hamid," she called.

He appeared moments later with a robe for her and a smile.

"I made breakfast. I wanted to eat with you before I leave."

"Let me shower, give me five minutes," Heaven said, slipping her arm into the robe, then kissing Hamid quickly and running into the shower.

When she arrived fully dressed in the kitchen, she was expecting *the look* from Hamid, the one that said, 'You don't have to.'

"Heaven."

"I want to. Saddia needs my help, so do you. Just let it be clear that you will not yell at me or anyone else there today. We're all doing our jobs, okay?"

"You don't have to."

"I know that, Hamid. When have I ever done anything that I didn't want to do?"

"Never," he answered truthfully. "Today we will start a new plan. We will not work such crazy hours." He laughed. "I didn't know I could be such a hard taskmaster."

"Neither did I," Heaven answered and kissed him. "Now let's go to work and behave like normal people." She kissed him again, leaning against his broad chest when he reached out an arm and pulled her to him. Regardless of what fate threw at them, they would be fine, she thought.

And two days later, they found they were not going to be parents, not yet anyway. They consoled themselves in each other's arms, knowing that babies were in their future and that they would be ready for them.

There were only two days left in Pakistan, and Heaven was feeling almost sad to be leaving. She'd made new family and friends, and she would miss them. But she thought of her friends waiting for her in America and she couldn't deny that she couldn't wait to go home to Chicago.

The goodbye party was in full swing. Heaven smiled at the dishes the women had made. *East met West and they compromised*, Heaven thought. The dishes were things they all enjoyed.

Family was family regardless of the culture, laughing, dancing, singing, eating, and telling tall tales. There was sadness for their leaving but joy that they'd found each other. Heaven turned from her musing as her father-in-law clapped his hands for attention.

"Hamid and Heaven, our new daughter. We are so honored to have finally met you and wish you could remain here forever, but accept that it's not to be. You are welcome here always; this is now your home.

"Hamid, I release you from your vow to the clinic. You have fulfilled your promise. You have done all that is required. Sometimes parents ask things of their children they have no right to, and I asked that of you simply because I wanted to keep you near me. The clinic will survive, Hamid, but you, my son, will not if you have to keep dividing your time between your vows. It is never right for a man to be separated from his wife. When you marry, your wife is your responsibility. You must cleave unto her as she cleaves unto you."

He smiled at Heaven. "As your wife said in her vow to you, Hamid, my son, let her people be your people and her land your land. Where she lodges, there you should lodge also. Follow your wife and be happy."

Everyone fell silent for a time. "When there are babies," Abba continued, "all that I ask is that you bring them so we may kiss their cheeks and that they may know us."

Heaven sat stunned, watching her husband's eyes fill with tears. She watched as he embraced his father, then his brothers and his mother and sisters. Heaven recognized the significance of the moment. They were all releasing Hamid to her. Tears streamed down her cheeks as well.

"Heaven, you are a true gift for my son. I have seen that you love him as much as he loves you. You have both chosen wisely. When you leave for America, you leave with our blessings."

"Thank you, Abba," Heaven said and bowed her head slightly before kissing his cheeks.

When he was able to steal a few minutes away from everyone, Hamid approached his father. "Abba, I told you Heaven's cycle came, that she isn't having a baby."

"Or maybe she was, but the hard hours were too much."

"Please don't make me feel guilty for this, Abba. I've thought of this myself. Why did you release me in front of everyone when you knew I was breaking my vow?"

"Call it a father's gift to his favorite son." He laughed. "I want you to know you have always made me proud. Your brothers have only teased you because it bothered you. They have always been proud of you. In fact, your brothers came to me and asked that I release you from your vow. They didn't know about the baby, but they saw the pain in your eyes and your love for Heaven. And they saw the same thing in her.

"They knew if ever two souls belonged together, it was yours and Heaven's. It would have been selfish of me to allow you to leave here with guilt when you were doing the right thing. I had the ability to take it from you, and I chose to do it with the blessing of your entire family. I meant it, Hamid. You married well. I do hope that this won't mean that Heaven will never come back."

"*Nah*, Abba, it doesn't mean that. In fact she's torn. She doesn't want to leave you all, and she doesn't want to leave the house that I rented. She loves it. She feels as I do, that it's our first true home. Do you know, Abba, in the beginning Heaven hated the clock for the Azzan. It took a bit of explaining to her that the Azzan was so much more than a clock, that it was a call to prayer, that there was a voice praying the prayer with you, making you feel more connected to Allah."

"What did she think it was?"

Hamid laughed. "She thought it was loud and annoying when she first heard it. She said if the person saying the prayer had a more pleasant voice maybe she could tolerate it."

"What did you do?"

"I put it in a room where the chiming and the prayer wouldn't bother her so much."

"Compromise?"

"Compromise. Besides, I could use a regular clock to remind me of the time for prayer. As for listening to the prayer of the *Azzan,* when the clock Heaven approved of would sound, I would go to the room where I had placed the *Azzan* and I would pray along with it."

"That seems like a lot of trouble."

"It was a small compromise, Abba."

"Humph."

"Do you want to know what Heaven thought of the *Azzan* when I left her for the first time?"

"I'm not sure."

"She told me that when I first left her, she listened for the sound of the prayer, that it made her think of me and that she knew I was here listening to the sound of the Azzan. Did you know the first purchase she bought here for our home was the *Azzan?*"

"You think this house you rented was the key to her understanding the importance of the *Azzan*?"

"*Nah*, Abba, that happened in America, but I think when we go back to America that we will have to buy a house that the two of us picked together. Thank you, Abba," Hamid said, and hugged his father to him. "Of all the gifts you've given me, releasing me from my vow is the greatest."

CHAPTER NINETEEN

After being back in the States for three months, Heaven and Hamid found things were not going as they planned. Heaven was puzzled that Hamid had not been able to secure a permanent position at a hospital. He thought it was because he'd not become board certified, but Heaven wasn't so sure. After all, Hamid was licensed in America.

While arranging certification, Hamid in the meantime was working whatever job Heaven could secure for him through her agency. But she knew he didn't like it. He'd once said to Sassa that Heaven was taking care of him. So far he was smiling and doing the freelance jobs she'd gotten for him, even working as a phlebotomist.

Heaven had cringed the first time she'd assigned a job to Hamid. Assigning him a phlebotomist job was even worse. Though he'd worked as a phlebotomist before he got his license, it pained her that he was forced to do it now.

"Hamid, you don't have to go out on jobs," Heaven said over breakfast one morning. "You can just help me run the business."

"Running a registry is your dream, Heaven, not mine." Then he smiled again. "Don't worry, Heaven, there is no shame in any honorable work. I don't mind doing it."

Heaven was putting dinner on the table when Hamid came in. He was angry. She wondered what had gone wrong. It couldn't be his assignment; she made sure he received the best ones that came in. Still, his anger seemed directed at her. In fact, he was glaring at her.

"Hamid, what's wrong?" Heaven asked, moving in for a kiss. He barely brushed her lips and didn't pull her in close as he usually did. That told her before he spoke that his problem was with her.

"What's wrong?" she asked again, moving away.

"How much do you pay your phlebotomists?"

"You know very well what I pay them."

"No, Heaven, suppose you tell me."

"Are you wanting a raise?" She attempted to laugh. "You've got it."

His hand slammed down on the table. "That's the problem, Heaven. I sent a friend to you for work as a phlebotomist. I make almost double what you paid him. Do you know how that made me feel, Heaven? Like a charity case, a man who can't take care of his family. I no longer want to work for your agency."

"Hamid, why are you angry with me? I wasn't trying to hurt you. I just wanted—"

"I know what you wanted. You wanted to make sure I felt like a man, so you decided to help me with that, and you gave me charity. *Nah,* Heaven, you will not do that."

Hamid went into the bathroom and Heaven could hear him muttering. Her accountant had warned her of possible legal ramifications for paying Hamid more than she paid anyone else, but she'd told him she thought, as a physician, Hamid deserved more. She wanted to explain this rationale to Hamid, but didn't think he would be willing to hear it. They both needed time to cool off.

She stuck her head in the bathroom door. "Hamid, I'm going to go to the gym to work out. I need the practice."

When he didn't answer, she went anyway, knowing that he'd heard her, knowing that his anger still had a hold on him, knowing that he was feeling bad because he couldn't get a job.

Heaven stepped into the *dojo* for the first time in months, feeling at first like a stranger. She did the customary bow and smiled as students rushed over to greet her. This felt good. She needed the contact of a normal life. It seemed that regardless of the country she and Hamid resided in, they were bound to have problems. They hadn't totally been happy in Pakistan but more so than they were here. She knew Hamid didn't blame her for his inability to get on staff somewhere. She'd asked him if he wanted to open his own office, but he didn't have the funds without accepting help from her or his family. Heaven had insisted that she didn't want him looking to his family and of course, he would not accept help from her. She should have known just returning to Chicago wouldn't solve all of her marital woes.

"Heaven, how are you and Hamid doing?"

Heaven smiled at the *sensei*. "Better some days than others."

"Has he found a permanent position?"

"No." Heaven shook her head.

"I never thought a doctor would have any problem."

"Neither did Hamid. In Pakistan he didn't need to be board certified; here he does. He'll get something soon because he's an excellent doctor." She smiled. "You should ask some of the patients at his clinic in Pakistan."

"Why did he return here? Why didn't he stay there?"

"We're married, *sensei*." Heaven knew the teacher wasn't passing judgment on her, but for the past three months she'd asked herself the same question. Hamid had been happy working at his clinic in Pakistan. He returned to America because of her, and now he couldn't even get a job. Of course, she wondered if he should have remained there.

"Heaven, I don't mean to pry, but I thought the two of you had an arrangement, that you'd reached a compromise, that he would work in his clinic for three months at a time, then return here."

"I didn't ask him to move here."

"Heaven, if you had, you would have had a right to do it. I just thought the two of you were okay with the way things were, the way you'd done them for a year."

For a second Heaven stared at the teacher. "If things had been fine, I never would have gone to Pakistan for three months. I missed my husband. Should I feel guilty for that? I love him, *sensei*, and I want to be with him."

The *sensei*'s eyes looked over her head and Heaven followed his line of vision, not surprised to find Hamid staring at her.

She walked away toward the bag and started kicking it. When she tired of that, she put on her gloves and punched the bag. Hamid held it for her.

"Are you done?" he asked when she bent over with her hands on her knees. Her breathing was ragged. "Yes, I'm done," she said.

"Then will you hold the bag for me?"

Heaven exhaled a couple more times, and then held the bag while Hamid burned off his frustrations.

When Hamid, too, bent over with his hands on his knees, Heaven grinned. "Do you feel better?"

He looked sideways at her. "I never blamed you, Heaven, not for my decision to return here." He took in a lungful of air. "And I never blamed you for my not finding a job. I was grateful that you had jobs for me to go out on."

"*Nah*, Hamid."

"I said grateful, Heaven, not joyful about it. I told myself that at least I was contributing, that it was honest labor, and I told myself that until I began to believe it. And then when I found that my wife was giving me charity, I no longer felt like a man." He rubbed his top lip with his thumb. "For that I do blame you, Heaven."

"Do you want to hit the bag a few more times?" she asked.

He smiled with just a tiny curling of his lips. "Yeah, I think so." He hit the bag several more times, then looked at Heaven. "Tomorrow I will apply at other agencies. Understood?"

"But Hamid, I really do need you."

"Do you need me more as your husband or as an employee?"

"My husband," she answered without hesitation.

"In that case, let's go home, Heaven."

LET'S GET IT ON

Heaven looked across the table at her husband. He was joking about his lack of work at the registry he'd signed up with. But she could tell from the look in his eyes that he wasn't amused.

She dared to say, "Hamid, I have more work than I can handle, I can—"

"Heaven, if you continue this, we are going to have the worst fight we've had in our marriage."

"I just want to help."

"You can help by loving me, by believing in me."

"I believe in you, Hamid, I always have." She went to him and he pulled her into his lap.

"Then there is something that you can do for me."

Heaven grinned. "Gladly," she said as she gazed up at him. His eyes darkened with desire as he carried her to the bedroom. They made love and Heaven kept looking up for the stars. "Hamid, I miss Pakistan."

Hamid chuckled. "I was wondering what was going on. I'm trying to recreate for you the things your prince did, and you're thousands of miles away. Now I know why."

"I miss the clinic."

"Heaven, stop that please, I don't want to discuss anything, I just want to make love to my wife. I just want to forget my worries in your arms."

She ceased the conversation but it still was in her mind. As her husband's hands caressed her, Heaven absentmindedly returned the caresses. As he thrust, an idea begin to develop. She wanted Hamid happy. She thought of giving up her dream to pursue Hamid's. She lifted her hips to meet his thrust and stared into his still unhappy eyes. She was going to change that. "I love you, Hamid."

"I know, Heaven," he whispered, softly, "I love you too, with all my heart and soul." Together they soared to the heavens.

Heaven had her plan in mind. She thought of discussing it with her husband. That would be the thing to do, she knew that. But she also was aware that Hamid was not about to allow anyone to bail him out, not even her.

Her dream had changed because of the love of her dark prince, the man who made her nights and her days pleasurable.

Heaven almost laughed. She'd pledged never to put anyone's needs above her own, and for the first year of her marriage, she'd followed through on that, refusing to go for a visit with Hamid to Pakistan.

She thought it must have been their second wedding and the vows she'd taken that changed her. She still didn't understand why she'd spoken the words she had, but she'd meant them. Hamid's people had become her people.

Heaven found she was bonding more and more with her new family in Pakistan. Since she and Hamid had returned home, they talked to the family once a week.

Whenever the subject of where Hamid was working was mentioned, Hamid put on a brave face and told them how much work he was getting. And then he would avoid Heaven's eyes, as if he thought he was failing her, and every night he would make love to her in the sweetest way possible.

It was in her arms that she knew Hamid found his peace, and it was in his arms that Heaven had found the answer. They would move to Pakistan. There they would work together. They would find another house as lovely as the one they'd left behind, and they would lie under the stars at night making love in their alcove. And in the morning, they would be awakened by the brightness of the sun.

Heaven asked her accountant whether he thought she could manage her business from out of the country. 'Haven't you ever heard of the Internet?' he'd asked. After the talk with her accountant, Heaven trained four managers, nurses she could trust to take over the day-to-day operations.

Her accountant would oversee everything with one exception. As much as she trusted him, Heaven knew enough to make sure the money was strictly in her name. She would open an account from which the accountant could draw funds, but the clients' checks would be deposited into Heaven's account, and Heaven would issue the payroll from Pakistan.

She was free to leave her dream and help her husband find his own. Besides that, Heaven had taken a test and found she was pregnant. She couldn't imagine anywhere she'd rather have their babies than surrounded by all the family that was ready to love them.

There were two things to do before they left. She wanted to see her father in San Francisco, and she wanted to have a party for her friends in Chicago. Before that, she would tell Hamid she wanted to return to Pakistan. They would fight, but in the end he would give in, because she had a trump card to play.

Hamid had the feeling that something was going on with Heaven. She was being secretive, and he didn't like it. After all, they'd promised not to have secrets. But he was too tired to call her on it. He was tired of jumping one hurdle after the other, and also tired of the look of pity in his wife's eyes.

The one thing Hamid had thought he could count on was their fighting. He'd tried it whenever she gave him that, I'm-so-sorry look, but then she'd kiss him and hug him, pressing her perfumed body against his, and his resolve would weaken. He would take her in his arms, make love to her, and would forget for a few hours how it felt to not be taking care of her.

It was only in the still of the night, when Heaven was asleep, that Hamid would remember the promise he'd made to take care of her. It was then that he felt he'd failed her.

Somehow Heaven always woke when he began to feel depressed. She would smile at him and whisper in his ear, telling him he was her prince, and immediately they would be back in their house in Pakistan.

The one thing they needed was to have a home of their own here, and he didn't have that to give her yet. Some favorite son he was. Some doctor.

Hamid walked into the kitchen where Heaven had been busy for a couple of hours while he read. There was not much else for him to do other than answering the calls for Heaven for her registry. He felt like an errand boy doing that while she remained in the kitchen. The feeling grew in his chest that his wife was hiding something, and that she wanted him out of her hair. He stood looking at her.

"Heaven, what are you doing? You're cooking a ton of food." His eyes narrowed. "Are we having guests?"

"Yes."

"Why didn't you tell me?"

"I didn't know I needed permission."

"Heaven, what are you up to?"

"I don't think I should tell you right now. I want tonight to be fun, and I think if I tell you we're going to fight."

"Since when have you ever worried about a fight? That's your middle name." Hamid backed away and glared at Heaven. "Listen, I'm not an invalid, I'm just unemployed. Don't treat me any differently than you normally would. I hate it, and I hate your pitying me."

"And I hate your feeling sorry for yourself. Grow up, Hamid. You're not the only one without a job." She returned his glare. "By the way, you're not even the only doctor without a job. And it's your choice. I have more than enough work to keep you busy but your silly male testerone pride has gotten in the way. Knock it off, and I'm not kidding. I'm not taking any crap from you." She pushed past him, then turned back and grinned. Hamid smiled.

"Thanks, Heaven, I needed that."

"Yeah, I know, but seriously, we haven't had anyone over for weeks. I invited Ongela, Peaches, Latanya, Sassa, and Isha." She smiled again. "Okay, I invited all of our friends. I want to have a party, a going-away party."

"Where are we going?"

"Back to where we can make love under the stars, where we can wake with the sun hitting us in the face." Heaven smiled as she saw the look that came into her husband's eyes.

"*Nah.*"

"Yes."

"*Nah*, Heaven."

"Yes, Hamid."

"Why?"

"Because I love you and you're not happy here. We tried, Hamid. I think it's time we try something else."

"You don't have to do this."

"I know I don't, Hamid. That's the reason I'm going to do it."

"Don't you think you should have asked my opinion before deciding this?"

"Don't you think you should have asked me before breaking your vow to run the clinic?"

"Is that what this is about? I told you before we came home that this was my decision, and that whatever happened was on my shoulders. It won't be like this forever, Heaven; I promise I'll get a position."

"Do you think this is about a job, Hamid? Whether you want to hear this or not, I make more than enough money to take care of both of us. This is about something more." Heaven put the pan she was carrying on the table and walked back to her husband. "This is about following your heart and finding your dream."

"But the business," Hamid said. "It's your dream."

"Even if it was before, it's not anymore. It hasn't been for a long time now."

"Heaven, I don't want you doing this."

"It's too late, I've done it. I've hired managers to take over, I've had accounts set up and I've called your family to tell them we're coming back."

"How long?"

"As long as it takes, a couple of years, or more, whatever it takes."

"A couple of years? Are you sure?" Hamid was looking at Heaven, not believing that she could possibly mean what she was saying.

"Or more. That's up to us. Just no vows, Hamid. We do what feels right for us."

"Why does this feel right?"

"I love making love under the stars. That was your dream, Hamid, and it became mine. More than anything I've ever wanted, I want that."

"What about your father?"

"Do you know how often we see each other? I could probably not even tell him, and he'd never know the difference. Just so I call him once a month or so, he won't care. And even if he does, your people have become my people and your land my land."

"Heaven."

Hamid crushed her in his arms. He'd never once thought this would happen, had never dared to dream it. He'd never once told Heaven how much he missed working in the clinic, how he'd enjoyed being needed.

"Heaven, I love you." He held her so tightly that he heard her gasping for air. Then he kissed her and kissed her, and kissed her some more, and then the bell rang.

"You are my soul mate, you are my dream, and fate knew what she was doing. Heaven, listen to me," Hamid said quickly. "There is no need to do this. We have no money worries. I have money, Heaven, we have money," he amended.

"Of course we have money. What's mine is yours. I'm not selling the business. We'll have more than enough money."

"Heaven, you don't understand. We will never have money worries." He looked toward the door as the buzzer sounded again.

"This isn't about money, Hamid. This is about us and how happy you were working in the clinic helping people who couldn't afford your services. That is, you were happy until the end when you went nuts. I have to let our guests in," Heaven said, and pushed the buzzer.

She kissed Hamid, then smiled at him. "This time we're going to do it right. We're going to work together, and we're going to work eight-hour days."

"We? Are you going to help?"

"Of course."

"But I thought you said you couldn't, that it was your dead dream, yours and Brandon's."

Heaven laughed. "So much has changed for me, Hamid. Being with you, being happy, really happy with you, is my dream. This isn't about money but about our being happy, and I think as long as we make love under the stars we will be." They both turned at the sound of Sassa's voice outside the door.

"Heaven, wait."

"Hamid, why are you resisting? What's the matter? You no longer want to make love to me under the stars?" Then Heaven opened the door to Sassa before Hamid could answer.

Hamid was astonished. He'd been in shock for a couple of hours, ever since his wife had sprung her plan on him. He couldn't believe she wanted to move back to Pakistan. Right before they'd left, she'd broken down in sobs saying she wanted to come home, and now she wanted to return because she thought it would make him happy.

"Pinch me, Sassa, I must be dreaming. Can you believe Heaven would come up with this?"

"I don't think even Heaven can believe she came up with this." Sassa laughed. "She worried about you. She called me a couple of weeks ago and asked my opinion on this." Sassa laughed again. "She thought you were worried about money. She's trying to ease that worry for you."

"I know." Hamid glanced toward Heaven talking with her friends and Isha.

"You never told her, did you?"

"I never saw a need."

"Two hundred million American dollars when you turn thirty-one and you never saw the need." Sassa also looked toward Heaven and the group of women. "Were you afraid that she would be marrying you for your money?"

"No, but knowing Heaven, she would never have married me if she had known. She's so damn independent, wanting to do everything her way, wanting her dreams to come true, that the thought of my having the ability to help her in her dreams..." He laughed. "She wouldn't have liked it."

"Hamid, she's going to kill you when she learns she didn't have to sell all of her belongings. She's having a moving sale to get money, and she's selling her condominium. In fact, Peaches is buying it."

Hamid sucked in a breath and closed his eyes briefly while he thought of the stars and making love to Heaven in their home. Somehow, Hamid would buy Heaven the home they'd made theirs in Pakistan. He didn't care who owned it. He'd do this if he had to move every mountain in Pakistan to accomplish it. His eyes opened and he gazed unabashedly at Heaven.

At last, he turned from staring at his wife to fixing his cousin with a stern look. "This isn't your business to tell, Sassa. Heaven is not moving to Pakistan because she thinks we will starve here. She's doing it to make me happy." He ignored the look in his cousin's eyes. "It's true, we found utopia for a time while we were in Pakistan, and she wants to return there."

"With everything that she has in America, why would she want to go and live in Pakistan? What could she possibly want there?"

"Me, Sassa," Hamid grinned. "My wife wants me." Hamid walked away, took his wife's hand, and danced with her.

"'Let's get it on,'" Hamid whispered in Heaven's ear as they danced and laughed, ignoring the others in the room. Hamid would not bother explaining to Sassa why Heaven wanted to go. It was only for him to know that she wanted to make love beneath the stars and wake with the sun shining down on them. Money had never been a factor and it wouldn't be in Pakistan.

Later, when everyone was gone, Hamid made love to his wife, knowing she was dreaming of the home they'd shared in Pakistan. He suckled her breast, looking up in surprise when she moaned. It wasn't a moan of pleasure but pain. He attempted to look at her but she wouldn't meet his gaze. She had a dreamy smile on her face as if she had a secret. He mentally calculated her last cycle and couldn't remember when she'd last had one.

"Stop that and make love to me, Hamid," Heaven whispered and he did. He kissed his way down her body, stopping at the small mound nestled in her belly. He knew her body intimately and was surprised he'd not noticed before. Maybe his eyes had been clouded, as Heaven had said. Now they weren't. Now they were clearer than they'd ever been.

Heaven and Hamid stood in the empty apartment looking around. There was nothing left. Their trunks of personal things had been sent ahead; even their luggage had been sent. They both were taking just a carry on bag with toiletries and a change of clothes. Hamid was attempting to look as American as possible, but when he'd suggested shaving off his beard, Heaven had objected vehemently. So now he was relying on the will of Allah.

Only when they were seated on the plane in first class did the knot in his stomach loosen. He thought their ease in getting through security had to do with Heaven and her smile that lit up the entire room. A pregnant woman's smile had the power to do that. She thought he didn't know, and he was content to wait until she told him.

The Pakistan airport was busy as usual. Hamid turned to Heaven and smiled. "It's not too late to change your mind. We can turn around and go back to Chicago if you want."

She gazed up at him. "Are you kidding? Already the spark is in your eyes, and I aim to keep it there. This is home, Hamid. Come what may, this is home."

They walked out the door together. "I can't believe all that you're giving up for me. You were not going to change, remember? You were going to stay as you were. The party that you threw before we left, all the ribs and Italian sausage side by side with all the hala meats? I got your message."

"Good." Heaven reached for his hand. "If the two of us can live together without killing each other, the entire world should be able to do it." She grinned and followed Hamid to the door, surprised when a caravan of family didn't rush out to greet them. "Where is everyone?" she asked. "I told them we were coming."

"And I told them not to meet us. I thought we could use a day to unwind."

She cocked her head at him. "So are we staying at the Avari Towers tonight?"

"We're staying somewhere that I believe you will like even better. Now stop asking so many questions." He put his hand in the air, waved for a taxi, and got in after Heaven.

Thirty minutes later, he heard Heaven's gasp as they pulled up in front of their new home.

"Hamid," Heaven said, running from the taxi before he could open the door for her. "You were able to rent the same house."

"Not this time," he answered, coming up behind her.

"Your family?"

"It's ours, Heaven. I bought it." He swung her up into his arms. "Does that make you happy?"

Heaven's face stretched with her smile. This was her dream. "Do you think our mattress is in the closet still?"

"Not that one, but I had Abba buy a new one and put it in the closet." For the second time he carried her over the threshold.

"Hamid, I don't believe it."

"Why not? You gave up a lot to come here to give me my dream, and I wanted to give you yours." She smiled and he kissed her.

"Do you think Abba put food in the fridge?"

"Ammi stocked this place, Heaven. She's so excited that we're coming here to live that she's practically bursting at the seams. I'm sure we have everything that we need." He looked at her. "Are you tired?"

"A little," she answered.

"Want to take a shower and a nap?"

"A shower, yes, a nap, *nah*."

He grinned.

She grinned.

And they took a shower together. Afterwards Heaven stood in the alcove trembling as Hamid brought out the mattress and laid it on the concrete. This one was thicker than the last one, she noticed. She looked up into the sky and saw the stars twinkling, welcoming them home. This was a good dream, one that she was more than willing to participate in with Hamid.

She turned and saw the look in her husband's eyes and a shiver of desire shot straight through to her womb. Had she known he would be looking at her like that she would have made this decision months ago.

Together they sank onto the mattress. He buried his mouth in the hollow at the base of her neck. "Hamid," she moaned.

"Yes?" he answered.

"I have something to tell you." Ripples of pleasure filled her and she sank into the soft mattress. "Later," she mumbled, "it can wait." She cringed as his hand lightly touched her breast before moving downward.

He smiled. He knew.

"Would you like some champagne, Heaven?"

She looked up at the bucket he'd brought out and wondered. "I don't think so," she answered after a moment's hesitation.

"It's non-alcoholic," he grinned.

"You do know."

"Of course I know. Now which name will we use?"

"There's time for that," Heaven answered, spreading her arms wide, looking again at the stars. "Right now I just want to make love under the stars."

And they did.

And when they woke, the sun was shining brightly on them. Heaven looked up and met her husband's gaze. He was looking down at her, his eyes bright, his dream fulfilled. There was no longer a continent dividing them. They were one, united by the stars, the sun and their love.

"Whither thou goest," Heaven began.

"I will go," Hamid answered.

"And thy people will be my people," Heaven chimed in.

"And your land will be my land," they both said in unison. "And naught but death part thee and me." And then they made love again. Both of their dreams had come true.

ABOUT THE AUTHOR

Award-winning author, **Dyanne Davis**, lives in a Chicago suburb with her husband, Bill, and their son, Bill Jr. Dyanne retired from nursing several years ago to pursue her lifelong dream of becoming a published author. She was able to accomplish this with her husband's blessing and financial support.

A member of Romance Writers of America, Dyanne now serves as chapter president for its Windy City chapter. She loves to hear feedback from her readers. You can reach her at her website, www.dyanne-davis.com. She also has an on-line blog where readers can post questions and photos: http://dyannedavis.blogspot.com. Dyanne has also started a romance reader and writer on-line book club with more than a dozen authors and would love to have you join them: http://book-marked.Target.com. The group is called Romancing the Book. Any problems getting in, send Dyanne an email and she will send you a personal invitation.

2006 Publication Schedule

January

A Lover's Legacy
Veronica Parker
1-58571-167-5
$9.95

Love Lasts Forever
Dominiqua Douglas
1-58571-187-X
$9.95

Under the Cherry
  Moon
Christal Jordan-Mims
1-58571-169-1
$12.95

February

Second Chances at Love
Cheris Hodges
1-58571-188-8
$9.95

Enchanted Desire
Wanda Y. Thomas
1-58571-176-4
$9.95

Caught Up
Deatri King Bey
1-58571-178-0
$12.95

March

I'm Gonna Make You
  Love Me
Gwyneth Bolton
1-58571-181-0
$9.95

Through the Fire
Seressia Glass
1-58571-173-X
$9.95

Notes When Summer
  Ends
Beverly Lauderdale
1-58571-180-2
$12.95

April

Sin and Surrender
J.M. Jeffries
1-58571-189-6
$9.95

Unearthing Passions
Elaine Sims
1-58571-184-5
$9.95

Between Tears
Pamela Ridley
1-58571-179-9
$12.95

May

Misty Blue
Dyanne Davis
1-58571-186-1
$9.95

Ironic
Pamela Leigh Starr
1-58571-168-3
$9.95

Cricket's Serenade
Carolita Blythe
1-58571-183-7
$12.95

June

Cupid
Barbara Keaton
1-58571-174-8
$9.95

Havana Sunrise
Kymberly Hunt
1-58571-182-9
$9.95

2006 Publication Schedule (continued)

July

Love Me Carefully	No Ordinary Love	Rehoboth Road
A.C. Arthur	Angela Weaver	Anita Ballard-Jones
1-58571-177-2	1-58571-198-5	1-58571-196-9
$9.95	$9.95	$12.95

August

Scent of Rain	Love in High Gear	Rise of the Phoenix
Annetta P. Lee	Charlotte Roy	Kenneth Whetstone
158571-199-3	158571-185-3	1-58571-197-7
$9.95	$9.95	$12.95

September

The Business of Love	Rock Star	A Dead Man Speaks
Cheris Hodges	Rosyln Hardy Holcomb	Lisa Jones Johnson
1-58571-193-4	1-58571-200-0	1-58571-203-5
$9.95	$9.95	$12.95

October

Rivers of the Soul-Part 1	A Dangerous Woman	Sinful Intentions
Leslie Esdaile	J.M. Jeffries	Crystal Rhodes
1-58571-223-X	1-58571-195-0	1-58571-201-9
$9.95	$9.95	$12.95

November

Only You	Ebony Eyes	Still Waters Run Deep –
Crystal Hubbard	Kei Swanson	Part 2
1-58571-208-6	1-58571-194-2	Leslie Esdaile
$9.95	$9.95	1-58571-224-8
		$9.95

December

Let's Get It On	Nights Over Egypt	A Pefect Place to Pray
Dyanne Davis	Barbara Keaton	I.L. Goodwin
1-58571-210-8	1-58571-192-6	1-58571-202-7
$9.95	$9.95	$12.95

Other Genesis Press, Inc. Titles

A Dangerous Deception	J.M. Jeffries	$8.95
A Dangerous Love	J.M. Jeffries	$8.95
A Dangerous Obsession	J.M. Jeffries	$8.95
A Drummer's Beat to Mend	Kei Swanson	$9.95
A Happy Life	Charlotte Harris	$9.95
A Heart's Awakening	Veronica Parker	$9.95
A Lark on the Wing	Phyliss Hamilton	$9.95
A Love of Her Own	Cheris F. Hodges	$9.95
A Love to Cherish	Beverly Clark	$8.95
A Risk of Rain	Dar Tomlinson	$8.95
A Twist of Fate	Beverly Clark	$8.95
A Will to Love	Angie Daniels	$9.95
Acquisitions	Kimberley White	$8.95
Across	Carol Payne	$12.95
After the Vows	Leslie Esdaile	$10.95
(Summer Anthology)	T.T. Henderson	
	Jacqueline Thomas	
Again My Love	Kayla Perrin	$10.95
Against the Wind	Gwynne Forster	$8.95
All I Ask	Barbara Keaton	$8.95
Ambrosia	T.T. Henderson	$8.95
An Unfinished Love Affair	Barbara Keaton	$8.95
And Then Came You	Dorothy Elizabeth Love	$8.95
Angel's Paradise	Janice Angelique	$9.95
At Last	Lisa G. Riley	$8.95
Best of Friends	Natalie Dunbar	$8.95
Beyond the Rapture	Beverly Clark	$9.95
Blaze	Barbara Keaton	$9.95
Blood Lust	J. M. Jeffries	$9.95
Bodyguard	Andrea Jackson	$9.95
Boss of Me	Diana Nyad	$8.95
Bound by Love	Beverly Clark	$8.95
Breeze	Robin Hampton Allen	$10.95

Other Genesis Press, Inc. Titles (continued)

Broken	Dar Tomlinson	$24.95
By Design	Barbara Keaton	$8.95
Cajun Heat	Charlene Berry	$8.95
Careless Whispers	Rochelle Alers	$8.95
Cats & Other Tales	Marilyn Wagner	$8.95
Caught in a Trap	Andre Michelle	$8.95
Caught Up In the Rapture	Lisa G. Riley	$9.95
Cautious Heart	Cheris F Hodges	$8.95
Chances	Pamela Leigh Starr	$8.95
Cherish the Flame	Beverly Clark	$8.95
Class Reunion	Irma Jenkins/John Brown	$12.95
Code Name: Diva	J.M. Jeffries	$9.95
Conquering Dr. Wexler's Heart	Kimberley White	$9.95
Crossing Paths, Tempting Memories	Dorothy Elizabeth Love	$9.95
Cypress Whisperings	Phyllis Hamilton	$8.95
Dark Embrace	Crystal Wilson Harris	$8.95
Dark Storm Rising	Chinelu Moore	$10.95
Daughter of the Wind	Joan Xian	$8.95
Deadly Sacrifice	Jack Kean	$22.95
Designer Passion	Dar Tomlinson	$8.95
Dreamtective	Liz Swados	$5.95
Ebony Butterfly II	Delilah Dawson	$14.95
Echoes of Yesterday	Beverly Clark	$9.95
Eden's Garden	Elizabeth Rose	$8.95
Everlastin' Love	Gay G. Gunn	$8.95
Everlasting Moments	Dorothy Elizabeth Love	$8.95
Everything and More	Sinclair Lebeau	$8.95
Everything but Love	Natalie Dunbar	$8.95
Eve's Prescription	Edwina Martin Arnold	$8.95
Falling	Natalie Dunbar	$9.95
Fate	Pamela Leigh Starr	$8.95
Finding Isabella	A.J. Garrotto	$8.95

Other Genesis Press, Inc. Titles (continued)

Forbidden Quest	Dar Tomlinson	$10.95
Forever Love	Wanda Thomas	$8.95
From the Ashes	Kathleen Suzanne	$8.95
	Jeanne Sumerix	
Gentle Yearning	Rochelle Alers	$10.95
Glory of Love	Sinclair LeBeau	$10.95
Go Gentle into that Good Night	Malcom Boyd	$12.95
Goldengroove	Mary Beth Craft	$16.95
Groove, Bang, and Jive	Steve Cannon	$8.99
Hand in Glove	Andrea Jackson	$9.95
Hard to Love	Kimberley White	$9.95
Hart & Soul	Angie Daniels	$8.95
Heartbeat	Stephanie Bedwell-Grime	$8.95
Hearts Remember	M. Loui Quezada	$8.95
Hidden Memories	Robin Allen	$10.95
Higher Ground	Leah Latimer	$19.95
Hitler, the War, and the Pope	Ronald Rychiak	$26.95
How to Write a Romance	Kathryn Falk	$18.95
I Married a Reclining Chair	Lisa M. Fuhs	$8.95
Indigo After Dark Vol. I	Nia Dixon/Angelique	$10.95
Indigo After Dark Vol. II	Dolores Bundy/Cole Riley	$10.95
Indigo After Dark Vol. III	Montana Blue/Coco Morena	$10.95
Indigo After Dark Vol. IV	Cassandra Colt/	$14.95
	Diana Richeaux	
Indigo After Dark Vol. V	Delilah Dawson	$14.95
Icie	Pamela Leigh Starr	$8.95
I'll Be Your Shelter	Giselle Carmichael	$8.95
I'll Paint a Sun	A.J. Garrotto	$9.95
Illusions	Pamela Leigh Starr	$8.95
Indiscretions	Donna Hill	$8.95
Intentional Mistakes	Michele Sudler	$9.95
Interlude	Donna Hill	$8.95
Intimate Intentions	Angie Daniels	$8.95

Other Genesis Press, Inc. Titles (continued)

Jolie's Surrender	Edwina Martin-Arnold	$8.95
Kiss or Keep	Debra Phillips	$8.95
Lace	. Giselle Carmichael	$9.95
Last Train to Memphis	Elsa Cook	$12.95
Lasting Valor	Ken Olsen	$24.95
Let Us Prey	Hunter Lundy	$25.95
Life Is Never As It Seems	J.J. Michael	$12.95
Lighter Shade of Brown	Vicki Andrews	$8.95
Love Always	Mildred E. Riley	$10.95
Love Doesn't Come Easy	Charlyne Dickerson	$8.95
Love Unveiled	Gloria Greene	$10.95
Love's Deception	Charlene Berry	$10.95
Love's Destiny	M. Loui Quezada	$8.95
Mae's Promise	Melody Walcott	$8.95
Magnolia Sunset	Giselle Carmichael	$8.95
Matters of Life and Death	Lesego Malepe, Ph.D.	$15.95
Meant to Be	Jeanne Sumerix	$8.95
Midnight Clear	Leslie Esdaile	$10.95
(Anthology)	Gwynne Forster	
	Carmen Green	
	Monica Jackson	
Midnight Magic	Gwynne Forster	$8.95
Midnight Peril	Vicki Andrews	$10.95
Misconceptions	Pamela Leigh Starr	$9.95
Montgomery's Children	Richard Perry	$14.95
My Buffalo Soldier	Barbara B. K. Reeves	$8.95
Naked Soul	Gwynne Forster	$8.95
Next to Last Chance	Louisa Dixon	$24.95
No Apologies	Seressia Glass	$8.95
No Commitment Required	Seressia Glass	$8.95
No Regrets	Mildred E. Riley	$8.95
Nowhere to Run	Gay G. Gunn	$10.95
O Bed! O Breakfast!	Rob Kuehnle	$14.95

Other Genesis Press, Inc. Titles (continued)

Object of His Desire	A. C. Arthur	$8.95
Office Policy	A. C. Arthur	$9.95
Once in a Blue Moon	Dorianne Cole	$9.95
One Day at a Time	Bella McFarland	$8.95
Outside Chance	Louisa Dixon	$24.95
Passion	T.T. Henderson	$10.95
Passion's Blood	Cherif Fortin	$22.95
Passion's Journey	Wanda Thomas	$8.95
Past Promises	Jahmel West	$8.95
Path of Fire	T.T. Henderson	$8.95
Path of Thorns	Annetta P. Lee	$9.95
Peace Be Still	Colette Haywood	$12.95
Picture Perfect	Reon Carter	$8.95
Playing for Keeps	Stephanie Salinas	$8.95
Pride & Joi	Gay G. Gunn	$15.95
Pride & Joi	Gay G. Gunn	$8.95
Promises to Keep	Alicia Wiggins	$8.95
Quiet Storm	Donna Hill	$10.95
Reckless Surrender	Rochelle Alers	$6.95
Red Polka Dot in a World of Plaid	Varian Johnson	$12.95
Reluctant Captive	Joyce Jackson	$8.95
Rendezvous with Fate	Jeanne Sumerix	$8.95
Revelations	Cheris F. Hodges	$8.95
Rivers of the Soul	Leslie Esdaile	$8.95
Rocky Mountain Romance	Kathleen Suzanne	$8.95
Rooms of the Heart	Donna Hill	$8.95
Rough on Rats and Tough on Cats	Chris Parker	$12.95
Secret Library Vol. 1	Nina Sheridan	$18.95
Secret Library Vol. 2	Cassandra Colt	$8.95
Shades of Brown	Denise Becker	$8.95
Shades of Desire	Monica White	$8.95

Other Genesis Press, Inc. Titles (continued)

Shadows in the Moonlight	Jeanne Sumerix	$8.95
Sin	Crystal Rhodes	$8.95
So Amazing	Sinclair LeBeau	$8.95
Somebody's Someone	Sinclair LeBeau	$8.95
Someone to Love	Alicia Wiggins	$8.95
Song in the Park	Martin Brant	$15.95
Soul Eyes	Wayne L. Wilson	$12.95
Soul to Soul	Donna Hill	$8.95
Southern Comfort	J.M. Jeffries	$8.95
Still the Storm	Sharon Robinson	$8.95
Still Waters Run Deep	Leslie Esdaile	$8.95
Stories to Excite You	Anna Forrest/Divine	$14.95
Subtle Secrets	Wanda Y. Thomas	$8.95
Suddenly You	Crystal Hubbard	$9.95
Sweet Repercussions	Kimberley White	$9.95
Sweet Tomorrows	Kimberly White	$8.95
Taken by You	Dorothy Elizabeth Love	$9.95
Tattooed Tears	T. T. Henderson	$8.95
The Color Line	Lizzette Grayson Carter	$9.95
The Color of Trouble	Dyanne Davis	$8.95
The Disappearance of Allison Jones	Kayla Perrin	$5.95
The Honey Dipper's Legacy	Pannell-Allen	$14.95
The Joker's Love Tune	Sidney Rickman	$15.95
The Little Pretender	Barbara Cartland	$10.95
The Love We Had	Natalie Dunbar	$8.95
The Man Who Could Fly	Bob & Milana Beamon	$18.95
The Missing Link	Charlyne Dickerson	$8.95
The Price of Love	Sinclair LeBeau	$8.95
The Smoking Life	Ilene Barth	$29.95
The Words of the Pitcher	Kei Swanson	$8.95
Three Wishes	Seressia Glass	$8.95
Ties That Bind	Kathleen Suzanne	$8.95
Tiger Woods	Libby Hughes	$5.95

Other Genesis Press, Inc. Titles (continued)

Time is of the Essence	Angie Daniels	$9.95
Timeless Devotion	Bella McFarland	$9.95
Tomorrow's Promise	Leslie Esdaile	$8.95
Truly Inseparable	Wanda Y. Thomas	$8.95
Unbreak My Heart	Dar Tomlinson	$8.95
Uncommon Prayer	Kenneth Swanson	$9.95
Unconditional	A.C. Arthur	$9.95
Unconditional Love	Alicia Wiggins	$8.95
Until Death Do Us Part	Susan Paul	$8.95
Vows of Passion	Bella McFarland	$9.95
Wedding Gown	Dyanne Davis	$8.95
What's Under Benjamin's Bed	Sandra Schaffer	$8.95
When Dreams Float	Dorothy Elizabeth Love	$8.95
Whispers in the Night	Dorothy Elizabeth Love	$8.95
Whispers in the Sand	LaFlorya Gauthier	$10.95
Wild Ravens	Altonya Washington	$9.95
Yesterday Is Gone	Beverly Clark	$10.95
Yesterday's Dreams, Tomorrow's Promises	Reon Laudat	$8.95
Your Precious Love	Sinclair LeBeau	$8.95

Order Form

Mail to: Genesis Press, Inc.
P.O. Box 101
Columbus, MS 39703

Name _____

Address _____

City/State _____ Zip _____

Telephone _____

Ship to (if different from above)

Name _____

Address _____

City/State _____ Zip _____

Telephone _____

Credit Card Information

Credit Card # _____ ☐ Visa   ☐ Mastercard

Expiration Date (mm/yy) _____ ☐ AmEx   ☐ Discover

Qty.	Author	Title	Price	Total

Use this order

form, or call

1-888-INDIGO-1

Total for books	_____
Shipping and handling:	
$5 first two books,	
$1 each additional book	_____
Total S & H	_____
Total amount enclosed	_____

Mississippi residents add 7% sales tax